OF
WINDMILLS
& War

Diane Moody

Published by

OBT·Bookz

Cover design by Hannah Moody

Dedication

To Glenn Howard Hale
proud veteran,
longsuffering Cubs fan,
and faithful father;
this one's for you, Dad.

To the men of the 390th Bomb Group (H),
Third Division of the Eighth Air Force.
For your service, sacrifice, and willingness
to stand in the gap for others
both at home and around the world.
You were so young and yet so brave—
truly, you were the Greatest Generation,
and we will never forget.

.

He rained down manna for them to eat;
He gave them grain from heaven.
So they ate the bread of angels;
He sent them all the food they could eat.

Psalms 78:24-25

On a personal note . . .

Since 1984, my mother and father attended the yearly reunions of the 390th Bomb Group, for which Dad served as a co-pilot in World War II. These reunions were always the highlight of Mom and Dad's year, seeing old friends and new. After Mom passed away in 2007, my sister and I started attending the reunions with Dad. We have the best time! These men who served our country at such a young age—eighteen, nineteen, and some even younger who lied about their age to get in—still love to get together to share war stories and never-forgotten memories. With each passing year, we find the descendents outnumbering our war heroes at these reunions. Still, our unique, common bond as we continue the legacy of these great men lives on.

Year after year, I began to notice something. Whenever one of the veterans talked about the Chowhound Missions, they would tear up. To a man, the mere mention of those food drops to the starving Dutch people in Occupied Holland would stir such strong emotions, they'd have to pause to collect themselves. How was that possible after all these decades later?

At the 2011 reunion in New Orleans, while discussing *Operation Chowhound* with our good friend Bob Penovich, I told him I was thinking about writing a novel to tell the story behind this little-known but life-changing mission at the end of World War II. I wish you could have seen how his eyes lit up. Bob was a B-17 pilot in the 390th who often speaks on behalf of his fellow veterans, and particularly about Chowhound. A few minutes later, I told my friend Wendy MacVicar about my idea, and mentioned how interesting it would be to have *both* sides of this story—from the perspectives of the men flying those missions and the people on the ground receiving them. Wendy grabbed my arm and told me of a friend whose mother had been a young Dutch girl when these food drops took place in Holland and had witnessed them herself. Wendy and I both got chills. Now there was no turning back, and I couldn't wait to start writing.

I have never written a historical novel before, and I must admit I was intimidated from the outset at the amount of research required to do the story justice. But once I started, I was totally consumed with the fascinating stories and accounts I read. What was it like for a young man barely out of his teens to sign up to fight in a war of this scope? What was it like for a young girl growing up in Occupied Holland? We're all familiar with the stories of Anne Frank and Corrie Ten Boom, but I knew there was so much more to tell. What was it like to be a part of the Dutch Resistance movement? And what must it have felt like to be starving during those brutal months of the Hunger Winter? How did it feel to be constantly consumed by death and despair all around you? And what was it like for those young men to fly missions bringing hope and life-saving provisions to these desperate Dutch survivors after years of dropping bombs of death and destruction?

These were the questions that set up camp in my soul. These were the stories I felt driven to tell. I don't pretend to be an expert historian. I pray I got it right, but please remember this is a work of fiction. My goal was to write the story in such a way that my readers would feel like they were there, experiencing this crucial moment in our history. And if I have done my job well, perhaps they will better understand in a new and fresh way the tremendous sacrifices of those who gave so much.

Before I wrote a single word, I dedicated this book to my father, Glenn Hale. In many ways, his story is similar to Danny's, though they are not the same person. I've grown up hearing my father talk of his experiences in the U.S. Army Air Force during WWII. Even now, at 89 years young, he can tell you where he was on any given date back in 1944 or 1945. Several years ago we convinced him to write a memoir about those years which have remained so deeply embedded in his heart. That memoir was a tremendous resource for my story. But for the record, while "Danny" has much in common with my father, Danny is a fictional character.

On 2 March 1945, Dad and his crew had to bail out of a crippled B-17 into Poland. It would be two months to the day before he got back to Framlingham on 2 May 1945—just in time to take part in *Operation Chowhound.* And like so many others who flew those food drops, Dad was tremendously moved by the experience. Not only gratified to be able to help the starving Dutch people, Dad felt it was a fitting way to thank the thousands of Dutch Resistance workers who had helped so many downed Allied airmen avoid capture by the Germans.

Over the years, Dad has had several opportunities to take some rather nostalgic rides in the vintage B-17s still flying, primarily the *Liberty Belle* and the *Memphis Belle.* On two of these occasions, I had the privilege of accompanying him on these flights. To see the local media gathering around my rock-star Dad was such a thrill. With all those microphones thrust in his face and cameras rolling, his message has always, always been the same—"We must never forget."

With textbooks sparing only a short paragraph or two to cover the entire scope of World War II, our future generations will know nothing about the great sacrifices made for them in the name of freedom. Not long ago we heard about a group of students visiting the Eighth Air Force Museum in Savannah, Georgia. The docent leading their tour, a P-47 veteran from WWII, was asked, "Did you serve in World War eleven?" Sadly, the person asking the question was the teacher.

God help us.

If my story helps remind even one person about the hard-fought and precious gift of freedom, then I shall consider it a success.

Diane Moody
November 2012

For more information on the 390th Bomb Group,
please visit their website at http://www.390th.org/

Or visit the 390th Memorial Museum
Located on the grounds of the Pima Air & Space Museum
6000 East Valencia Road
Tucson, Arizona 85756
520.574.0287

Part I

1

June 1938

Chicago, Illinois

"For Your many provisions, we give thanks, O Lord. For Your grace and mercy and love beyond measure . . ."

With his head still bowed as his mother prayed, fifteen-year-old Danny McClain slowly crawled his fingers into the basket of biscuits resting just beyond his glass of tea. Working his hand beneath the cloth napkin covering the warm biscuits, he grabbed the closest one and slid it silently onto his plate.

"And today, we thank You especially for the occasion of Joey's graduation. Bless him as he begins this new chapter in his life."

Danny peeked across the table at his brother, surprised to find Joey's head bowed. Ever the family clown, Joey had been his role model for mischief as far back as Danny could remember. Sneaking biscuits during Mom's prayer was practically a ritual between them.

"And now, O Lord, we ask You to bless this food for our nourishment and us for Thy service. Amen."

"Amen," they echoed around the table. Everyone except Dad, that is. Danny's father tolerated Mom's prayers, but otherwise he just ignored God. As usual, he quickly changed the subject.

"I want you to run the route with me tonight, Joey. I'll expect you ready to go at midnight sharp."

"Tonight?" Joey stabbed a pork chop and dropped it onto his plate. "But I'm meeting up with the guys tonight. We just graduated and we're all going down to the—"

"Precisely," Dad snapped, plopping a mound of mashed potatoes on his plate. "That little stunt you pulled at graduation was a disgrace. If you weren't eighteen, I'd take you out to the shed and make sure that never happened again. But you're out of school now, and it's time to grow up. You'll have plenty of time for your friends later. Tonight you come with me. It's time you learned the family business. Might as well be tonight."

Danny looked at Joey and watched his brother's face crimson as he spooned green beans onto his plate. He noticed the little nerve along his brother's jaw line twitching. Never a good sign.

"Frank, don't you think Joey deserves a night off?" Mom asked quietly. "This should be a night of celebration with his friends, and—

"And when I want your opinion, Betty, I'll ask for it."

Mom didn't respond. She took a small bite of her potatoes but said nothing.

Why does she let him talk to her that way? Why does she

2

put up with him? Danny hated dinners that started this way. You could cut the tension with a butter knife. They always ended the same—with everyone all worked up and saying stuff he didn't like hearing. He focused on the butter he was slathering on each half of his biscuit, hoping to tune them out.

After a few moments of uneasy silence, Danny said, "Hey Joey, did you see the carrot cake Mom made you? Five layers!"

"Yeah, Danny, I saw it." Joey put his fork down. "I keep telling you, Dad. It's *your* business, not mine. I never wanted it. I'm real proud of you and all you've done, but it's not what I want to do with my life."

"It's good work and you're mighty lucky to have it," Dad answered, mumbling a few choice words.

Danny heard his mother's long sigh. "Frank, please," she said.

"I'll say what I want to say. It's my home. I built it. And no one's gonna tell me how to talk in my own house."

Danny mouthed his father's words along with him. The discussion was another family ritual, one he didn't like at all. He snuck a peek at Mom and wasn't surprised to see her eyes glistening. *How come she always cries? She's heard it a thousand times before. Surely she's used to it by now.* Still, Danny often marveled at his mother's gentle ways and wondered how on earth someone so kind and loving ended up with someone so hateful and mean.

She cleared her throat and tried to smile. Danny didn't even try.

Suddenly Joey stood, the legs of his chair scraping against the hard wood floor. "May I be excused?"

"Sit down and finish your dinner," his father growled. "There's plenty of folks that would be happy to have a hot plate of home-cooked food right now, so you just park yourself back in that chair and clean your plate."

Danny rolled his eyes. He watched Joey take a long, deep breath then turn toward his mother. "Mom, thanks for dinner." He gave her a quick peck on the cheek, picked up his plate and glass, then left the room.

"You get back here this instant!" Dad yelled.

The squeaky hinge of the back door preceded a mighty slam. His dad launched into a tirade laced generously with four-letter words. He cursed the day Joey was born and railed at Mom for being too easy on him. Then he threw down his knife and fork and stormed out of the room.

Danny and his mother sat there listening as the door slammed a second time and the colorful language gradually faded. He just hoped Joey had high-tailed it out of the neighborhood.

Danny forked another bite of potatoes and smushed it into the remaining beans on his plate. "Joey's never gonna work for Dad. How come Dad won't let him just do what he wants?"

Mom carefully folded her napkin and set it beside her plate. "Your father's a complicated man, Danny."

"That's putting it mildly. He knows Joey wants to join the Navy. If you ask me, he's just being stubborn."

She peered over her glasses. "It's not your concern, son. Best you stay out of it."

"But Mom, it *is* my concern. I see the way he treats Joey. He treats me the same way. It's not right!"

"That's enough."

Something in her tone slowed the anger boiling inside him. He finished off his biscuit and washed it down with a gulp of tea. He waited, wondering if his father would come back. He waited, wondering what his mother would say if he did. But he'd heard it all before.

In the fall Danny would be a junior in high school. In two years, he'd be the one graduating. He wasn't about to let this scenario play out when his turn came. He wanted to go to college and get a degree. Like his brother, he didn't want to carry film cans from one theater to another all night every night. He'd go crazy doing the same thing over and over, night after night.

Right then and there, Danny decided to make a plan. He'd work extra hard to make good grades so he'd be accepted at Northwestern—maybe even get a scholarship. He'd work hard each summer mowing yards and doing as many odd jobs as he could. In the winter, he'd shovel snow for his neighbors and see if Mr. Chaney needed help at the corner grocery store. He'd open a savings account and save every dime he made.

Because when it was his turn to walk across that stage in a cap and gown, and his turn to sit down to a family dinner afterward, Mom and Dad would both know Daniel Howard McClain had plans. Big plans!

With his newly resolved determination, a wave of relief washed over him. He reached over and squeezed his mother's hand. "Mom?"

"Yes?"

"I'd like to celebrate. How about we cut us a couple pieces of that carrot cake?"

Danny sat straight up in bed, his heart pounding. "What?" He looked around in the darkness, wondering what had awakened him. He turned on his bedside lamp and looked at his clock. Eleven fifty-five. He'd only been asleep for a couple hours. He could hear the yelling downstairs and wondered what on earth could have happened. Suddenly his mother appeared at his door.

"Mom? What is it? What's going on?"

She covered her face with her hands and wept, her shoulders shaking.

Danny threw back the covers and crossed the room, grabbing his mother's arm. "Mom, you're scaring me. What's happened?"

She took a moment to compose herself, wiping her eyes with a handkerchief. "It's Joey. He's gone."

"What? You mean he still hasn't come back since dinner?"

"No, he came back. He told us he was going to lie down for a little while before going with Dad on his routes. And . . . and I went to bed. Your father had set the alarm to get up at eleven forty-five like he always does. And when he did, he went to Joey's room to wake him up and he was gone. His bed was made. He was just gone. He left a note . . ."

"A note?"

"It said he'd enlisted in the Navy way back in March. He was leaving to report for duty." Suddenly she looked up at him. "Danny, did you know? Did he tell you he was doing this?"

"No! I would have told you if he had, Mom. He never said a word to me about it."

She sniffed a couple more times and wiped her eyes again. "Your father . . ."

"Dad must've hit the roof."

"I've never seen him so angry. He said such horrible things."

"Every time Joey brought up going into the service, Dad got upset. Why? Why's he so dead set against it?"

She walked over and sat on the end of Danny's bed. "I don't really know. He lost a lot of friends in the Great War. I suppose maybe he's afraid of losing Joey if we should get pulled back into the trouble over in Europe."

"But if Joey wants to serve his country, why can't Dad just be proud of him and let him do it?"

She smoothed her cotton robe and took a deep breath. "I can't speak for your father." She shook her head. "Oh Joey, what have you done? What have you done!"

Danny patted her arm, trying to think what to say. He was shocked, but mostly he was happy for Joey. He was free! He'd always wanted to see the world and now he would. Danny tried to picture him standing at attention in a crisp white uniform . . . even now, he couldn't help feeling proud of him.

"He didn't even say goodbye," Mom whimpered.

Danny stood beside her and wrapped his arm around her trembling shoulders. "Because he couldn't, Mom. With Dad so angry, he didn't dare tell you. He'll be okay," he said over her soft cries. "Joey'll be okay, Mom."

They heard the front door slam and his father's heavy footsteps coming up the stairs. His mother gave him a quick hug and slipped out the door, closing it behind her. For the next hour he heard nothing. Not a sound. His mind ran wild, wondering what it would be like not having Joey around. *That makes me the only kid in the house now. That'll be weird. Will Dad take out his frustration about Joey on me?*

When sleep eluded him, he got up and turned on his desk light. As quietly as he could, he opened the bottom drawer and pulled out the cigar box. Lifting the stack of letters from the box, Danny looked at the postmarks from The Netherlands and wondered what Hans would do if something like this happened in his family.

At the beginning of school last year, his geography teacher made an assignment. Each student had to pick a country and learn as much as they could about it—and they had to choose a pen pal from that country. Mr. Chesterton had a master list of names and addresses from kids all over the world. Danny groaned when he first heard the assignment. He wasn't much of a writer, and he sure didn't want to write letters to some kid he didn't know half-way around the world. But as others started picking names and countries, he knew he had no choice. Browsing through the list, he saw the name *Hans Versteeg* from The Netherlands. He'd always been fascinated by those *National Geographic* pictures of Holland's windmills, so why not pick a Dutch kid?

It took him three days to write his first letter. It was only a page long but Danny hadn't been able to think of anything interesting to write. After several rewrites, he'd finally finished his "Letter of Introduction" as Mr. Chesterton called it.

Dear Hans,

You don't know me but I got your name from a list my teacher gave us. He's making us have pen pals, so I was wondering if you'd write me now and then. It's for a grade so maybe just a couple of letters or so.

My name is Danny McClain and I live in Chicago, Illinois in the United States. Chicago's a real big city. It's always windy here because we're right by Lake Michigan which is more like the ocean than a lake. It's huge. We have a football team called the Bears and a couple of baseball teams—the Cubs and the White Sox. I'm a big Cubs fan, and sometimes I go to Wrigley Field with my brother to watch them play. That's my favorite thing to do.

I live on the south side of Chicago with my mom and dad and my big brother Joey. My dad has his own business delivering movie reels to theaters. Have you ever seen a movie? My mom is real nice and she cooks really good food. She also sings in the church choir. My brother Joey is two years older than me. He's real funny. Everybody loves him.

I don't know much about The Netherlands. How come it's also called Holland? And what's with all those windmills? Do you have one? What language do you speak? I sure hope you can read this or my grade is in the toilet.

I hope you write me back. In <u>English</u>.

Danny McClain

Danny smiled, recalling that first letter he'd written. He never expected to hear back from the Dutch kid named Hans. Then one day, about three or four weeks later, he got a letter from The Netherlands addressed to him, with a strange stamp and all. It had surprised him how excited he was to get that first letter. And to his great relief, it was written in English.

Dear Danny,

Thank you very much for your letter. I would be happy to be your pen pal. Our teacher also submitted our names to an international pen pal club, and I was very afraid I'd get stuck writing a girl.

I looked up America on a map in our classroom. The United States is very big compared to my country. I found Chicago on that map and the big lake you mentioned. Do you ice skate on your lake? In Holland, everyone skates in the winter. It's my favorite thing to do. I do not know much about baseball and football. Maybe you can tell me about them.

I live in a small town named Utrecht (not far from The Hague) with my mother, father, and my sister, Anya. My father is a pastor so we live in the parsonage beside the church. He grew up in England, so we speak both Dutch and English in our home, and we're learning German at school.

You asked why we call our country by two names. There are twelve provinces in our country. North Holland and South Holland are two of them, located on the west coast where most of our ports are found. Our larger cities are found there as well—Amsterdam, The Hague, and Rotterdam. That area is called Holland while the rest of the country is called The Netherlands. ("Nether" means below which makes sense because more than 2/3 of our country is below sea level.) What's strange is that most Dutch people keep the distinction, calling their country The Netherlands. It's the outsiders and foreigners who lump us all together and call it Holland.

Now I must ask you. Why do some people call your country America and others call it the United States?

Holland is not like the other countries in Europe, so we do not take part in their wars. It's a good thing, because there are many struggles in countries near us.

I hope you will write again.

Hans

Danny leafed through the many envelopes he kept stored in the old cigar box. To think he'd dreaded writing that first letter. Now, less than a year later, Hans had practically become his best friend. Page after page, he'd write his new friend, sharing everything from the silliest thoughts to his deepest concerns. He always looked forward to hearing back from Hans. During the months at school, he always checked to see if a letter had come when he got home. Mom always placed the familiar envelopes on his pillow. Sometimes he'd get two letters a week, but most of the time just one.

And now, here he was—after midnight, unable to sleep, sharing this latest family turmoil with his Dutch friend. He took out a sheet of notebook paper and started writing.

Dear Hans,

I wish you lived just down the street. Even though it's really late, I'd sneak out and come knock on your window to tell you what happened. Today, Joey graduated. I'd never been to a graduation ceremony before. It was boring at times, with so many students walking across the stage to receive their diplomas. And then at last, my brother made that walk. He was dressed like the others in a black cap and gown, but as he approached the principal to receive his diploma, he stuck his arms out and acted as if he was flying! The gown billowed around him and everyone laughed. Well, everyone except my dad. Then once he shook the principal's hand and took his diploma, he turned to the audience and gave the grandest bow you've ever seen. Everyone loves Joey, so they all applauded and cheered. It was hilarious!

Unfortunately, when we sat down for dinner this evening, Dad was really mad about the whole thing. Then, he didn't ask—he <u>told</u> Joey that he expected him to start working for him tonight. Mom tried to convince Dad that Joey should get to celebrate with his friends, but Dad wouldn't listen. Joey got mad and left the house which only made Dad madder.

But that's not the worst of it. After we all went to bed, Joey packed his bags and left. He wrote a note saying he'd already enlisted in the Navy, and he was leaving to report for duty. I couldn't believe it! Dad's yelling woke me up, then Mom came in and told me what had happened. He's been quiet ever since. For some reason, that's even worse—him being quiet like that. I've told you before that my dad can be a real pain. But being so quiet these last few hours? It really worries me.

I can't believe Joey's gone. But at the same time, I'm real proud of him. I just hope he writes or calls me. I'm sure gonna miss him.

Your friend,

Danny

2

Danny wiped his brow with his bandana, wishing he was done for the day. He'd already mowed five lawns and had one more to go before he could head home. Just then, Mrs. Zankowski stepped out on the back porch and waved at him. She held up a mason jar filled with lemonade and ice. Danny stuffed the bandana in his pocket and walked across the fresh-cut grass.

"Awful hot this afternoon, Danny. I thought you could use something ice cold to drink."

He took the glass from her. "Thanks, Mrs. Z. I sure appreciate it." He took a sip, trying hard not to gulp it down in one swallow. "That's real good lemonade. Thanks."

She sat down on her porch swing. "Any news from your brother?"

"Yes, ma'am. We had a letter just yesterday. Joey's doing fine. He finished boot camp. He was kinda disappointed—he was hoping to make it into aviation training, but he didn't pass some of the tests. But you know Joey. He'll make the best of it. Said they're sending him to Norfolk, Virginia for some kind of training."

His neighbor smiled as she fanned herself with a magazine. "Well, Joey never did take his studies too seriously, but I'm sorry he didn't get to be a pilot if that's what he wanted. Then again, I can't imagine that brother of yours up there flying an airplane. Good heavens, what a scary thought!"

Danny laughed with her as he wiped the sweat off his neck. "I see your point."

"But good for him joining up to serve our country. You and your parents must be so proud of him. That brother of yours about drove me crazy with all his antics. Never could keep a straight face when he was in my classroom. But he kept things interesting, that's for sure." She shaded her eyes with the magazine and looked up in the sky. "Lord have mercy, Danny. What I'd give to see him toe the line for his superiors in the Navy. That would be a sight to behold, wouldn't it?"

"Yes, ma'am, it would." He took another drink remembering how much Joey liked Mrs. Zankowski. She taught history at Calumet High School. Everyone loved her classes because she always made history interesting and fun. Danny hoped he'd be assigned to one of her classes before he graduated.

She stood up. "Well, you be sure and tell him hello for me next time you write him, okay? I'm mighty proud of him for following his dream." She reached into her apron pocket and handed him two neatly folded dollar bills. "Thank you,

Danny. You always do a real nice job."

"Thanks. I'll see you next week." He snapped his fingers. "Oh, that reminds me—next week I'll be mowing on Saturday instead of Friday. I've got tickets for the Cubs game on Friday."

"Good for you! Great season so far, isn't it?"

"We're going all the way this year. I can feel it!"

"I hope you're right. Well, we'll see you next Saturday then. Have a good week."

"You too, Mrs. Z."

Danny finished the backyard, swept the patio and front sidewalks, then headed out for his next lawn, dragging his mower behind him. School would be starting in a few weeks and his income would slow way down. He'd already talked to Mr. Chaney about helping out after school at his grocery store. He liked the old guy and looked forward to working for him.

As he mowed the Smithson's lawn, back and forth across their broad front yard, he couldn't help thinking about his dad. Danny had avoided him as much as possible over the course of the summer. Ever since Joey left, Dad had grown more quiet with each passing day. He'd grumble and growl if something didn't go his way, but mostly he was just quiet. *Too* quiet. It made Danny and his mother uneasy, though they both welcomed the silent meal times.

After Joey's first letter, they learned to keep quiet about the news they'd read. Danny had tried to share a funny story his brother had written—something about a prank someone in his unit had played on a bunkmate. Dad had slowly placed his knife and fork on his plate, then folded his hands.

Looking back and forth between them, he said, "There will be no discussion about Joey at this table. Is that understood?"

Danny had stared into his father's tired, bloodshot eyes, then looked at Mom. Her head was bowed as she seemed to study her plate, not saying a word. She just sat there with a bite of meatloaf on her fork. Danny looked back to see Dad's reaction.

"I said, is that understood?"

"Yes, sir," Danny croaked. Mom nodded her head.

From that moment on, they never mentioned Joey again at the dinner table. Instead, Danny and his mother found stolen moments to talk about Joey's letters when his dad was out of the house. Sometimes it meant waiting until he left late at night on his film routes. Then they'd sit at the kitchen table and read the letter together, even though they'd both read it separately when it first arrived. He hated having to hide the fact he was interested in his brother's news. But even more troubling was the silence that so often filled their home.

Danny quickly finished his last lawn for the day, collected his pay from Mr. Smithson, and hurried home. He stopped first in the garage, grabbing the broom to sweep the remaining blades of grass off the old mower, then stepped out of his filthy shoes. He took the back steps two at a time and found his mother snapping beans on the back porch.

"How was your afternoon? Get all your yards done?"

He leaned over, planting a noisy kiss on her cheek. "Sure did. And for a change, they all paid me today." He dug the bills out of his pocket and waved them at her. "I need to make another deposit."

"Good for you, son. Why, at the rate you're going, you'll own that bank one of these days."

"Not hardly. Hey, did I get any mail today?"

Mom smiled. "Letter from Hans on your pillow."

"Anything from Joey?"

"No," she said, her voice dropping a notch, "but we can read yesterday's letter again if you'd like. Your father's leaving early tonight." She winked at him and patted her pocket.

"Sounds good. I'm gonna go wash up then read my letter from Hans."

"Dinner's in about an hour."

Ten minutes later, Danny got dressed after his shower and tossed his dirty clothes in the hamper. He reached for Hans' letter, then stretched out on his bed to read it.

Dear Danny,

It is hard for me to imagine such temperatures as you have in Chicago! Today it is 19.1° C. here. I believe that is 66.4° F. Much cooler than your 99°! Today I had to help my sister Anya fix her bicycle. Everyone rides bicycles in The Netherlands, as I told you before. And most everyone takes very good care of their bicycles because we have to depend on them. But my little Anya (she's only a year younger than me but she's really small for her age) is not so careful. And with all our rain lately, her bicycle has rusted once again. She's terribly hard on things and always frustrated when things go wrong. I told you before what a tomboy she is, but have I mentioned she's also bull-headed?

Such fights the two of us have!

Congratulations on the new job at the grocery store. I would think you would be very busy working and going to school in the fall. Here, most everything is brought to us so that we do not often need to go to the market. It's considered an honor to supply the local pastor with bread, vegetables, milk, and even meat from the butcher. But this is also done for many other residents as well.

What have you heard from Joey? Any news?

Everyone here seems quite nervous. None of us believed Hitler could take Austria, yet he did. We thought that England and France would step up and try to stop him, but they have not. Our country always stays out of war, but the news we hear is still troubling. It's quite hard to understand all that is happening.

I have enclosed a picture of our family as you requested. This was taken by my cousin Piet. The windmill behind us is not far from our home. It is called Mollen De Ster (Star Windmill) and it is my favorite. This picture was taken when we had a family picnic with Piet and his family. That is Anya standing to my left. Mother was upset with her for scraping her knee while chasing Piet through a tulip field.

By the time you get this letter, perhaps your letter and picture will arrive here. I wonder if you look as I imagine you to look!

Your friend,

Hans

Danny carefully unwrapped the tissue paper folded around the photograph. He too had been curious what his Dutch friend looked like. It was strange to be good friends with someone he'd never met. Immediately he spotted Hans standing next to his father. Danny smiled seeing his picture for the first time. Hans had a thick head of blond hair brushed straight back. His face was oval, his chin squared a bit. He assumed Hans' eyes were blue, though he couldn't be sure in the gray tones of the photograph. He had a friendly smile, just as he'd expected. Now he had a face to go with the name.

Hans looked a good deal like his father, except for the round glasses perched on his father's nose and the bushy mustache below it. He too had a friendly smile. Danny wondered what it was like to hear him preach. Was he soft spoken and kind, or one of those who shouted his sermons? Then he looked at Hans' mother, her face quite beautiful despite the firm set of her lips. Danny recognized that expression, so similar to his own mother's when she got upset. And then he glanced at Anya standing there with her arms folded across her chest and a pronounced scowl on her face. Sure enough, her pant leg was stained and dirty at the knee. Two messy pigtails hung down three or four inches below her shoulders. Danny chuckled, having no trouble imagining the girl's mischief.

He studied the windmill in the background, its four outstretched wings lending an air of majesty to the photograph. Hans had explained the important role of the *windmolen* helping pump water from Holland's precious land to prevent flooding. The Dutch had a long history battling their below-sea level ground, and the windmills stood at the forefront of those battles, dating all the way back to the thirteenth century—a fact Danny had included in his latest report for Mr. Chesterton's class.

He leaned his head back on the pillow, crossing one arm over his head. As he often did after reading Hans' letters, he tried to picture himself in their world. He wondered what it would be like to live in a land dotted with those big windmills. He wondered what it must look like to see everyone riding bicycles to and from their destinations. And he wondered what it felt like to have that Hitler nut just across the border breathing down your neck. Hans said everyone in The Netherlands was nervous about the Germans.

Danny's only worry was if the Cubs would make it to the World Series.

How different, their worlds.

3

October 1938

Dear Hans,

I still can't believe it. Our Cubs made it all the way to the World Series, then they lost the first four games! FOUR GAMES! The first two games were played here at Wrigley. We couldn't get tickets. Probably just as well. Dad would've killed me if he found out I skipped school to go, but I sure wanted to. But everybody's real upset. We were so sure this was our year! People keep blaming Dizzy Dean for letting us down, but I think they should get off his back. If it wasn't for him, the Cubs never would've made it to the World Series. I don't know, I'm just real sore we lost.

In your last letter, you said your mother was not well. Is she better now? I told Mom about her and she promised to pray for her.

Joey said he's getting used to being in the

military. He seems to like being stationed in Norfolk, but hopes to get assigned to a ship soon. I wish I could go see him. He said I'd love living near the ocean.

Well, I need to do some homework. I have a test in English Literature tomorrow. I just realized you all probably don't have any kind of English classes. Do you study Dutch writers?

Bye for now,

Danny

The months flew by as fall gave way to winter. But for Danny, Christmas 1938 just wouldn't be the same. He couldn't get used to holidays without his big brother around. On Christmas Eve, they drove out to his grandparents' farm in Sandwich, a rural community west of town. He loved visiting the big farmhouse and helping his grandfather feed the livestock. He wished he could spend the holidays there, but Dad never took much time off work and wouldn't hear of leaving his wife and son in the company of her family for that long. Dad didn't much care for Mom's kin, and the feeling was mutual. Still, Danny was glad they could spend most of the day on the farm. A light snow fell all day which made it just about perfect.

The following week, Danny worked as many hours as he could at the grocery store. One night, as he was helping Mr. Chaney close up, he put on his jacket to take out the trash. As he rolled the big trash barrel out to the alley, he heard the faintest whimper. Following the sound, he discovered a puppy hiding behind the big garbage bin.

Danny squatted down to get a better look at the pup.

"Hey, little fella. What're you doing back there?" The pup pulled back when Danny reached out his hand toward him. "Don't be afraid. I won't hurt you." He could tell it was some kind of beagle mix, though dirt and mud covered much of its coat. He could see the dog's ribs under all that mess.

"Danny? Where are you? Let's call it a night."

"Over here, Mr. Chaney." He waved the older man over. "There's a little puppy back here. Looks like he could use something to eat. Okay if I give him some scraps out of the trash here?"

His boss came closer to take a look. "Well, hello there, little fella. Look at him—he's shaking like a leaf. Think we should take him inside to warm up?"

"Not a bad idea. Awful cold out here."

As Danny slowly leaned closer to the pooch, it backed up against the brick wall and let out the most pitiful cry. "At least he's not growling or baring his teeth at me," Danny said as he moved in closer. He carefully held out his hand for the dog to sniff. "There you go, little fella. I just want to help." The puppy sniffed and sniffed, then slowly started licking Danny's hand.

"He probably smells those vegetables you were sorting earlier. See if he'll let you pick him up."

And in one gentle, swift move, Danny scooped the pup into his arms and held him tight. Mr. Chaney opened the door and followed Danny and his new friend inside.

"Let's give him some dog food just to be safe. I'll be right back," the grocer said.

A couple minutes later they watched as the dirty hound gobbled down the contents of a large can of Alpo.

"Whoa! I can't believe how fast he ate that. Think we should give him more?" Danny asked.

"Actually the question is, should we give *her* more."

Danny took a peek, and sure enough the he was a she. He laughed, giving the dog a rub behind her ears. She immediately crawled up in his lap and started nuzzling around inside his jacket.

"I'd say she's probably had enough to eat. Don't want to give her too much too fast. Might make her sick if she hasn't eaten in a few days."

Danny pulled her head out of his jacket and took a long look at her. "Well, little lady, what are we going to do with you?"

Mr. Chaney stood up. "Can't leave her here. That's for sure. I reckon you're going to have to take her home for the night."

Danny wondered what his dad would say, but realized he had no choice. For years, he and Joey had begged their dad for a dog until they finally just gave up. But surely Dad would understand. Poor little dog couldn't be left out in the cold on a winter's night in Chicago.

Thankfully, Dad was gone by the time he got home and his mother was already in bed. Danny snuck the dog up the stairs and into his room. "Now, whatever you do, keep quiet." He grabbed some blankets out of the hall closet and made a bed for her beside his own bed. She seemed content to curl up in its warmth, her big brown eyes following Danny's every move. After brushing his teeth, he quietly made his way back to bed where, for the next half hour, she whined as she tried over and over to climb up onto the bed with him.

"All right, all right. But just for tonight. And keep it down, will ya?"

He put the blankets at the foot of his bed and lifted her onto them. She walked in circles, sniffing here, scratching there. She made one final circle and curled herself against Danny's leg. He reached down and scratched her head. "No matter what Dad says, first thing we do tomorrow is give you a bath," he whispered. "You stink!"

She let out a long sigh and quickly fell asleep. As his eyes grew heavy, Danny couldn't help thinking this might not be such a bad Christmas after all.

By New Year's Day, the scrawny little pup had already begun to put on some much-needed weight. She'd also won the hearts of his mom—*and* his father. Danny couldn't have been more shocked when his dad finally agreed to let him keep her.

"It's a big responsibility. First time I find her making a mess on the floor or tearing up the furniture, she's gone. Understood?"

"Yes, sir. I'll take good care of her. I promise."

"See that you do."

Then, the strangest thing happened. Dad knelt down on one knee and gave her a good long rub on the back of her neck. Danny watched, surprised at the tender display of affection.

"She's a fine girl. Reminds me of a dog I had when I was a kid." His dad sniffed then stood up as if he'd had enough.

"You had a dog once?"

"A beagle. Looked a lot like her. Named him Barney. That dog went everywhere with me."

For the first time, Danny looked at his father with different eyes. He tried to imagine a younger version of Frank McClain and the dog named Barney. The image didn't come easily in his mind, but he liked the idea of it.

"What happened to him?"

"Idiot neighbor accidentally ran over him. Took me a long time to get over it." He leaned back down and patted the pup's head. "See that you keep her out of the street. We'll get the backyard fence all fixed up so she can't wander off."

"Thanks, Dad. I'll take real good care of her. You'll see."

His father stood and headed for the stairs. "What are you going to call her?"

"Sophie. I think I'll call her Sophie."

January 2, 1939

"Danny?" his mother called up the stairs. "Mail's here. You have a letter from Hans and we have a postcard from Joey!"

Danny flew down the stairs with Sophie at his heels. "Holy cow, I lost all track of time. Mail man came early today, huh?"

"Maybe he knew how anxious we were to hear from Joey." She handed him the letter from Holland with the familiar lettering as he followed her down the hall to the kitchen.

"Whoa—this letter was stamped more than a month ago. I wondered why I hadn't heard from him in a while. That's slow, even for The Netherlands."

"Perhaps the holidays slowed down their mail service. I hope all is well with Hans and his family," Mom said. "But first, let's take a look." She flipped the postcard over to look at the picture. "Goodness me—this is Times Square in New York City! Although this picture looks like it was taken in the spring or summer. I'd expect folks to be wrapped up in coats and hats in the dead of winter, not linen suits and cotton dresses."

Danny took a closer look at the picture. "Imagine that. New York City! Think he's rubbing it in?"

"Your brother? Of course he's rubbing it in. Now, let's see what he has to say."

Happy New Year from New York!

Me and the guys got a last minute leave so we caught a bus up here for a couple of days. But I sure missed spending Christmas with you. Thanks for the nifty sweater and the socks and cookies. I had to hide the cookies so the guys wouldn't eat them all! Right before I left the base, I got my orders. I've been assigned to the USS Oklahoma in the Pacific Fleet! They'll fly me out to San Francisco to board her 1 March 1939. I'll try to call you before I leave Norfolk.

Miss you!

Love, Joey

"Wow! He's going to the Pacific," Danny said. "He's gotta be excited about that."

"But that's so far away."

"And he gets to fly all the way to San Francisco! Man, I wish I could fly in an airplane. That's gotta be swell, way up there above the clouds. I wonder how long a flight all the way across the country will take?"

She shook her head. "I wish they weren't sending him so far away. Now we'll never get a chance to visit him. I'd hoped we could make a trip to see him sometime this year."

"Really? You think Dad would be okay with that?"

Her countenance fell. "Oh, sweetheart, I doubt it. You know how he is."

"But Mom, Joey sounds really happy, don't you think?"

She tilted her head to one side. "Yes, yes he does. I just hope and pray he won't go near all that trouble overseas."

"Oh, don't worry. That doesn't involve the U.S. He'll probably be having the time of his life. You'll see."

She looked at him over her glasses. "Danny, I wish I was as optimistic as you. You always look for the best in situations. I wish I had more faith so I didn't worry so much."

"But you're a mom. Moms are supposed to worry," Danny teased, grabbing his letter and heading down the hall. "C'mon, Sophie. Let's go find out what's happening in Holland."

The beagle followed him up the stairs and into his room, jumping up on the bed before he even sat down. She never left his side when he was home, never happier than when she was curled up beside him on the bed.

He used the letter opener his mom had given him for Christmas to slit open the envelope. He sat on his bed beside Sophie and unfolded the pages.

Dear Danny,

How was your Thanksgiving? From what you described, it sounds like such a special holiday for you and all Americans. Although I cannot imagine what this "stuffing" you mentioned must taste like. But I do think I would like your pumpkin pie.

I know well these cranberries! They are quite popular here in The Netherlands. We learned about them last year at school. A long, long time ago, an American shipwreck came ashore in the northern Netherlands province on the island of Terschelling— including a barrel of cranberries. The man who found them was disappointed to find the sour berries, hoping the barrel was full of wine. He dumped the barrel in the dunes. My teacher said the sandy bog was the perfect ground for the berries to grow and we've had them ever since. When I read of your Thanksgiving tradition of cranberries, I thought of that shipwrecked crate as a gift from your America to my homeland and I laughed. Should I say thank you? Bedankt!

We just celebrated Sinterklaas on December 5, and had a wonderful time. As is custom, we give each other presents that we make ourselves—sometimes silly, sometimes thoughtful and nice. You have to wrap each present and write a poem to go with it, then the person who opens the gift must read the poem aloud.

It's very funny, going around the room hearing all these poems, most of them very clever. I gave my sister Anya a small wooden pig which I had carved myself. Whenever I ask my little Anya to do a favor for me, she always says, "When pigs fly!" So I carved little wings on this pig and made up a funny poem about Anya flying away on her little pig. She laughed and laughed, then suddenly she started to cry. When I asked her why, she gave me a hug and said, "Because you did something nice for me, and I am always such a nuisance to you." I have no understanding of why that made her cry. Perhaps I shall never understand girls.

We're about to go skating, so I must close. Most of the kids our age in the village are going. We plan to make a day of it, skating on the canals past all the windmills. It is very common to do this, and all along the way families set up tents to feed the skaters. Everyone joins in and has a wonderful time. Some day you must visit me and we shall skate by all those windmills you like so much!

Prettige Kerstdagen en een Gelukkig Nieuwjaar, Danny! That means "Merry Christmas and a Happy New Year." I thank God for the American friend He gave me in you, and I hope He will make us life-long good friends.

Hans

4

February 1939

"I love snow as much as the next guy, but this is ridiculous."

The blustering snows off Lake Michigan kept Danny busy each day after school and most of Saturday if he wasn't working for Mr. Chaney. He'd get home, have a quick snack and play with Sophie for a couple of minutes before bundling back up and heading out to shovel snow for his neighbors. Lots of his friends made money this way too. They all had their own territories. Danny did his best to keep the sidewalks and driveways of the two block area surrounding his home near the corner of Yale Avenue and 80th Street. Ordinarily that was an easy task, but 1939 had brought layer upon layer of the white stuff, often negating his efforts from the previous day.

As he stepped out on his front porch, he looked up, noticing the sky was clouding up again. *Better get to it.* He yanked his knit cap down low to cover his ears then pulled on his heavy work gloves and grabbed his shovel. He always stopped first at Mrs. Martello's house across the street and two doors down. Recently widowed, the portly old lady insisted on a clear pathway to her sister's house next door. Danny knew if he didn't keep it clear, she'd try to make the short walk and probably end up falling.

"Oh, there you are! I was wondering if I'd see you today. I need to take a loaf of bread over to Angelica's, but as you can see my walkway is covered again."

"No problem, Mrs. Martello. You know I always come here first. I'll have it cleared for you in just a jiffy."

"Thank you, Danny," she called, already heading back into her house.

Danny got right to work, all too aware the snow had begun to fall again. Twenty minutes later, he stomped his snow-covered boots up the steps of her house and knocked on the door. When she opened it, she was putting on her heavy coat.

"Mrs. Martello, it's snowing again. I cleared the sidewalk, but it already has another fine layer. Why don't you let me take that bread over to your sister?"

"Nonsense and horse feathers. I go every day. Why would I let a little snow stop me? I'll be fine. See you tomorrow, Danny."

He looked down the street at the six houses he'd hoped to shovel, but knew he couldn't let her make the walk alone. "Well, if that's the case, then I insist you let me come along. Wouldn't want Miss Angelica to go without that loaf of bread." He offered his elbow to her.

"Why, aren't you the nicest young man! I'd be most grateful. Now, just give me a minute while I put on my gloves."

He felt sure the minute was more like five, but he tried to wait patiently. When she was finally covered from head to toe, he helped her down the porch steps and across the brick walkway. Once there, she had a chatty visit with her sister. *It's not like you all don't talk on the phone several times a day,* he thought. Why the two women didn't just move in together, he had no idea.

Fifteen minutes later, he returned her safely to her home, in spite of a couple of close calls coming up the steps. She tipped him an extra dollar for the favor and sent him on his way.

The snow twirled about in heavy, silent rhythms. He was used to shoveling in all kinds of weather, so he stuck it out. By five o'clock, he'd finished the McPherson's, the Lendowski's, and the Langley's houses, and decided to stop. The streetlights helped, but shoveling in the dark could be dangerous. He'd have to do the other two tomorrow. Hopefully the snow would let up by then.

His mother opened the door as he stepped onto the porch. "I was about to come looking for you. It's late, Danny. Come inside and get warm. I don't want you catching your death of cold out there."

"Be right in. Something sure smells good. What's for dinner?"

"Fried chicken." She suddenly covered her mouth with her hand. "Oh, for goodness sake. I forgot to tell you earlier. You have a letter from Hans."

"Yeah? It's about time. I was starting to worry."

"I know, that's why I'm so sorry I didn't mention it earlier. It's up on your pillow."

"No problem, Mom. I was in a hurry this afternoon and never thought to go up and check."

"Do you want me to get it for you?"

"No, I'd rather read it after dinner and a bath. That'll give me something to look forward to." He set the shovel in the corner of the covered porch and sat on one of the rockers to take off his boots. He hadn't heard from Hans in over two months. From the beginning they'd always written at least once a week, though their letters often took three weeks to be delivered—two if they were lucky. Danny assumed the recent long delay was probably a Dutch postal problem and tried not to worry.

Sophie broke his train of thought, standing inside the window behind him, barking in delight, her breath frosting the glass. "Hey girl, I'll be right in. Did ya' miss me?" He could swear she smiled at him. "Well, just for the record, I missed you too, Sophie."

After dinner, Danny dragged himself up the stairs. He pulled his sweater over his head and tossed it on his bed. He was tempted to read Hans' letter but decided he'd rather take a nice hot bath first. Once he was clean and finally warm again, he picked up the letter and noticed something different. *That's strange. It's from his address but that's not his handwriting.* He sat down on his bed and carefully opened the letter.

Dear Danny,

I have tried to write you many times, but I simply could not find the words. I am so very heartbroken, but

I must tell you of the recent death of my brother Hans. It happened back in December on a day of skating. We had such a wonderful day, all of us, skating the canal. Late in the afternoon, as we skated our way home, there was a terrible scream from behind us. Hans immediately skated back and found our young friend Rieky had fallen and hit her head on the ice. Hans tried to calm her down as we all turned back to see what had happened. Just as we approached them we heard a loud crack in the ice. We know whenever that happens we must get off the ice as fast as possible. We all skated away as fast as we could, but Hans stayed with Rieky who was crying hysterically and clinging to him. Suddenly, with a sound I shall never forget, the crack split wide open. We could not see Hans or Rieky! I started to skate back to them, but the others held me back. Some of the older boys tried to reach them, but the ice kept cracking and they had to turn back. We could hear Hans and Rieky crying out for help in that freezing water, but we could not reach them. I yelled and yelled, screaming at Hans not to give up. But soon their cries were silent and we knew the water below had pushed them beyond the gaping split in the ice.

Even now, these many weeks later, I cannot forget the sound of their desperate cries going silent. I cannot erase from my mind the image of my brother and little Rieky dying in that icy water. I will never forgive myself for not breaking through the arms of those who held me back. I could have saved them! I know I could have saved them!

Our home is filled with sorrow. My mother's broken heart has kept her bedridden. Father tries so hard to be strong, but in the quiet of the night I hear him crying. I do not know how we will go on.

I know how much your friendship meant to Hans. He talked about you constantly, telling us all about his American friend Danny in Chicago, America. He has a cigar box where he kept all your letters. When they continued to come after he died, I knew I must find the courage one day to write you.

More than anything, I live each day with the regret that I never told Hans how much he meant to me. It seemed my quest in life to annoy him as much as I could, but deep down I adored him and loved him more than words can say. Now he shall never know.

I know Hans hoped to someday meet you, and now that shall never happen. I'm so sorry you must now mourn the loss of your friend, as we have mourned these many weeks.

Anya

Danny's hands trembled as he stared at the page. A drop splashed on the words, causing the ink to run. He hadn't even realized he was crying. He brushed away the tear, not wanting the words to smear, but at the same time wishing he could blot out the horrible message they told.

He heard himself moan as he set the letter aside. He dropped his head in his hands and gave in to the ache in his chest. "Tell me it's not true. Please tell me Hans didn't die . . ." He squeezed his eyes, wiping away his tears when a thought hit him. *Maybe it's just a joke. Hans always talks about how mischievous his little sister is. Could this be some sick retaliation for another of their fights?* But almost as soon as the notion drifted through his mind, it disappeared. *No one is that cruel. Not even a bratty kid sister.*

He knew the despair in Anya's letter was genuine. He could feel it in his gut. Hans had drowned in the frigid waters beneath the ice he'd always loved to skate on. The friend he'd hoped to one day meet was now gone forever.

Sophie began to whimper quietly, her mournful eyes locked on Danny's. He drew in a ragged breath and pulled her into his arms. "I don't understand. How could something so bad happen to someone so good?" Still whimpering, she nuzzled up to his face and began licking the tears from his cheek.

They sat like that for several minutes as Danny tried to make sense of it all. He tried to picture Anya and her parents . . . how they must have suffered with a grief so much worse than what rocked him now half a world away.

He wasn't sure how long he'd sat there when another thought came to him. He knew what he had to do. He set Sophie aside and got up, making his way over to his desk. He opened the drawer and reached inside to lift out the old cigar box. He slowly opened the lid and placed his hand on the stack of letters. His eyes tracked to the mirror above his desk where he'd tucked the picture of Hans and his family in the frame. The pain in his chest ached again, but he pushed through it, reaching into another drawer for a clean sheet of paper. With his pen poised above the first line, he froze. How could he possibly express what he was feeling in his heart?

Dear Anya,

I have just received your letter and cannot begin to tell you how sorry I am to read of Hans' death. Even seeing the words on the paper, I find it impossible to believe he's gone. We never had the chance to meet face to face, but I can honestly say, over the past year and a half we've been writing, he's become my best friend. I don't even know what to do with that—losing someone so special to me. Even still, it's nothing compared to the grief you and your parents have shared these past weeks.

But I want you to know how often he wrote of you and how fond he was of his "little Anya." He loved giving you a hard time, but deep down he was crazy about you. Don't ever think differently.

I can't even find the words to say how sorry I am for you and your parents. I promise to keep all of you in my prayers. Maybe someday God will help us make sense of this.

Danny

5

Over the next couple of weeks, Danny lived in a fog. He went to school, continued to work for Mr. Chaney at the grocery store, and shoveled snow when it fell. But he merely went through the motions, his mind and his heart thousands of miles away. His mother seemed to understand. She told him she'd lost a young sister when she was just a girl. She encouraged him to talk about Hans and not hold in his grief, or let her know if she could help. But it was too hard. Too soon. He knew it was crazy, but it seemed like talking about it only made it more painful. In some strange way, it validated the truth that Hans was dead.

At first his father seemed sympathetic, but only for a day or two. Then came the grumbled comments across the dinner table.

"Nothing you can do about it, so stop all this moping around."

"You never met the kid. Get over it."

"Enough of this. Grow up and take it like a man."

Whenever one of these missiles came his way, Danny just let it roll over him, ignoring the intended barb. For some reason, he felt completely numb, unwilling to muster any kind of response. Always, his mother would later commend him for not taking his father's bait, but truth be told, he just didn't care anymore.

Joey called near the end of February before crossing the country to his new home aboard the USS *Oklahoma*. He seemed anxious to go, but regretted not getting to see his family before he deployed. Danny thought he sounded a little homesick, but couldn't be sure. He wondered if Joey would have come home if Dad hadn't kept his grudge all these months. The thought depressed him. He'd give anything to get to spend some time with his brother. Who knew how long it might be before he'd be stateside again?

Gradually, as winter gave way to spring, he began to feel the fog lifting and made an extra effort to pour himself into his school work. He took as many hours at the grocery store as he could. When April finally rolled around, he started looking forward to the Cubs' new season and another chance at the pennant. Still, never a day passed that he didn't think of Hans. He always looked for a letter on his pillow when he came home from school, then glanced at the picture on his mirror and tried to be thankful for the friendship they'd shared instead of living with the grief.

Then one sunny afternoon in late April, Danny hurried home from school and took the porch steps two at a time. In less than two minutes, he scratched Sophie behind the ears, threw an old knotted sock down the hall for her to chase, said hi to his mom who was peeling carrots at the kitchen sink, and sliced himself a piece of pound cake for a snack.

"Good heavens, what's the hurry, Danny?"

"Opening day! Cubs and Cardinals in St. Louis. Don't wanna miss it!"

As he flew down the hall and up the stairs, he heard his mom yell, "Danny, don't forget to feed Sophie, and by the way, there's a—"

He missed whatever else his mother said when he flipped on the radio on his bedside table and tuned it to WLS. Just as he was ready to plop down on his bed, he saw it—an envelope resting on his pillow. His heart nearly stopped until he realized the handwriting was that of Anya, not Hans.

He turned the volume down on his radio, picked up the letter, and studied the postmark as he reached for his letter opener. He noticed she'd sent the letter on April 1—three weeks ago.

Dear Danny,

I thank you for the letter you wrote after hearing our sad news. It was kind of you and we were grateful for your prayers. It's been hard, but we're trying to put our lives back together as best we can. Mother has had a very difficult time. She stays in bed most days, and I'm very much afraid she may never be the same. I try to cheer her up, but it doesn't seem to help.

I hope you don't mind, but one day I read all of your letters to Hans. I often spend time in his room. It makes me feel close to him. Now I understand why you and my brother were such good friends. You sound so

*very much like him in many ways. I was wondering if
you would like me to send the letters back to you along
with your picture?*

I don't know what else to say so I'll end this.

Anya

For some reason, the idea of Anya reading his letters
startled him. A lot. He glanced over at the picture of Hans
and his family still stuck in the frame of his mirror. He'd
often thought she looked like a real pill, but maybe that was
more about the stories Hans had written about her and all
the trouble she used to give him. His mind wandered off,
picturing his friend's feisty sister and the mischief that
seemed to follow her every step. He remembered the time
Hans wrote about her getting kicked out of the Girl Scouts.
Danny had been shocked to hear Holland even had Girl
Scouts, but apparently the organization had roots in England
which had quickly spread throughout Europe. Mrs. Versteeg
had insisted her daughter join, much to Anya's displeasure.

Hans once wrote him that Anya got into a fight one day
with a girl named Tilly who happened to be the scoutmaster's
daughter. Tilly fancied herself quite the beauty and loved to
tease Anya in front of the other girls for her rough and
tumble behavior and unkempt appearance. On that
particular day Tilly made up some silly song about Anya's
stubby fingernails and freckles. As all the other girls laughed
and laughed, Anya ran headfirst into Tilly's stomach, tackling
her in the dirt outside the windmill where their meetings were
held. By the time the two were separated, Tilly had the wind
knocked out of her and her uniform was covered with dirt.

The scoutmaster immediately ended the meeting and dragged Anya to her home where she told Reverend and Mrs. Versteeg their daughter was no longer welcome in their club. Of course Anya was delighted by the news and didn't even mind when she was grounded for a month. Far worse, her parents made her apologize to Tilly in front of the entire congregation. Hans had found the whole incident hilarious, though he worried about his little sister. "Will she never learn?" he'd written.

Danny had smiled when he read about the scuffle, envisioning Anya wrestling on the ground with that girl and the humiliation she must have felt having to apologize in front of everyone. Now, as he looked back at the letter he still held in his hand, he decided he was glad she'd written. It made missing Hans a little easier somehow. It still felt odd to know she'd read all his letters, but maybe that was okay too.

Dear Anya,

I'm glad you wrote. I was thinking about your family a lot and wondering how you were doing. I'm sorry your mom is still having a hard time. I can't imagine what my mom would do if she lost me or my brother.

There's no need to return the letters. You can keep them or just throw them out, whatever you want to do.

Hans told me you're just a year younger than he was, but real smart. Do you like school? I can't wait until I graduate. I want to go to college and all, but sometimes I get tired of studying. He also said you liked to draw. I'm lousy at art stuff.

If you want, you can write me again. I'm kinda used to getting letters from The Netherlands, so I wouldn't mind. You're the only girl I ever wrote a letter to, but since you're Hans' little sister, it's okay.

Danny

p.s. I think it's funny you decked that Tilly girl.

Danny folded the letter, stuck it in an envelope, licked the flap and dug around in his drawer to find a stamp. That's when he remembered the Cubs game and leaped across his bed to turn up the radio.

"Bottom of the first with the Cubs leading their opening game against the Cardinals, one to nothing. We'll be right back."

"Did ya hear that, Sophie? Cubs are ahead! I think this could be the year we go all the way! C'mon, girl, let's go tell Mom."

As Danny and Sophie made their way downstairs, he heard his mother's voice calling from the kitchen. "So you had another letter from Hans' sister?"

His pace slowed as he felt his face warm. Would his mother still ask lots of questions as she'd always done when Hans wrote? The thought of it sent a prickly, odd wave over him.

He wasn't at all sure he was ready to be pen pals with—*a girl.*

6

June 1939

With another year of school under his belt, Danny looked forward to the summer ahead. He would soon celebrate his seventeenth birthday, but dreaded his last year of high school. He was itching to go to college, tired of working two jobs, and weary of the strained air filling his home. Sure, he had friends he hung out with, but he missed Joey terribly. Had it really been a whole year since Joey left to join the Navy? Thankfully, his brother sent frequent postcards describing life on a battleship and all the colorful places he'd visited. Once he'd even called when the *Oklahoma* was in port on Guam, but spent half his time reassuring his worried mother.

"Yes, I'm doing fine. Yes, I'm staying out of trouble, and yes, I'm healthy as an ox, Mom. But please stop fussing about how much this call is costing me! I saved plenty of money to pay for it. I promise you!"

Despite the static-filled connection, Danny could hear the growing confidence and pride in his brother's voice each time he called. He tried to imagine the smell of the salt water Joey always talked about and the feel of the ocean wind against his skin. He couldn't help it—he was just plain jealous.

Nevertheless, Danny quickly settled back into his familiar summer routine, mowing lawns and helping out at Mr. Chaney's grocery store. Sophie often accompanied him on his mowing days, tagging along from house to house, usually finding a spot of shade as she waited on him. She seemed to enjoy all the attention from neighbors who stopped to pet her or offer her a dish of water. Danny couldn't imagine how he'd ever lived without her companionship. It seemed the feeling was mutual.

Then one Sunday, out of the blue, he and his dad went to a Cubs' double-header against the Brooklyn Dodgers. Normally Mom didn't like them doing things on Sunday, but the tickets were a gift from one of his dad's theater clients, and rather than cause a heated discussion, she relented. "Just this once," she added, with a touch of warning. This was a first—Dad had never included him on *anything* this special. He wasn't sure how much fun it would be, but for a double-header at Wrigley, he'd take his chances.

On June 18, the Windy City felt hotter than usual by the time Danny and his dad switched from the trolley car at 59th and Wentworth to catch the El to Wrigley. When they got off at the Addison exit, even the breeze off Lake Michigan couldn't keep Danny's shirt from sticking to his skin. Using his baseball glove to fan himself, they joined the bustling crowd filing into the stadium and found their seats just minutes before the first pitch. The bleacher seats weren't the greatest, located behind the right outfield, but Danny didn't care. The Cubs were finally home after a five-game losing streak away, and the faithful fans seemed energized to cheer on their beloved team. Win or lose, Danny loved the games at Wrigley. There, he felt a part of something special, something so much bigger than his own little world.

Dad hadn't said much of anything since they left the house. Saturday nights were tough for Frank McClain. Those nights, his film routes kept him out until seven or eight the following morning. With Hollywood studios releasing one blockbuster after another in 1939, the movie business stayed busier than ever. But for Danny, Hollywood's success meant a tired, cranky father. He knew his dad had slept a few hours before the game, but fatigue only dialed up his father's perpetually sour moods. By the top of the fourth inning of the first game, he started grumbling about the scoreless game, letting Danny know he wanted to leave early.

"Dad, c'mon. With Dizzy Dean on the mound, you know something's gonna happen. He hasn't lost a game yet this year. Besides, there's a whole other game after this one. Why can't we stay?"

His father chewed on some peanuts, tossing the shells beneath his seat. He wiped his hands on his pants and stared a hole into Danny. "If nothing happens by the end of this inning, we're leaving. Not another word."

Danny huffed, tamping down his simmering frustration. *What's the point of coming to a double-header if you're not gonna stay til the end? Sure it's hot and windy, but you never know when something exciting might happen.* He remembered all the times he and Joey had come to Wrigley, chasing balls, shouting at the opposing team, and cutting up with their friends. Didn't matter where they sat, they always had a good time. Not like today. He should have known his dad would spoil it all.

The announcer's voice boomed across the field. "Next up at the plate, number eleven, catcher Gabby Hartnett."

Danny stood and applauded, cheering with the crowd for the manager-player, one of his favorites. "Come on, Gabby! Knock it outta here!"

"Sit down, Danny."

A split second after the words growled from his father's mouth, the loud, promising crack of bat-connecting-with-ball echoed across the ball park. As he looked up, Danny couldn't believe it—the ball was coming right at him!

"I got it! I got it!" Just as he stretched his gloved hand high above him, the man in front of him blocked his view with a glove of his own.

"Let me get it, mister! Let me get it!"

"No way, kid! That ball is mine!"

As the ball began to drop from the sky, the glove in front of him disappeared. The ball smacked hard in Danny's glove.

"I got it! Dad, look! I got!"

As he turned to show the ball to his father, his smile faded. The guy in front of him had a fistful of Dad's shirt, spewing a stream of beer-stained expletives at him. "I had as much a right to that ball as your stupid kid. I oughta knock you out of this park for that, you jerk! That was MY BALL!"

Danny couldn't believe it. His father must have pulled the guy's arm down so Danny could catch the ball. His dad had never done anything like that before! Danny's heart pounded.

His father calmly untangled his shirt from the man's hand then grabbed both the man's wrists in a vice grip. In a quiet, methodical tone he said, "Keep your filthy hands off me. Understood?"

The guy stood there blinking bloodshot eyes, wincing as he finally yanked his hands free. He mumbled a few more choice words and rubbed his wrists as he turned then dropped into his seat.

Danny could see the nerve twitching on his father's jaw. He knew this kind of situation could easily be volatile for Dad, but he refused to let it spoil the thrill of catching Hartnett's home run ball. He reached out, slowly putting his hand on his father's arm. "Dad?"

He watched as his father stood silent for a couple of seconds, his eyes still glued on the drunken fan seated in front of them. Then he slowly exhaled, gradually turning to let his eyes fall on the ball still resting in Danny's glove. His smile, almost imperceptible, sent of rush of relief through Danny.

"That was a real fine catch, Danny."

The idea came to him immediately. He lifted the ball out of his glove, stared at it, and without a second thought placed it his father's hand, curling his fingers around it. "Thanks, Dad. It's yours."

His father rolled the ball around in his hand and tossed it a few inches in the air. When he caught it, he handed it back to his son with a wink. "No, Danny, it's yours. You keep it."

Danny smiled and looked away. Maybe this wouldn't be such a bad summer after all.

Later that night, he wrote a five-page letter to Anya, telling her all about the Cubs' 1-0 win in the first game, and the 9-1 tromp over the Brooklyn Dodgers in the second, giving her an inning-by-inning run down of both games. He told her all about catching Gabby Hartnett's winning home run ball, and how his dad had intervened when the drunken man tried to grab the ball.

Three weeks later, he had a response.

> *Dear Danny,*
>
> *I do not like this game baseball.*
>
> *Anya*

7

As the heat and humidity steamed the summer of 1939, something strange happened to Danny McClain. He knew it all started the day his dad took him to that double-header at Wrigley. Something about that whole exchange surrounding the Gabby Hartnett home run ball had sliced open the tiniest fissure in the arm's-length relationship his father had with him. Ever since Joey joined the Navy, Dad had remained stoic, distant, silent—even more than usual. But Danny noticed something different as each day passed. A kinder comment here and there. An unexpected interest in Danny's routine activities. An occasional scratch behind Sophie's ears. And perhaps most noticeable, the gradual ease in the features of the pronounced scowl that usually framed his father's face. That, along with a noticeable shift in the atmosphere around the house added up to a much more relaxed home life.

Since Anya made it clear she wasn't interested in baseball, Danny took care not to mention the subject in his letters to her. In his latest, he'd written about the change in his father over the past few weeks.

. . . I guess you'd have to know Dad to understand his ways. But it's all really strange to me. For the first time in my life, he actually seems interested in what I'm thinking or doing. Stranger still, last night he invited me to ride along on his delivery route. First time he's ever asked! We've had a lot of rain lately, so I haven't been able to mow many lawns, which meant I could stay out all night with him.

Every night he has to be at Film Row downtown at 1:00 a.m. Each studio has an "exchange" office where they stock their films. Dad's job is to pick up the film reels ordered by the theaters on his route, then deliver the reels to each theater. Most movies have four or five reels of film for each movie. They're transported in these narrow, octagonal-shaped cans. So we loaded up the cans from MGM, Warner Brothers, 20th Century Fox, Columbia Pictures, and all the other big name studios, then headed off on Dad's route. It's a big area, even crossing over into neighboring Indiana (that's the state next to Illinois). We'd drop off the film cans, pick up the ones they'd already shown, and drive to the next theater. We did that all night long. Then, once all the deliveries and pick-ups were made, we made our way back to Film Row to drop off the ones we'd picked up along the way.

It was kinda fun, being out all night. We didn't get home until 8:00 a.m. I found out it's a real different world that time of night in Chicago. Even the folks working at the studio exchanges were a little shady. Nice, but ruffians, even the women. Dad talked a lot (which was _real_ unusual), telling me about the people we met along the way, and all about the movies we were toting around. My favorite is "Stagecoach" with that new Western star, John Wayne. It came out in February and I've seen it at least a dozen times. (I get to go free to the theater "The Hounds of Baskerville" with Basil Rathbone playing Sherlock Holmes. That's a real scary one! And I'm kinda curious about this new one coming out next month called "The Wizard of Oz." Sounds weird, but there's a lot of buzz around it.

Do you have movie theaters in Holland? If so, do they show American films? What are your favorites? Any favorite movie stars? I like Hoot Gibson, Johnny Mack Brown, Ken Maynard—they're all Western cowboy stars. But I also like Jimmy Stewart, Clark Cable, Laurence Olivier, and lots of others.

Well, I hope I didn't bore you with all this. I just thought you might find it interesting.

I hope you're having a good summer.

Danny

Over the next few weeks, Dad invited him to ride along now and then, whenever it wouldn't interfere with his sleep schedule for his other jobs. Danny liked going along and found it all really exciting. At least at first. Then, one night near the end of August, as they were heading back to Film

Row after their deliveries, his dad surprised him as their conversation took a sharp turn.

"Son, I've been impressed with your interest in my work. Seems you enjoy these nights, making the deliveries."

"I do. Kinda makes me feel like I'm a part of the movie business. Like ol' Hoot Gibson is a buddy we know." He laughed at the silly thought. "Kinda like we're rubbing elbows with all these stars or something."

"Well, I'm glad you enjoy it, Danny. Which has made me start thinking you'd be a natural at this when the time comes."

"What do you mean?"

"When you graduate next year. No need to waste money on college. Book learning won't pay the bills. You're already learning the business. Soon as you're all squared away, you can have your own route. We could be partners. Increase our territory. Your brother . . . well, Joey never could sit still or finish a job. Probably just as well he's gone. But you've got real promise."

Danny's head began to swim. He knew enough to nod his head and act like he was pondering the idea, but truth be told, he wanted to scream. His mind flashed back to that night at the dinner table when Joey told Dad he didn't want to follow in his footsteps. He remembered his dad's unmasked anger. And he remembered the vow he'd made that night, promising himself to make sure Mom and Dad knew precisely what his plans were so he could avoid this exact conversation. Yet here he was.

Think! he warned himself, *but be careful what you say.*

He knew if he shrugged or acted with indifference, their relationship would go right back to how it used to be—frigid.

He faked a coughing fit to stall for more time then cleared his throat.

"Wow, Dad. It's a real honor you'd even consider me for that."

His dad reached over and squeezed his shoulder. "I was hoping you'd say something like that."

No no no! Don't leave it like this! He'll think you said yes!

"But the thing is . . . well, something this big, I probably ought to think it over for a while. Spend some time making sure, you know?"

His dad's face fell a fraction as he stared at the road ahead. "I can accept that. But you'll see it makes a world of sense."

Danny kept nodding, but mostly wondered how on earth he'd ever get out of it.

Dear Danny,

I had to laugh when I read your last letter. You asked if we had movie theaters, as if you think we're still living in caves here! I believe if you read your history books you'll find out Holland has been around <u>much</u> longer than your America. We are quite modern here. In fact, my father discovered how to make fire just last year. Soon we shall have running water in our house! Ha ha. I laughed and laughed. You are so silly, Danny McClain.

We go to cinemas every time a new one comes to town. Many of our films come from England and France, but we also have American films. Last week we saw "Wuthering Heights." What a stupid movie. I wanted to punch that Heathcliff. Such an idiot. But a few weeks ago we saw "Good Bye, Mr. Chips." I liked it very much. Did you see it?

The problem with going to cinemas here are the newsreels shown before they start the movie. Lately they are longer and longer because of all that's happening around us. I hate Hitler. He and his stupid army are stirring up trouble in half the countries in Europe. What did they ever do to him? On and on, the newsreels run. Once, my friend Diet threw her hairbrush at the screen and yelled for them to show the movie.

It's not much better at home. With everyone so worried about all these threats of war, our doorbell rings day and night as parishioners come asking my father for prayer and wisdom. Yesterday there was a long line of them on the front sidewalk waiting to see him, and dozens crammed inside our zitkamer (what you would call a living room) while he met them one by one in his home office. Mother is still bedridden, so I have to be hostess. This is not something I like to do. I'd rather be outside with my animals.

Did I tell you my cat had kittens? Six little ones. Their meowing is the sweetest sound. Do you like cats?

I worry too. I wish Hans was here so I could talk to him. He always made things better.

Anya

8

September 1939

For the first time in his life, Danny was glad to be back at school. Sure, he had looked forward to being a senior, but even more important, it meant fewer all-nighters running deliveries with his dad. He'd carefully side-stepped the subject of his father's invitation to partner his work. Dad hadn't mentioned it directly, though traces of it drifted into conversations now and then. For the life of him, Danny didn't have a clue how to tell his dad no.

He was pleased to finally have a U.S. History class with Mrs. Zankowski. With everything going on in Europe, she kept her students engaged in an on-going discussion about the situation escalating over there. The parents of both Mrs. Z and her husband were Polish immigrants, and many of her family members still lived in their home country. When classes began in September, just a few days after the Nazis invaded Poland, Mrs. Z came to class visibly shaken, her eyes still red and puffy. She struggled to get through her lessons, expressing deep sorrow for her Polish countrymen and family, yet determined to use the invasion as a teaching tool.

"Living in our great democracy, we take our freedoms for granted every day we live. We are so blessed here, with our roots firmly established in liberty, but we must never let our guard down. If Hitler and his regime can storm into Poland, he can surely storm the rest of Europe, picking off one country after another, squishing them as if they were nothing more than bugs to be annihilated. And we must pay attention to what is happening there and be ever mindful of the potential danger to us here at home.

"Thank God the British have now stepped in with the other Allies to help those poor countries fight the aggressors. I do not understand why the United States has turned such a blind eye to these invasions, as if it is no affair of ours. Those nations haven't the military resources to withstand the hungry Nazi machine. They need us. Must we wait until the enemy is on our own doorstep?"

Dashing away tears with trembling hands, she continued. But all Danny could think about was Anya's family over in The Netherlands. Hans once told him Holland always remained neutral in these conflicts, sitting out the Great War as their European neighbors fought to the death. But how could the Dutch possibly withstand an attack this time around since they shared a border with the Germans who seemed bent on taking over the world? He'd always brushed off Anya's mention of war nerves in her country, thinking she might be over-reacting and a bit melodramatic. But the more Mrs. Z spoke, detailing what she knew about the fall of her beloved Poland, the more Danny finally began to grasp the seriousness of this war and its proximity to Anya and her family.

Still, here in America life went on. By the end of September the die-hard Chicago Cubs fans knew their team wouldn't make it back to the World Series, sliding back to fourth place in the National League. Once again the New York Yankees made it to the World Series, and just as they'd swept the Cubs the year before, they beat the Cincinnati Reds in four straight games.

With a growing savings account, Danny kept thinking ahead to next year when he would start college. He'd sent off a letter asking Northwestern University for admission forms and immediately filled them out the day they arrived. He asked his mother not to mention any of this to his father. Unless he was accepted, there was no point. He continued studying hard, making excellent grades, working as many hours as Mr. Chaney would give him at the grocery store, and picking up odd jobs from neighbors here and there.

Joey's postcards arrived sporadically, though whether it was the slow mail service or a lack on Joey's part, they didn't know. Last they heard the USS *Oklahoma* was somewhere in the Pacific involved in joint fleet operations with the Army and training reservists.

Whenever he could, Danny would shoot a letter off to Anya. She'd eventually fallen into the rhythm of writing back almost as often as her brother had. Danny made a concerted effort to keep his letters light and funny, hoping to distract her from the gravity of the situation there in Holland. He couldn't imagine living with such constant fear.

Then one day when he was almost finished writing her about a freshman who got stuck inside a locker, he stopped cold with his pen poised above the notebook paper.

Anya's a girl.

I'm writing a girl.

I've been writing a girl for months now.

He glanced up at the photo of her family on the mirror above his desk. He stared at it for a moment before realizing he always looked at Anya's face first before the others. *How long have I been doing that?*

Alarmed at the realization, he pulled the old photograph down from the mirror. Just as he no longer looked much like the kid in the photo he'd sent Hans over a year ago, surely Anya had changed too. But how? Had she grown taller as he had? Last time he checked, he was almost six feet, two inches. Was she tall now too? Had that little girl pout given way to a nice smile? He doubted she wore pigtails anymore, but he sure hoped she still had those freckles.

Freckles? What difference does it make if she has freckles now?

That's when it hit him. Anya wasn't just Hans' kid sister anymore. *She's my friend now.*

Whoa.

His mind took a strange detour. *Most guys my age have had lots of girlfriends by the time they're seniors. I've never even been out on a date. Although it's not for lack of interest. Jenny McPherson has been sitting behind me in most of my classes for the last two years since we're seated alphabetically but she doesn't even know I'm alive. Well, except for that time she borrowed my eraser in geometry. Man,*

61

she's got knockout blue eyes. She's so pretty . . . but how do I get her to stop treating me like I'm invisible? Then again, the one time I tried to start a conversation with her after class, I couldn't get two words out thanks to those stupid hiccups. She laughed at me, even patted me on the back before taking off with her friends. Yeah, I'm a real Don Juan.

But Anya's different. We're just friends. At least I think we are? Wonder what she thinks about me? She said she likes my letters because they remind her of Hans. Probably nothing more. But does she at least consider me a friend?

He shook his head, hoping to clear the silly notions from his mind, then continued writing.

. . . then when everyone else went to class, the janitor was sweeping the hall and heard that kid crying in his locker and let him out. They said he took off running for home. Can't say as I blame him. But it was pretty funny, if you think about it.

That's about all. I hope everything's okay where you are. Sure hope someone drops a bomb on Hitler soon and puts the world out of its misery—or at least shears off that ugly mustache of his.

Danny

Dear Danny,

I would have laughed myself silly at the boy in the locker. I might even have locked him in there myself if he was annoying! I used to play pranks like that all the time, much to my parents' disapproval. Now, with all that's going on, I'm trying very hard to behave. It's terribly dull, but I force myself.

I wish to share some good news with you. Mother has finally recovered from her illness and the sorrow of losing Hans. She's still weak, but at least she's up and about and trying to get back into a routine. My father and I try hard to help out and lift her spirits. How Hans would laugh if he could see his "little Anya" trying so hard to be nice and cheerful for a change.

The house is still filled with the pesky parishioners. I told Father we should tell them all to go home then shut the door and lock it. Of course, he is much more sympathetic with them than I am. It's so hard not to be grouchy since none of us get much sleep with the constant roar of airplanes overhead on their way to Germany. I too hope one of these bombs hits the maniac with the awful mustache. Many times, I have imagined myself shooting him down as a favor to the world.

One of Father's parishioners has a farm just outside of town. We've known the Boormans for years. I ran into Mrs. Boorman the other day and found out their son Wim has a broken leg and cannot help Mr. Boorman with the many chores on their small farm. She knows I love animals. When I was young I used to *play for hours with their piglets and chicks. I told her I would like to come tomorrow after school to help with chores.*

I thought of you. I'm just like you, Danny, because I cannot tell Mother and Father some things— like working out at the Boormans' farm. They believe I should be more of a young lady. They will not approve of my plans to muck about with the livestock—though I would love nothing more than to quit school and help the Boormans all day. Do you suppose either of us will ever get to do what we want?

Anya

9

November 1939

An unexpected early snow ruined lots of Thanksgiving plans, blanketing most of Illinois under a foot or more of snow. Danny and his mother were disappointed they would have to miss the family dinner out at his grandparents' farm, but they tried to make the best of it. He got up early that morning, trying to shovel the deep snow from as many sidewalks and driveways as he could before their noontime meal. He made sure he got home in time, stomping the snow off his boots and pulling his tired feet out of them as fast as he could.

When he opened the front door, the aromas wafting from the kitchen about knocked him over. "Mom! It smells fantastic in here!"

"Good. Now hurry and get cleaned up. We're about ready to sit down."

His mother hadn't bought a turkey, of course, thinking they'd be out at the farm, but she made do by roasting a chicken with all the usual side dishes. The three of them enjoyed a quiet meal together, though Danny insisted they could have made it out to the farm with the chains Dad had put on the tires. But Dad said no and that was that.

Over slices of pumpkin pie and coffee, they chatted about the war news, the neighbors, and the latest big movie, *Mr. Smith Goes to Washington.* The movie had caused quite a stir in some political circles. They'd heard Joseph Kennedy had tried to have the movie banned, calling in favors from some of the biggest names in Hollywood. In the end, his attempt failed and the Jimmy Stewart drama was a big hit with folks all over the country.

Danny added a little more whipped cream to his pie. "I liked the part where he was so tired from that long speech that he passed out."

Just then, Dad tapped his water glass with his knife. Danny looked at his mother who shrugged as though she had no idea what this was about.

"I have an announcement to make," his father began.

Danny swallowed hard. *Oh dear Lord, please don't let this be about me going to work with Dad.*

"The old Windsor Place Theater went up for sale, and I've decided to buy it."

His mother's fork dropped, clattering on her plate. "What?"

"Lester Gentry told me he wants to retire and asked if I'd be interested. I thought it over and decided I'm going to do it."

Danny breathed a long sigh, relieved his quick prayer had been answered. "Sounds great, Dad."

"I'm glad you think so because you'll be helping me run it."

An expletive shot through Danny's brain, but he caught it before it slipped from his lips. He tried to act grateful but failed miserably. "Uh, well, we can, uh, talk about it, I guess."

"Nothing to talk about. I'll teach you the ropes over the next few months, and by graduation you'll know everything you need to know."

Danny looked at his mother, hoping the expression on his face conveyed his frustration.

She set her coffee cup on its saucer. "Frank, Danny needs to be the one to plan his future. Not you."

"Nonsense. Why, if it was up to him, he'd go spend all my hard-earned money at that fool college in Evanston."

"Not your money. *His* money."

"That's ridiculous. He could never—"

"He has and he will. He's worked hard, saved every penny, and has more than enough to pay for his first year."

Danny swallowed hard before turning back to face his father. "It's true, Dad. I don't need your money because—"

"Well, it's a good thing, because you won't get a dime from me."

"Fine."

"Fine," his mother added.

Dad looked back and forth between them, his face darkening. "So, I see the two of you have made an alliance against me. Well, isn't that nice. A man works hard to provide for his family, and they gang up on him behind his back. Well, to hell with both of you." He threw his napkin on his plate, shoved his chair back, and stormed from the room.

His mother closed her eyes as she raised her palm toward Danny. When the door to the basement slammed, she pointed in that direction and opened her eyes. "Sorry, I've learned to wait for the slamming of the door. It's his punctuation mark whenever he gets this way. Which you surely know by now."

"I'm sorry, Mom. I'd hoped we could stay off the subject since it's a holiday."

She reached over and covered his hand with hers. "Not your fault, honey. And besides, we're long overdue telling him your plans. We both know there was no easy way to do it, so today was as good a day as any. At least you and I have something to be extra thankful for this Thanksgiving." She smiled, squeezing his hand.

Danny leaned over and planted a kiss on her cheek. "Thanks. And you're right. What a relief. Finally!"

"He'll huff and puff for a few weeks, but he'll eventually accept it."

"You think so?"

"I hope so. But even if he doesn't, what's done is done. And you, my son, are going to college!"

"I can't believe it. It's really happening, isn't it?"

"It sure is. I never doubted it would. Every night before I go to bed, I get down on my knees and ask God to intervene for you and help you see your dream of college come true. Of course, I pray for your brother, too—even when he doesn't bother to write home." She rolled her eyes. "I believe God has opened this door for you. This is an answer to our prayers, Danny. Never forget that."

"I won't. And thanks, Mom. Not just for praying, but for understanding."

"You're most welcome."

Danny stood. "Tell you what. As a token of my appreciation, I'll clean the kitchen. You go sit by the fire and I'll bring you another cup of coffee. Then Sophie and I will do the dishes."

She looked up at the ceiling. "Oh, Lord Jesus, thank You for a son who knows how to bless his mother." Then she pulled him toward her, put her hands on his cheeks and gave him a long kiss on the forehead. "I am a blessed, blessed woman."

"Go. Sit. Sophie, you wash and I'll dry."

"What?!"

"I'm kidding, Mom. Now scoot. Can't you see we're busy clearing the table?"

Later that evening, with the kitchen scrubbed and sparkling, Danny sliced another piece of pumpkin pie and tiptoed past his mother who was napping on the sofa. He could hear his dad still down in the basement banging around with his tools, probably still grumbling to himself. Danny hoped he stayed down there a while. He headed upstairs, looking forward to writing Anya a letter. Snow was falling again, so any more shoveling would have to wait.

Sophie hopped up on the bed, her long ears swaying back and forth until she circled twice and settled in for a snooze. Danny grabbed a pen and paper, using last year's Calumet yearbook as a writing surface.

"Sophie, do you mind?" He pushed her to the side, allowing himself enough room to sit on his bed to write. She snorted once for good measure, then lay her head back down.

Dear Anya,

It was great to get your letter yesterday. It sounds like you're already quite popular with all the farm animals, which is no surprise. I've tried to imagine you squatting beside Josephine as you milk her, but I'm sure the images in my head don't do it justice. And congratulations on the new litter of piglets—or "biggetjes" as you called them. Why, you must be in hog heaven! (Ha ha) Have your parents accepted your new job?

You won't believe what happened today . . .

Danny wrote out the details of their most unusual Thanksgiving, the unexpected table conversation, and the great relief he now felt. He knew she'd understand. Three pages later, he began to wrap it up.

I realize this may be the last letter you receive from me before Sinterklaas. You'll have to write and tell me all about the special gifts you and your parents made for each other. I know it will be hard for you without Hans, but maybe you can focus on the good memories and celebrate his life. I still miss him too.

Merry Christmas to you and your family.

Danny

10

February 19, 1940

Dear Danny,

Today is my birthday, though there's little to celebrate. I don't think Hans ever told you that he and I shared the same birthday. Mother always told me that when I was born, Hans thought I was one of his birthday gifts. I smile whenever I think of it and how happy he must have been. But today, I find it hard to smile. This is now my second birthday without my brother.

In The Netherlands birthdays are very special. We normally get up early and open all our gifts, then have a special breakfast of our favorite foods. But the air is filled with such tension now, none of us felt like celebrating. Mother and Father tried to make a nice morning for me, but we are all much too nervous. And it's very difficult to get certain kinds of food now, certainly nothing for a cake.

The weather turned bitterly cold this week and

coal is already scarce. We wear several layers of clothing on the days the coal runs out and sleep under many blankets. I still ride my bicycle out to the Boormans' farm to help out. My piglets are growing much too fast. With food so scarce, I worry they will be slaughtered to provide the family and others with food to eat or sell. I've named them all. I can't stand thinking their little lives may soon be over.

Wim is on a crutch now, but he's too slow to help much. Sometimes he keeps me company in the barn as I help with the chores. He's very nice. The other day I caught him staring at me. At first it made me mad. Then the more I thought about it, I liked it. All my friends have dated, but always I have found that most boys are stupid. Now I'm not so sure anymore.

You must write to tell me of new movies that have come to your father's theater. I think it is nice that you offered to help him out. I'm glad to hear he's stopped being so mad at you. I wonder if you see the same newsreels we see at the cinema. They seem longer and longer. They trouble me, always showing bombs dropped here and there. We heard on the BBC that all of Britain is now on food rationing, though they already evacuated most of their civilians last fall. Between Britain, France, Australia, New Zealand, and Canada, you'd think the Allies could finish off Hitler once and for all. I don't know how much longer we can hold out.

I apologize for rambling so. I can't seem to keep my mind focused on anything right now.

Anya

Danny still found it hard to believe the United States had not joined the Allies to fight the Germans. How long would America continue to turn its back on all those countries falling to the Nazis? He wished someone like Jimmy Stewart's Mr. Smith could stand up to the government and convince them to help win the war.

He reminded himself to send a small belated gift to Anya for her birthday. Though what he might get her, he had no idea. His mother loved to embroider delicate handkerchiefs. Then again, he never thought of Anya as the "delicate" type. It was hard to visualize her with something so refined. He would have to give it more thought.

As he finished getting ready to head to the theater, something felt off-balance. Something wasn't quite right, and the sense of feeling so unsettled bugged him. It wasn't until he was going down the stairs with Sophie at his side that he figured it out.

Wim. The farmer's son who apparently has a crush on Anya.

Yes, something was definitely off-balance, and Danny had a feeling he knew exactly what it was. For the first time in his life, he was jealous.

Danny climbed the rungs leading up to the projection booth. As much as he'd dreaded the thought of working for his dad, he had to admit he really liked it. For the first time he could remember, he'd stood up to his father, telling him he'd like to help out, but only with the understanding it was just temporary until fall when he'd be a full-time student at Northwestern. Of course, his dad had moaned and groaned about it, but in the end Danny could tell he was pleased his son had offered to help. As long as he could keep Dad from strong-arming him when it came time to leave, he'd be okay.

He crawled into the booth—an enclosed closet built in the back of the room above the theater. He flipped on the small lamp, pulled the bag off his shoulder, then lifted the sliding door to the dumbwaiter behind him to retrieve the film cans. He was relieved to see a new horror film in the rotation. Since *Gone With the Wind* had released in January, the blockbuster had remained in the evening show time at Windsor Place Theater for more than a month. Thankfully, the afternoon slot still had some variety.

"*Son of Frankenstein.* It's about time," he muttered out loud.

The long-awaited sequel to *The Bride of Frankenstein* had caused quite a stir the last couple of months—at least by those not obsessing over *Gone With the Wind.* David O'Selznick's epic saga ran three hours and forty-four minutes plus a fifteen-minute intermission. Danny often caught himself dozing off after the first three times he saw the film. Still, it gave him more than enough time to finish his homework, write a letter to Anya, read the latest sports news in the paper, and anything else he could think of to fill the time.

But this afternoon, he would get to watch Boris Karloff as the ugly Monster, Basil Rathbone as Wolf von Frankenstein, and Bela Lugosi as Ygor. He couldn't wait.

"All set up there?"

Danny leaned out the door of the booth. "All set, Dad. Who's doing the intermission today?"

Dad grumbled under his breath.

"What's that?"

"Marco Polo. Dumbest act I ever saw, but the fools who come here seem to like him."

"Ah, he's not so bad. The man can juggle just about anything."

"Yeah, he can juggle all right. The other night he juggled a bunch of kittens. I'll never hear the end of it. Some lady got all worked up and reported it to the police."

Danny laughed. "What'd they do?"

"Nothing. Some stooge from downtown came out here and tried to tell me I owed the city a fine of $500. I let him know that would happen when hell froze over. I think I put the fear of God in him. Haven't heard another peep outta that little jerk."

Oh, the wrath of Frank McClain.

Dad pulled out his pocket watch and opened it. "I'm gonna head home for dinner. Your mom send you something to eat?" He closed the watch and slipped it back in his pocket.

"She sure did. Pot roast, carrots and potatoes, and a piece of chocolate cake for dessert."

"Alrighty then. You take care. Steve's in the lobby on concessions, and Katherine's in the ticket booth. Any problem, give me a call at the house."

"Will do. Bye, Dad."

Half an hour later, the theater was almost at capacity. Danny played the dreaded newsreel, wincing as he watched the troubling war news. He'd grown to despise the menacing tone of the reporter's voice as he droned on and on about one attack after another. When it finally ended, he clicked on the projector with the first reel of *Son of Frankenstein*.

Two hours later, as the patrons returned to their seats following the intermission between shows, he flipped the switch on the first of eight reels for *Gone With the Wind*. As Scarlett O'Hara sashayed her way across the screen, he settled into his chair and pulled his notebook from his bag. Long before the melodramatic heroine proclaimed her loyalty to Tara, Danny would have plenty of time to write Anya another novel-length letter. She hadn't complained so he kept writing them.

Dear Anya,

Once again, Atlanta is burning, and I have over three hours to kill. Lucky you. Ha ha. If they ever show "Gone With the Wind" in The Netherlands, you'll know what I'm talking about. I've grown to hate watching the newsreels, especially knowing you're not far from the action. With all the Allies, I sure would've thought the war would be over by now. I'll be anxious to hear the latest news from your side of things.

It's been cold here too. We've had an awful lot of snow this year. It's a good thing Smitty Truesdale wanted my shoveling territory. Working here doesn't leave me any time to help neighbors like Mrs. Martello and her sister. She still calls the house, complaining about Smitty and asking me to come over and do it right. I've tried and tried to tell her I'm no longer available. Did I tell you Mr. Chaney's grandson is helping him out at the grocery store now? I really miss working there, but I figure this is where I'm supposed to be right now.

I just saw Son of Frankenstein. It was great! I hope you get to see it. Course, being a girl and all you'd probably be <u>too</u> <u>scared</u>. (I just ducked in case you threw your "klompen" at me. That would hurt! By the way, why do you all wear wooden shoes anyway? Seems to me they'd be hard to walk in.)

Dad was all hot and bothered the other day about the Chicago Theater. It's in the heart of downtown Chicago and boy, is it ritzy. I've been there a couple of times. Real fancy. You should see it. Red velvet seats. Big balcony. Great big stage. Girls in uniforms with short skirts who go up and down the aisles offering candy and cigarettes during the intermission.

But it's those amazing intermissions that had Dad all riled up. See, because it's a top-of-the-line theater, they can book big name talent for their intermissions—like the Glenn Miller Band, Kay Kyser, Harry James. Wait—I just realized you won't know who these bands are. I sure wish you could hear them. They're the best. Glenn Miller's my favorite. He always has Tex Beneke with him, singing along and cutting up. He's famous for singing the Glenn Miller hit, "Chattanooga Choo Choo." Oh, and then there's Hildegard. First time I saw her play, the whole theater went pitch black. Then all of a sudden a spotlight appeared right on her hands on the keyboard of that grand piano! Everyone went wild cheering. Crazy thing is, she always wears elbow-length gloves when she performs. I guess the fingers of the gloves are cut out. I don't know. But she sure can heat up the keyboard. She plays all the latest tunes.

Anyway, Dad kept hearing about all "the hoopla" as he calls it, and went on a tirade because he can't compete. The thing is, I don't see the problem. Some folks like all that "hoopla" and others just want to see a movie at a neighborhood theater. Course, if he wasn't ranting about this, it would just be something else. I sometimes think he was born just to complain.

How are your animals out at the farm? Any more new ones? I'm glad to hear Wim is up and walking again. Swell news.

We had another postcard from Joey. He said most of the guys on his ship are itching to get into the war. That made Mom real nervous. Dad finally started reading Joey's mail, though he never says anything about it. Mom just leaves Joey's postcards out where he can see them. She knows he reads them because they're never in the same exact spot she left them. Isn't it silly? Two grown adults, playing games like that? If I ever get married I sure don't want that kind of relationship. Seems to me a man and his wife ought to be best friends. One thing's for sure—I've learned a whole lot from my dad about how NOT to be a husband or father. Guess that's good for something.

How's your mother doing? Must be hard having a house full of people day in and day out, especially in her condition. What's wrong with those people? You'd think by now they'd lay off expecting your dad to have all the answers. Has to be tough on him, too—carrying the burden of so many people's needs. I never thought about it before, but being a pastor is probably much harder than most people think. From some of your letters, I can tell you love your father a lot. Count your blessings.

I've told Sophie how much you love animals. I'm quite confident she would melt at your feet. She's a wonderful dog. I sure was lucky to find her that night. I wish there was some way to take her to college with me.

I'm determined to work hard at college and maybe even graduate early. I'm still not sure what degree to pursue, but I've got a couple of possibilities. Don't laugh, but I've even considered an education major with an emphasis in history. I wish you could meet my U.S. History teacher, Mrs. Zankowski. I've never had a teacher who has so much passion for her subject. Every kid in her class goes a little crazy about history after sitting under her teaching. Sometimes she even dresses up as the historical characters she's teaching. One day she came in dressed like Abraham Lincoln, the 16th president of the United States—beard and all! We laughed so hard, but she never once came out of character, telling us all about the difficulties of governing a nation divided. (America was in a civil war when Lincoln was president.) Last week she showed up as Teddy Roosevelt who was our 26th president. He was a fifth cousin of our current President Roosevelt. Teddy Roosevelt was quite a character and Mrs. Zankowski really brought him to life.

Something about her zeal for our history, and her unabashed quest to teach us the important lessons of our forefathers and the cause of freedom. It's almost contagious—that's how good she is. I'm probably not explaining it very well. You could probably tell by her name—her parents immigrated from Poland. So the battle against the Nazis over there is very near and dear to her heart. She's real emotional about it.

Of course, the other reason I'm interested in history is because of you—well, I should probably say, you and Hans. Your letters have given me a real "glimpse" into your world and the history that brought us to this point in time. I just wonder if I could teach the next generation about the past and its implications for our future. It's all very confusing. Mom keeps telling me to pray, but she's a much better prayer warrior than I've ever been.

Do you ever wonder what God must think of all this war stuff? I keep wondering why He doesn't do something about it.

Now I'm the one who's rambling. It's about time to change another reel, so I'll close now. Take care of yourself, Anya. Stay safe. Write soon.

Danny

11

March 1940

Once winter finally gave up, another spring blew through Chicago, bringing with it the usual explosive thunderstorms and heavy rains. Despite the gloomy weather, Danny kept a running countdown as he moved ever closer to graduation. His grades reflected his hard work, and at this point, it was a downhill slide toward that walk across the stage in cap and gown.

He'd grown accustomed to his routine at the theater, enjoying the solitude of the projection booth. There, he could plan his future with plenty of time to think it through. And that's exactly what he was doing one evening when he heard some shouting downstairs in the lobby.

"I said, GET OUT OF HERE!"

Danny recognized his dad's booming voice immediately. He flew down the rungs and into the lobby, almost running into three men he didn't recognize. They had his father cornered.

"What's going on here?"

"None of your business, kid," the tall one snapped, adjusting his cuff links.

"These lugheads came in here trying to scare me with their lousy threats, and I told them to get out. No one strong-arms Frank McClain!"

Danny hadn't seen his dad this angry in a long time, which was saying something. He tried to diffuse the situation. "Gentlemen, I believe you heard the man."

"Yeah? And who are *you*?" the same guy asked, pressing closer to Danny now. The man must have eaten a clove of garlic and washed it down with bourbon.

Danny stiffened his back. "I was about to ask you the same question."

The man touched the rim of his rain-spattered Fedora, nudging it up on an inch or so on his head. "We just came by to make a neighborly visit to welcome Mr. McClain here to our district. That's all. No need for all the drama."

His father broke free of the two men who'd stayed close, pinning him against the counter. "You're nothing but a bunch of thugs. I'll give you thirty seconds to get out or I'm calling the police."

"No need, no need," said the shortest of the three, a stubby little guy in a shiny damp suit at least a size too small. He stepped closer to Dad, took a puff on his cigar, and blew it in his face. "We'll be on our way. Wouldn't want to interrupt the show or nothin'."

"But we'll be back. You can count on that," the tall one added as he made his way to the door. "Tomorrow? The next day? Who's to say?" He tossed a broad smile over his shoulder. "Real nice meetin' ya, Mr. McClain."

"Yeah, a real pleasure," his short accomplice said.

The third one bumped Danny's shoulder as he followed the other two out the door into the rain.

"Bunch of no good—"

"Dad, what did they want?"

His father wiped his brow with his handkerchief. "Tried to tell me I needed some kind of 'insurance' to stay here. They said it's a rough part of town and they could provide protection against the 'unsavory elements'. Who do they think they are, coming in here trying to muscle up on me? Well, they picked the wrong guy to—"

"Dad, let it go. Take a deep breath. Don't let 'em get to you."

"I've seen their type before. Used to run into them all the time on my film routes. Always trying to scare everybody with their big threats. Well, NO one comes in my place and threatens ME!"

"Dad!" Danny put his arm around his father's shoulders. "They're gone. Relax."

His dad looked at him, his eyes wild with barely-restrained anger. Then he seemed to focus, staring into Danny's eyes before looking away. "Yeah. They're gone." He broke free of his son's embrace and headed back behind the counter for a cup of water.

Just then, Steve opened the side door and slid behind the concession stand. "Sorry, Mr. McClain. I had to go to the bathroom."

"Huh? Oh. Yeah, okay."

Steve shot a questioning glance at Danny.

Danny shrugged. "No problem. Well, I guess I better get back up in the booth. Reel change coming up. Dad, are you okay?"

His father waved him off. "Fine. Get back to work. Both of you."

As Danny climbed back up the rungs, a sense of dread grew with each step. He had a feeling those men would keep their word and come back. Thugs like them tried to strong-arm Chicago businesses; the stories of their exploitations were the stuff of legends. But who could possibly care about a little neighborhood movie theater? Surely they had bigger fish to fry. He wondered if the Chicago Theater ever had visits like the one they'd just had.

Thankfully, over the next few weeks, the men never showed their faces again at Windsor Park Theater. Dad remained tense and uneasy for weeks following their visit, and made Danny promise not to mention the incident to Mom. Danny was glad to see the whole thing put behind them.

In April, the Cubs got off on the wrong foot losing their first two games to Cincinnati. Of course, any Cubs fan knew the ups and downs comprising the rhythm of their team's schedule. Still, Danny hoped by the end of the season, his Cubs would be in the World Series. When he realized he'd be at Northwestern when that happened, he couldn't help smiling.

On a beautiful spring afternoon in the last week of April, he was late leaving school after a required fitting for his cap and gown. He hustled to get home in time to grab his gear, hop on the trolley, and make it to the theater in time for the afternoon matinee.

"Where've you been?" his father barked. "Movie starts in fifteen minutes."

Danny dashed past him toward the auditorium. "I know. Had to get measured for my cap and gown. But I'm here, so take it easy. What's our movie today?"

"If you'd ever stop and read the marquee you'd know," he grumbled heading toward his office.

"Yeah?" Danny whispered to himself as he climbed the rungs, "and if you'd ever stop trying to be the crankiest man on the planet, you'd know there's more to life than your stupid marquee."

Once in the booth, he quickly stashed his gear and slid open the door to the dumbwaiter to get the film can.

"Well, looky here. *The Oklahoma Kid* has come back for a visit."

Americans still loved Westerns, and the Cagney-Bogart oater had been a favorite since its release the end of March. Danny was a big fan of both actors and enjoyed the on-screen tension between Cagney's Jim Kincaid character and Bogart's Whip McCord.

But when he'd stopped by the house, he'd found a letter from Anya on his pillow. He was anxious to read it, so he threaded the film through the projectors and checked his watch, waiting for the exact moment to start the newsreel. He sat down to tear open Anya's envelope just as the voice-over on the newsreel fretted over the recent fall of Denmark and Norway.

Too close, too close . . . Thoughts bounced around and around in Danny's head. *Who will be next? France? Belgium? The Netherlands?*

Danny wished he had ear plugs to silence the disturbing news. He leaned back in his chair, stretched out his long legs in front of him, and settled in to read Anya's letter. He took another look at the envelope to see the postmark. The date was April 5, 1940—just four days before Norway and Denmark fell. She didn't even know that troubling news when she wrote the letter.

Dear Danny,

How I wish I could climb into this envelope and escape the madness! Day and night, our skies are filled with aircraft. We know well the sound of the engines—which are Allies, which are Luftwaffe. It's as if we're sinking in someone else's quicksand, knowing it's only a matter of time until we're pulled in over our heads. The fear eats at me constantly. It makes me sick. My only refuge is the Boormans' farm where I surround myself with the animals I love and force all my attention on them.

Everywhere, everywhere—Jews from Germany slip over our border seeking refuge in our midst. The stories they tell us, Danny . . . at first I thought they must be exaggerating. I thought, surely no such atrocities actually exist? Who could do such things to another human being? Homes raided, families thrown out on the street, fathers executed right in front of their children, mothers taken from their babies, food and shelter withheld from innocent people whose only crime is their Jewish faith. This can't be happening, I tell myself.

But as new arrivals continue to stream over the border bringing tales of far worse torture and destruction, I realized it's all true.

Father was approached last week about hiding Jews in our home. He desperately wanted to help, but Mother has been paralyzed with fear, unable to get out of bed again. I want so much for her to be strong, but I am so afraid she is losing her mind. Father is concerned she could not handle strangers in our home. Or worse, that she would not understand how confidential the arrangement would have to be. Could we trust her not to say anything to anyone?

Finally, when Father was told of a young family with three small children who had no place to go, he couldn't say no. They are the sweetest people, so thankful, their hearts overflowing with gratitude. We pray constantly for them—mostly for their little ones to be quiet. As parishioners continue to come seeking Father's counsel, we must be sure no one hears the cries of a baby from the back of the house or the secret place in the attic. Already, it is hard to know who to trust. We have enough food to feed them, at least at this point. The Boormans send me home with milk and eggs and butter and vegetables almost daily. And yes, pork as well. I try not to think about it, in light of the despair all around us. Of course, the Jews do not eat the pork. We share with others whenever we can. The Boormans have also taken in Jews. I helped Wim and his father build an enormous basement beneath the barn with a door easily hidden. Already the basement is full.

My hand shakes as I write you, so great is the fear in my heart for my country. How I wish Hans was here. Always he made things better. Our house is full, but a hole remains in our hearts for dear Hans.

I can't help but wonder how much longer I will receive your letters or be able to send you mine. Such uncertainty stirs constantly inside me and causes me to say things I might not otherwise say . . . You have been the dearest of friends, Danny. I shall never forget how you wrote me, week after week, month after month, lifting me up from the darkness of losing my brother. Always giving me a reason to smile, a thought or two to ponder, and a reason to write you back. I've even learned to tolerate your beloved Cubs.

One of the Jewish ladies hidden away beneath the Boormans' barn told me something yesterday I shall never forget. She reached her hands up to cradle my face, then said, "We cannot know what the future holds, but we know who holds the future." As she spoke those words, she had the most serene smile in her eyes and on her wrinkled face. In spite of all the horrible things she has witnessed, still she smiled. I repeat those words to myself whenever I feel the fear taking over. I shall cling to them in the days ahead.

Forgive me, that I never thanked you for the beautiful handkerchief with the little tulips on it. I've never seen anything so lovely. I shall cherish it always. Please tell your mother how much it means to me.

And please know always how much you mean to me.

Anya

12

Danny stared at the last page of Anya's letter. He noticed several smears throughout the page. *Tear stains?* An overwhelming sense of loss consumed him. "She's saying goodbye." Hearing the croak of his own voice didn't surprise him. But the knowledge that she was probably right shocked him to his core. He shuffled back to the first page to read the letter again. Surely he'd missed something.

The matinee showing came and went. Well into the evening showing, Danny lost count how many times he'd read Anya's letter. He stared at the wall of the projector booth with unseeing eyes as he tried to imagine what was happening at that moment half way around the world. He felt so helpless.

Eventually he noticed the final reel of *The Oklahoma Kid* had run out. He reached over to stop the *click-click-click* flapping of the reel. Looking down into the auditorium, he found it completely empty. With a heavy sigh, he gathered his things and climbed down the rungs, his mind rounding in circles much like that reel on the projector.

"There you are." Steve turned off the concession stand lights. "I'm done here so I'm leaving. That okay with you?"

"Sure. Is Dad in his office?"

"No, I haven't seen him. I thought maybe he was checking inventory or something. You know your dad."

"Huh? Oh, yeah."

"You okay, Danny?"

"Huh?"

"I said, are you okay?"

"Yeah. See you tomorrow, Steve."

"Goodnight."

Danny's mind traveled thousands of miles away to a Dutch parsonage. As hard as he tried, he couldn't picture Anya's face as it must now look. All he had was the old family picture of the Versteegs in front of a windmill. Back then she ran through tulip fields and sucker-punched snotty Girl Scouts. He couldn't imagine how she must have matured or how the worry might be etched on her face now.

He noticed the overflowing trash can by the auditorium door. "Nice, Steve," he muttered to himself. "How many times do we have to tell you?" He picked up the large container and made his way out the side door to the alley. He tossed the trash into the bin, but noticed a huge wad of bubblegum still stuck on the bottom of the can with candy wrappers and popcorn stuck in its gooey clutches. "Great. Just great."

He froze.

What was that? A shot of adrenaline skittered down his spine. He didn't move a muscle. He heard it again—a low moan, barely audible. It seemed to come from further down the darkened alley. As he debated what to do, he heard it again.

"Who's there?"

He couldn't be sure but he thought he heard his name. Danny rounded the trash bin and tried to make his eyes adjust to the pitch black alleyway. He spotted the slightest movement and rushed to the form lying on the ground.

"Danny . . ."

"Dad! What happened? I can't see—are you hurt?"

"Those guys . . ."

His father cried out as Danny gently lifted his father's head off the ground.

"Dad, let me go call an ambulance. I'll be right—"

His father lifted his hand, reaching for him. Danny took hold of his hand—and the sticky substance covering it. "Dad, you're covered in blood! Where are you hurt?"

His father moaned. "My legs . . . they smashed . . . my legs . . . baseball bat . . ."

Danny looked down at his father's legs, for the first time noticing the dark stains all over his pant legs and the pool of blood beneath them. He clenched his fists as his gaze fell on the impossible angles of his father's splayed legs.

"Those thugs . . ."

Their faces, the garlic on their breath, the rain-pelted Fedora, the cigar smoke, the sneer of their smiles—all exploded in Danny's mind in a split second. "Dad, I'll be right back. I'll call for an ambulance and be right back. Hold on, okay?"

"Hurry . . ." It was more of a breath than a plea.

Danny knew seconds counted. He rushed inside, made the call, grabbed a jacket from the back of the office door, and hurried back to his father's side.

"I'm here, Dad. I'm gonna lift your head, okay?" He balled up the jacket and slid it carefully beneath his father's head. "There you go. Just take it easy. One breath at a time. Help is on the way, so hold on."

His father groaned. "Tell your mother . . ."

As his eyes readjusted once again to the partial moonlight, Danny could see a tear slip from his father's eye.

"No, *you* tell her. You're gonna make it. So don't you give up on me, you hear?"

His dad squeezed his eyes shut. "Joey . . . tell Joey . . . I'm . . . I'm so sorry."

"Dad, please hold on. You've gotta hold on!"

The siren grew louder as Danny stroked his father's face. "I love you, Dad. Hold on. Just hold on."

"We got 'em!"

"Excuse me?" Mom asked the police officer. Danny's father lay unconscious in the hospital bed, his two legs in casts suspended in a maze of traction.

"We got 'em," Officer Cameron Fuller said. "All three of 'em. Locked up so tight they'll never see sunlight again."

"How?" Danny asked in disbelief. "It's only been two days."

"We've been watching these guys for a long time. Arrested 'em dozens of time but nothing ever stuck. Til now. This time we applied a little pressure, if you will. Little Rocco

Feeney sang like a bird. We've got 'em on so many charges, they'll be old and senile before they ever walk free again."

"Are you sure?" Danny asked. "I mean, how do you know there aren't others who'll just move in and fill their shoes? Make the same threats?"

"We made a sweet deal with Rocco. He'll be out in ten, but he's not the problem. Rocco's just a stooge. A follower. Doesn't have enough sense to connect the dots, let alone pull off anything on his own. Mulrooney was the brains of this operation. Called all the shots. Tried to scare folks like your dad here real bad, making 'em think they'd be robbed or roughed up or even killed without his protection, when the only ones robbing and roughing up were his own flunkies. It's not very original, but Mickey Mulrooney was good at it. Real good."

His mother wiped her eyes. "Do you mean we don't have to worry about another attack? Is Danny safe working at the theater?"

"He'll be fine, Mrs. McClain. And we've been ordered to move more officers to cover that part of town. Kid, you'll be sick of seeing our boys, but you'll be safe. You have my word on that."

They chatted a few moments more before Officer Fuller left. Danny stood across the bed from his mother looking down at his father. "Sure wish he could've heard the good news."

His mother pushed a strand of her husband's graying hair off his forehead. "Oh, he'll be plenty happy to hear it once he comes out from under all the medication. Doctor Mercer seemed to think he'd start coming around sometime in the next day or two."

Danny dropped back into a chair. "I guess this means I need to re-open the theater."

His mother's eyes fell on him. "That's entirely up to you."

"I know, but you and I both know that's what he'd want. Besides, he's gonna be here in the hospital for a long time. How else are we gonna pay the bills if we have no income?"

She made her way around bed and sat in the chair next to his. "I don't want you worrying about the money. God will take care of us. He always has and He always will. Maybe we could find someone to run the theater for us while you're in school."

"Who? That's why Dad wanted me to work for him. He doesn't trust anyone else."

"Well, for heaven's sake, surely there's someone who can pitch in and help? How about that young man who works at the concession stand?"

"Steve? He works two other jobs. He's nineteen and already has two kids. I can't expect him to give up one of his other jobs just for a few weeks until I graduate." Danny dropped his head in his hands then ran them through his hair. "Look, maybe we can talk to someone at school. Explain the situation. I've only got a few more weeks. Maybe they'd work with us to let me cut my afternoon class. I've already got enough credits to graduate."

"I'll be happy to talk to someone, honey."

He looked over at his father's sleeping face. Even at rest, the creases of a face always scowling made him look mad. Danny thought back on those moments before the ambulance came when his dad whispered for Danny to tell Joey he was sorry, to tell his mother—well, he could only assume he wanted her to know how much he loved her. Such a striking difference from the indifferent, brusque, and angry father he knew. Would he still be different when he woke up? Would he still ask Joey to forgive him? Tell his mother how much he loved her?

He blew out a sigh. "It'll all work out, I guess. I'm just thankful he pulled through."

She reached over and placed her hand on her husband's. "I couldn't bear it if we'd lost him."

Danny thought back on all the times his dad had belittled her in front of him. All the times he'd silenced her with his glare. And still, she couldn't bear it if she'd lost him?

Danny needed some fresh air. "I need to run some errands. I'll be back in a little while. Do you need anything?"

"No, dear. I'm fine." She took hold of his father's lifeless hand. "I've got all I need right here."

13

May 1940

Danny sat at his father's desk going over the ledger. As much as he didn't want to learn the business, he wished at some point he'd asked his dad to explain the books. He felt sure it all made sense to his father, but to him it looked like chicken-scratched numbers in nameless columns. He rubbed his hand over his face and sighed.

I can't do this on my own. I've got to take the ledger to Dad at the hospital and have him explain it. If he can stay lucid long enough.

Danny stared out the window, fighting the despair consuming him. Ever since he accompanied his mother to yesterday's consultation with Dr. Mercer, he'd known his hopes of starting college in the fall had just gone up in smoke. The doctor's words buzzed through his head over and over . . . *With luck Mr. McClain might be able to leave the hospital by the holidays. But don't count on him walking for at least a year. He'll require months of physical therapy to retrain mobility of his legs. Of course the head trauma and other internal injuries are far more serious. As I told you before, Mrs. McClain, your husband is lucky to be alive.*

Danny dropped his head in his hands. *At least a year . . .* Even if his dad made it home by Christmas, his mother would need help caring for him. He'd be an invalid. Who knew when he'd be able to go back to work? Danny could fight it all he wanted, but nothing would change the fact he'd have to wait another year to start college.

He stood up and stretched, then decided to go across the street for a cup of coffee. He had another half hour before opening the theater doors for the matinee. He locked the alley door behind him then made his way across 75th Street to the diner. He was about to climb the steps when a newsie stepped in front of him.

"Hey mister, want a paper?"

He started to brush past the kid when the big bold letters of the Chicago Tribune headline jumped out at him:

GERMANS INVADE HOLLAND

For a second, he stood motionless, staring at the headline as it seared into his brain. He dug in his pocket for coins and quickly swapped the newsie for a copy of the paper. Danny devoured the front page story as fast as he could, his heart beating faster with every sentence. The story began the evening of May 9 when Hitler gave another of his ranting speeches. In it, he said The Netherlands had nothing to fear. Because of their neutrality during the Great War, he said he respected their wish to remain neutral in the current war.

Then, in the wee hours the following morning, the Dutch were awakened by the deafening sounds of an air battle overhead. Hundreds of planes roared above them, many dropping bombs at strategic locations. Others dropped so many paratroopers, the sky resembled a snow storm with all the white parachutes fluttering down. At the same time German soldiers poured over the border into every town and village, many disguised as Dutch citizens, priests, and soldiers. When the real Dutch soldiers rushed to load their weapons, they found their ammunition cases filled with sand, further evidence of sabotage.

Danny remembered Anya once telling him her country didn't believe in war and therefore didn't have a fully trained military. She'd told him how hard she had laughed at a group of Dutch soldiers riding bicycles with their rifles slung over their shoulders. How could such an "army" fight the mighty Germans? With war all around them, why hadn't they better prepared to fight?

He scanned the rest of the article, hating what he read and sick with worry about Anya and her family. Had they survived? Were they safe? As the questions raced through his mind, he remembered Anya's last letter. Would it be her last? Would his letters get through to her? No, of course not. The Germans immediately cut off every form of communication in the countries they took over.

Danny cursed and wadded the paper in his hands. He sat down hard on the steps of the diner ignoring the customers coming and going. He stared across at the theater. Had it really been only moments before when he'd groaned about having to put off college for another year? His eyes tracked downward to the paper in his hands. He carefully spread it across his lap, smoothing out the wrinkles and refolding it. Somehow it felt like Anya was in those pages and he wanted nothing more than to protect her. What was a delay in his plans for college compared to the horror she must surely be facing?

He closed his eyes, imagining the dark sky over Holland, the ghost-like shapes of the German Luftwaffe flying overhead, the inky blotches of flak dotting the sky, the massive explosions blowing up bridges and buildings.

He pushed the thoughts from his mind, trying to stuff them somewhere so he could think of some way to help, some way to get through to Anya. But what could he do?

Nothing.

Nothing except pray.

And right there, on the steps of the 75th Street Diner, he prayed. *Oh Lord, keep Anya safe. Keep all of them safe.*

Part II

14

Utrecht, The Netherlands

Anya sat across the kitchen table from her father. She studied the new creases on his face, the stubble on his chin; his eyes, normally shining with hope and laughter, now shrouded and troubled. But it was his silence that unnerved her, almost as much as the distant gunfire echoing through the streets. His hand, still poised around his coffee cup, trembled ever so slightly. Anya reached across the table and placed her hand over his.

"Father?"

As if snapping out of a trance, he looked up. "Yes?"

"So quiet you are. Tell me what you're thinking."

He turned his hand, taking hers in his, as a tired smile tried to form. "I was thinking of the day I married your mother."

"Tell me about it."

"It was such a beautiful day. The sky so blue. Birdsong

filled the air. A cool breeze danced through the flowers in her hair. How lovely she looked, her hand in mine, as we walked from the church to the parsonage surrounded by those we loved. The parishioners had prepared a great feast in our honor."

A distant explosion rumbled through the air, shaking the foundation below them. They'd grown wearily accustomed to such interruptions over the past few days. Since 3:30 on Friday morning, when the Germans invaded in spite of Dutch anti-aircraft and ground-to-air artillery, Anya and her father had watched their way of life turn upside down. The Germans quickly made themselves at home, emptying homes and warehouses, stealing everything in sight, even forcing families out of their homes so they could move in. They gathered food from shopkeepers, raiding shelves until nothing was left. While pillaging, they ordered residents to give up all their metal treasures—copper, brass, pewter, silver, serving pitchers, plates, and anything else they could melt down for ammunition. Anya had watched her neighbor dig several holes in his backyard to hide his treasures. *How has it come to this?* she'd wondered

The Germans demanded all radios be turned in. But like many others, Anya and her father hid their radio—in their case, behind a wall in the pantry. They drilled a hole for access then placed a framed picture over it. Listening late at night to the BBC, they'd heard that Queen Wilhelmina and most of the Dutch government had fled to England just before the invasion. Anya was furious. *How could our queen turn her back on her people at such a time? How could they care only for themselves, leaving the rest of us to ruin?* Her father had cautioned her, speculating the queen surely had good reason to go to England. Hours later they heard the voice of Wilhelmina explaining her actions. Unwilling to be arrested or shot as a lamb unto slaughter, the wise queen and her government had taken all of the national treasures and money to England. There, they set up a temporary station where they could continue to govern from a safe place. Wilhelmina could speak to her people via *Radio Orange*—a broadcasting service in cooperation with the BBC—at least to those who kept hidden radios.

Now, Anya and her father waited, listening to determine how far away the bomb must have hit. Father and daughter looked once again at each other, confident there was no need to take shelter.

"Go on, Father. Tell me about the wedding feast."

"So much food, so lovingly prepared. And yet I don't remember what was served. Only the cake we cut together. Lemon cake with a pale yellow icing." He paused again.

"Mother once told me how nervous she was in front of all those people, but she stood by your side because she loved you so dearly."

His eyes glistened. "Yes, we loved each other very much. Even as a girl she was very shy. Yet she was willing to become a pastor's wife because she believed God himself had drawn us together."

A moment passed. "Will Mother recover? Will she ever be herself again?"

Sadness fell across his face. "I don't know, Anya. This war will be very hard on her. Even now I don't think she truly understands that the Germans now occupy our homeland. I can't bring myself to tell her. She's so fragile . . ."

"What's to become of us?"

He squeezed her hand again. "Only God knows the answer to that question, Anya. He has allowed this travesty to occur for reasons we may never fully understand. But we trust Him, no matter what befalls us. Always we trust Him."

Anya pushed her chair back and stood. "Why would a loving God do such a thing? How can He just sit back and watch the suffering? Where is His heart if not with His people?"

Her father gazed at her with sympathetic eyes. "This, you must ask Him. I cannot speak for Him."

She reached for the dish rag and began wiping the countertop in busy circles. "I don't have your faith, Father. I have no patience for God playing games with people's lives. He must stop this at once!"

He made his way to her side, stilling her hands with his own. "Oh Anya, do not presume to tell God what He must or must not do."

She untangled herself from his grip, lifting her face to mere inches from his. "Then what are we to do with our guests?" She jerked her chin in the direction of the attic. "Huh? How can we promise them safety when our own lives are in peril? What will we do when our home is searched and they are discovered? Even in the hidden space between the attic and the ceiling—if the baby were to whimper, we'd all be arrested. You've heard the stories. You know what the Gestapo does to those hiding Jews!"

"Lower your voice, Anya."

She huffed, planting her fists on her hips. "Tell me," she

whispered coarsely, "tell me how we shall endure this. Tell me how!" A sob stopped her cold as she began to weep. "Oh Father, I'm so scared!"

He wrapped her in his arms, shushing her whimpers. She *hated* crying and always had. Tears were for sissies. At least that's what she'd always thought until Hans died. Then, nothing could stop the flow of her tears. How frustrated she'd been! And now, the day her country knelt for surrender before Hitler's machine, giving up after only five days—now she fought the tears all over again. *This must stop. I will not cry again!*

Anya straightened herself, wiping her face as she tried to find her composure.

"Dear Anya," her father said, holding her face in his hands. "I don't have the answers you need, and I cannot speak for God. But this I promise you—we will get through this together. And if God allows us to live through it all, then we shall look back and know we stood together and did what we had to do."

She couldn't respond and didn't try.

He gently tweaked the tip of her nose, just as he'd done a thousand times before. "And now I shall check on your mother and our guests. Are you all right?"

She took a deep breath and blew it out. "Yes, Father. As much as I can be, under the circumstances."

As he left the room, Anya stood at the window looking out on the deserted road in front of the parsonage. No children played in the street. No vendors knocked on their door. No parishioners waved as they took a stroll by the house. Only the constant sounds of war in the distance. That's when she knew she and God must come to some kind of understanding.

"You will answer my questions one day, Lord. In the meantime, I will do whatever it takes to survive this Occupation."

Whatever it takes.

15

How odd, Anya thought. *We sit here in our classrooms, acting as if soldiers aren't in the halls watching our every move. We listen to our teacher, study our books as though the streets aren't lined with armored tanks. How can we put our heads in the sand as if nothing has changed?*

Anya fidgeted in her seat, her foot bouncing in rhythm with her nerves. How anyone expected them to learn in such a situation was utterly ridiculous. Already the Germans had mandated that all Jewish students must go to a special school for Jews only across town. More than half the desks in her classroom sat vacant, including that of her friend Lieke. She felt a knot in her stomach each time she thought of Lieke and her large family. There was talk of Jews forced to board trains to be transported to some kind of camp. Anya knew it wasn't the kind of camp they'd gone to as Girl Scouts. She had to talk to Lieke, to convince her and her family to hide before it was too late. But would her family take the risk? For them to follow German orders would mean certain death.

I must find a way to help. There must be a way!

As Anya left school that day, she vowed it would be her last. Who could study in such an atmosphere? What was the point? Even her teachers seemed distracted and on edge. Every one of those empty seats in her classroom seemed to cry out, "Help us! We have done nothing wrong! Please help us before it's too late!"

Anya ran the rest of the way home. "Father?" she called as she burst through the front door.

"Anya? Is that you?"

But the voice wasn't her father's. It belonged to Helga, her mother's dearest friend. Whenever she was gone and her father was called away, Helga would stay with her mother. Anya was relieved her father wasn't home. Now she could go to see the Boormans without him telling her she couldn't.

"How is Mother today?" Anya asked as she entered her parents' bedroom.

Helga stood to hug her. "The same. Always the same. As if her mind is locked away in some prison. Still, I talk to her and sing to her. I tell myself it calms her spirit."

"You are so good to her."

"She would do the same for me."

Anya leaned over her mother's resting body. "Hello, Mother. It's Anya. I love you." She kissed her mother's forehead and turned to go. "I must go to the Boormans for a while, but I'll be back. Don't wait dinner on me."

"Oh Anya, do you think you should be out and about? What if you run into some Germans on your way there?"

"Then I shall speak Dutch and tell them what idiots they are."

"Child! Don't talk like that! These are dangerous times. People have been shot for less."

Anya turned and tried to appease her mother's friend. "I'm teasing. I shall act like I haven't a brain in my head and sputter so much Dutch, they'll wish me gone. Don't worry, Helga. And please, don't tell Father."

"But if he asks—"

"Then change the subject."

She changed her clothes and hurried outside to get her bicycle. It had seen better days, but it still rolled. She'd often thought of using Hans' bike which stood in the shed collecting dust. Not yet, she always told herself. As her wheels offered a repetitive scraping and squeaking rhythm, she pedaled hard with the urgency of her mission. The farm was only fifteen miles away, an easy trip before the Occupation began. Now, she wasn't so sure. Her father hadn't allowed her to venture out except to school. He wouldn't be pleased, but she was desperate to know how the Boormans were doing, and she had an urgent favor to ask of them.

As she crested the last hill, she spotted a group of people ahead walking her direction. *Germans!* Her heart skipped a beat. She yanked the handlebars a hard right, steering herself off the road and into a thick cluster of bushes. Quickly pushing her bicycle under the brush, she crawled in beside it. Panting hard, she scolded herself. *Breathe. Just breathe. Don't move a muscle.*

She couldn't see through the bushes and prayed they couldn't see her either. As their voices grew closer, she held her breath. She knew enough German to catch the drift of their conversation. One of the soldiers was bragging about the beautiful Dutch girl he'd bedded the night before. His comments and their responses disgusted her. *Any Dutch girl who gives herself to lie with these pigs should be shot. Who would do such a thing?*

Eventually the soldiers passed by, but Anya waited several minutes more. Finally, she crept from cover and peeked out to make sure they were gone. She struggled to pull the old bicycle from the bushes, but finally broke it free. She climbed on the seat and pedaled as fast as she could.

Two miles more and she turned left, bouncing along the rutted dirt lane that led to the farm.

"Anya!" Wim cried, hobbling toward her with the help of his cane. "Thank God you're alive! We've been so worried!"

She dropped her bicycle and ran into his embrace. Something caught in her throat as she realized Wim had worried about her. She'd never allowed herself to have feelings for him, though he was always kind and attentive. In many ways she'd thought of him as a brother, though she knew no one would ever take the place of Hans.

He put his arm over her shoulders as they made their way to the farmhouse. "Your parents? They are safe too?"

"Yes, they're fine. Well, except for Mother. She's the same, but safe. Everyone is safe. At least for now." She hoped he understood the implied meaning.

"Ah, yes. We are all well here too. All of us."

"Oh, thank God. I've been so worried."

"Come. Mother and Father will want to see you."

Later, as they sat around the kitchen table, they shared their experiences since the fall of their country to the Germans.

Ella Boorman poured hot tea into Anya's cup. "The paratroopers landed all over our fields! They came storming into the house, shouting their demands, taking whatever they wanted—"

"You must have been so frightened!"

"Ja, we were very afraid. But Bram, he told them we're just poor farmers, we have nothing—"

"But that didn't stop them. They started poking around the house," Bram said, his deep voice agitated, "and into our closets, our cellar—"

Anya sucked in a breath.

"Our guests were tucked safely in the hidden cellar beneath the barn. We have practiced many times what to do if Germans come. They were quiet as church mice. Even the little ones. It was surely an act of God. The Germans poked around in the hay, disturbed our livestock, but they found nothing."

Anya put her hand over her heart. "Oh, thank God. They must have been terrified!"

"They are safe now, Father," Wim said, "but what about next time? It was dangerous enough before the Occupation. Now, we could be shot for hiding our Jews."

"I asked my father the same question," Anya said. "There must be *something* we can do?"

Wim looked at his father and raised his brows.

"What?" Anya asked, picking up on the unspoken message.

Bram shook his head and looked away.

"Stop that! Tell me," she insisted, looking back and forth between them.

Ella patted Anya's hand. "There are some things best not discussed."

Anya pulled her hand free. "No. Do not treat me as if I'm a child." She pushed her hair out of her face. "In fact, you should know that I came here today to ask you to help."

"Help? What kind of help do you need?" Wim asked.

She paused. "I know you have more guests than you can handle. We have so little room in our home, we can't take more. So many Jews . . . but my friend Lieke and her family, I must do something to help them. What shall become of them and all the others if we don't help them? There *has* to be something we can do."

Wim's eyes stayed on her. "And what might that be?"

She looked from Wim to his father then his mother. "How should I know? I was hoping you had some ideas. Surely if we work together, we can do something?"

Bram stood and walked over to the kitchen sink where he poured out the rest of his tea. "Anya, have you mentioned this to anyone else?" He turned, looking over his shoulder at her.

"No. No one. Not even Father. He knows of my concern but until today, I hadn't thought beyond my own needs—only how the war would affect me. But today as I sat in my classroom surrounded by so many empty desks . . . something happened inside my heart. I can't explain it, I only know I have to do something!" she growled. "Father doesn't know it yet, but I'm not going back to school. It's a waste of time and there's too much to be done. Tell me—you have to tell me what we can do!"

Anya studied Bram's weathered face. Such a kind man,

always ready to lend a hand, gracious with everyone he met. She'd grown to love her time with this family. As she looked into his deep set eyes beneath those bushy brows, she knew he was holding something back. But why would he?

She turned to find Wim looking at her, his gaze dropping when their eyes met. Such a strong face, his messy blond hair falling across his forehead, his eyes so blue. She felt herself blushing and pursed her lips, unsettled that she'd reacted like such a school girl.

"Anya . . . there are people . . ."

16

"Yes?" Anya said. "Go on, Bram. There are people?"

The farmer took his seat again. Resting his elbows on the table, he leaned in toward her, lowering his voice. "There are people who are organizing."

She pushed her chair closer, leaning in as far as she could. "I'm listening."

"They're coming together, people just like you, wanting to help those in grave danger in our country. They have begun an effort to mobilize individuals like you, like Wim and Ella and myself—people who are tired of the injustices against their Jewish countrymen."

Wim spoke as quietly as his father. "Anya, it's very dangerous. The things they do could get all of them—all of *us* killed. Are you sure this is something you want to do?"

She swallowed hard. "Yes. I want to be a part of this group that is organizing. Tell me what I must do."

"First, you must understand you can tell no one of your involvement," Bram began. "And I mean no one. A slip of the tongue could cost any one of us our lives. I would never ask you to keep something from your parents, but I'm afraid I must. It's as much for their safety as yours. The less they know, the better."

She looked down at her tea cup resting on its saucer. Could she be a part of this without telling her father? He seemed to know her so well—how she thought, how she acted. Would he see through her? Still, she knew what she must do.

"Yes, I'll do it. I may have to be creative in explaining my absences to Father, but I can do it. I must do it."

"Good," Bram said, folding his arms. "Your help will be greatly appreciated."

"What can I do?"

"At this point, much of our work is primarily that of communication. When so many of our people handed over their radios to the Germans, they cut themselves off from the truth. The German newspapers are filled with lies and propaganda. We must get the truth to our people. Every night at the 8:00 broadcast on the BBC, we have people who take down the information in shorthand. They transcribe their notes, then others print the news which is then carefully, so very carefully distributed.

"As we inform our people by spreading the news, we shall grow stronger in numbers. But I warn you again—not everyone wants the truth. Some have already fallen for the lies."

"Only yesterday, I delivered milk to some homes just inside the city," Wim said. "When the woman at the first home opened her door, I was shocked to see a huge picture of Hitler on the wall behind her."

"A Dutch woman?" Anya cried. "How can she be so stupid?!"

"That is between her and God," Bram said. "But Wim learned quickly how to shield his feelings. Didn't you, son?"

"I forced myself to act like I hadn't seen it. I went about my business. But I realized what my father has said is true. We can trust no one."

"Ja, and we must work faster, husband," Ella said then turned to Anya. "Today we heard such horrible news. It seems the Germans have already started rounding up the Jews. The curfews they have set are merely a way to try to hide their dirty work. These *razzias* are nothing more than mass kidnappings under darkness. Entire families rounded up and put on trains," she said, shaking her head.

"Many are taken to labor camps where they are forced to build ammunition. Imagine, being forced to build the very weapons used to annihilate your own people! And these are the most deadly locations because these factories are prime targets for our Allies. It's an impossible situation. We must stop as many of these transports as we can."

Anya noticed Wim nervously tapping his spoon on the table. He continued where his mother left off. "The Jews are frightened and with good reason. Many of those who came here to escape the persecution in Germany are refusing to surrender. They receive notices, ordering them to show up at a certain time and place. They are allowed only one suitcase. Some are told to show up at the train station for immediate transport to Poland."

"Surely they do not show up as instructed? Surely they know not to—"

"Many of them are confused. They think it's just a temporary situation. They think the war will be over in a few months and they can return to their homes. And some actually believe the lies in the German papers telling them this is for the Jews' own protection—'from the barbaric Dutch people who despise them.' Lies, all of it. Still, some are naïve and do as they're told. But not all. The ones who came here from Germany know all too well what the Nazis are capable of. They give up. We heard that more than 300 of them committed suicide rather than surrender to the Germans."

"I cannot believe this is happening," Anya cried, shaking her fists.

"The others," Wim continued, "the other Jews ordered to show up are taken to certain Jew-only neighborhoods which the Germans are calling 'ghettos'. They tell us it is because the Jews are all infected with terrible diseases. But we are not fooled. To keep them all together makes it easier for the Germans to rule over them or deport them."

Anya raised her hand. "Wait a minute. Back up. Why are they transporting the Jews to Poland? Why would they move them out of the country?"

"Not all of them are taken out of the country," Bram answered. "Some are taken to labor camps not so far away— just down the road at Amersfoort or on the coast at Scheveningen. But the things we are hearing about these camps, especially the ones in Poland . . ." Bram closed his eyes, shaking his head. "It is urgent that we keep as many as we can from getting on those trains."

"How?" Anya asked, her voice thick with emotion. "How do we do that?"

Bram folded his hands, his index fingers pointing at her. "Anya, we have to hide as many of them as we can. We have to transport them away from our cities and villages. But unlike the Germans, we can't just round up large groups of them. No, we must take them a few at a time. A couple here, a child there . . . nothing so as to attract attention or arouse suspicion."

Anya sat up straighter, her resolve growing. "Let me help. Show me how. Teach me. I have to help my friend Lieke and her family as soon as possible. I must help them—take them far from here! How soon can I do this?"

Bram looked at his wife, then his son, then back to Anya as a broad smile widened on his weathered face. "Anya, I'm glad you asked."

17

Anya still couldn't understand God's silence in the Occupation of her country, but she thanked Him anyway for protecting her ride home that evening. How else could she have traveled that distance after curfew without encountering a single German? As she tiptoed into the house she asked God for a second favor—to be able to sneak in without disturbing her father.

"Anya!"

She cringed, recognizing the aggravated tone in her father's voice. "Yes, Father?"

"Where have you been? I've been out of my mind with worry!" By the time the sentence was out of his mouth, his hands were clamped tightly on her shoulders.

"I'm sorry, Father! I should have—"

His hands gripped tighter. "You should never have left without asking me!"

"I know, but I—"

"Anya, what if something had happened to you? What if

the Germans had taken you away from me?! What if—"

"But they didn't! I'm here! I'm home, Father! I'm so sorry!"

He held her at arm's length, his face wild with anger. Then, in a split second he crumbled, gathering her into his arms. "Oh my little Anya! I was so frightened. I thought I'd lost you!" He wept quietly as she hugged him back. "I thought I'd lost you."

Anya bit back her own tears, still vowing to keep her resolve even as her eyes burned. "I'm sorry, Father," she whispered. "I should have told you."

Finally, he pulled back to look her in the eye, struggling to find his voice. "Helga told me you went to the Boormans. How could you disobey me? You knew I would worry, but more than that, you disobeyed me. How could you?"

She pulled out of his grasp, avoiding his penetrating stare. "It was wrong. I know it was wrong. But I . . . I had to go, Father. I was so upset."

"Why? Why were you so upset?"

She turned back to face him. "Because I cannot continue living my life as if nothing's changed! *Everything* has changed! We're at war. Our friends, our neighbors . . . they're not just hiding behind closed doors. The Germans are rounding them up like so many cattle to be slaughtered! I cannot turn a blind eye to them anymore!"

Her father wiped his face with a handkerchief, letting out a long sigh. "Anya, sit."

"What? I don't want to sit."

"Sit! Do as I say." He motioned toward the kitchen table.

She dreaded the lecture, but knew she deserved it. She

slowly took a seat as her father sat across from her. She kept her head bowed, unable to face him. His fingers tapped slowly on the table. She waited.

"I am not blind, Anya. I know what is going on around us. Today I met with other ministers in our city. We talked. For many hours we talked. The things I heard, well, it all made me sick."

Anya looked up. "What?"

"The atrocities against our Jewish friends and neighbors—unspeakable."

Had he heard the same things the Boormans told her today?

"All afternoon, one after another—such horrors against them, I cannot tell you. Then I come home only to find you gone? Dear Helga tried so hard to cover for you until I told her what those Nazi animals are capable of. She burst into tears, begging my forgiveness as she ran from the house. I could not leave your mother, and so I paced. And with each step I imagined another despicable act forced upon you by German monsters."

Anya looked away again, sickened that she'd caused her father so much pain. "I'm sorry. I'm so sorry, Father."

He blew his nose into his handkerchief.

"It was wrong of me to burden Helga like that. I will apologize to her."

"It's not just Helga. It's not even me, Anya. It's the danger you put yourself in! You said it yourself—everything has changed. We are at war. And we are smothered by these godless Germans who make a sport of torturing anyone in their way, Jew or non-Jew. When I told you not to leave the house except to go to school, it was for your own protection."

"I know."

"Then what am I to do with a sixteen-year-old daughter who disobeys me? How can I make her—make *you* understand the risk of wandering about alone when evil lurks all around us?"

"That's precisely why I had to go to the Boormans!"

"Why? What could possibly be so important, you would risk your life to go there?"

His question hung between them. What could she tell him? Hadn't Bram warned her to keep her mouth shut, even to her father?

"Well?"

She dug deep inside for the courage to say what must be said. Bram was wrong. She could not take part in this movement behind her father's back. She would not. Lowering her voice in case their guests might be listening, she began. "I went to ask for their help, Father. I've decided I'm not going back to school—"

"That's ridiculous. Of course you'll go back to school. I won't allow you to quit."

She clenched her teeth. "No, I will not. I cannot waste another moment when lives are at stake."

For a fleeting second, her father narrowed his eyes. Then just as fast, he blinked. "Go on."

Go on? She tried to read his expression but couldn't. "I cannot sit in a class half-empty because all the Jews are gone. I cannot sit by and watch Lieke and her family dragged off to some death camp in Poland! I have to save them, Father. Don't you see?" He said nothing so she continued.

"The Boormans are like family to me now. I trust them. They too have guests, many more than we do. So I knew they would understand the urgency I feel in my veins. This calling in my heart to *do* something!"

"And what is this you think you can do?"

"I had no idea until I spoke to Bram and Ella and Wim." She paused, still hesitant. Her father tilted his head just so, the way he always did when he listened with his heart. It was one of the things she loved about him. "They told me of many others."

"Others?"

"People like me, like the Boormans, who are desperate to do what we can to help the Jews."

Again, something flickered in her father's eyes along with the slightest hint of a smile. "And that would be?"

"To hide them. As many as we can. And not just in *our* homes, but everywhere—to shuffle them here and there, put them in safe houses away from the hideous shadow of the swastika."

He sat back, folding his arms over his chest. "Anya, Anya. When did you grow up on me? Eh? One moment you were this little girl, covered in dirt, your wooden clogs always covered in mud, your braids flying in the wind as you climbed the wings of our windmill . . . and suddenly, the next moment I look across the table and see this beautiful young woman whose heart beats for her country, her friends. Such a remarkable change. But one, it seems, I had not noticed. How did this happen?"

"It happened when we lost Hans." She searched for the right words. "Nothing was ever the same after he died. Not me, not you, not Mother. We all changed. Then the Germans began to breathe down our necks. They stormed our borders and fell from the sky, destroying everything in their way. I believe they stole our innocence as well."

"I'm afraid you're right."

She reached for his hand. "So you understand? You accept my decision?"

He took a deep breath. "Yes and no. Yes, I understand why you're so passionate. But no, I'm not sure how wise it is for one so young to walk such a dangerous tightrope."

"But you just said—"

"I know, I know."

"Father, may I ask you a question?"

"Of course."

"This meeting of ministers you attended today. Is it possible some of these men of God are also organizing to help our friends? Could you and I both be stepping into the same organization?"

He gazed at his hand over hers for a moment, then raised his eyes to meet hers. "It seems your mother and I raised a very smart girl." He winked. "A very smart girl, indeed."

18

"Anya, they won't listen. I know my parents," Lieke Grünfeld argued. "They think if we just do as we're told, we'll be treated fairly. Besides, the papers said it's just until the war is over. We'll be back in—"

"The papers? The German papers?" Anya cried. "You believe the lies of the Nazis over the truth of your friends?"

"Shhh! Mama will hear you!" she snapped. "She's scared enough as it is." Lieke lifted her young sister into the high chair. "There, little Inge. Eat your *koekje* like a good girl." She broke the cookie in two and handed it to the child.

"Lieke, you have to listen to me." Anya followed her friend around the kitchen table. "There's no time to argue. You must convince your parents to let us help them. To help you and your brothers and sisters." She looked toward the door then lowered her voice just above a whisper. "There is a whole network of people who will take you and your family to a safe place. You can stay together."

"That's only asking for trouble," Lieke insisted. "Who

knows what the Germans would do if they caught us all sneaking out in the middle of the night."

Anya held her tongue, afraid she might say something she regretted. She blew out a slow breath. "And if you stay, they will split you up, put you in cattle cars, and send all of you off in different directions where you'll all be baked alive in ovens!"

Lieke spun around and slapped Anya's cheek. "How dare you! What an awful thing to say!"

Anya touched her hand to her stinging cheek. "BECAUSE IT'S TRUE!"

Inge wailed at the outburst, wailing at the top of her lungs.

"Now look what you've done!" She lifted the child from her high chair.

"Look what *I've* done? You're the one who's too stubborn to listen to truth!"

"No, *you're* the one who's trying to get us all arrested. Honestly, Anya, how can you believe all that gossip? Father says the Resistance crusaders are the ones causing the most harm. He spoke to a member of the Gestapo the other day, and he promised we will all travel together. He said—"

"Lieke! Listen to yourself! You might as well lie down on the railroad tracks and let them roll their trains right over you and your family."

"Get out, Anya."

"What? You can't—"

"I said GET OUT! You are no longer my friend. You and your ignorant friends will get all of us killed. So get out and don't come back. I never want to see your face again!"

Anya froze, too stunned to move.

"GET. OUT!"

She pulled in a long, rugged breath, staring in disbelief at the friend she'd known her whole life. The one friend who had always loved mischief as much as she did. The only friend she'd ever trusted. Anya wanted nothing more than to drag her from the house and force her into hiding, with or without her family. But even as she blinked back the wretched tears, she knew that would never happen. As a haunting groan took root inside her, she turned on her heel and ran.

By the time Anya reached home, she was panting, angry, and so frustrated she could hardly think. Pausing to catch her breath before going inside, she rested on a bench under the tree in her front yard.

"Hello, Anya."

She looked up to see Mr. van Oostra coming out of her house. Most likely he'd been to visit her father. She smiled but didn't return his greeting.

"What's wrong, my dear? You look like you've lost your last friend." He adjusted his spectacles, then donned a cap over the ring of gray on his head.

She knew he couldn't have known, but the question caught her off guard. "I fear that's exactly what's happened."

He took a seat on the bench beside her. "Really? My dear child, you're much too young to have the weight of the world on your shoulders. Would you like to tell me about it? Perhaps I could help?"

Bram's warning echoed through her mind, though she wasn't remotely tempted to tell the church busybody anything, much less what had just happened. She stood up and walked toward the front porch steps. "I'll be all right."

"Of course you will. Your father will see to that. Still, if you ever need to chat, I'm always happy to offer a listening ear."

And a big mouth. "Thank you. Goodbye." She hurried up the steps and into her house. "Father, what did that windbag Mr.—"

"Anya, you remember Mrs. van Oostra?" her father interrupted with a warning glare. "She and Mr. van Oostra just stopped by to invite us to a gathering tomorrow night at their home. A chance to get to know our new German friends one-on-one and perhaps find some way to get along."

Anya felt her mouth drop open.

"What's the matter, my dear? Mrs. van Oostra said. "Be careful lest you catch a fly," she teased with a giggle.

Anya snapped her mouth shut and glared at her father.

"Yes, well, so nice of you to drop by, Mrs. van Oostra. We look forward to seeing you tomorrow night."

"Good. Good! I'll be on my way now to catch up with that husband of mine. Good day, Reverend Versteeg. Anya, we'll see you tomorrow."

Once the door was closed Anya turned to her father. "What is wrong with you? How could you even consider going to such a meeting? I can't believe you'd—"

"Enough, Anya! What was I to do? If I declined, the van

Oostras would most likely report me to their new Nazi friends. That would only lead to more scrutiny and perhaps another more thorough search of our home. Yes, I agreed to go to their stupid meeting, but I have no intention of going. God forgive me for the lie, but it seemed the wiser thing to do, all things considered."

Anya flopped down onto the sofa. "Thank goodness. I thought you'd lost your mind, Father."

He lifted his wire eyeglasses from his face and began cleaning them with a handkerchief. "Nevertheless, young lady, I will not tolerate such behavior as that which was displayed when you walked into this house. You have no way of knowing who might or might not be here, and I will not stand for such disrespect."

"But Father—"

"No buts! Were it Hitler himself, I will not allow you to come in here calling him names or throwing your attitude around like some brat of a child. Do you understand?"

"No, I do *not* understand. If Hitler were your guest, I'd rip off his ugly mustache and kick him in the shins. And if I had a gun, I'd blow his brains out without so much as a second thought!"

"ANYA!" Her father shook visibly as he neared her, as though trying to calm a caged beast inside. "How can I make you understand how dangerous such words are now? You cannot continue to speak your mind so recklessly when all around us are ears listening for any excuse to take us into custody. You can't tease about such things. You must not!"

She planted her elbows on her knees, then dropped her head into her hands. "I can't help myself, Father. It's as if everyone around here has handed their brains over to our enemies. How on earth will we ever survive such madness?"

She heard him blow out a heavy sigh, then felt him sit beside her. "You're right, of course. I'm completely baffled by such actions. Still, we cannot for a single moment be careless or let an unguarded thought slip from our mouths."

She leaned back against the sofa. "Today I begged Lieke to let us help her family escape."

"No! Anya, what did you say?"

"How could I *not* say something to her? But it did no good. She threw me out of her house, Father, and told me we could no longer be friends."

He put his arm over her shoulder and drew her close to his side. "I'm sure she didn't mean it. Perhaps under the circumstances she only—"

"No, Father, she meant it." She put her hand to her cheek. "She slapped me and told me never to come there again."

He grew quiet. Anya wondered what he was thinking.

"Father?"

"You won't want to hear this, but I must say it anyway. I ran into Lieke's father earlier today. In our conversation, he assured me the Germans would take good care of them. I was careful in choosing my words when I responded. Still, he made it clear to me they intend to follow the edicts of the Germans and comply as instructed."

"But how can they be so blind?"

"I haven't a clue. And yet, even as we spoke, I realized the danger in trying to reason with him. Which is what I must insist you do as well. Anya, we can't save them all. We can try.

We can state our case, but in the end the decision is theirs."

She tried to make sense of it. "You're telling me to give up on Lieke? To let her and her family go knowing full well we may never see them again?"

He tucked her head under his chin. "I'm telling you we can only help those who want to be helped."

She ground her jaws together, feeling an acidic burn in her gut. And there, in that moment, as her mind reeled along with her imagination, she saw the Grünfelds—all twelve of them—board a cattle car already crammed with other Jews, never to return.

She closed her eyes and tried to pray, quite sure it was already too late.

19

Anya awoke with a start. It took a moment to realize something was scratching against her bedroom window. She gazed at the clock on her nightstand. It showed 2:45. Heart pounding, she tiptoed across her room, assuring herself it was probably nothing but a branch blowing in the night breeze.

"Anya!" a voice whispered.

She jumped back out of sight, wondering who would come calling at such an hour.

"Please, Anya, it's me, Lieke!"

Anya threw open the window. "Lieke! What are you—"

"Let me in. Hurry!"

She looked at the bundle in her friend's arms. "Meet me at the back door." She rushed down the hall to open the door as quietly as she could.

Lieke pushed her way inside, quickly closing the door behind her. When she turned to her friend, her face crumbled. "Oh, Anya!"

"Lieke, what's wrong?"

She removed the blanket, revealing the angelic face of her youngest sister Inge.

Anya looked at the drowsy child then back at Lieke. "I don't understand. What has happened? Why are you here?" She lifted the child from her friend's embrace.

Lieke tried to stifle her sobs, clamping her hand over her mouth. She fell into a chair at the kitchen table, crying so hard her shoulders were shaking. "They came . . ."

"Who came?"

"The Germans. Anya, you were right! It must have been one of their razzias—they broke down our door and stormed into our house yelling and shouting in their horrible language!"

"Oh, Lieke, no!"

Lieke pulled a scarf from her coat pocket and wiped at her tears. "Mother and Father—they rushed from room to room, gathering my sisters and brothers. But as she and Father opened my door, Mother shoved little Inge into my arms, covered me with her coat, and told me to run! I begged her not to make me go, but she pushed us out the back door just as the German soldiers came running down the hall. I was so afraid they'd come after us! I ran as fast as I could. I didn't know where else to go!"

Anya cradled Inge in her arms as she sat down at the table. "Of course you came here. Where else would you go?"

Lieke covered her face. "But I said such awful things to you yesterday!"

Anya reached out to pull her friend's hand into her own. "It's all right. I knew you didn't mean any of them. You were scared as much as I was."

Lieke cried harder. "I'm so sorry, Anya. How could I have been such a fool?"

"Shhh, it's all right."

"Hans, is that you?"

They both looked up to find Anya's mother standing in the kitchen doorway in her nightgown.

"Mother, what are you doing up?"

Her mother shuffled toward the table as she pushed her tangled hair out of her face. "I thought I heard Hans, and I wanted to make him some breakfast." She blinked, looking at Lieke, her face falling. "You're not Hans."

Lieke wiped her face, trying to compose herself. "No, Mrs. Versteeg. I'm Lieke. I'm sorry I woke you."

Anya watched her mother's vacant eyes track toward the child in her arms. "Mother, do you remember little Inge?"

She came closer, taking a seat next to her daughter as she gently reached out to touch the child's head. "Anya? You had a baby?"

"No, Mother. This is Lieke's sister, Inge. Remember when we took them flowers and cookies when she was born?"

"Flowers?"

Anya bit her lip, her patience wearing thin. She'd tried to accept the diagnosis of her mother's illness as a serious psychological problem. But whenever she was tired, Anya couldn't help thinking her mother was merely weak, choosing to remain lost in her perpetual fog. Weak and fragile, unable to function as anything more than an echo of the person she used to be.

"Trüi?" her father called out as he entered the kitchen. "What are you doing up?"

Anya watched as her father took in the situation, obviously understanding at once what had transpired. "Father, I was just telling Mother about little Inge here."

He winked, his face awash with compassion for Lieke and the baby in Anya's arms. "Well, isn't that nice." He put his arm around his wife, helping her to her feet. "But it's not time to get up yet, dear. Let's get you back to bed. Perhaps tomorrow you can visit with Lieke and Inge."

"Do you think? Will Hans be here too?"

He herded her back down the hall. "There, now. Let's just worry about all that tomorrow. Come along, dear."

When her parents disappeared down the hall, Anya turned to Lieke. "We must hide you here until we can find a safe place for you and your sister."

"What do you mean? How can you hide us here?" Lieke wiped her nose with her scarf.

"There are others already here. A young family with three little ones. We took them in when they had nowhere else to go. They're in our attic right this moment."

"I don't understand, Anya."

"It's what I was trying to tell you yesterday. There's a whole network of people who want to protect their Jewish friends and neighbors. In secret attics. In hidden cellars. Everywhere, people are taking in those who need to escape before the Germans arrest them. Tonight you can stay with our guests. Then tomorrow, I'll see what I can do to find you and Inge a place to disappear until it's safe again."

Lieke's face mirrored the confusion obviously traipsing through her mind.

"You don't have to understand all of it tonight." She

reached for Lieke's hand once more. "You'll see. But for now, you're safe. I promise you're safe."

"But what about Mother and Father?" Lieke asked, her voice quivering again. "What about the rest of my brothers and sisters?"

"We must pray for them. And we will, but right now we have to focus on you and Inge."

Half an hour later, Lieke and her sister had been introduced to Margrit and Bernard Wolff, the young couple who'd been hidden away in the parsonage attic along with their three children. Margrit's maternal instincts took over as she took Inge into her arms and welcomed Lieke into their tight quarters.

As Anya turned to leave, she hugged Lieke. "Get some rest. We'll talk in the morning, all right?"

Lieke simply nodded, hugging her back.

Anya closed the door and found her father there to help move the heavy bookcase back in front of it.

"And so it continues," he mused, "as we add two more."

She laced her arm around his waist as he draped his arm across her shoulders. "Yes, Father. Our little secret grows larger, it seems. Just promise me Mother won't remember any of this in the morning."

"The bigger concern tomorrow is to find more hideaways for many more of our Jewish friends. I fear time has run out for them. Perhaps for all of us."

The following morning, Anya rode her rusty bicycle out to the farm. Thankfully, she encountered no more Germans and made the trip in record time. There, she asked the Boormans what to do with Lieke and her baby sister.

Bram scratched his head as he led her and Wim into the house. "I don't know what to tell you, Anya. Already our cellar is at capacity. Even now, we are securing false identification papers to move them farther south into the farmland near the Belgian border. Perhaps we could—"

"Oh, please don't send them away! Lieke is so frightened. I couldn't bear to send her and her little sister so far away."

"But can't you see? Everywhere we turn, another family needs shelter. How can we help one and not another? You would want us to send away one family to make room for your friend? How do we choose? Tell me."

Anya paced the large kitchen. "There has to be a way, Bram. I can't make her go. Not now."

"Maybe there is a way," Wim said, leaning against the kitchen counter. "Father, we can send the Kleins and the Emmerings to the van Deen's farm. They still have a little more room left."

"Why the Kleins and Emmerings?" Bram asked.

"Because if I hear one more complaint from either of those men, I shall turn them into the Gestapo myself."

Bram laughed. "That's true enough. Perhaps it will do them good to have a change of scenery."

"It will do *me* good to have them out of here."

"How will you take them?" Anya asked. "Will you hide them in your wagon?"

"No, it's too risky. We get them new IDs then we act as if

139

they're family traveling with us to visit our grandparents or some such."

Anya studied him. How easily he offered to solve the problem for her, willing to make a way for Lieke and Inge to remain close by. "I'm coming with you," she said, surprised to hear the words come from her own lips.

"No, you're not," Wim answered, dismissing the idea with a chuckle.

"I'm coming and you can't stop me. Just tell me what to do and when we'll go."

"It's very kind of you to offer, Anya," Bram said. "But Wim is right. You cannot go."

"Why not?" she asked, folding her arms across her chest. "You accepted my offer to help the Resistance the other night. You're making this move in order to help my friend. I'm going and you can't stop me."

They looked at each other, back and forth, back and forth. Finally, Bram shrugged. "Fine. You want to go, you go. But hear me, Anya, and hear me well. This is not a Sunday school picnic. This is very dangerous. The slightest mistake or slip up could be your last. Whatever Wim tells you to do, you must do it with no questions asked and no arguing. Is that understood?"

A chill raced down her spine at the serious tone of Bram's warning. "I understand."

Wim rubbed his hand over his face. "I still don't think she's ready, Father."

"I am too ready," Anya said, stomping her foot. "Stop treating me like I'm a child." She flushed immediately, embarrassed by the irony of her reaction.

He held up his hands in defense. "All right! All right!"

"She'll do fine, Wim. You'll explain the routine step by step and she'll comply. Won't you, Anya?"

"Of course. Now when do we go?"

20

November 1940

"You will do as I say or I shall leave you here on the road to fend for yourselves!"

Wim's anger startled Anya as they stood at the back of the truck. Over and over, they had rehearsed the scenario with the Klein and the Emmering families, yet still they argued.

"You have no right to talk to me that way!" Samuel Klein ranted. "I will not stand for this in front of my wife and children!"

Wim jumped up into the crowded truck bed where the two families sat huddled together. He grabbed the stubborn Jew and lifted him to his feet. "Fine, Samuel. Have it your way. I hope you and your family have a nice walk back to Utrecht, because I refuse to take you another mile unless you stop arguing!"

Esther Klein tugged at her husband's arm. "Samuel, stop! The Germans will send us to the camps if he leaves us here. For the sake of your children, sit down and do as you are told."

Rebecca Emmering wailed, begging Mr. Klein to be quiet. The louder her cries, the more her five children cried with her. Her husband blasted Samuel, blaming him for putting his family in danger.

"STOP THIS!" Wim threw his hat on the truck's straw-covered floor. His chest heaved as he fought the last ounce of frustration. "One more word . . . *one more word* and I shall abandon ALL of you right here right now. Is that understood?"

The mothers shushed their children as the men glared back at Wim. To Anya they looked as if they were debating his threat. Now she too jumped up, joining Wim. "Please, everyone, let's just calm down and continue our journey. The train station is only a few miles more."

She watched their faces turn from anger once again to apprehension. They all knew the extreme risks they were taking. "If you would only follow Wim's lead as you promised to do, you will soon be on your way to a safer place."

"Yes, we shall do as we are told," Esther said, pulling on her husband's sleeve until he sat back down.

Wim wiped his neck with his handkerchief and reached down for his hat. With great restraint, he reminded them, "Remember, hold your heads up as you walk through the station. Do not look as if you are trying to hide something. At all times, make sure you do not speak unless spoken to. Mothers, make sure your children understand how important it is to remain absolutely silent. Not one word."

In a few moments, Wim started the engine and steered the truck back onto the road. Knowing the Kleins and Emmerings would be recognized in Utrecht, his father suggested driving them to the train station in Amersfoort where they would board the train for Roosendaal. Half a mile outside of town, Wim pulled over and parked behind an old building. Warning them again to keep silent, he and Anya helped the two families out of the truck so they could walk the rest of the way. With each step, Anya prayed God would protect them.

When at last they approached the station, Wim took the Kleins one direction and Anya took the Emmerings the other. Both families were told to follow at a distance and have their falsified IDs ready. As she made her way to the ticket booth, she noticed Wim at the booth three windows down from her. They would both purchase tickets for their *families on holiday* then casually find the corresponding gates.

Confident her prayers had been answered, Anya helped the Emmerings into a train in a car near Wim and the Kleins. As they stowed away their belongings, she reminded Rebecca to keep the children quiet and try to get them all to sleep as soon as possible. But that was not to be. Having never ridden a train before the children were much too excited, chatting like magpies.

"Please!" Anya whispered loudly. "You must keep them quiet."

Just then, a door banged open as a German soldier entered the compartment. The children flew into their seats, the youngest hiding behind her mother.

He held out a gloved hand to Anya. "Ausweis." *Identification papers.*

"Graag gedaan," she answered. *Our pleasure.* She handed her ID card to the soldier and tried to still her nerves as he examined the picture and compared her to it. He handed the card back to her and demanded the same of all the others. When at last he held his hand out to Jakob Emmering, she swallowed hard, hoping the man would keep his mouth shut. He held out the ID to the soldier, his hand shaking violently.

The soldier looked up, narrowing his eyes at the man whose card named him Maarten van der Rol. "Why are you traveling?" he asked in German.

Emmering shot his eyes at Anya, not understanding. She faked a silly giggle, then spoke in Dutch. "Oh, Papa, tell the nice man we are going to visit Grandmother and Grandfather. We're on vacation!"

Jakob repeated the lie in Dutch, punctuating the information with a nervous smile.

The soldier looked back at Anya with a furrowed brow, clearly not able to understand their language. She rattled on, stringing together a bunch of nonsensical statements, as if she were providing him with all the information he could possibly need.

"Ja, ja," he muttered before handing back their IDS and moving on to the next compartment.

Anya closed her eyes and took a deep breath. Once the train began moving the children watched out the windows until the gentle, rhythmic motion rocked them to sleep. An hour and a half later, Wim motioned for Anya to come to him. Steadying herself along the way, she joined him at the rear of the car.

"We'll be at the station in about ten minutes. When we get off, you and the Emmerings will look for a man smoking a pipe and wearing a red beret. Greet him as if he's a long lost relative. He will load you and the family into his truck and drive you to the farm."

"What if I do not see such a man?"

"You will. The arrangements were made yesterday. He'll be there."

"And you? What will you and the Kleins do?"

"We'll look for a woman in a straw hat with a red ribbon around it. She will escort us to the same farm, though we'll travel a different route. I'll see you there later. Once the families are settled, we'll make our way back to the train station."

Just then the train lurched, throwing Anya against him. She felt her face warm at his nearness. "Sorry."

He held her even as she tried to regain her footing. "I'm not."

Anya looked into his eyes, thinking she might have imagined his comment. For a moment she lost herself, wondering what it would be like if he should lean over and kiss her.

Even as the thought whispered through her mind, he leaned closer . . . then bypassed her lips to whisper in her ear, "You're welcome."

His breath tickled her ear, sending a strange sensation over her. *Is he toying with my affections?* Still, she couldn't deny the desire already filling her heart. She moved back, better able to gaze into his startling blue eyes as she tried to read his thoughts. How many times had she dreamed of this moment?

"Anya?"

She turned, hearing Jakob Emmering call her name. The moment was lost. She nodded, then backed away out of Wim's embrace. She only hoped her face had returned to its normal shade as she returned to her seat. "Yes?"

He pointed out the window. "Look."

There as the train eased to a stop, she saw a sea of German uniforms. She turned, searching for Wim and found him rooted in place, staring out the window. His eyes cut away, catching hers. And though his countenance reflected her fear, he tossed her a subtle wink of assurance. *Go with God,* he mouthed.

Go with God, she mouthed in return.

As they helped their charges down the aisle to get off the train, Anya thought her heart would surely thunder out of her chest. Wim had escorted the Kleins toward the opposite end of the compartment, while Anya and the Emmerings took the closer exit. Going before them down the steps, she stopped short as shrill whistles filled the air. Suddenly the mass of green just below her bolted to her left as the soldiers shouted, "Halt! Halt!"

Anya turned back, pushing the Emmerings back into the car as shots rang out. The children screamed and clung to their parents.

"What's happening?" Jakob shouted.

"Stay down! Cover the children!"

Against the chaos of screeching whistles and gunfire, Anya crouched down, wrapping her arms around the two eldest children. "I'm here, I'm here. We'll be all right. You'll see," she yelled, shielding them with her body. The children whimpered, shaking as they crouched down.

"Joosie!"

She jerked her head up at the sound of Wim's voice calling her code name. He was pushing the Kleins the other direction, twisting back toward her.

"Go! Go! Get them off the train! NOW!"

"But—"

"I said GO!"

She popped up, grabbing the two children closest to her while shouting at Jakob and Rebecca. "Hurry! We must go now!"

They spilled out of the train onto the platform into a cloud of steam belching from the train's engine. The children wailed as guns continued firing in the distance now.

"Hurry! We must hurry!"

Suddenly, a man wearing a red beret with a pipe clamped between his teeth appeared before her. "Ah, my dear Joosie! Thank goodness you are safe!" He hugged her, lowering his voice to speak urgently against her ear. "God has smiled on us, providing a distraction, but we must get everyone out of here at once. Quickly! Quickly!"

"Opa! How good to see you!" she played along. "Look and see all your grandchildren!"

"Ah, my little ones! Come! Come! We must hurry home. Your grandmother has prepared a dinner in your honor!"

As if masterfully performing before a theater audience, the actors played their parts, all the while rushing the frightened family out of the station as fast as possible. It wasn't until they'd all loaded into the farmer's truck that Anya was able to breathe again. And only then, did she think to look for Wim, but of course it was too late.

21

"Anya! Wim! I was so worried about you!"

She fell into her father's arms, relieved to finally be home. "I'm sorry, Father. We couldn't risk trying to get word to you."

"Come inside! It's after curfew," he said, shutting the door after them. "I expected you two days ago! What happened?"

Wim stepped into the living room then shook hands with her father. "Complications. But we're fine. We made our deliveries and all is well. Just a few unexpected surprises along the way. My apologies for making you worry, Reverend Versteeg."

"Come, let me make you some tea. There is much to tell you."

They followed Anya's father to the kitchen where he busied himself preparing tea.

"How is Mother?"

"The same. She sleeps most of the time. Helga sits with

her most of the day. Helga is such a kindhearted woman, always insisting it is her ministry to care for her dear friend. Such a godsend, she is."

"Reverend Versteeg, you said you had much to tell us."

"Yes, and none of it good, I'm afraid." He poured the hot water into the teapot to let it steep. "There has been quite a run on the banks as people are withdrawing their funds in fear of the Germans who will most likely steal what's there. Likewise, the stores are depleted as everyone seems to be hoarding as much food and as many supplies as they can. Of course, there wasn't much left. From the beginning, the Germans helped themselves to our store shelves. There's little left to be had except at farms like that of your family, Wim. Otherwise, there's a sense of panic everywhere you turn."

"Have the Germans continued their razzias?" Anya asked. "Are they still rounding up the Jews every night?"

Her father poured their tea. "Yes, every night. I peek from the windows when I hear their trucks roaring down the street. I watch as our neighbors are pushed and shoved into the trucks, then whisked away. I grieve for them and pray for their protection. Already our street is almost deserted with so many of our Jewish friends gone."

"What have you heard over the BBC?" Wim asked.

Anya's father took a seat at the table with them. "They've now confirmed that more than ten thousand innocent men, women, and children were killed in the initial attack on Rotterdam."

Anya covered her mouth unable to speak.

"Of course, the Germans didn't stop there. Similar reports have come from all across our country. We've sustained many more losses than any of us ever imagined. We've also begun to hear troubling news of these concentration camps where many of our citizens have been taken in Poland and Germany. Apparently many have already been killed in what's been described as gas chambers. It's unspeakable . . ."

Anya had heard the rumors. She thought back to the night she'd told Lieke of these camps and their "ovens," still grimacing to think she'd said such a horrible thing to her friend.

Anya heard Wim groan as he dropped his head in his hands. "We have to work harder. We've got to do whatever it takes to stop these—"

Someone banged on the front door. Anya, Wim and her father jumped up. "Father, what if it's—"

"Shh! Wim, stay here with Anya. Whoever it might be, you let me do the talking." A moment later they heard him open the door. "Good evening. How may I help you?"

Suddenly the house was filled with soldiers all shouting at the same time. Anya hadn't even thought to ask her father if Lieke and the Wolffs were still hidden in the attic. She prayed for their silence as Wim came to her, tucking her under his arm.

Her father reappeared at the kitchen door. "I'm more than willing to help if you'll tell us what it is you want?"

Again, a flurry of harsh German commands. One of the soldiers poked his rifle against her father's back while yelling at him to sit. "HINSETZEN!"

"Fine. No problem. See? I'm sitting." He motioned for Wim and Anya to do the same.

An S.S. officer strolled into the kitchen as he pulled off his gloves. "Ah, Reverend Versteeg. We meet at last."

"And you are?"

"I am Standartenführer von Kilmer. Since you speak English so well, perhaps it is easier if you call me Colonel von Kilmer. It is my privilege to assist these gentlemen as they acquire information concerning you and your family for our census. According to our records, you have not submitted this information as required. Why would that be, Reverend?"

"My apologies, but you see I've been quite busy with my congregation. These are difficult times, you know. And my wife is very ill which makes it difficult for me to—"

"Very busy. Of course you are. A minister of God must be available for his flock."

"Yes, I try to—"

"And who might these two be?" he asked, nodding with his head. "Your children?"

"My daughter Anya, yes. And this is our friend, Wim."

Colonel von Kilmer waited. "And?"

"I don't follow," her father responded.

"And what is your friend Wim doing here? Are you not aware it is well past curfew?"

"Yes, well, Anya and Wim just returned from a visit to my parents' home—her grandparents. And as you stated, since it's well past curfew I suggested Wim stay the night and return home in the morning."

The officer smiled. "Ah, I see. I see. Now tell me, where is it you live, Wim?"

Wim folded his arms across his chest. "I live outside of town. My parents have a farm."

"A farm." He snapped his fingers at a short man who appeared to be his assistant. The man handed him a clipboard with many pages attached. "And what did you say your last name was?"

Wim paused, causing Anya's heart to skip a beat. If the colonel asked for Wim's ID, it would not match his name. Of course her father had no way of knowing his alias, or hers for that matter. She prayed they wouldn't have to show their IDs.

Finally, he leveled his gaze at the officer. "Boorman. I am Wim Boorman."

Von Kilmer looked down his list, lifting page after page. "Boorman . . . Boorman . . . ah! Here it is. Ja, it appears our people also had to make a visit at your home to collect information as well. He looked up at Wim. "Now why do you suppose both of your families refused to comply with our simple instructions to report to our office for the census?" He looked at Anya then at her father.

"I suppose we all have better things to do than stand in long lines to give you names which you already have," Wim said. "All Dutch citizens are enrolled at birth with their local governments. It's no secret."

Colonel von Kilmer's smile faded, his words spoken quietly and deliberately. "Ja, but when you are ordered by the Third Reich to be personally counted on our rolls, you must comply. It's really very easy."

Anya despised the condescension in his tone. She bit the inside of her lip to stifle the angry retorts flying through her head.

"And who have we here?" von Kilmer asked, looking behind them. A tall soldier with a hideous jagged scar across his cheek entered the kitchen pushing Anya's mother in front of him.

"Mother!" Anya gasped, rushing to her side.

"I don't understand," she began. "Who are these people?"

Reverend Versteeg and Wim both stood. "Please, Colonel von Kilmer, as I told you, my wife is quite ill."

"Ah, Frau Versteeg, I must apologize for disturbing you at this hour. Come, have a seat. Would you like some tea?"

Anya watched the confusion skitter across her mother's face. "Here, Mother, let's get you seated."

"But shouldn't I make them breakfast?"

"No, dear, it's the middle of the night," Anya's father said. "These gentlemen just came by to ask a few questions. Nothing to worry about."

"Your husband's right," von Kilmer said. "Not a thing to worry about. We're just here to add your family to our census rolls."

Anya watched her mother blink several times.

"Frau Versteeg, we were just getting to know your family here. Your husband, your daughter Anya and her friend Wim—"

"But where's Hans?"

"Sweetheart, you know Hans is gone," her husband reminded her, taking her hand in his.

"Hans? Would that be your son perhaps?" the officer asked, once again checking his clipboard.

"My brother Hans died last year," Anya snapped. "You'll not find his name on your list."

"How sad. I'm very sorry to hear of your loss," he answered, addressing her mother. "Would there be other

154

children in your home?"

"Lieke and Inge were here—"

"Now Mother," Anya interrupted. "You know it's just us now." She stepped between von Kilmer and her mother, attempting an air of sympathy. "You must forgive my mother. Since my brother died, she has not been the same." Turning, she addressed her father. "Perhaps these gentlemen would allow you to take Mother back to bed."

"How very sad," von Kilmer said, stepping around her to motion her mother toward him. "But as long as you are up, Fraü Versteeg, let's you and I have a little chat."

The heat of Anya's anger surged through her veins. She looked to her father for help. "But surely—"

"Now, now, it won't take but a few moments," von Kilmer chided. He pulled out a chair. "Please, help your mother take a seat."

Anya prayed silently as she and her father helped her mother into the remaining chair at the kitchen table. Anya took her seat again, frightened by her mother's confused countenance.

"Now, here we are. Fraü Versteeg, you mentioned someone named Lieke and—"

"My mother is confused. I told you she—"

"Stop!" Von Kilmer ordered, his hand raised in Anya's face. "I am speaking to your mother. You will not interrupt me again."

Her father's hand trembled as he reached out for his wife's hand. He patted it but kept silent.

"I was asking you about these names you mentioned. Who is Lieke?"

Wim stood behind Anya, resting his hands on her shoulders.

Anya's mother looked from face to face as if trying to make sense of it all. "Lieke?" She looked at Anya who tried to communicate with her eyes ever so slightly. "Lieke is Anya's friend from school."

"I see," the officer responded. "And who is this Inge you mentioned? Also a classmate of your daughter?"

Her mother scoffed. "Goodness, no. Inge is just a baby." She looked around as if everyone should have known. "The Grünfelds have a very large family. Ten children, I think?" She looked at Anya for confirmation.

"Yes, Mother." *Please don't say another word!*

"Ah, the Grünfelds. I know this name." Von Kilmer looked at his assistant. "I believe we assisted a family named Grünfeld to the ghetto a few weeks ago, did we not?"

His assistant leafed through another sheaf of papers. "Grünfelds . . . yes, here it is. Isaac and Eliza Grünfeld. But our records show there were only eight children." His finger traced along the paper. "I see no one named Lieke or Inge here." He looked up, first at Anya's mother, then at von Kilmer.

"When did you last see these Grünfeld children, Fraü Versteeg?"

Her mother looked for help from Anya's father, then to Anya. "I . . . I don't know. Everything is . . . I can't—"

"Please, Colonel von Kilmer," her father began, his voice hushed. "You can see for yourself her mind is not right. She is confused. Lieke and her brothers and sisters were often in our home. They were friends of Anya and Hans. In my wife's mind, names and dates—they're all mixed up."

The officer leaned back in his chair, drumming his fingers on the table. "Yes, I can see she is confused. Still, how would you explain that these Grünfelds are obviously missing two of their children—two daughters? Furthermore, these two daughters just happened to be the ones your wife mentioned. How would you explain that, Reverend Versteeg?"

Anya watched her father swallow hard. "I'm sure I wouldn't know."

"And you, Anya? Have you talked to your friend Lieke recently? Have you seen her or this young sister of hers?"

His narrowed eyes seemed to see right through her soul. Anya sat straighter. "No. I told you. I've been away visiting my grandparents."

Von Kilmer looked back and forth between Wim, Anya, and her father. He stilled his fingers, pressing his hands flat on the table. "Forgive me, but I must ask. Could it be you have given refuge to these two Jewish girls?"

Anya felt her face heating.

"There are no Jews here, Colonel," Wim said with authority, moving to stand beside Anya's father. "Reverend Versteeg is a man of God. To ask him such a thing is to question his integrity as a minister and a leader of our town. You owe him an apology."

Anya took a breath, thankful for Wim's quick thinking. She suddenly stood up, shoving her chair back. "I agree with Wim. You owe my father an apology, as well as my mother. To come into our home at this hour, and to question my mother when she's obviously so ill, then insult my father with your accusatory questions? Enough. I shall ask you to leave at once."

Von Kilmer tapped his fingers twice, fixing a polite smile on his face as he slowly stood. "Very well." He nodded at Anya's mother and father. "I trust you will accept my apologies. I meant no harm." He took great care putting his hat back on his head. "We shall leave now." He turned, then stopped. "However, as many of our questions have not been adequately answered, I should warn you that we will return for another chat. Perhaps then your wife will be feeling better and more inclined to put our concerns to rest."

Anya, Wim, and her father remained silent.

"Very well, then." He turned, starting down the hall. "It was a pleasure to meet you. We shall see ourselves out now. Guten Nacht."

Wim followed them down the hall then closed the door after them. As he stepped back into the kitchen, Anya's mother rose to her feet and cried out, "Hans! There you are! You've come home!"

"Mother!" Anya snapped again. "This is not Hans! This is Wim. Hans is DEAD! When are you going to get that through your head?"

Her father grabbed her arm. "Anya! You will not speak to your mother in that tone!"

"Hans is dead?" Her mother fell back into her chair. "My Hans?"

Reverend Versteeg immediately helped his wife to her feet. "Trüi, let's get you back to bed. We've had enough excitement for one night."

As they made their way down the hall, Anya heard her mother's whimpers. "My baby? My dear Hans?"

"Wim, what will we do? Von Kilmer and his men will be

back. They know. They'll be watching our every move. They'll tear this house apart looking for Lieke and Inge. What will we do?"

He gathered her into his arms, holding her tight. "We will find a way, Anya."

She relaxed in his embrace but fought the sting threatening her eyes. Wim rubbed her back trying to calm her. When she looked up, he kissed her forehead.

"Shhhh. God will make a way for us, Anya. We must trust Him."

"I'm so scared, Wim. I'm just so scared."

"I know you are. And God knows too. He knows all our fears. He will make a way. We will trust Him." He rested his chin on her head. "We will trust Him. We *must* trust Him. There's nothing else we can do."

Just two days later, word spread quickly of an uprising in the Utrecht ghetto. Anya and her father nervously peeked out the front window, watching wave after wave of German soldiers rush by in trucks, on motorcycles, and even on foot. Anya couldn't imagine how the poor Jewish residents could fight off such a force. She wanted to pray for their safety but lately, it felt as if God wasn't hearing her prayers.

Suddenly her father jumped up. "Anya! This is it!" He quickly grabbed her hand. "This is our chance to move our guests! Hurry! We haven't a moment to lose!"

In less than ten minutes, Reverend Versteeg and his daughter had sent word to their Resistance contacts, asking for immediate help to move Lieke, her sister Inge, and the Wolff family. By the time they'd gathered their belongings, a horse-drawn carriage driven by Helga's husband Lars arrived at the back entrance of the church.

"I cannot thank you enough," the reverend said to their good friend.

"It is my honor," Lars answered as he covered his passengers with a tarp. "Now, you must remain silent. Not a word until we get to the Boormans' farm. Then you must do exactly as I tell you."

"Father, I'm going too," Anya announced, hopping onto the cart. "I'll ride back with Lars once everyone is settled."

"All right, but be careful. And hurry home. We have no idea how long the Germans will stay preoccupied with the uprising."

"Yes, Father. I'll be home as soon as possible."

As the cart began to move pulled by Lars' horse, Anya heard her father call her name. She peeked from beneath the tarp. "Yes, Father?"

"You see? He did it! God has answered our prayers. He has made a way for us!"

22

As the Jewish residents of Utrecht scattered into homes and farmhouses across Holland, tucked safely away from the Germans, their non-Jewish friends and neighbors tried to make the best of life under German Occupation. Like so many others involved with the Dutch Resistance, Anya and her father grew strangely accustomed to leading double lives. Reverend Versteeg kept up appearances going about his daily routine while his daughter tried to do the same. She no longer attended school, instead playing the charade of the Reverend's assistant, helping her father manage the affairs of the church while acting as parsonage hostess in her mother's absence. Most of the church members marveled at the change in her, admiring the maturing young lady, no longer the Versteeg's "problem child."

"Never thought I'd see the day," she heard them gossip. "That wild child has become such a beautiful young lady, don't you think?"

"Can you believe she has such lovely hair? It was always such a rat's nest before!"

"It's about time. Look how lean and poised she is. Why, even with those freckles, she's quite striking, don't you think?"

Anya heard their comments and noticed their stares, but chose to ignore them all. She'd made a conscious effort to work on her appearance, better able to play the role she'd taken. She'd even learned to walk with an air of grace when she had to, especially whenever she encountered German soldiers. For such occasions, she'd quickly learned how to play another role—that of a daft young Dutch woman.

"Guten Morgen, Fräulein," they'd say with their wide smiles.

"Ah," she'd answer, giggling as if she hadn't a thought in her head. Then speaking Dutch in her most flirtatious tone she'd say, "I would never speak your filthy language, you pathetic maggots!"

Oblivious to her meaning, they'd laugh as she laughed, circling her like bees to the hive. "Sprechen Sie Deutsch, Fräulein?"

Laughing even harder, she'd respond, "How hilarious you are, you disgusting, good for nothing swine! As if I would lower myself to speak your horrible language!" While they joined in laughing, she'd break through their midst and go along her merry way, sometimes turning back to give them a dainty wave while cursing them under her breath.

Anya had learned to play the game and play it well.

But she also learned to play other roles. Throughout the summer and fall of 1940, Wim and Anya helped transport many more families—*onderduikers*—or "underwater" which was code for hidden Jews and other Dutch who needed to be safely hidden away. Each time taking a different route, they constantly used different strategies to avoid detection by the ever-present German soldiers. Sometimes, these charades fell into place seamlessly; others made for close calls as they'd narrowly make their "deliveries" as planned.

As the Resistance grew stronger, Anya learned more about the various arms of the vast underground movement. While some worked feverishly to produce falsified IDs and papers, others ran illegal printing presses to provide publications and bogus food stamps. Eventually, the Allies began dropping paratroopers into Holland for the specific purpose of coding and decoding messages to and from England. These messages were then sent by couriers to other members of the Resistance throughout The Netherlands keeping them informed of the latest war news. Likewise, they'd report developments back to Queen Wilhelmina and her administration still governing from London.

Others handled the finances, vital to keep the Resistance movement in motion. The National Relief Organization, made up of brilliant financiers, kept the flow of money moving as needed to each arm of the Resistance, all the while staying in close touch with their counterparts in London.

Still others handled the sabotage necessary to cover the movement's tracks and do the dirty work as required. These men and women functioned under the radar, blowing up bridges and buildings when required, freeing political prisoners whenever possible, and killing as many Germans as necessary along the way.

No task was too small. Even young boys and girls did their part, setting up intricate schemes to steal bicycles, a mainstay for transportation in Holland. When tires became scarce, they'd scrounge up wooden wheels to keep the bicycles moving.

Back at home, Anya's father maintained his role pastoring over his membership while using the parsonage to help the cause in any way he could. Like everyone else in his beloved country, he learned to trust no one. Through the church grapevine he and Anya learned that members like the van Oostras had not-so-secretely partnered with the Germans, keeping them informed of friends and neighbors who assisted the Jews. While the van Oostras and others grew wealthier with each tip provided to the Germans, those arrested were often shot or sent to one of the many concentration camps springing up throughout the country.

Such news grieved Anya and her father, but it also fueled their commitment to the cause. Time after time, Anya's father reminded her that God alone would have to deal with traitors like the van Oostras, but it took every ounce of resolve for her to be civil to them when their paths crossed.

In the elaborate system of transporting Jews here and there, Anya insisted that Lieke and her sister Inge must remain at the Boormans' farm. Ella Boorman had grown to love Lieke and her young sister, treating them like family. Lieke never stopped hoping to find out about her parents and siblings, but with Ella's help, she'd learned to take life one day at a time.

As the months passed, more and more of Anya's charges were young children. As the Germans rounded up all the

Jews and forced them to live in ghettos, Jewish mothers and fathers looked desperately for ways to find a safe haven for their children. The Resistance provided passage for these little ones, though they were often moved constantly to avoid suspicion. Even with her self-imposed vow not to cry, Anya couldn't help the tears which moistened her eyes every time a mother or father placed their child in her care. As much as she wanted to help, she despised those heart-wrenching moments when anguished mothers or fathers had to walk away from their screaming, confused children. Instead of caving in to the constant grief, she funneled her emotions into ever-increasing hate toward the evil Occupiers.

On a frigid, blustery day near the end of January, she and Wim were accompanying a young five-year-old girl and her three-year-old brother to the train station in Amsterdam. From there, they would travel north to a village near Leeuwarden in the province of Friesland. Just outside of Amsterdam, the dairy truck they were riding in broke down.

Their driver, a fellow member of the Resistance named Dirk, rolled the truck to the side of the road where it sputtered to a stop.

He pulled an unlit pipe from his mouth. "Sorry, folks. I had a feeling we'd run out of gas. Hard to come by these days. I'm afraid you'll have to walk the rest of the way."

"How much farther is it?" Anya asked, already chilled to the bone.

"About four more kilometers. I'm terribly sorry."

Wim checked his pocket watch then opened the passenger door of the truck's cab. He stepped out, juggling the sleeping girl in his arms. "We still have time to make it.

Thank you for bringing us this far, Dirk. Come, Anya." He helped her lift the young boy out of the truck. "We'll have to walk fast. If we miss the train we'll have to wait til tomorrow. The longer we stay in the station, the more likely we'll arouse suspicion."

"Thank goodness the doctor supplied us with sedatives for the children," Anya said. "Better they sleep through all this. I just hope this cold wind doesn't wake them." She covered the little boy's head with her knitted scarf as she plodded along beside Wim.

Half an hour later, Wim adjusted little Liesbeth onto his other shoulder. "Anya, hurry. We haven't much time."

"I'm walking as fast as I can, Wim. I can't feel my feet anymore."

He stopped, waiting for her to catch up. "Here, let me take Henri."

"You can't carry them both. Don't be silly." She picked up her pace. When she matched his stride, she made a face at him.

He laughed and reached over, draping his arm over her shoulder. "After we tuck these little ones safely away in their new home, I think you need to take a break."

"I can't. There's too much to be done."

"You haven't had a break in months, Anya."

"Neither have you, so why should I?"

"Because fatigue can be deadly. You know that as well as I do. These little ones are precious cargo, and they deserve the best we can give them. When you're tired, you can't possibly function at—"

"I was thinking of Hans just now."

166

He exhaled, his breath a brief puff of air whipped away by the wind. "What?"

"Hans believed a person could do extraordinary things by simply pushing through disappointment or fear or fatigue."

"Well, that's true, I suppose, but—"

"I still miss him so much."

He was silent for a moment.

"I wish you could have known him."

"But I did. We met a few times."

"No, I mean I wish you could have known him. Like I knew him."

He gently squeezed her shoulder before shifting Liesbeth to his other side. "I do too. I think we might have been good friends."

She smiled up at him. "You do?"

"Of course. Now hurry. We're almost there."

Moments later as they rushed into the old train station, Anya heard someone call her name.

Wim closed in, stepping just behind her. "Don't look back. Ignore it and keep walking."

They'd been trained for situations like this, warned to maintain their falsified identities under all circumstances. A blown cover could land them in a cold dark cell. Or worse.

"Anya Versteeg!"

Anya's heart pounded as she tried to keep up with Wim. "What do I do?" she whispered. "It's obviously someone who knows me!"

"We're almost there. You are not Anya Versteeg. You are Hannie Hendriks."

Someone pulled at her elbow. "Anya! I knew it was you!"

She stopped cold, staring into the face of Franz van Oostra.

Wim intervened, smiling as he extended his hand to their fellow church member. "Hello, Mr. van Oostra. What a surprise! What brings you to Amsterdam?"

Anya watched as he shook Wim's hand. "Business. Always business. But I should ask the same of you. What brings the two of you here?" His eyes flitted back and forth on the children in their arms.

"Well, it's actually a most unusual circumstance," Wim began. "You see, Anya agreed to accompany me on my journey. My niece and nephew here were staying with us at the farm while their parents were on holiday. They've just returned from their travels, so we're taking the children home to their parents."

Van Oostra's eyes narrowed. "I see. How nice they could get away, though you'd have to agree it's a most unusual time to take a holiday."

"How so?" Wim asked, his face a blank page.

"Why, the Occupation, of course. I would think most parents would want to keep their children close at hand. Who knows what dangers could befall them?"

"True, I suppose, but they're safe with us. We would never let anything happen to them."

Anya could tell the church busybody wasn't buying a word of it.

Van Oostra nodded without smiling. "Yes. Yes, of course." He patted Henri on the back. "And where might you be taking the children?"

As if it's any of your business?

"Oh, I'm quite sure you've never heard of their village. It's on the coast near the Belgian border." Anya hoped he didn't hear the quiver coating her lie. She glanced at the massive clock on wall above them. "But you must excuse us now as it's time to board our train." She turned to go. "How very nice to see you. Please give our best to Mrs. van Oostra."

"I shall." He nodded slowly, his smile now vanished.

Wim touched his hand to the brim of his hat. "Good day."

"Yes, good day to you as well. I trust you'll have a safe journey."

Anya forced a smile and kept walking. She half expected him to alert the Gestapo right then and there and have them all arrested before they neared their train.

"Hurry, Anya," Wim urged, his hand at the small of her back. "We're almost there."

They quickly made their way to the platform and boarded their train. Much of the train was already occupied, and it took several minutes until they found a compartment with room enough for the four of them. Once they settled in with the children curled on the seats beside them, Anya leaned her head back. "Oh Wim," she whispered. "He knew we were lying. I could see it in his eyes."

Wim gently patted Liesbeth's head which rested in his lap. "I'm afraid you're right."

Anya leaned her head on his shoulder and closed her eyes, the implication of what had just happened hanging over them like a shroud.

After several moments, Wim took her hand, lacing his fingers with hers. "I'm afraid it will be a long, long time before we can return home."

23

Anya awakened as the train began to slow. She lifted her head off Wim's shoulder. "Why are we stopping? Is this Leeuwarden?"

"No, we're approaching the station at Alkmaar."

She looked out the window into the darkness wishing they were already at their destination.

"Mama?"

"Shhhh," Anya warned quietly, hoping to lull Henri back to sleep. "Everything's all right."

He looked around, confusion drawing his brows together. "Where's Mama? I want Mama!"

"Perhaps you'd like a lemon drop, Henri," Wim said, digging a small paper packet out of his shirt pocket. "Would you like that?"

The little boy's chin wobbled as his eyes began to fill. "I want Mama," he whimpered.

"Yes, Henri. I know," Anya cooed, whispering into his ear. "But Mama's not here right now. Let's see if this lemon drop tastes like lemon, all right? Do you suppose it might be grape instead? Or perhaps cherry? What do you think?"

With his chin still trembling, he reached out and grasped the yellow candy out of Wim's hand then slowly put it in his mouth. Moving it from side to side, he looked pensive. "Lemon. Just like the last one."

"Ah," Anya said. "So it is. I was hoping it would be grape. But it's yummy like the last one, right?"

He sniffed, wiped his eyes, and nodded. "Where's Mama?"

"She's safe and sound, and she loves you very much." Anya tousled his hair and watched as his eyes grew heavy. In a couple of moments he slumped against her shoulder, sound asleep.

"We must remember to thank Dr. Bakker," Wim said quietly. "What a brilliant idea to coat lemon drops with sedatives."

Before Anya could answer, the door to the compartment flew open. A huge German soldier stuck out his beefy hand.

"Ausweiss!"

Once again their papers were checked and identification photos compared to their faces. Anya doubted she would ever get used to these impromptu inspections. The soldier studied the children's faces, tipping Liesbeth's chin with his stubby finger for a better look. Her eyes popped open.

"Papa? Mama?"

"I'm here," Wim said, wrapping his arm around her.

She pushed back from Wim's embrace. "You're not my papa . . ."

"What is wrong with this child?" the soldier grunted in

German. "Why is she crying?"

Both Wim and Anya feigned ignorance, as if they didn't understand.

He pursed his lips in frustration, stared them down, but moved on.

Anya let out a long sigh.

"I'm afraid our friend is not alone. Look," Wim said, pointing out the window. The platform was crammed with German soldiers, each with a rifle slung over his shoulder. They appeared to be crowding in toward the train. "It looks like they're boarding."

"Should we get off?"

He shook his head. "Too risky. Our tickets are stamped for Leeuwarden."

One after another, the soldiers passed their compartment door as they boarded. Some looked in, most didn't. Anya knew most trains had special cars reserved for the German soldiers. Often, only one or two rode in the special cars while the rest of the passengers were crammed into others. This time, the car with the *Nur für Wehrmacht* sign would surely be filled. Regardless, Anya was uneasy knowing so many of them were on the train.

Wim bumped his shoulder next to hers. "We'll be fine. Just try to get some sleep."

"It's hard to sleep with such an overwhelming stench on board."

He smiled. "Would you like a lemon drop, little Anya?"

"And then what would you do? Carry all three of us off the train?"

"Of course," he said with a wink. "I'm strong and virile.

I'd just pile all of you on my back and off we'd go."

"Very well. Hand me a lemon drop." She held out her open palm.

He shook his head. "Sorry, I'm afraid we must save these for the little ones."

"Convenient response."

He grinned. "Ja, it is."

Moments later the train lurched forward as it started down the track again. Anya wished she could sleep as soundly as Liesbeth and Henri, knowing they still had a ferry ride across the bay before making it to the province of Friesland. It would take most of the night to reach their final destination. As she thought about the journey still ahead of them, she tried to remember what life was like before every waking thought was consumed with fear—a fear so strong, it seeped into every pore in every situation. She dreamed of living free from such constant fear, wondering if that day would ever come again.

Fatigue tugged at her even as renegade thoughts nudged her down a troubling path. There in her mind, she watched Franz van Oostra whispering into the ear of the gruff German who'd just checked their IDS. The scene played out as the soldier blew his whistle hard, signaling hundreds more of his comrades to assist. They were everywhere—their ugly olive coats and helmets multiplying before her eyes. Suddenly they all stormed a familiar house, dragging a man and his wife outside and holding them at gunpoint.

"WO SIND SIE?! the soldiers shouted. *Where are they?!*

"I don't know!" the man answered in Dutch, his face streaming with tears. "I don't know where they are!"

"Sagen Sie uns!" *Tell us!*

"I can't because I don't know! You have to believe me!"

"Ja?" the huge German said. He laughed out loud, reaching over to drag the woman to her feet then placed his gun against her temple.

"Mother!" Anya cried out. "No!—"

A single gunshot rang out. "Nooooo!"

"Anya! Shhhh! Wake up!"

Her eyes blinked open, finding Wim's face next to hers.

"You must have been dreaming. You cried out." He cupped her cheek in his hand. "I'm here. You're all right." He kissed her forehead.

"Wim, it was horrible! They shot—"

"Shhh, Anya," he whispered urgently. "You must be quiet."

She looked up, startled to find an elderly man and woman in their compartment looking at her. "I'm, uh . . . it was—"

"A bad dream?" asked the old lady sitting across from her.

Anya nodded, her hand trembling as she pushed her hair out of her eyes.

"We all have them, dear," she said, shaking her head. "Such a nightmare we're all living."

"It's been a long night," Wim answered, as if an explanation was needed.

"Ja," Anya added, "a very long night."

Suddenly the train lurched again followed by the high-pitched screeching of wheels braking against the rails.

"What now?" the old man asked, gazing out the window.

Anya and Wim looked out the window nearest them. "We're in the middle of nowhere," he said quietly. "This can't be good."

As they speculated the cause for such a stop, Liesbeth and Henri both woke up.

"Mama?" Liesbeth blinked, her eyes bloodshot. "Mama?"

Without a word, Wim slipped his finger into his shirt pocket then pushed a lemon drop into the little girl's mouth before she knew what was happening. She sucked on it, still looking bewildered by her surroundings.

"That's a good girl," Wim whispered, tucking a strand of her dark curls behind her ear. "Go back to sleep."

The train jolted to a final stop. "Why do you think we've stopped?" Anya asked.

"I don't know."

Just then, their compartment door opened and a conductor stepped in. "The bridge ahead has been damaged and the train can't cross it. Remain where you're seated until you're told what to do." Just as quickly, he was gone.

Wim closed his eyes.

"What are you doing?" Anya whispered.

"Praying." His eyes fluttered opened. He leaned closer, his mouth to her ear. "We have to get off the train and disappear. We can't risk another outburst by the children if we're escorted by the Germans. We need to casually gather our things then slip away before anyone notices us."

Anya nodded. She looked over toward the elderly couple who seemed glued to the window. "What about them?"

"Don't worry about them. Let's go."

As they stood and hoisted the children over their

shoulders, the woman looked back at them. "What are you doing?"

"Oh, we just need to stretch. Maybe get some fresh air," Wim said as he opened the compartment door.

"We'll save your seats for you," she said, smiling.

"Thank you. That's very kind."

Wim leaned out to check the passageway. "It's clear. Follow me and stay close."

Anya held on to the hem of his coat as he led the way. Suddenly he stopped.

"Soldiers ahead. Turn around—slowly, slowly."

As nonchalantly as possible, they reversed their direction and made their way down the passageway. At the door, Wim looked through its window. "No one's here. Once we step into the connection corridor, I want you to wait while I jump, then when I signal, you jump. Hold onto Henri extra tight. I'll help you land."

Anya's heart raced. "Are you sure? What if someone sees us?"

"Anya, do as I say!" And with that, he leapt from the train into the darkness. A moment later she heard her name. "Jump, Anya!"

Without a second thought, she clutched Henri, tucking his head beneath her chin then jumped. She crashed into Wim, taking all three of them to the ground.

"Are you all right?" he whispered.

"I think so." She checked Henri, surprised to find him still sleeping. "Where is Liesbeth?" she asked, her eyes not yet adjusted to the darkness.

"She's right here. I'm picking her back up. Now stay

close to me. Hurry!"

Blindly, they disappeared into the nearby woods, uttering a prayer of protection with each footfall. An hour later, Anya stopped, grabbing hold of Wim's arm. "I can't go on. I have to stop."

He turned around. "All right, but we need to stay out of sight. There, in that thicket of trees." He helped her along, easing her down against the base of an enormous tree. They remained silent except for their panting as they tried to catch their breath. The children settled back in their laps, rousing but never fully wakening.

"Wim, what will we do?"

"We must look for help. Perhaps a farmhouse or a church."

"We're in the middle of nowhere. How will we find such places?"

"I don't know. Let's rest for just a moment and think."

She rested her head back against the tree, hoping no snakes or wild animals roamed the forest. As her breathing returned to normal, she tried to pray. Instead, she fell sound asleep.

"Anya."

She blinked, startled by the sound of her name. "What is it?"

Wim stood, offering his hand to help her up. "You've been asleep for ten minutes. We have to get moving."

He pulled her up, helping her readjust Henri in her arms. "I'm so tired, Wim."

"I know. But the sooner we go, the sooner we find refuge."

Near the break of dawn, they came upon a small village. Wim approached a farmhouse on the edge of town. "This way," he said motioning her to follow him toward the barn. As they rounded the back of the weathered structure, he held his arm out, stopping her. "There, Anya. Do you see?"

"See what?"

"God has smiled on us yet again." He pointed to a spot barely visible on the corner of the barn.

There, in the dusty light of dawn she recognized the three-inch square of orange—the Dutch royal family's color— atop a mini-version of the red, white and blue Dutch flag. "They are one of us?"

"Shhh. Yes, it appears they are. But we cannot be too careful."

A rifle cocked into place. "Wie gaat daar?" someone behind them barked. *Who goes there?*

They turned to find a farmer looking down the barrel of his shotgun at them. "We mean no harm," Wim answered in Dutch, his hand raised to assure the old man. "We're trying to get to Scheveningen. We seem to have lost our way."

Anya held her breath, waiting to see if the farmer understood. Members of the Resistance used the city's name as a verbal test, knowing Germans could not pronounce the uniquely Dutch word.

The man straightened, lowering his rifle. "Ah! Scheveningen," he said, his pronunciation perfect. "Then you've come to the right place." He approached them with a wide, toothy grin, holding out his hand to Wim. "I'm Joris Hildebrand."

Wim shook his hand heartily. "I am Wim Boorman. This

is Anya Versteeg. We are from Utrecht. We were taking these children to a safe house in Leeuwarden when our train was stopped in the middle of nowhere."

"The train was full of German soldiers," Anya continued. "We couldn't risk being questioned about the children, so we fled on foot."

"You made a wise choice. You must be exhausted," the farmer said. "Come along. Let's get you something to eat and let you rest a while."

Wim pulled her against his side as they followed the kind stranger. "That would be most kind. You are an answer to prayer."

Joris stopped and turned back to face them. Pointing to the two sleeping children, he said, "No, I would say *you* are an answer to prayer to these little ones . . . and to their parents as well." He shook his head. "So hard it would be to send your own children away."

24

Anya rolled over, suddenly startled by her surroundings. Then she remembered. The kind farmer, also a member of the Dutch Resistance. His wife Roos, who readily took charge of Liesbeth and Henri, giving Anya and Wim a chance to rest. The soft glow of a lantern on the bedside table helped her get her bearings as she sat up in bed. *It's dark again. I wonder how long I have slept?*

A few moments later, she opened the bedroom door and walked down the hall. She followed the sound of Wim's voice, glad to know he was awake as well.

He turned as she entered the kitchen. "Anya—at last, you are up," he said coming to her.

Anya tried to read something which flickered across his face, then decided she must still be groggy. "It is already night again?" she asked, stifling a yawn.

Wim put his arm over her shoulder and kissed the top of her head. "Night then day then night again. You've slept almost thirty-six hours. I was beginning to worry."

"What?" She twisted to look up at him. "No, that's not possible."

"Ja, but you needed your rest and so we let you rest," the farmer's wife said.

Panic cut through her. "The children—where are the children?"

Roos crossed the kitchen, taking Anya's hands into hers. "The children are fine. They've been fed, they've played with our own grandchildren, and now they're once again in bed. Not to worry about the little ones." She patted Anya's hand. "Now. What can I cook for you? You must be starving."

Anya looked at Wim again for assurance. "The kids are fine. Mrs. Hildebrand took good care of them. I promise."

"Please. I insist. Call me Roos. Yes, those poor dears. They were so frightened when they first woke up. It took a while but slowly they began to warm to us. Especially when our grandchildren stopped by. It was good for them, I think. Playmates, ja?"

"We can't thank you enough," Wim answered, taking the words out of Anya's mouth.

"Come. Sit. I'll warm you some dinner."

Wim led her to the kitchen table where he pulled out a chair.

"Thank you. I am rather hungry."

Wim sat beside her, rubbing his hand along her forearm. "You'll love it. Mrs. Hildebrand—I mean Roos—made the most delicious *erwtensoep*. I confess I had two bowls of it myself."

Anya loved her mother's Dutch pea soup, so thick and flavored with leeks and carrots and sausage.

Mother . . . She wondered how her mother and father

were getting along.

"There you go. Nice and hot. Don't burn your tongue. Would you like *een sneetje brood?*"

"Yes, that would be wonderful."

Roos placed the warm bread on a small dish then spread butter on top. "Now. Eat up."

Every bite was better than the one before. Anya couldn't remember ever being so hungry. Only a farmer and his wife would offer such hearty food. At home, only the bare necessities could be found in the stores. And even then, you had to be there when the merchandise arrived or the shelves would be emptied. Everyone in Holland had already learned to do without.

Mr. Hildebrand entered the kitchen through a second door that looked to come from somewhere beneath the house. "Good evening, Anya," he said. "You are rested, I hope?"

She smiled, embarrassed. "Yes, apparently I'm *well* rested."

"Nothing to be ashamed of, child. From what Wim tells me you have worked tirelessly for some time now. I'm glad we could offer you a pillow on which to lay your head." He held up the coffee pot. "*Koffie?*"

"Yes, thank you," Anya said between bites.

He filled a cup for her then refilled Wim's mug. The farmer caught Wim's eye and made a gesture with his eyes.

Anya caught the exchange between them. "What is it?"

Wim shook his head. "It can wait. Go ahead, finish your dinner."

She took a big bite of the buttered bread and set down her spoon. "No. Tell me now."

"Anya, please. You need to—"

"Don't tell me what I need to do, Wim," she snapped. She looked back at the farmer, who'd turned to leave. "What is it, Mr. Hildebrand? What hasn't he told me?"

Joris turned, his hand on the doorknob. "I'll be downstairs." He disappeared down the steps.

Anya turned, grabbing Wim's wrist as she searched his face. "Tell me."

He took a deep breath, blowing it out with gusto. "Joris has an elaborate secret phone system. He's in close contact with many in the Resistance. Not just here but all over the country." He paused, tracing his finger around the rim of his coffee mug. "I asked him to contact our people in Utrecht."

"And?"

He kept his eyes locked on his mug. "And . . ." He reached for her hand then looked into her eyes. "And it seems your parents were arrested, Anya."

She stared at him, positive she'd misheard him. "No, you must be mistaken."

"I wish I was."

She withdrew her hand from his. She couldn't blink. She couldn't even breathe.

He tried to put his arm around her shoulder, but she batted it away. "No! Don't touch me. You're mistaken. There's no way my parents could have—" But in that split second, she knew. The face of Colonel von Kilmer flashed in her mind. His veiled threats. His accusations.

Before they'd left home, several weeks had passed with no more visits from the suspicious officer. They'd presumed they'd been lost in the paperwork; his accusations nothing more than idle chatter meant to make them nervous. And yet, as the thoughts peppered her mind now, she knew he'd come back to her home.

She looked up at Wim. A single tear rolled down her cheek. "Von Kilmer?"

He nodded, pulling her into his arms. "Yes, Anya. He came back. Only this time he brought a dozen soldiers with him and they literally tore the house apart."

She jerked her head up. "But we moved them—the Wolffs and Lieke and Inge—we took them to your farm!"

"Yes, we did. But in our haste, we neglected to go back and check the attic space where they'd hidden. It never crossed my mind, and apparently it didn't cross anyone else's. When the soldiers came and tore through your home, they ripped the bookcase apart and discovered the hidden attic. They found a worn copy of a Hebrew Bible under the floor board. Bernard must have hidden it there and forgot it. Inside the cover of the Bible, it listed his name, his wife's name, and the names of their two children—all of them wanted by the Gestapo for not showing up to be transported months ago."

"How could Bernard be so stupid?" she cried out.

"Anya, it wasn't his fault. It all happened so fast that night, remember? We rushed them out during the ghetto uprising. It was all very sudden and none of us thought to look for hidden things beneath floor boards. Only the Germans would think to rip the wooden floors apart in the home of a Christian minister."

"But . . . where did they take them, my parents? My poor mother—"

"Joris is trying to find out." He stroked her hair. "Some

of our people in Utrecht saw them loaded onto a cattle car filled with Jews."

Anya shook her head and covered her face with her hands. "No, no, no . . . this is all a mistake."

"The last they heard, the train was headed for Westerbork. But Westerbork is only a holding camp. By now they've most likely been sent to one of the concentration camps, either here or perhaps in Germany."

As the words fell from Wim's mouth, Anya couldn't breathe. She collapsed into his arms, the wails rattling her lungs sounding distant somehow.

Suddenly, she felt herself lifted up in his arms and cradled against his chest. She grabbed hold of his shirt, tightening her grip as she cried. He walked her to the bedroom, then gently laid her down on the bed. As the sobs shook her body, she curled onto her side, pulling her knees up tight. She felt him lie down beside her, tucking himself against her back as his arm wrapped around her waist.

Finally, much later, she felt each breath catch in little hiccups as she tried to calm down. As exhaustion slowly took over, she felt herself drifting off to sleep.

And prayed she would never wake up.

25

"I'm going and you can't stop me!"

Two full days had passed since Anya learned about her parents' arrest. For two days she'd cried and thrown up and slept, only to do it all over again. On the third day, she'd had enough. She'd made her way down the dark stairs to the room below the house where she found Wim and Joris, huddled over a map.

"What are you doing?" she had asked, startling them both. They had hemmed and hawed, giving her vague responses until she stomped her foot and demanded they tell her what was going on.

"Very well," Wim had answered, planting his hands deep in his pockets. "We've learned there's to be a massive raid on Utrecht and the surrounding areas. Someone has tipped them off to our work there, moving Jewish families to safety. One of our Resistance workers is planted inside the Gestapo office there in Utrecht. He said they're waiting for reinforcements which could arrive at any time."

"Your family?"

"No word. I've tried to reach them. I've contacted others to find out if they know what's happening, but so far nothing. Which is why I'm leaving shortly to go home."

"Then I'm coming with you."

"No, Anya. It isn't safe. You need to stay here until I can come back for you."

"Wim, I said I'm going and you can't stop me."

"Don't be ridiculous!"

"*I'm* the one who's ridiculous? If it was my family, don't you think I'd do whatever I could to save them? But no, I didn't have that chance, did I? Now it's your family, but don't forget—my friend Lieke and little Inge are in your parents' care. If I couldn't save my parents, at least I can try to save my friend and her sister."

Wim pulled at his hair. "You make me crazy! You are SO STUBBORN!"

"Ja, they tend to do that," Joris added casually. They both looked at him. He held up his hands. "It's true. Do yourself a favor, Wim, and let her go. You'll save a lot of time and frustration in the long run. They always get their way. It's a woman's way."

Anya hugged the farmer. "Finally, someone understands. Thank you, Joris." She planted a loud kiss on his cheek. "Oh—wait a minute. What about Liesbeth and Henri?"

"Actually, I've already discussed that with Joris and Roos," Wim said.

"What do you mean?"

"What he means," Joris said, "is that Roos and I would like to keep the children here with us. There's no need to take them north. They've had enough to deal with; they don't need to be uprooted again. But even beyond that, we *want* to keep them here. We love having little ones in the house. Besides, having them here draws our own grandchildren like magnets. We get to see more of them as well. So you see? It's best for everyone."

"Wim? Is this all right with you?"

"Yes, in fact I think it's what's best for Liesbeth and Henri. We will make the necessary contacts with the Resistance headquarters so their parents will know where they are when the time comes for them to go home. And we can always come back to see them once things settle down."

"You mean, *if* things settle down."

"It will," Joris insisted. "You'll see. One day we'll be rid of these German idiots and we'll all return to our lives as we once knew them."

"I hope you're right," Wim said, then turned to point Anya up the stairs. "We must be ready to go. They're sending a truck to take us home as quickly as possible. He should be here any moment."

Over the bumpy back roads heading home to Utrecht, Anya and Wim's driver filled them in on more of the war news. The man who introduced himself as Nathan told them that Jews sequestered in the ghettos all across the country were barely holding on, cut off completely from supplies of food and other staples. The Germans didn't seem to care of their plight knowing it was a temporary situation until all of them could be transported to the death camps, as they were now called.

"My kids have learned to hate the sound of the train whistle. Always before, they loved running to watch the trains go by. Now, we do not let them because the cattle cars are filled with people."

Anya closed her eyes as she tried to push the image of her parents in such a cattle car to the back of her mind. Wim entwined her fingers with his, his thoughts no doubt the same as hers.

Nathan continued. "They're packed in those cars so tight they can't even move. Oftentimes they'll hold up their little ones, just so their children can catch a breath of air. I've never seen anything like it. The sadness in their faces . . . it's unspeakable. My wife and I have told our children to stay away from the tracks. It's too much for their young minds, you know? Children their age shouldn't have to see such things." He paused, then added, "Of course, when I think about all those little Jewish children and what they face?" He shook his head.

Wim squeezed her hand. "What do you hear of Utrecht?" he asked, steering the subject a different direction.

"Utrecht. You'll see for yourself soon enough. The synagogues are all boarded up now, and the Germans have painted obscene messages on most of the synagogue walls. Horrible, vile things as you can't even imagine. I just hope and pray God unleashes His wrath on these vermin.

"Everyone is on edge, weary from the constant bombing, rushing down into the bomb shelters half the night. Between that and the shortage of food getting worse every day, I don't know how long we can continue our work. But we have no choice. If we don't, who will?"

They continued the next couple kilometers in silence. As they drew close to the outskirts of Utrecht, Wim gave the driver directions to his farm. "But let us out a kilometer or so before we get there. We don't want to take any chances."

A few minutes later, their driver pulled over to the side of the road near a wooded area backing up to the Boormans' farm. Wim reached across Anya to shake his hand. "Thanks for the lift."

"You're welcome. And just so you know, I'll be staying at a friend's home here in Utrecht. If you run into any trouble, contact the Resistance headquarters and they'll get word to me."

Wim said, stepping out of the vehicle. "Will do. Thank you, Nathan."

"Thank you." Anya shook his hand then joined Wim on the side of the road.

"Take care," Nathan said, putting the truck in gear.

As the old truck rattled off into the distance, Wim and Anya headed into the woods, walking hand in hand. Anya wanted to be grateful for the sunlight streaming through the branches, but being so close to home filled her with sadness. She wanted nothing more than to turn and run to her house, throw open the door and find her mother and father at the kitchen table having tea.

They walked in silence, Wim helping her step over fallen branches and rocks here and there. As they neared the farmhouse, Wim dropped her hand, motioning her behind him.

"What's wrong?" she whispered.

"I'm not sure."

She looked through the cluster of trees before them, then across a cultivated field, trying to see what had stopped him in his tracks. "Wim, what is it?"

He held his finger to his lips.

Following his gaze, she looked out across the straight crop rows between them and the house. Suddenly something moved in her line of sight. Wim's hand clamped over her mouth just as she gasped. She blinked, hoping against hope her eyes had somehow deceived her. There, crawling down the dirt row moved Lieke's baby sister Inge.

"Shhh," Wim whispered in her ear. "I'll remove my hand but you must not make a sound." She nodded, her eyes stinging as she watched the toddler crawl slowly along the dirt path, her movements wobbly and uneven. Wim gently pulled his hand away, keeping his mouth over her ear. "We'll get to her, I promise. But we must first wait. Something's very wrong here."

Anya couldn't breathe. As they watched, Inge plopped back on her haunches. Her face was filthy, covered and streaked with dirt. How long had she been out in the field? Why was she out here alone? Lieke would never . . .

A sickening feeling knotted her stomach. Wim's mother would never let a child so young out of her sight.

Oh God, please no.

Inge began to whimper, rubbing her eyes. The baby rubbed harder and harder, losing her balance and tipping over. Her cry pierced the air.

"Wim, we have to—"

He was halfway to the child by the time she'd opened her mouth. He moved like a bolt of lightning, grabbing the baby and dashing back into the woods.

"Quick—stick your finger in her mouth!" he whispered urgently.

Just as the child sucked in a breath to wail, Anya stuck two of her fingertips in her mouth and held her close to her chest. "Inge, Inge, it's Anya. I'm here, sweetheart. I'm here." The baby tried to open her eyes, but opened her mouth again to cry instead. "Shhh, no, no, Inge, don't cry," she whispered, wiggling her fingertips in the baby's mouth. "Wim, try to clear her left eye. That's the one she's rubbed."

"How? What should I do?"

"She's got plenty of tears. See if you can hold her eye open to clear whatever's in there."

Wim took out his handkerchief and tried to pry open the child's eye. As gently as he could, he touched the edge of his handkerchief to her eye, hoping to free the specks of dirt that were lodged there. Inge jerked back, whimpering and chomping down on Anya's fingers.

Anya winced. "Try it again. You almost got it."

Wim spit into the cloth, dampening it, then tried again. This time the handkerchief pulled another cluster of dirt particles from the baby's tearing eye. She blinked repeatedly then looked back and forth between them, clearly frightened.

"Inge, you're all right. Shhh, little one. Don't be afraid," Anya whispered, rocking her gently in her arms.

The baby began to suck on Anya's fingers and slowly, gradually relaxed in her arms. Anya looked up at Wim. His eyes were fixed on the farmhouse in the distance. "What do you think happened?"

He turned to grip her shoulders. "You stay here. No matter what happens, you stay here until I come back. Stay out of sight. And whatever you do, try to keep Inge quiet."

They both looked down at the child, her eyelids drooping as she continued to suck on Anya's fingertips. She pushed the child's dirty curls out of her flushed face. "She must have been out here a long time." Her chin began to tremble at the implication.

He pulled her against him. "I know."

She listened to his heart pounding against her ear. "Please be careful."

He tipped her chin with his finger, turning her face toward his. "I will. But if anything should happen to me—"

"Stop. Do not say it," she whispered. "Don't you dare say it."

He cupped her face in his hand then leaned over, touching his lips to hers. Anya kissed him back, curling her other hand around his neck. *Oh, let this moment never end,* she prayed. When he lifted his lips from hers, her eyes remained closed for a moment longer.

"I've wanted to do that for as long as I can remember," he whispered, his breath warm against her cheek.

She opened her eyes. "And I've *wanted* you to do that for as long as I can remember."

He touched his nose to hers. "I must go." He kissed her once more then he was gone.

She watched him crouched over, dashing along the outer perimeter of the field, working his way to the far side of the barn. Reaching it, he stood with his back against it, stealing a quick look around the corner.

"Oh God," she prayed. "Please protect him. Please—"

Anya gasped as something hard pressed against the back of her skull.

"Perhaps your prayer is misplaced, Fräulein."

Her heart thundering in her chest, she clutched Inge tightly. "Please don't—"

"Zum Schweigen bringen," he whispered into her ear as he clicked the hammer on his gun. "Not a sound or you and the baby are dead."

Anya looked across the field for Wim, unable to find him. *Oh God! Let him save us before it's too late!*

"On your feet."

She clumsily stood up bracing herself against the tree. He moved the barrel of the gun against her forehead, coming into view for the first time. She recognized him immediately. One of the soldiers who'd come to her home with von Kilmer. She remembered the ugly jagged scar across his cheek and his deep-set eyes.

"Ja, Fräulein, we've met before. That night in your home."

She nodded, her whole body shaking. *Lord, please . . .*

"We wondered where you were the last time we paid your parents a visit. Did you know we shipped them off to Auschwitz? By now, who knows what fate may have befallen them."

"Please," Anya croaked. "I beg you. Let us go."

His wheezing laughter frightened her. "Surely you're not that stupid? Why would I let you go? You and that farm boy are going to earn me a commendation from my superiors. And as for this precious little Jew in your arms?"

Anya screamed as the shot rang out. "Nooooo!"

Inge went limp in her arms. Anya dropped to her knees as blood poured from the hole in the baby's forehead. "She's just a BABY! How could you—"

"Correction, Fräulein. She's just a *Jew*."

Anya rocked the child's lifeless body in her arms as her own cries filled the air.

"Zum Schweigen bringen!" *Silence!* He grabbed her by the elbow and pulled her to her feet. "Enough of the melodrama. Start walking." He shoved her with his gun in her back. When her cries continued he shoved the barrel against her head again. "I said, SHUT UP!"

Anya could barely see through the blur of her tears as she stumbled into the field, the baby's limp body in her arms. She looked down at the blood covering them both, her own body shaking so hard she could barely lift her hand to close the child's eyelids. Her mouth burned with bile at the sight and she fell to her knees, setting the child on the ground before vomiting the other direction.

"You Dutch are all alike," her captor said. "So weak and stupid."

Anya wept as her stomach emptied, her wails sounding distant as she heaved.

"Aufstehen." He poked her in the back with his weapon again. "I said, GET UP!"

She wiped her mouth with the back of her hand then turned to reach for Inge's body. The German kicked the child's body away from Anya as if it were nothing more than a rag doll. "Leave her. Let her body rot and serve as fertilizer for the crops." He snickered. "Perhaps she'll be worth something after all."

"No! I won't leave her!" Anya cried, scrambling over to the lifeless child.

"Oh, but you will," he said, kicking Anya in her ribs. She doubled over, clutching her side. "Really, Fräulein, you're making this so much harder than it needs to be." He pulled her up by her hair. I said, GET—"

She heard the wind knocked out of his body as she fell from his grasp.

"Anya!"

She jumped at the sound of Wim's voice as he fell to his knees beside her. "No! Wim, the German! He—"

"He's dead, Anya. Look!" He turned to show her the soldier, collapsed in a heap on the ground behind him. "I smashed his head with that stone. He can't hurt us now. Oh, Anya! I should never have left you all alone." He pulled her into his arms but she pushed back.

"Wim, he killed . . ." She covered her face with her bloodied hands. "He killed her," she cried, falling back on the ground.

"I know, I know. I'm so sorry." He pulled her back into his arms. "I'm so sorry."

"I wished he'd killed *me*. Not Inge! She was only a baby!"

He held her as she wept, wishing she could just die and be done with it. Suddenly, she looked up at him. "What about the others? Your mother? Your father? Is Lieke—"

He shook his head slowly. "They're gone. They're all gone. I'd only glimpsed their bodies in the barn when I heard the shot ring out. I was so afraid you'd been killed too."

"You mean they're all dead?"

He nodded, a lone tear running down his face. "It looks as though they lined them all up and executed them. All of them . . . they must have hidden little Inge somewhere before they were captured. If only she'd—"

Another shot rang out. Anya jumped, turning in the direction of it. A wisp of smoke from the German's gun drifted upward, his hand clutched around it. Still lying on the ground, he cocked it again, aiming it straight at her. Just as she started to scream the gun fell from his hand and he dropped face first in the dirt.

"Wim! He's—" She stopped, realizing Wim was slumped against her. "Wim? No! No!" She tried to push his body to a sitting position, but he fell backward. "WIM! Oh God!"

"Anya . . ."

She rested his head in her lap. "Wim, please, hold on! I'll go for help. Just hold on!"

He reached for her hand, as his eyelids drifted shut. "No . . . no time."

"Stop it. Stop it! Open your eyes, Wim. Open them!"

His eyes flickered open then squeezed shut as he tried to swallow. "Anya, it's too late."

She cried out but not a sound came from her mouth. She had nothing left. She rocked him in her arms just as she'd rocked little Inge only moments before. Surely this was just a nightmare? Hadn't she fought the nightmares, night after night?

"Anya, you must run . . . please . . . go . . ."

"No! I won't leave you!"

He reached for her face and pulled it toward him, his eyes struggling to focus on her. "I love you, Anya. I have always . . ."

His eyes rolled back as his head fell against her lap.

"Wim! WIM!" Anya pulled his lifeless body against her, his arms flopping at awkward angles. She tried to gather them, make them stay in place. "Why? Oh Why? Oh God, where ARE YOU? Why would You . . . how *could* You?"

She wasn't sure how long she sat there, cradling him in her arms. The sun was starting to set in the western sky. But no sooner had that realization crossed her mind than she heard shouts in the distance. German shouts.

She squeezed Wim's body one last time, kissing his pale cheek. "I love you, Wim. I've always loved you." She gently laid his body down, kissed him once more, then got to her feet and tried to discern which direction the German voices had come from. As the wind carried more of their despicable language, she grabbed the gun, turned the opposite direction, and ran as fast as she could.

Part III

26

October 1941

Northwestern University

Evanston, Illinois

Danny stared out the window of his dorm room. He'd been studying for more than an hour, but his mind kept drifting. He still couldn't believe he was finally here—a college freshman living on campus. During all those months he'd managed the theater during his dad's recovery, he'd constantly stewed over the delay. While the rest of his friends went off to college or enlisted to serve in the military, he'd kept the theater running. But his mind seemed to constantly chronicle everything he was missing out on. He'd missed a year.

One full year.

His mother had encouraged him not to look at it that way. "You have to stop agonizing over this change of plans. God allowed it for a purpose, Danny. Your father will never forget the sacrifice you made to provide for our family during his recovery. And I know God will bless you. You'll see."

He wished he had his mother's simple faith. She accepted whatever crisis or roadblock fell in their path. When his father was finally released from the hospital late last year, their lives had changed drastically. Again. Since Dad couldn't manage the stairs up to the bedroom, they'd rented a hospital bed and set it up in the living room. Day and night he barked at them, always needing something just out of reach—the newspaper, a glass of water, the ledger from the theater, a pain pill. Danny's mother took it all in stride, maintaining a cheerful attitude no matter how belligerent he was.

Danny did his best to stay out of the house, spending as much time as possible at the theater. He didn't possess a single ounce of his mother's patience and resented the way his dad treated both of them. At first, he'd felt compassion toward his dad, realizing how close they came to losing him. But once the initial shock wore off, Frank McClain was back to his old grouchy self, only worse. Like a caged animal, he'd snap at anyone near him—usually Mom.

Sophie seemed to be the only companion Dad could tolerate. She parked herself at his side whenever possible. It occurred to Danny that his dad related better to dogs than humans.

By summer, Frank had learned to walk again, though his gait was jerky at best. He hated using what he called "that blasted cane." Refusing to stay bedridden the rest of his life, he gradually forced himself to get used to walking with a cane. Eventually he eased back into his routine managing the theater. Naturally, he made quite a production of pointing out all the things Danny had done wrong in his absence. But Danny took it in stride, knowing it was just his father's way.

Even then, all Danny could think about was starting classes at Northwestern in the fall. Even with all his savings, he'd come up short for housing primarily because of the ongoing medical bills. His mother continued praying over the matter, and much to his surprise, Danny was able to secure a job working at the campus soda fountain. It helped with expenses, it was easy work and a good place to meet people.

Which is exactly how he met Beverly Grayson.

Danny never had time to date much in high school. Which wasn't a problem since he always had crushes on the popular girls whose eyes were set solely on the football and basketball players. With everything else going on, he figured there'd be plenty of time for romance when he got to Northwestern. Still, he was surprised when the cute little coed from Wisconsin seemed to frequent the snack bar whenever he was working.

"Hi there, Danny," she'd said that first week of school.

He'd never laid eyes on the attractive brunette before, but somehow she knew his name. He looked around then leaned across the counter toward her. "I'm sorry, do I know you?"

"Of course not, silly." She pointed at his name tag. "I just thought we should get acquainted since we'll be seeing each other a lot." She'd tossed him a subtle wink then ordered a cup of coffee and a brownie.

"Coming right up." He poured a mug of fresh coffee from the urn then plucked the largest brownie from the display case and put it in a small paper bag. "That'll be twenty-five cents."

She dug in her purse and placed fifty cents in his open palm. "Thanks, Danny. You can keep the change."

"Thank you, Miss . . .?"

"Miss Grayson. But you can call me Beverly." She picked up her brownie and coffee.

"Thank you, Beverly Grayson. Nice to meet you."

As she turned to go, she waggled her eyebrows and smiled at him. "The pleasure's all mine, Danny McClain. See you tomorrow."

He was fairly sure it was the most gorgeous smile he'd ever seen. And by the time he'd slipped her tip into his pocket, he was head over heels for her.

The door banged open. "Well, if it isn't my roommate, the bookworm."

Danny blinked out of his daydream as Craig Gilmore sauntered into the room and threw his books on his desk. Danny doubted there were two more mismatched roommates on the entire Northwestern campus, but he couldn't help but like the Indiana transplant.

"I'm just trying to keep up." Danny turned around. "Where've you been?"

"I thought you'd never ask. I've been tutoring the *sweetest* little Georgia peach."

Danny laughed. "For two days? Somehow I doubt there was much 'tutoring' going on."

Craig flopped onto his bed, locking his hands behind his head. "I suppose that depends on your definition of the word. I feel it's my duty to welcome as many coeds as possible to our sacred institution. I see myself as a one-man hospitality committee. In fact, the university should probably pay me for my services."

Danny shook his head. "I'm afraid that's still illegal in the state of Illinois, but I'm sure they appreciate your endeavors."

Craig rolled onto his side to face his roommate. "And what about you, Saint Daniel? Have you found any bewildered young coeds in need of a more personal introduction to the vast exploitations of our beloved campus?"

"Not in your context of the word. But yeah, I met someone."

"And?"

Danny closed his textbook and shoved it aside. "And we've gone out a couple of times."

"And? C'mon, McClain. Out with it."

"Out with what? We've gone out. In fact we're going to the movies tonight. She's a nice girl. There's not much else to tell."

Craig rolled onto his back again, covering his face with his hands. "Please don't tell me you haven't scored yet. Because I refuse to give you a lecture on the birds and the bees. Let's be absolutely clear on that."

Danny stood up and pulled a clean shirt from his closet. "Ah shucks. I guess I'm on my own then. Whatever shall I do?" A pillow sailed by his head as he opened the door. "Nice try, Gilmore. Where I come from, a gentleman doesn't kiss and tell."

"Yeah? And where I come from, guys who don't tell aren't getting any."

Danny shook his head. "See you later, Mr. Hospitality."

After he showered and shaved, Danny returned to his room to find Craig sound asleep and snoring like a freight train. He finished getting dressed, ran a comb through his damp hair, and splashed on a little aftershave before heading out. As he walked to Beverly's dorm in the south quad, he had to appreciate the fact that she kept things light and fun.

He'd waited a long time to find someone special and wasn't in a big hurry. He wanted to savor the experience. Craig could keep his conquests. Danny preferred the all-American girl-next-door type.

It still embarrassed him, thinking about the first time he asked her out. True to her word, she'd stopped by The Grill every day and said hello. Whether she actually wanted a morning snack between classes or whether she stopped by just to see him, he couldn't be sure. He just knew he'd grown awfully fond of seeing her smiling face every day at 9:50. By Wednesday of the second week of school, he'd convinced himself to ask her out. Unfortunately, he lost his nerve, kicking himself as she waved goodbye like she always did. On Thursday morning, his boss asked him to get some straws and napkins out of the store room right at 9:50. As he hurried to grab the supplies, he dropped the carton of straws, spilling them all over the floor. By the time he'd cleaned up his mess and returned to the counter, he saw her rounding the corner as she left.

By Friday, he vowed to ask her out no matter what else transpired. But on that particular day, she wasn't alone. A tall, good looking guy walked in with her, then sat beside her at the counter.

"Hey Danny! How's it going?"

"Good. How about you?"

"I'll have a cherry Coke and a Danish," the guy with her ordered.

She swatted the guy's arm. "Where are your manners? Whatever happened to ladies first?"

"Fine. The lady can order whatever she likes, but I'll have

a cherry Coke and a Danish."

Danny wanted to deck the guy. Wise guys like him were a dime a dozen on this campus. But it bothered him even more that Beverly would hook up with a smart mouth like this one.

"Coffee and a brownie?" Danny asked her, avoiding the chump beside her.

"Yes, thank you." She smiled at him like she always did, which felt a little strange under the circumstances. So much for asking her out.

He put their order together, serving her first. As he finished pouring the cherry syrup into the Coke, someone yelled, "Heads up, Grayson!"

Danny turned just in time to see a football sail across The Grill toward Beverly's friend who thankfully caught it. As he spun the football in his hands, he yelled back, "Dawson, if you'd throw like that on Saturday, we might just beat Kansas State!"

Danny slid the coke and Danish across the counter.

"Danny, you'll have to forgive my big brother."

"Your brother?"

"Oh, that's right. You probably don't know him." She tugged at her brother's sleeve. "Billy, turn around. I want to introduce you to Danny. Danny, this is my obnoxious brother Billy."

Billy tucked the football under his arm and held out his hand. "Nice to meet you, Danny. Oh wait—did you say Danny?" he asked, looking at his sister. "So this is the guy you keep talking about?"

She dropped her face behind her hand. "Gee, thanks, Billy."

"Huh? Oh. I probably wasn't supposed to say that. Well, it's nice meeting you, Danny."

Danny returned the handshake. "Billy, it's my pleasure."

Beverly lifted her head, her face flushed as she pasted a smile on it. "Okay. Now that we've got that straight . . ."

"Hey Sis, I'm gonna go sit with the guys. I'll catch up with you later." He was halfway across the room before the words were out of his mouth.

She faked another smile. "Sure, brother dearest. By all means."

Suddenly Danny laughed out loud.

"And what, pray tell, are you laughing at?"

He pushed his paper hat back on his head. "Ah, nothing. I'm just relieved."

"Relieved?"

"Well, sure. I mean, I was all set to ask you out and then you walked in with that guy and I thought he was your boyfriend or something. So I—"

"You were going to ask me out?"

He watched her face fill with expectation. He didn't know much about girls and dating, but he had a feeling that was a good sign. "Well, yeah. In fact . . . I've been wanting to ask you out for several days now but I—"

"I'd love to."

"You would?"

"Of course I would."

He laughed again.

"Now what are you laughing at?"

He scratched his eyebrow. "I was going to ask if you'd like to go to the football game with me tomorrow."

She laughed out loud. "What a great idea! I would love to go to the football game with you. As long as you don't make me root for my brother."

They'd had a great time at the game, cheering the Wildcats—and Billy Grayson—to a 51 to 3 victory over K-State despite a drenching rain. Afterward they'd huddled under Beverly's umbrella and walked to Cooley's Cupboard for dinner followed by a slow, chatty walk back to campus.

"I must look like a drowned rat, but I had a really nice time today, Danny," she'd said, taking his hand as they walked up the steps to her dorm. "I hope we can do it again sometime. Preferably without the monsoon."

"I'd like that, Beverly. I'd like that a lot."

Standing on a step above him, she'd suddenly turned around and gave him a quick peck on the cheek. "Good night, Danny McClain."

"Good night, Beverly Grayson."

Not a bad first date. Not bad at all.

Now, as he approached her dorm, the sound of her voice snapped him out of his stroll down memory lane.

"There you are." She hopped up from the steps of the dorm where she'd been seated. "I was hoping you didn't forget me." She looped her arm through his.

"How could I forget someone like you?" He pulled his arm free and wrapped it over her shoulder. "Whoa, you smell really good."

"Yeah? It's a new fragrance called *Deception*." She stretched her neck, inviting him for another whiff. "Daring, isn't it?"

He took the bait and pressed his nose against her perfect

neck. "Scandalously daring, my dear." He couldn't stop grinning at her. He honestly couldn't help it. She was so pretty, so full of life, and so obviously happy to see him.

Wow.

"I've been *dying* to see this new Bogart movie!" Beverly intertwined her fingers with his as they headed across campus. "It's supposed to be quite the mystery."

"Oh, it is. Why, just last week Bogie called and told me how they—"

"Sure he did." She pinched his arm.

"Ouch!"

"And last week it was Gary Cooper who dropped by to see you. You forget I called you out on all that name dropping. Just because you and your dad were movie theater moguls doesn't mean you rubbed elbows with all the stars. Except maybe in your dreams."

He braced his grip around the back of her neck and gently squeezed.

"Noooooo! Danny, stop stop stop! You know I'm ticklish!"

"Yeah? Guess I forgot or something."

"Stop, stop, stop!" She wrangled out of his grasp and ran ahead, wrapping her sweater around her shoulders as her long plaid skirt billowed in the strong breeze off Lake Michigan.

He held up his hands. "Okay, okay. Truce. No more tickling. I promise."

She walked backward just ahead of him. "I don't believe you."

"Oh, I forgot to tell you! I had a postcard from Joey today."

"No kidding? What'd he say?"

"He said his ship just got out of dry dock in San Francisco and they're headed back to Pearl Harbor, Hawaii. He was disappointed he couldn't make it back to see all of us before they shipped out, but he didn't have the money to get home. Dad thinks he's probably losing all his money in poker games, but I don't know if that's true or not. Mom was pretty disappointed, though. We haven't seen him since he enlisted."

Beverly resumed her place beside him, taking his hand again as they walked. "I can't even imagine how beautiful it must be in Hawaii. I've always dreamed of going there some day."

"Is that so?"

"Well, sure it is! I want to travel the whole world. Don't you?"

"I don't know. Guess I never gave it that much thought."

She looked at him as if he'd sprouted a third eye. "You can't be serious. Who *wouldn't* want to travel to exotic places? Think about all the amazing sights you'd see—the Taj Mahal, the Parthenon in Athens, the Eiffel Tower, the London Bridge—"

"Maybe so, but this isn't exactly the optimal time to travel the world. Unless, Fräulein," he said with a thick German accent, "you'd like mein goose-stepping Nazis to give you a tour?"

"Your accent needs work, Herr McClain." She slowed her pace. "Whoa, look at the long line."

Danny followed her gaze across the street where a line of movie-goers had already wrapped around the corner of the theater. "Gee, I hope they don't sell out."

"Then c'mon. We better hurry!" She started to run,

tugging on his arm. He didn't budge. She turned. "What are you doing?"

"Oh. Wait." He dug in his pocket with great theatrics, finally pulling out two tickets.

"I knew there was some reason I let you tag along." She plucked the tickets out of his hand and giggled.

He watched her dance her way to the main doors of the old theater. As she turned to summon him to catch up, he stared at her . . . the soft waves in her shiny brown hair, the flirty little smile, the twinkle in her eye . . . and wondered how on earth he'd ever lived a day before knowing her.

27

November 1941

On the Sunday evening after Thanksgiving, Danny kicked open the door to his dorm room and turned on the light.

"Do you mind?" his roommate growled, peeking out from under his covers.

Danny tossed his keys on his desk and dropped his duffel bag on the floor. "What are you doing in bed? And why is this place such a mess?" Remnants of half-eaten food covered both desks, the floor, and most of Danny's bed.

"None of your business," Craig mumbled, pulling the covers over his head.

Danny yanked them back. "I thought you were going home. Did you stay on campus over break?"

"So what if I did?"

"Because I invited you to come home with me, but you said you had plans of your own."

"Well, then. You've found me out. I lied. Happy?"

Danny shrugged and started unpacking his clean

laundry. "Suit yourself, Gilmore."

Craig sat up in bed. "What is that I smell?"

"You mean the hamburger you left rotting on the floor or the spoiled milk on your desk?"

"Neither. It's turkey. And if I'm not mistaken, dressing as well." He closed his eyes and inhaled deeply. "And I must say, it smells *wonderful.*"

Danny shook his head at his roommate's antics. "Mom sent me back with some leftovers."

Craig threw back his covers. "So, what are we waiting for?" He pulled on a robe and rubbed his hands together eagerly. "Well?"

"Fine. Clear some room off your desk. Honestly, Gilmore, you're a pig. Look at this place!"

"Is this the part where I'm supposed to feel bad and rush around, picking up all the evidence of my pathetic lonely weekend?"

Danny pulled a metal lunch box from the top of his duffel. "I could only hope."

"Look, McClain. Not everyone has the happy little home life you do. Some of us dread the very idea of going home."

"Yet you're too proud to accept an invitation to come home with your roommate." He pulled the wax paper wrapping off a sandwich piled thick with slices of fresh turkey. "Here, help yourself."

"No, I can't take your sandwich."

"Take it before I change my mind. Besides, I'm not that hungry."

"In that case . . ." Craig grabbed the sandwich with both hands and took a mammoth bite out of it. He closed his eyes in obvious bliss. "Oh, this . . . this is—"

"Fantastic. I know. Just save your comments and don't talk with your mouth full. Here's some dressing. You like cranberry sauce?"

Gilmore nodded emphatically, motioning for his roommate to hand over the rest of the food. "Mmm-mmm-mmm."

"Yeah? Mom makes a pretty mean pumpkin pie. She sent half a pie with me, so save me some, will ya?"

Craig mumbled something over a mouthful of dressing.

"I think you asked where I was going?"

Gilmore nodded.

"I'm headed over to Bev's. She was supposed to get in about an hour ago. There'd better be some pie left when I get back." He shot a scowl over his shoulder which his roommate waved off as he forked another bite of cranberry sauce.

As Danny descended the steps of his dormitory, he climbed back into his coat and wrapped the wool muffler around his neck. It felt good to be back. As much as he'd loved seeing his mom, he'd barely tolerated his father's incessant lectures about "those idiotic Nazis" and "that maniac Hitler" over the course of his three-day visit. And what holiday dinner would be complete without a blistering session about "that irresponsible brother of yours working on his tan over in Hawaii." As if Joey had nothing better to do than hang out on the beach. Danny wondered if his dad would ever give Joey credit for serving his country.

Sophie had stuck to him like glue, dancing in circles when he first arrived. Her tail never stopped wagging from the moment he got home until he left on Sunday evening. If there was any way to sneak her into his dorm room, he would've done it. He'd missed her unconditional love and admiration. But in a strange way, he knew she kept his mom and dad company.

Chilled to the bone, he raced up the steps of Beverly's dorm and into the lobby where he stopped at the front desk to have her paged. A few minutes later, she stepped off the elevator.

"Hey Danny."

He took in her pasty complexion, messy hair, and the pink bathrobe she was wearing over flannel pajamas. "You look awful," he said, meaning it. When he leaned in to give her a hug, she backed up with her hands raised.

"You don't want to come near me. I'm sick as a dog. Must've picked up something."

"Hey, I'm sorry, Bev. Not a good weekend?"

She blew her bangs out of her eyes. "I was sick from the minute I got home. I've just now stopped throwing up. I wanted to say hi, but I've gotta get back in bed. You don't want my germs. Trust me. I'm just hoping I feel better tomorrow so I don't miss classes."

"Poor baby . . . I'm so sorry. Go get some rest. I'll check in on you after I get out of English tomorrow, okay?"

It would be two more weeks before Beverly completely recovered. She spent most of that time in the campus infirmary, but she wasn't alone. Twelve of her floor mates shared the same nasty flu bug. Danny was glad she'd spared him the germs, but he missed her, unable to visit her quarantined wing of the clinic.

He stayed busy, going to class, studying and working as

many hours as possible at The Grill. His roommate disappeared for days at a time, insisting he'd met some "heavenly goddess" who understood his needs. Danny just hoped she could convince him to make an occasional visit to class before he got kicked out of school.

The first Sunday in December, on a brisk, beautiful afternoon, Danny had just finished his shift at The Grill when he noticed a crowd of students gathered around a radio in the lobby of Scott Hall. He was supposed to meet Beverly at the library to study together, but curiosity got the best of him. He slowly joined the crowd, pressing in to see what everyone was listening to.

"I repeat," the tinny voice on the radio said. "President Roosevelt said in a statement today that the Japanese have attacked Pearl Harbor in Hawaii from the air. The attack was also made on all naval and military activity on the principle island of Oahu. We now take you to Washington."

Danny grabbed the arm of the guy next to him. "Did he say Pearl Harbor?"

"Yeah. The Japanese attacked Pearl Harbor. It sounds bad. Really bad."

Danny stared at the guy as the sound of his own heartbeat started pounding in his ears. The picture postcard of the Hawaiian island of Oahu flashed through his mind. The same postcard where his brother had scribbled on the back how nice it was to be back in the islands . . . and something about the USS *Oklahoma* being docked on Battleship Row.

Danny's eyes slowly tracked back toward the radio.

"The White House is now giving out a statement," the

reporter continued. "The President's brief statement was made to Stephen Early, the President's secretary. A Japanese attack on Pearl Harbor would naturally mean war. Such an attack would naturally mean a counter-attack. Hostilities of this kind would naturally mean that the President would ask Congress for a declaration of war—"

"Danny!"

He turned at the sound of his name and found Craig running toward him.

"Danny, your mother's trying to reach you," he said, gasping to catch his breath. It was only then that Danny realized his roommate was wearing his maroon bath robe. "She called the dorm and they came to our room looking for you. They said she's really upset. Did you hear the news?"

"Mom?"

Craig grabbed him by both arms. "Danny! Did you hear what I said?"

"My mother called?"

Craig steered him away from the crowd. "Buddy, you need to snap out of it. Your mom wants you to call her back. Obviously she's heard about the attack on Pearl Harbor. You need to come with me back to the dorm so you can call her."

Danny ran a hand through his hair. "Yeah, sorry. I must've—"

"Doesn't matter. C'mon." Craig pulled him by the arm. "I need to get you back there."

Five minutes later, he dialed the hall phone to call home. It rang only once before his mother answered.

"Danny, is that you?" her voice trembled.

"Mom, I just heard. Have you heard from Joey?"

"What? No, not yet. Oh son, I'm so scared. What if—"

"Don't say it, Mom. Don't even think it. Listen, I'm coming home. I'll be there as soon as I can. Where's Dad?"

"He's on his way home. He cancelled the showings and locked the theater once he heard the news. Danny, he couldn't even talk when I called him."

"Mom, take it easy. I'll be home soon."

The two-hour commute from Evanston to his home in Chicago were the longest two hours of his life. Over and over the images on that postcard kept dancing through his mind, and all of them covered in smoke. The chaos, the panic, the sounds, the smells . . . all of it horrible, beyond comprehension. He pushed every thought of what Joey might or might not be experiencing to the deepest corner of his mind, refusing to dwell on it. In the midst of all the outrageous thoughts bouncing around in his head, he knew with certainty that his life would forever be changed by this day in history. Whether it meant he'd be drafted to go fight the inevitable war, or whether his family would be reduced to just three, nothing would ever be the same.

When he finally stormed into his house on Yale Avenue, his mother fell into his embrace.

"Oh, Danny. Thank God you're home. Thank God!"

He held her for several moments, feeling her shake in his arms as she wept. Sophie jumped on him, excited in all the commotion. He scratched her behind the ears, then turned with his mother, keeping his arm around her as they walked into the living room. His father, seated next to the radio with his head in his hands, didn't even acknowledge his entrance. Danny knew his dad was never one to show emotion—except for that night in the alley behind the theater. He knew his father would handle this situation in his own way. As they walked past him, Danny patted his dad on the back then took a seat beside his mother on the sofa.

"All afternoon we've listened," his mother began, wiping tears with her handkerchief. "It's so frustrating because the radio networks keep going back to their regular programming. Why would anyone want to hear music or listen to a football game when our country has been attacked?"

"Because they're all idiots, Betty!" his father snapped. "I keep telling you. Those people have no idea what they're doing. Bunch of imbeciles, the whole lot of them."

She ignored him, digging something out of her pocket—a postcard from Joey, its edges frayed. "I keep looking at this picture of this beautiful island." She turned it over, holding it out with trembling hands for him to see. "Joey wrote that the entire Pacific fleet was stationed there in Hawaii. When I got this a couple of days ago, it didn't even cross my mind how—" She looked up at him. "Why would they put all their ships in one place? I don't understand. Why would they make such an easy target for the Japanese?"

The same question had bothered Danny all the way home. Wouldn't such a bold move arouse suspicion to American's enemies? Especially the Japanese? Surely the military strategists had their reasons.

"Because our president and the so-called military 'geniuses' have no idea how to fight a war," his father bellowed as he got to his feet. "They play their ridiculous war games, sending those ships all over kingdom come, but when push comes to shove, they don't have a single blasted clue what they're doing! They might as well have taken our boys and just handed 'em over to the Japs on a silver platter."

Suddenly he spun around, put one hand on the fireplace mantel and aimed his cane at Danny with the other. "If you ever get a lame-brain idea to join up and do like your brother, then you don't ever come home. You got that? The day you join the military is the day I disown you."

"Frank! What a horrible thing to say!"

"Stay out of this, Betty. I've lost one son. I'm sure as hell not going to lose another."

"Dad, we don't know that Joey's—"

"Of course, we do. If he was alive, he would've called your mother by now. You know it and I know it."

"That's not true!" Danny shouted, closing the gap between them. "He probably couldn't get a call out even if he wanted to! After something like this? It may be days or weeks before we find out anything. So don't say . . . if you can't . . . just keep your mouth shut, Dad!"

"Fine. Live in your fairy dream land. Think whatever you like. But the sooner you accept that your brother died in that attack today, the sooner you get over it."

Danny lost his temper, letting a string of expletives fly as he stood toe to toe with his father. When he finished, his chest heaved from the outburst as he stared into his dad's darkening face. Dad narrowed his eyes as he clenched his teeth together, but he didn't say a word. Finally, he hobbled off, cursing under his breath as he went downstairs to the basement.

He turned to his mother who held a handkerchief over her mouth. "Mom, I'm sorry you heard that. I just couldn't take it. Not now. Not when we don't know anything yet."

She composed herself and gave him a hug. "Don't mind him, Danny. You can't let him get to you like that. He doesn't know how to handle things like this. You know that."

"Yeah, so we all just keep making excuses for him? Wouldn't you think after everything that happened to him, he would've learned something? If nothing else, to at least keep his mouth shut at a time like this?"

"Hush, Danny. Let it go."

They listened to the radio long into the night, clinging to any special bulletin that updated the news coming out of Hawaii. Details remained sketchy, but there was no question about the overwhelming destruction at Pearl Harbor. Some reports mentioned ships already sunk in the shallow bay, others capsized. The loss of life would be beyond any of their imaginations.

His mother had asked him to pray with her around ten. As they knelt beside the sofa, he listened as she poured her heart out, asking God to protect Joey and keep him safe through the night. Danny fought the nagging traces of his father's earlier remark. *The sooner you accept that your brother died in that attack today, the sooner you get over it.* No matter what his father thought, Danny chose to cling to his mother's faith. She trusted God to watch over Joey; so would he.

Later, after his mother finally drifted off to sleep on the sofa, Danny heard the radio station sign off for the night. As the troubling images continued parading through his imagination, he too gave in to the fatigue and fell asleep.

28

"Yesterday, December 7, 1941—a date which will live in infamy—the United States of America was suddenly and deliberately attacked by naval and air forces of the Empire of Japan. The United States was at peace with that nation, and at the solicitation of Japan, was still in conversation with the government and its emperor looking toward the maintenance of peace in the Pacific. Indeed, one hour after Japanese air squadrons had commenced bombing in Oahu, the Japanese ambassador to the United States and his colleagues delivered to the Secretary of State a formal reply to a recent American message. While this reply stated that it seemed useless to continue the existing diplomatic negotiations, it contained no threat or hint of war or armed attack.

"It will be recorded that the distance of Hawaii from Japan makes it obvious that the attack was deliberately planned many days or even weeks ago. During the intervening time, the Japanese government has deliberately sought to deceive the United States by false statements and expressions of hope for continued peace.

"The attack yesterday on the Hawaiian islands has caused severe damage to American naval and military forces. Very many American lives have been lost. In addition, American ships have been reported torpedoed on the high seas between San Francisco and Honolulu.

"Yesterday, the Japanese government also launched an attack against Malaya. Last night, Japanese forces attacked Hong Kong. Last night, Japanese forces attacked Guam. Last night, Japanese forces attacked the Philippine Islands. Last night, Japanese forces attacked Wake Island. This morning, the Japanese attacked Midway Island.

"Japan has, therefore, undertaken a surprise offensive extending throughout the Pacific area. The facts of yesterday speak for themselves. The people of the United States have already formed their opinions and well understand the implications to the very life and safety of our nation.

"As commander in chief of the Army and Navy, I have directed that all measures be taken for our defense. Always we will remember the character of the onslaught against us. No matter how long it may take us to overcome this premeditated invasion, the American people in their righteous might will win through to absolute victory.

"I believe I interpret the will of the Congress and of the people when I assert that we will not only defend ourselves to the uttermost, but will make very certain that this form of treachery shall never endanger us again. Hostilities exist. There is no blinking at the fact that our people, our territory, and our interests are in grave danger.

"With confidence in our armed forces—with the unbounding determination of our people—we will gain the inevitable triumph—so help us God.

"I ask that the Congress declare that since the unprovoked and dastardly attack by Japan on Sunday, December 7, a state of war has existed between the United States and the Japanese empire."

As the roar of applause punctuated President Franklin D. Roosevelt's address to Congress, Betty McClain motioned for Danny to turn off the radio. Like most Americans, they'd waited anxiously that Monday for the president's speech, needing reassurances and hoping to hear his declaration of war. They weren't disappointed.

Danny's father had remained downstairs in the basement for most of the night, returning there after a silent breakfast the next morning served by his wife. After he disappeared downstairs, Danny and his mother listened to the ongoing radio broadcast. Earlier reports had already confirmed the massive damage of the Japanese attack on Pearl Harbor. When the announcement was made that eight Navy battleships and more than 100 planes had been damaged or destroyed in the attack, Danny reached for his mother's hand. The death toll, including military and civilians alike, was predicted to be substantial.

"There's to be a special church service at 1:00 this afternoon," she said. "I think we should go."

"Sure, Mom. Will Dad—?"

"No, I'm afraid not. I think it's best we let him be. But when we return from the service, I want you to catch the El and go back to school."

He locked eyes with her as he shook his head. "No. Not yet. Not until we know."

"Sweetheart, that could take weeks. You can't miss your classes, and more important, you can't miss finals."

"How can I possibly concentrate on finals with all this going on? Everything's changed now. Who knows, maybe they'll cancel school for the rest of the semester."

"I doubt that. Go back and throw yourself into your studies. If—I mean, *when* we hear something, I'll call you immediately. I promise."

He released her hand, raking his fingers through his hair. "I suppose that makes sense. I guess."

"Of course it does. Now go put your suit on. I don't want to be late to church."

Later, as they walked the five blocks to church, they were shocked to find a steady stream of cars and pedestrians all headed in the same direction. Along the way, American flags waved in the brisk breeze, on one front porch after another. Turning the corner, they were stunned to see a long line of people all trying to get into the church building.

"Look at that, son. And don't ever forget what you see. The United States may be many things, but we are above all a nation that loves and trusts God. When we are troubled or worried, we come together and ask for God's mercy and protection."

In the days following the tragedy at Pearl Harbor, Americans slowly began learning details of the unprecedented attack by the Japanese. On November 26, just six days after Americans celebrated Thanksgiving, the massive fleet had left its home base in the waters of Tankan Bay back in Japan. Aboard six aircraft carriers—*Akagi, Kaga, Hiryu, Shokakus, Soryu,* and *Zuikaku*—hundreds of planes were transported on the quiet ten day voyage to the waters just shy of the island of Oahu. Under strict order of radio silence, the fleet sailed under the command of Vice Admiral Chuichi Nagumo at the directive of Admiral Isoroku Yamamoto, Commander in Chief of the entire Japanese fleet and architect of the attack on Pearl Harbor.

Around 7:00 on the morning of the attack, two young Army privates on duty at the Opana Point Radar Station in Oahu reported seeing a large group of planes on radar heading their direction. When the morning duty officer informed them it was probably a squadron of B-17s that were due in that morning, the privates relaxed and ignored the large blips on their screens.

By 7:30, the first squadron of Japanese fighter planes flew over Oahu, circling the island as they waited for the rest of the 183 planes in that first wave. They struck their first target on Pearl's naval base and the nearby air base at Hickam Field at 7:53. The second wave of attacks began dropping their bombs at 8:55. Many civilian areas of the island, including Honolulu, were also targeted. By 10:00 that morning it was all over. The Japanese, having successfully achieved the ultimate element of surprise, headed back to their aircraft carriers some 200 miles off the coast of Oahu. In the end, the entire Pacific fleet was gutted, and America hungered for revenge.

Not knowing Joey's fate was excruciating. With each passing day, Danny and his parents grew more frustrated at the inability to find out if Joey's ship was one of those sunk or damaged, and whether or not he was still alive. They'd tried calling, they'd sent telegrams, they'd contacted their elected representatives. But America was in a state of mass confusion, and so they waited.

Listening to radio reports and reading newspaper stories only added to the confusion. Stories were told as fact only to be retracted later as false. News and radio sources in Hawaii were immediately shut down after the attack. Early on, it was reported that the Battleship *West Virginia* had been sunk and the USS *Oklahoma* was badly damaged and eventually capsized. Those reports were quickly flagged as false, but caused tremendous anxiety for the McClains and the other families of those on board those ships. Soon after, the Secretary of War issued a statement that families would be notified first by letter or telegram. When such casualties were made public, the Navy refused to list which ship the individuals had served on, hoping to slow the rumors.

In a radio address on the evening of December 10, President Roosevelt assured the loved ones of those injured or killed in the attack on Pearl Harbor they would be contacted as quickly as possible. Then he blasted those who gave out "disinformation" in the form of half-truths, unsubstantiated reports, or blatant rumors, while reminding the newspapers and radio stations of their "grave responsibility" for the duration of the war:

"But in the absence of all the facts, as revealed by official sources—you have no right in the ethics of patriotism to deal out unconfirmed reports in such a way as to make people believe they are the gospel truth. The lives of our soldiers and sailors—the whole future of this nation—depend upon the manner in which each and every one of us fulfills his obligation to our country."

But rumors continued to run wild. Some claimed Japan was simultaneously attacking other Allied countries. Many believed Washington D.C. would be Japan's next target. Others warned that Germany would soon follow Japan's lead, including supposed sightings of swastikas on some of the planes that attacked Hawaii. The mayor of New York City told his citizens they could expect a visit from the Axis bombers at any time, causing extreme panic throughout the large metropolitan city. The entire west coast, fearful of Japanese attack, sabotage, and infiltration, started immediate blackouts and began rounding up Japanese nationals. These roundups would eventually spread across America, placing these individuals and their families in immigration detention centers or internment camps while all Japanese banks, businesses, and newspapers were forced to shut down.

At the same time, Americans united as never before and stepped up to serve however they could. Nowhere was that more evident than the recruiting stations of the various branches of the military. As early as the evening of December 7, these offices began staying open around the clock to accommodate the huge numbers of those wanting to enlist. Red Cross stations were swarmed with Americans wanting to donate and help out however they could.

But none of that mattered to Danny and his family as they waited for news about Joey.

Then, early on the morning of Christmas Eve, the McClain's doorbell rang. Danny and his mother and father looked at each other across the kitchen table as Sophie barked and rushed to the door. Over the past two and a half weeks, the ringing of the telephone, a knock on the door, or the sound of the doorbell had filled them with a sense of dread mixed with hope. Danny bolted for the front door, his parents close behind him.

"Telegram," the Western Union messenger announced, handing Danny the yellow envelope.

"Thanks," he said without thinking as he handed it to his mother.

With trembling hands she dropped the precious telegram. Frank bent down and picked it up then tore it open. He quickly scanned the message. A gasp caught somewhere inside, prompting him to raise a fist to his mouth.

Then, with a quivering voice barely audible he said, "He's alive."

29

When Pearl Harbor was attacked on December 7, the USS *Oklahoma* was moored in Battleship Row next to the USS *Maryland*. The *Oklahoma* was one of the first ships attacked, taking three torpedo hits almost as soon as the Japanese began dropping bombs. As she began to capsize, two more torpedoes struck her causing her to roll over until her masts touched bottom. It took only twelve minutes before she came to rest with her starboard side above water.

Apparently that previous "unsubstantiated" report had been accurate after all.

Four hundred and twenty-nine of her officers and enlisted men were killed that day. Only thirty-two survived—including Petty Officer Joey McClain of Chicago, Illinois.

The telegram from the Department of War informed them he was "seriously wounded" but alive.

As his mother wept freely, she kept saying over and over, "The best Christmas present ever—our Joey's alive! He's alive!"

Dad had quickly retreated to his downstairs refuge. Through the course of the day, Danny and his mother had voiced all kinds of speculations concerning Joey's injuries and when they might hear from him. But in the end, all that mattered was that he was alive.

The day after Christmas, another telegram arrived. In it, a Navy doctor by the name of Benjamin Hurley wrote them a brief message about the extent of Joey's injuries.

PETTY OFFICER JOSEPH FRANK MCCLAIN
REMAINS SEDATED. SEVERE BURNS ON 50% OF
HIS BODY. WILL UPDATE RECOVERY FORTHWITH.

January 1942

Danny still felt numb as he returned to Northwestern after the Christmas break. The image of his brother lying helpless in a military hospital gnawed at him day and night, balanced only by the burning frustration of the thousands of miles between them. He wanted nothing more than to hop on a plane with his mother and be at Joey's bedside to encourage him through his recovery. But in the aftermath of the attack on Pearl Harbor, civilians were not yet permitted to travel to Hawaii.

He hated to leave his mother, especially since his dad was no support whatsoever, still in a shroud of silence since receiving word of Joey's injuries. Danny had to admire his mother's faith. She didn't care what shape her oldest son was in, as long as he was alive. He wished with all his heart he felt the same way, but he didn't. Danny kept trying to put himself in Joey's place. Would he want to live with a body so severely damaged? Or worse, could he handle the mental and emotional trauma inflicted by such injuries? He knew Joey would be able to handle it much better than he would. Still, Danny hated all the thoughts that buzzed incessantly in his head.

For now, at least he had school to help distract his thoughts.

School and Beverly.

They had talked a couple of times over Christmas break. He'd missed her terribly, and even contemplated taking the train up to see her in Madison. But he knew his place was at home, helping his mother get through the long days of waiting for more news about Joey. Once he and Beverly both returned to campus, she'd been the perfect antidote for the darkness of the holidays. Any moment he wasn't in class or working, they were together.

The campus they returned to was not the Northwestern they'd left. In fact, most of America had changed drastically in the weeks since the attack on Pearl Harbor. As the country moved into a lock-down mindset, students at Northwestern made adjustments to the necessary restrictions. Normally, most of the college dances were held off-campus—primarily because NU was an alcohol-free campus. But with the country at war, most campus activities were confined to campus-only events. The Wildcat Capers, the Second Semester Stomp, and the Sophomore Cotillion relocated to Scott Hall or the new Patten Gym.

Perhaps the most noticeable change on campus was the large presence of Navy personnel. Northwestern administrators welcomed the servicemen who resided on campus while completing their military training. At first Danny warmed to the idea of sharing a campus with the cadets, admiring them for their service. The familiar uniforms always reminded him of Joey and his sacrifice.

But a strange thing began to happen. With the pervasive sense of patriotism sweeping across America, these cadets didn't hesitate to taunt the other males on campus who'd received deferments simply because they were enrolled in college. Harassing their male counterparts became a favorite pastime for the sailors.

"Think you're too good to fight for your country, boy?"

"Scared you might break a nail, freshman?"

"Not my fault your girl prefers a man in uniform!"

Danny made a conscious decision not to engage the sailors and their verbal abuse when they crossed paths. They had no way of knowing his brother had paid dearly at Pearl Harbor, but it didn't mean he liked it.

By the end of January, Danny's parents had finally received the long-awaited phone call from Joey.

"He sounded good, Danny, all things considered," Mom said. "You know your brother—he cracked a few jokes, insisting he'd faked his burns just so the pretty nurses would fuss over him. But when he tried to tell us about the attack, he broke down. I'm ashamed to say, while I was so worried about Joey and his injuries, I'd never once thought about all the friends he'd lost. He was more concerned about the families of his buddies and their loss than about his own situation."

She'd paused, and Danny had wondered if he'd lost their phone connection. "Mom? Are you there?"

She sniffed then answered, "Yes, honey, I'm here. I'm just so proud of Joey and how he's handling all this. He's grown up so much since he left home. But I guess war does that."

"It's made us all grow up in one way or another."

"I suppose it has. Anyway, the good news is that Joey will be moved stateside in the next few weeks. They're sending him to Bethesda Naval Hospital near Washington, D.C."

"We'll go see him as soon as he gets there, okay?"

"Yes, dear. As soon as we can."

When their call ended, Danny stood still, his forehead pressed against the wall above the telephone on his dorm floor. *I can't believe I ever wallowed in pity for Joey, wondering how I would handle getting burned and maimed if it had been me. Joey's twice the man I'll ever be.* Then he chuckled, imagining his brother carrying on with all those pretty nurses and realized he couldn't wait to see him again.

On a surprisingly warm Thursday in March, Danny and his parents made the long drive to Washington after learning Joey had finally arrived stateside. Even his father's ever-grumpy demeanor couldn't deter Danny and his mother's anticipation of finally getting to see Joey face to face. As they arrived at Bethesda Naval Hospital, they were escorted up to the burn unit. After a quick meeting with Joey's doctor, briefing them about his prognosis and anticipated recovery, they were finally led down the hall to Joey's room.

"Petty Officer McClain, you have some special visitors who are quite anxious to see you," Dr. Shepherd announced, leading them into the six-bed room.

There, third bed on the right, Danny spotted the lazy smile of his only brother. His eyes filled as a lump lodged in his throat. An unexpected rush of relief washed over him. As Mom rushed to Joey's side, Danny tried to compose himself.

"Mom . . . Dad," Joey started, coughing over his emotion. "It's about time you got here."

Dr. Shepherd pulled the white curtain around Joey's bed. "I wish we could offer you more privacy, but please—have a seat and take your time. I'll check back with you later." He shook Dad's hand and disappeared behind the curtain.

"Joey . . . oh, son," Mom cried, leaning over to kiss his forehead. "I want so much to hug you, but—"

Danny hadn't known what to expect. None of the reports had ever specified where Joey's burns were. Now, seeing his gauze-wrapped arms, torso, and neck, he silently thanked God that his brother's face had been spared.

"I know, Mom, but we'll have time for that later after all this heals up. I promise." Joey gave her his signature wink.

Dad had made his way to the other side of Joey's bed, removing his hat. "Joey . . . I, uh . . ." His face crumbled as he too was overcome by emotion.

Joey slowly raised his arm toward his father, extending the only two fingers not bandaged. As his fingers reached his dad's hand, Frank looked up with tears streaming down his face. He gently grasped those two fingers then leaned over to bring them to his lips.

"Now, Dad, don't go all mushy on me."

For the first time in more than three months, Danny heard the sound of his father's laughter. "I'm afraid it's a little late for that, son."

"Danny! Come here and let me take a look at you."

As Dad stepped aside, Danny slid in closer to his brother's bedside. "Hey, Joey. It's good to see you."

"I'd muss up that hair of yours, but I'm a little indisposed at the moment." He shrugged, reaching out his fingers.

Danny reached out for them, tweaking them gently. "It's a good thing you look good in white."

"No kidding. So what's it like being at college? I was hoping you'd show up in purple, Mr. Wildcat."

"Not gonna happen, sailor."

"That's *Petty Officer McClain* to you, boy."

The banter continued, bridging the emotion swirling around them. They avoided any mention of the war or Pearl Harbor, finding refuge in the mere joy of being together again. Over the next two days, they spent as much time with Joey as visiting hours allowed.

On Sunday morning, they stopped by for one last visit before heading back home. None of them wanted to say goodbye, stalling until the last possible moment.

"Dad, before you go there's something I want to ask," Joey said after taking a sip of water through a straw.

"What's that?"

"I know it's gonna be a while before I get out of here, and I know I've got a lot of physical therapy before I get to come home. But I was wondering . . ." He scratched his left eyebrow. "I was kind of hoping you'd consider letting me come to work for you at the theater. Maybe teach me about the movie business."

Frank blinked, then blinked again. "Well, now." He looked across at his wife whose smile brightened her whole face. He coughed a couple of times, then looked back at Joey. "I think we might be able to work that out. If that's what you'd really like?"

Joey nodded. "I've been thinking about it a lot lately. I think it's exactly what I'd like."

30

Spring 1942

With spring in the air, the Northwestern campus came alive much like the lustrous green ivy crawling up the walls of Deering Library. Spring fever drew students out for sunny picnics on the Quad and moonlight strolls along Lake Michigan. Even professors couldn't resist the warm weather, many holding classes outdoors in the Deering meadow. Baseball games, track meets, Navy ROTC parades accompanied by the Drum and Bugle Corps, glee club concerts, stage plays, and interfraternity competitions all kept students entertained. The 1942 Waa-Mu Show, the annual musical production always written and produced by Northwestern students, was the most popular event of the spring semester. This year's musical, "Wish You Were Here," drew record crowds for every performance.

Danny's roommate once again disappeared for weeks on end, only stopping by to pick up his mail, do some laundry, or search for a missing textbook.

"You know, people pay a lot of money to have a dorm room all to themselves," Craig quipped one afternoon while digging in his closet. "You should thank me. Better yet, you should pay me for the privacy I've given you all these months. Ah, there it is," he said, straightening as he placed a pipe between his teeth. "I don't suppose you have any fresh tobacco on you?"

Danny leaned back in his chair, chuckling. "No, my elusive roommate, I don't. Haven't taken up the habit."

"Oh, but you should! It makes you look dashing and debonair. Drives the ladies mad with passion."

"Does it, now. Well, I'm happy to report the only lady I'm interested in doesn't care a thing about tobacco."

"Ah! And how is Lady Grayson? Still just holding hands, are we?"

Danny threw a tennis ball at Gilmore, smacking him in the back.

"I'll take that as a yes. Well then, I'm off again," he said, opening the door with the unlit pipe still wedged between his teeth. "Mustn't keep the ladies waiting."

"Ladies? As in plural?"

"Yes, well. The current love of my life and her suite mates like to share and share alike, shall we say? What's a casanova to do?"

"A casanova? Gilmore, you bring new meaning to the word."

"Why, thank you. See you in a few weeks, McClain."

It was actually a month before their paths crossed again. By then, Danny was well into finals, already dreading the upcoming summer. He'd planned to stay home for a couple weeks to help Joey get settled then return for summer classes. He'd tried to convince Beverly to take some classes so they wouldn't have to be apart, but that wasn't to be.

"Danny, I told you before. My family always spends summers together up at Squirrel Lake. We've been going to our cabin there since I was a little girl. I couldn't bear to stay here and miss seeing all our friends and family!"

He'd taken her hand in his as he walked her back to her dorm one night late in April. "Not even to be with me?"

"Now, don't put it that way. It's not that I don't want to be with you. I just need a break from school. That's all. Besides, it's so beautiful up there, and we water ski every day and soak up the sun and have cookouts and bonfires . . . promise me you'll come up one weekend?"

"I'll see if I can work it into my busy schedule."

"Very funny." She'd come to a stop, facing him. "Now close your eyes."

"What?"

"Just do it! Close your eyes."

"Fine. My eyes are closed."

He heard her jostling her books then felt her lift his hand to place something soft but solid in it.

"Okay, you can open your eyes now."

He looked down, finding a thick, soft leather book resting in his hand. Embossed across the front was the word JOURNAL.

"Beverly, this is beautiful."

"I hoped you'd like it. I thought you might like to write down your thoughts. You know, like a diary only more grown up."

He ran his hand over the dark caramel-tinted leather. "I don't know what to say."

"Well, we both know *that's* a lie. You always have something to say. And since I won't be here, I thought this might be the next best thing."

He looked up at her. "I love it. Thank you." He leaned over to kiss her softly. She kissed him back and he wished all over again that she didn't have to go.

When she finally pulled back, she leaned over to whisper in his ear, "Of course, I'll expect you to fill it with all your passionate longings for me while I'm away."

"Gee, I don't know. I'll be so busy here, what with staring at the walls of my dorm room and all. I don't know how I'd find the time . . ."

"Very funny." She pulled him along the walkway as a group of sailors passed them by. "Behave yourself or I might ask one of those guys to come up to the cabin instead of you."

"Hey!" He yanked her playfully back toward him and pressed his forehead against hers. "Look at me. What do you see?"

Her brows drew together, her face suddenly serious in the moonlight. "Uh, well, I don't—"

"See me all green with envy." He smirked and planted a noisy kiss on her cheek.

"Danny, that's not funny." She huffed and took off up the steps of Willard Hall.

"Goodnight, Grayson."

"Goodnight, McClain."

He watched her walk toward the dormitory doors, knowing she'd turn and wave like she always did. Instead, she marched in and never looked back.

He tucked the journal under his arm and dug his hands deep in his pockets as he turned to go, wondering if he'd somehow crossed a line. But he couldn't help it. It was the first time she'd ever teased about seeing someone else. Even if it was just a harmless joke, he didn't like the way it made him feel. He didn't like it at all.

"Hey McClain!"

He turned to find her poking her head out a second story window. She stuck her tongue out at him, wiggling her fingers with her thumbs stuck in her ears. Then she kissed her fingers and blew him a kiss. "I love you, Danny McClain!"

He shook his head, laughing. "I love you too, Beverly Grayson. Sweet dreams."

June 1942

Joey arrived home with a hero's welcome. Neighbors, classmates, teachers, and complete strangers turned out to show their gratitude and welcome him back home. Danny couldn't have been prouder of his big brother—or the outpouring of kindnesses toward him. For days, a steady stream of well wishers stopped by to thank him and fill their home with baked goods, flowers, and all kinds of unusual gifts.

"Thank God for bringing you home to us," Mrs.

Zankowski said, arriving with a large tin of homemade chocolate chip cookies. "I prayed for you every day, Joey."

"I appreciate that, Mrs. Z. Can't tell you how many times I thought about all that history you taught us in school. Sure never thought I'd be smack dab in the middle of it like that."

"But you're home, and we're all so thankful that you are."

Mrs. Martello and her sister from across the street brought over a red, white, and blue afghan they'd made for Joey.

"We started it December the eighth," Angelica said. "Went right out and bought the yarn as soon as we heard you were over there in Hawaii when the Japs attacked."

Mrs. Martello dabbed at her eyes. "We didn't even know if you were alive or not. We just figured as long as we worked on your afghan, you'd come home."

"Crocheted just as fast as we could to have it ready for you."

"That's so nice!" Joey said as they covered his legs with the colorful afghan. "I'll think of you every time I look at it."

The two ladies fussed over him, promising to stop by regularly. They both choked up after planting ruby red kisses on his cheeks before saying goodbye.

Danny plopped down on the armchair beside Joey's makeshift bed in the living room. "Seriously, Joey, you could charm the habit off a nun. I'm pretty sure both those widows have a serious crush on you."

"Ah, they're just being neighborly."

"Maybe so, but you might want to wipe all that lipstick off your cheeks."

The visits continued, day after day. Joey wore out easily, so Mom started posting a sign on the door whenever he needed a break. Folks respected her wishes, often leaving a vase of flowers or a loaf of blueberry bread—his favorite—wrapped in aluminum foil inside a paper bag.

Danny loved having some time home with his brother. It gave him a chance to help his folks get Joey settled into a routine. The hospital sent him home with lots of instructions on caring for the wounds that hadn't yet healed, as well as a calendar of appointments they'd set up at the VA Hospital in Chicago.

But those two weeks also gave the brothers a chance to talk, often long into the night after their parents went to bed. At first Joey didn't say much about Pearl Harbor, then gradually he began to open up. He'd get emotional, sharing snippets of memories from that fateful day in December. The clear blue sky filled with Japanese zeros as far as they could see. The panic that set in as the call went out . . . *Battle stations! Battle stations! This is not a drill!* The deafening explosions that ripped apart the mighty battleships, one after another. The oil-soaked bodies of his shipmates floating in the water.

Joey squeezed his eyes, wiping away tears. "I just thank God I don't remember the worst of it. The Navy chaplain told me that was a real blessing, and I know he's right. But every once in a while, I ask God why me? Why didn't I die with the rest of my buddies? Why'd He let me live when every single one of my friends on board died?

"Then one day, when I was lying in that bed at Bethesda, I felt as if God told me not to ask Him that any more." He looked over at Danny. "I mean, it wasn't like I heard Him say it out loud or anything. But I knew I'd heard it all the same. And that's what I did. I stopped asking why and started asking what He wanted me to do with the rest of my life. For the longest time, I couldn't figure it out. But I knew in my heart God saved me that day for a reason, and I told Him I'd try to figure that out if it took me the rest of my life." Joey leaned his head back on the pillow. "And that's what I'm going to do."

"And somehow you think working for Dad at the theater is why God saved you?"

Joey snickered at first. Then his snicker rolled into unrestrained, guffawing laughter which made Danny laugh just as hard. Sophie jumped up on Joey's bed, wagging her tail as if wanting in on the joke.

Joey rubbed behind her ears, sending her into canine bliss. "Oh girl, you are the best medicine." He looked at his brother. "Although I still don't get how you convinced Dad to let you keep her."

Danny wiped tears of laughter from his eyes. "Well, I guess it's time I told you."

Joey looked back at his brother. "Told me what?"

"It's time you knew. Dad's always loved me more than you." He couldn't stop the wheezing laughter that crept out.

"Yeah, that's it. Have your fun. Kick a sailor when he's down," Joey teased. "Sophie, should we tell him? Or do you think he already knows you love me more than him?"

Danny dreaded the thought of returning to school after his two weeks home. He'd loved every minute he spent with Joey. It was like they'd become more than just brothers. They were friends. But Danny had already enrolled for summer classes, already paid his deposits, and he was already scheduled to work at The Grill. He said his goodbyes, promising to get home as often as he could. On the train ride back to Evanston, he broke in the journal Beverly had given him, writing of the special times he'd shared with his brother . . . and how much he missed his girl.

As he wrote down his thoughts and feelings, he remembered the letters he used to write to his pen pal Hans and then to Anya, sharing similar thoughts. He'd often thought of Anya whenever newsreels mentioned Occupied Holland, often showing grainy images of blown up bridges or long food lines. It all seemed so strange. One minute they'd been friends, sharing thoughts and musings in weekly letters. Then The Netherlands fell and Germany cut all avenues of communication from that little country. He'd never heard from her again. He wondered where she was and how she was doing. He knew it was altogether possible she hadn't survived the war. The thought unsettled him. He wondered how her parents were handling the war, if they'd survived. Was her mother still bedridden? Her father still pastoring? What was it like to live under the jackboot of the hated Nazis? Danny shook his head, scattering the troubling thoughts from his mind.

The campus in Evanston seemed strangely deserted compared to the fall and spring semesters, but Danny didn't mind the more relaxed pace. Craig showed up now and then, still paying his half of the dorm room cost. He'd once talked about Reginald Craig Gilmore Senior, his millionaire father who traveled the world with the fourth Mrs. Gilmore.

Like father, like son.

Twice over the summer, he'd made plans to visit Beverly up at the family cabin on Squirrel Lake. The first time she'd called just before he left for the train station, telling him of some kind of family emergency that had come up and asking if he'd mind postponing til later in the summer. The second time, Mrs. Grayson had called to tell him her daughter had come down with a nasty summer cold and was too contagious to risk a visit. He wondered why Beverly couldn't have just called herself, but didn't give it another thought, heading home for the weekend instead.

Every time he went home, he found his brother growing stronger. Joey was finally walking again, though he required a cane. His father clearly enjoyed buying him a hand-carved cane much like his own. Danny couldn't believe the difference in the atmosphere at home. He almost didn't know the Frank McClain who could be heard whistling down in his workshop, helping Mother with the dishes, or playing chess with his oldest son. He didn't recognize this man, but he sure liked him better.

How ironic. The world was at war, but for the first time, theirs was a home filled with peace.

31

September 1942

Danny checked his watch again. Ten after nine. Beverly, who'd just returned to campus earlier that day, had said she'd meet him at The Grill after his shift ended that evening. Classes hadn't yet started, but the endless lines of fall registration had sent droves of excited students downstairs to The Grill. He'd never seen the hangout so busy, the booths and counter seats all crammed with both wide-eyed freshmen and seasoned upper classmen. When they'd finally closed down for the night, Danny was exhausted but anxious to finally see his girlfriend again after the long summer.

He was surprised she hadn't come back to Evanston sooner. He'd missed her terribly and couldn't wait to hold her in his arms and tell her how much he loved her. All summer he'd dreamed about the possibility of marrying Beverly Grayson. He knew they were still fairly young to get engaged, but he couldn't help imagining how he might propose to her, when they might get married, and where they might honeymoon. Even now the thought brought a smile to his face.

But all those thoughts quickly disappeared once he saw her. She approached him in the now-quiet hall outside The Grill, never once making eye contact.

"Beverly! I thought you'd never get—"

"Hi, Danny."

Her monotone greeting stabbed something deep in the vicinity of his heart. When he tried to hug her, she was stiff as a board. She kept her head down, only briefly glimpsing up at him.

"What—Bev, what's wrong?"

He watched her swallow then press her lips together.

"Danny, we have to talk."

He stepped back. "I don't think I like the sound of that."

She took a seat on the second step of the staircase and folded her arms across her chest. He slowly took a seat beside her wondering what could be so wrong.

He reached for her hand. "I really missed you this summer," he said, hoping to keep the conversation light. "I'm sorry it didn't work out for us to—"

"Danny, I'm engaged."

His mind went completely blank. He stared at her, certain he'd misunderstood. She looked down, smoothing and re-smoothing the pleats in her skirt. He couldn't begin to think, much less respond.

"I'm sorry. I really am. Last year was . . . we had a lot of fun. We did. And I really like you. From the very beginning, I liked you."

"You *liked* me?" he heard himself croak.

"Well, sure," she answered, still not looking at him.

251

"What we had was really nice and all. But, well, over the summer I . . . I met someone."

He stared down at his shoes noticing how scuffed up they were. He'd need to get some new ones before classes started. These would have to be his work shoes. *Work shoes? Why am I focusing on my shoes at a time like this? Wait. What did she just say?*

"—and, well, I never meant to fall in love with Ronnie, but—"

He looked over at her brown and white saddle oxfords. Not a smudge on them. Her rolled-down socks, perfectly white.

Ronnie. Did she say Ronnie? . . ."Ronnie?"

"Ronnie Wentworth. I don't think you know him."

"Ronnie Wentworth, the halfback?"

"Yes. See, my brother invited him up to the cabin that first weekend and—"

"That *first* weekend?"

"Yes. And, I don't know, we just started having a lot of fun together and—"

"That first weekend."

A film reel of the summer started flashing through his mind. The phone calls she didn't return. The visits he'd planned that never worked out. That disinterested tone in her call the day before yesterday. He'd convinced himself she was just busy, trying to pack up for school.

"Yes, that first weekend." She paused and finally looked up at him. "Danny, there's no easy way to say it. Ronnie and I just fell in love. And last Sunday he asked me to marry him."

He stood up, shoved his hands in his pockets, and slowly began walking up the stairs.

"Danny, I'm so sorry."

I bet.

He picked up his pace until he reached the first floor and headed for the doors. A thousand thoughts raced through his mind as he shoved the doors open and stepped out of Scott Hall. He started walking with no destination in mind. Even at 9:30, the campus still bustled with activity. He ignored the happy chatter of giggling coeds catching up on each other's summers. He ignored the dance tunes and raucous laughter drifting out of the Sigma Nu house. And he especially ignored the young couples strolling arm in arm.

He didn't stop walking for several hours. But not once in all that time—*not once*—did what just happened make any sense at all to him.

Danny skipped the first week of classes. He'd called his boss at The Grill and said he was sick. He was, of course. Sick at heart and kicking himself for being so blinded by love. He'd taken refuge in his dorm room, thankful Craig was missing in action again. He'd thought about going home but wasn't up to the scrutiny.

Occasionally he'd take long walks in the middle of the night, trying to sort it all out. How could he have been so stupid? How could he have let himself be so vulnerable? Had she played him? Or was he just too naïve when it came to romance?

Eventually he talked himself out of his self-imposed pity party and went back to class. He had a mountain of school work to catch up on, including a Greek mythology paper and an upcoming test in Western Civilization. He forced himself to focus on his studies and nothing else. He also made a job switch to something more invisible. He gladly took a maintenance job, cleaning classroom buildings and the library after hours.

The one thing he dreaded was running into Beverly on campus. The first time it happened was the Sunday afternoon following Saturday's homecoming. Danny had camped out in Deering Library to work on a term paper for his Econ class. After sitting for two hours, he stood up to stretch and decided to get a drink at the water fountain. As he leaned over for a sip, he heard a familiar giggle. He wiped his chin just as Beverly and her fiancé rounded the corner.

"Danny," she said, startled.

He took a step back. "Beverly."

She smiled shyly at him. "It's nice to see you."

Wish I could say the same. He said nothing.

She seemed flustered that he didn't respond. "I'd like you to meet Ronnie Wentworth. Ronnie, this is Danny McClain."

Ronnie stuck his hand out. "Nice to meet you."

Danny shook it. "I'm sure it is. Nice game yesterday." The halfback blanched and started to say something, but Danny didn't give him the chance. "Beverly. Ronnie." He turned to leave.

As he made his way back to his stack of books on the other side of the room, a slow smile tugged at his lips. *Yeah, nice game, Wentworth. The Buckeyes stomped you guys*

20-6. That puts us at one for five for the season.

Couldn't happen to a nicer guy.

Northwestern went on to lose nine of its ten games on the season, the worst Wildcat record in twenty years—a fact that delighted Danny immensely. The last game of the season, a home game played at Dyche Stadium, was the worst yet as the midshipmen of Great Lakes shut out the Wildcats 48-0. It was Northwestern's worst defeat since 1899.

In all fairness, the entire student body had been gutted with so many students, faculty members, and coaches enlisting to help fight the war. In fact, everything at Northwestern had changed. Everyone on campus had joined in to help the cause, from blood drives for the Red Cross to war bond sales and relief contributions. Social activities and dances were scaled back in line with war time restrictions.

For the first time, physical education became compulsory for all male students. More than 2,800 students took part in the program which was designed to help build endurance through body conditioning and competitive sports in compliance with Army and Navy requirements. During half-time activities at the Northwestern-Illinois game, the entire football field was covered with these students in a mass demonstration of their new physical capabilities.

The military had its strongest presence ever on the Evanston campus. Navy sailors moved into Foster House and the Naval Air cadets moved into Haven House. While Danny could appreciate the campus opening its arms to these young men, it didn't make it any easier to put up with their constant taunts and teasing. If anything, the verbal harassment got worse as fall progressed.

"Hey, coward. Think Uncle Sam doesn't see you hiding behind those text books?"

"What's the matter, chump? Mommy won't let you go to war?"

"Too scared to enlist? Afraid of those scary little Japs?"

By the time Thanksgiving break rolled around, Danny couldn't wait to get off campus and spend a few days at home. On the way home, he'd opened the leather journal Beverly had given him. He'd actually tossed it in his trash can right after she broke up with him. Then a day later, he dug it out of the trash in his room. He ripped out all the pages he'd written previously—most of them about her—and started writing in it again. It seemed like a symbolic way of starting over and facing life again. His own personal therapy. Most of the time his thoughts rambled, jumping from one topic to another, but it didn't matter. It just helped getting the knotted up thoughts in his head down on paper.

He was still writing when the El reached the 59th Station. He stashed his journal and grabbed his gear. After exiting the station, he took the streetcar and jumped off close to home.

Sophie greeted him at the door, smothering him with slobbering kisses and a tail that wagged incessantly. The familiar aromas wafting from the kitchen were just as he'd expected, drawing him into the heart of home. The hugs and laughter shared with his family felt like a soothing balm to his troubled soul. On Thursday, when Joey winked across the table at him after snatching a biscuit during Mom's Thanksgiving prayer, Danny felt restored.

Well, almost.

"Danny, pass the dressing to your father, please," Mom said as she buttered a biscuit. "Has Joey told you about his new girlfriend?"

Danny held his turkey-loaded fork mid-air as he looked across the table at his brother. "Girlfriend? You have a girlfriend?"

"Well, you don't have to say it like that. Even war-scarred sailors have a chance at love now and then."

"No, Joey. I didn't mean it like that. It's just that this is the first I've heard about this. How come you never told me?"

"We haven't seen much of you around here, son," his father added after taking a sip of tea.

"That's a fact," Joey said. "It's like all of a sudden you were allergic to home. We couldn't lure you back for nothing."

Danny concentrated on the food on his plate. "Just a rough semester. That's all. So who's the lucky girl? Anyone I know?"

Joey swallowed a bite of mashed potatoes. "I doubt you know her, but you'll get a kick out of this. Remember Mrs. Zankowski from high school?"

"You're *dating* Mrs. Zankowski?" he teased. "Does Mr. Zankowski know about this?"

"No, goofball. Her niece, Millie Davis. She got a job working for Armour, and she's staying at her aunt's house."

"Lara brought her down to meet Joey," Mom continued,

beaming. "The minute they laid eyes on each other, I knew it was something special. Never saw anything quite like it."

"Was it that obvious?" Joey asked.

Dad pointed a carrot stick at him. "I'm hardly the romantic type, but even I could tell she was head over heels for you."

If he hadn't heard it with his own ears, Danny never would've believed such words could come from his dad's mouth. He'd been quite sure his father wouldn't know romance if it hit him up side the head.

Danny cleared his throat. "Clearly, I've missed out. So what's she like?"

"You'll love her, Danny. She's fantastic. Not to mention the fact she's easy on the eyes."

"Yeah? Davis . . . doesn't sound very Polish to me."

"Lara's sister Melanie married a dentist named Clayton Davis," Mother said, passing Danny the cranberries. "Millie is their daughter."

"I see. Well, when do I get to meet this angel?"

"Patience, little brother. She went home to Boston for the weekend. She'll be back early Sunday evening if you want to stick around."

"I'll do it."

"Your brother's doing a real fine job at the theater, Danny," Dad said. "Seems to like the work. And they like him too, I can tell you that much. I think half the folks come just so they can talk to a war hero."

"Ah, they're just being nice, Dad. Hey, Danny. We just got in the reels for *The Flying Tigers*. John Wayne is in it— that actor you like. The theater's closed today. Wanna go get a sneak peek? Just the two of us?"

"Sure thing. Let me help Mom clean up then we can—"

"Nonsense," Dad said. "I'll help with the dishes. You boys go on and have a good time."

He looks like Dad. He sounds like Dad. But the man is helping with the dishes? Danny shook his head. "Well, okay. Just promise you'll save us some of that pumpkin pie."

"I made two pies. I doubt we'll run out," Mom said, gathering their empty plates. "Go on. Have a good time, boys."

Two and a half hours later, they sat in the middle of the empty theater as the final credits rolled.

"Not too bad," Joey said. "Of course, I heard the movie was already in production before Pearl. Did you notice the date on the calendar behind John Wayne's character when he was firing Woody? December seventh. Kind of blows the whole story. But still, I enjoyed it."

Danny let the music fade as the credits rolled to a stop. "Yeah, it was good. I liked the aerial cat fights. Made you feel like you were really up there with them. What's it like seeing something like that after being in the service?"

Joey scratched the crinkled scars on his left hand. "Good question. We'd run war games and all, but we were pretty much blown out of the water before the U.S. got into the war."

"True." They sat in silence for a moment. "I think if I ever joined up, I'd want to be a pilot."

"Can't blame you. Better up there than sitting ducks like we were on the *Oklahoma*."

"I didn't mean it that way, Joey."

"No, I understand. I wanted to fly, but I didn't have the

grades for it. You'd have no problem, academic genius that you are."

"I don't know about that. My grades have really taken a nose dive this semester."

"I doubt that."

"It's true. Don't say anything to Mom and Dad, okay?"

"I won't. But how'd that happen? Grades have always come easy for you."

"They used to."

"Wait—does this have something to do with that girl who dumped you for the football player?"

Danny scowled. "Thanks a lot. Would you like to throw a match on the gasoline you just poured over me?"

"Not hardly. I still get a little nervous around fire."

"Oh my gosh," Danny said as he dropped his head in his hands. "I'm sorry, Joey. That was thoughtless of me to say."

Joey laughed. "No kidding! Look, Danny. I didn't mean to make light of what happened to you. Women can trample a guy's pride like nothing else can. But don't let her ruin your life. I'm sure she was a real peach and all, but no matter who she is, she's not worth cashing in all you've worked for. You've got to let her go."

"Says the brother with the perfect girlfriend."

"Well, that's true." Joey smiled. "But what I was trying to say is don't let a broken heart define you for the rest of your life."

They sat in silence again, then Danny sat up a little straighter. "Can I ask you something?"

"Sure."

"If you had to do it all over, would you? I mean, if you

knew then that you would've been burned so badly because you were serving your country at Pearl Harbor, would you have still gone off and joined the Navy?"

"I had a lot of time to think about stuff like that when I was in the burn ward. I asked myself that and a million other questions. But I can honestly say—absolutely, positively yes. I wouldn't trade anything for my years in service. I left home a kid and came back a man. Yeah, I've got the battle scars to show for it, but I loved everything about it. Well, except for . . . except for losing all my friends. That was the hardest. Those guys were like family to me, Danny. We lived together, worked together, played together. I would've given my life for any one of them. And they'd have said the same."

Danny ran his fingernail in a groove of the upholstered armrest, back and forth, back and forth, as his mind jumped around.

"And I'll tell you this much. If they hadn't sent me home, I'd still be there fighting today. I'd give anything to help win this war."

"You're serious?"

"That's what keeps me awake at night. Not the what-ifs or the ugly scars I see in the mirror. I'd give anything to be back on a battleship doing whatever it takes to beat our enemies. I envy every man in uniform right now. Would I go back? In a heartbeat."

32

As Danny rode the El back to Evanston late Sunday night, he felt unusually restless. He'd enjoyed being home for Thanksgiving break. He'd especially enjoyed meeting Joey's girl, Millie. Mom and Dad were right. She was crazy about Joey. Just observing the way she watched over him and looked at him with such a transparent affection was a visible reminder that there are still a few decent, good women out there. Millie had a great sense of humor, teasing Joey playfully as he bantered back and forth with her. Danny wouldn't be surprised at all if Joey popped the question before Christmas.

Then he started thinking about the conversation he'd had with his brother that night at the theater. In fact, he hadn't stopped thinking about it. He stared out the window into the darkness, wishing he could stop the restless, uneasy feeling that continued to gnaw at him. He tried writing in his journal, but shoved it back in his duffle, just anxious to get back to his dorm.

It was after nine when he made his way down the hall toward his room. That's when he saw someone walk out of his room with a suitcase.

"Hey! What do you think you're doing?"

The man set the suitcase down beside two others and turned to face him. "Are you Mr. McClain?"

Danny dropped his duffle. "Yes, I am and this is my room. Who are you?"

He was probably fifty years old, maybe fifty-five, with salt and pepper hair, a tanned complexion, and pale blue eyes. Then it hit him. *Just like Craig's eyes.*

"I'm Reginald Gilmore, Craig's father." He dug his hands in his coat pocket and blew out a loud breath. "I'm afraid Craig won't be coming back to school."

Danny wasn't too surprised. He'd figured this would happen at some point. Craig had played at being a student, but never took it seriously. He'd actually been surprised that his roommate returned for the fall semester. Of course, he never saw that much of him. A whole string of college coeds kept Craig busy most of the time.

"I'm sorry to hear that. Is he here?" Danny tried to look into their room.

"No. No, he's not here. He, uh . . . he was killed in an automobile accident Wednesday night."

"What?" Danny felt the air rush from his chest. "No! He can't . . ."

Mr. Gilmore's eyes glistened. He coughed then looked back up at him. "Yes, well, we're all still in shock, of course. Craig was our only child. He . . . he was on his way home for the holidays and apparently his car swerved off the road. There was ice on the road and they said a truck rammed him from behind and Craig's car flew down a ravine. They said he most likely died on impact."

Danny kept shaking his head, unable to speak.

"I know my son was a bit of a character most of the time, but deep down—well, deep down, he was a good boy. I . . ." He pulled a handkerchief out of his pocket and wiped his eyes. "I'm not sure how we'll go on without him."

Danny clenched his jaw and rubbed his hands together. "Mr. Gilmore, I'm so sorry. I just can't believe it. Craig was—I mean, he was . . ."

Mr. Gilmore put his hand on Danny's shoulder. "It's hard on all of us."

Danny pinched the bridge of his nose. "Is there anything I can do?"

"No, I'm just about finished gathering his things. The RA downstairs let me in. I'm sorry if I startled you."

"No, I'm sorry I sounded suspicious when I first saw you. Here, let me help you carry these downstairs."

"Thank you, Mr. McClain."

A few minutes later, after helping Craig's father load the car, Danny shook his hand and said goodbye. He shook off a chill as the biting wind off Lake Michigan danced around him. He wasn't about to go back upstairs. He was used to having the room to himself, but not like this.

Danny started walking across campus. How many times had he done the very same thing this last semester? How many miles had he walked around Evanston and along the beach late at night while trying to make sense of everything? He could taste the bile in his mouth, and for a moment he thought he might throw up. But what good would it do?

When he finally started heading back to his dorm near dawn, he was numb from the blustering wind. Somewhere behind him, drunken voices pierced the quiet solitude. Probably some frat boys about to call it a night.

"Well looky what we have here. It's one of those sissy deferment boys!"

Not again.

"That's sissy deferment boy SIR to you!"

They laughed as they caught up, flanking each side of him as the sailor on his right draped an arm over Danny's shoulder. "How's it going, sissy boy?"

They could barely walk and reeked of alcohol. He decided to ignore them, hoping they'd get bored and move on, or just pass out and be done with it.

"Cat got your tongue, boy? I believe Midshipman Clancy here asked you a question."

"Ah, sissy boy can't answer. He's got a pacifier in his mouth."

The sailor beside him got right in his face. "Is that right, sissy boy? You got a widdle pacifier in yo mouth, sweetie pie?"

Danny elbowed him away and picked up his pace. "Guys, let it go."

The one on his left, a short guy with red hair, grabbed his arm and whipped him around. "Oh, I don't think so, prissy pants! Just because you're too much of a weanie to serve your country—"

"I said, let it go," Danny growled, jerking his arm free.

"Let what go? Oh—you mean this?" The redhead unzipped his fly and urinated on Danny's shoes.

Danny jumped out of the way, but the damage was done. In a split second, he cold-cocked the guy's nose, the snap of cartilage breaking loud in all the commotion. As blood began to pour from the guy's nose, Danny felt his arms pulled tight behind him, almost yanked out of their sockets. The first punch to his gut took his breath away, but he kept fighting back. He was outnumbered but sober, and that had to count for something.

They cursed, they punched, they stomped, and they twisted him in knots, but he didn't give up. He wasn't about to give in, but he wasn't sure how much longer he could last.

"You sorry little mama's boy—this one's for Pearl!" The kick landed right in his groin sending Danny to his knees. Stars danced before his eyes as his kneecaps slammed into the pavement.

"MY BROTHER WAS AT PEARL, you idiot!" he wheezed.

"What'd he say?"

"Did he say his brother was at Pearl?"

A lot of scuffling. Cussing. Accusations.

Then silence.

A moment later, the darkness swallowed him whole.

"How'd the other guy look?"

Danny held the cold compress against his jaw wishing he could put it down where the pain really hurt. "Guys. Plural. There were eight of them."

"Eight? Well then, now I'm impressed!"

"Don't be. They were sailors."

The Army sergeant laughed heartily, leaning back in his chair. "Even better! Any day's a good day when you whack some of those Navy fruitcakes! Son, we may have just opened but you've already made my day!"

"I know. I've been sitting outside since the sun came up."

"Is that a fact? What can I do for you, Mr. McClain?"

Danny moved the compress from his face. "You can sign me up for the Army Air Force. I'm here to enlist."

Part IV

33

January 1943

Danny breezed through all the written and physical tests required by the Army Air Force, then spent the Christmas holidays and remaining weeks with his family before reporting for duty at a recruiting office near Chicago's Union Station. After finalizing the necessary paper work, he and a group of recruits were marched to the station where they boarded a Pullman car headed for Texas. The two day trip gave him more than enough time to think about his recent past and immediate future.

His parents didn't take the news of his enlistment well, which didn't surprise him. Having Joey there to talk them through it helped a lot, but it didn't stop the steady flow of his mother's tears. She was gravely concerned about his safety as a pilot "up there with all those Germans or Japanese trying to shoot you out of the sky." But in the end, she accepted his decision and promised she would pray for him every waking moment.

As for Dad? That was an entirely different situation. While his father had changed considerably since Joey came back after Pearl, he still didn't want a son fighting in this war. At first he'd lost his temper like the Frank McClain of old, ranting about his son making "such an idiotic decision" when he was almost half way through college. He kept pointing at Joey, saying, "Haven't you learned anything from your brother's example?" Thankfully, Joey came to his rescue, letting his father know he was proud of Danny's decision and fully supported it. Dad had disappeared downstairs as he so often did and didn't say much for a few days.

When the morning of January 19 arrived, Danny said his goodbyes to his mother, to Joey, and also Millie who'd gladly accepted Joey's proposal of marriage on Christmas Eve. He looked around for his dad, hoping to at least get a chance to say goodbye. He'd insisted on making the trip into Chicago alone on the El. But as he stepped outside, there was his father—sitting behind the wheel of his Packard with the engine going. Danny looked back at his mom. She held a handkerchief to her mouth and motioned for him to go. On the drive into town, his dad kept his eyes glued to the road, not saying a word. When they got to the station, Danny got out, grabbed his bag, and turned to thank him for the ride. His father cut the engine, got out of the car, and just stood there for a moment. Then suddenly, he pulled Danny into a tight embrace.

He patted Danny on the back. "You come back, son," he croaked. "You come back."

"I will, Dad. I promise."

Another moment passed before his father pulled back. Without a second look, he climbed back in his car and drove away.

Now, as the train pulled into the Wichita Falls station, Danny only had one thought—to be the best aviator in the Army Air Force. Nothing else mattered at this point. They were quickly transported to nearby Sheppard Field Army Air Base where they were greeted by a grizzled sergeant named Walker and two of his staff.

"Welcome to the Army, ladies!" the sergeant shouted. "Now GET YOUR BUTTS OFF THAT BUS AND FALL IN LINE!"

And that was just the nice part.

Shortly after their arrival, they were ushered into the barbershop and all given the same cut. Danny ran his hand through his new crew cut, liking it immediately. Next stop, uniforms and barrack assignment.

At noon, his unit was marched over to the mess hall for lunch. The metal trays with divided sections also served as their plates. The guys working KP duty seemed really friendly, loading up the plates of all the newcomers. "Enjoy!" they said. Danny was amazed at the quantity of food on his tray. Only a few minutes later, he realized those guys weren't being friendly—they'd played an age-old prank on the recruits.

"You will leave absolutely NOTHING on your trays, gentlemen," Sergeant Walker barked. "You have three minutes. EAT UP!"

"I'm sorry, sir, but I can't eat any more," the kid next to him said.

"Son, are you deaf? I said you WILL leave NOTHING on your tray. Now you and your friends get your butts back over to that table and CLEAN YOUR PLATE!"

That was one lesson Danny wouldn't forget. He quickly learned how to handle those KPs.

He wasn't particularly impressed with what he'd seen of Texas so far. The erratic weather made it impossible to dress appropriately. One day would be freezing, the next could be warm as a summer's day. At least back in Chicago you knew what to expect from Mother Nature. Still, Danny learned to adjust. He knew how to dress for the long hours they spent marching in formation and running obstacle courses. And he quickly learned how to layer extra clothing for those chilly nights in the barracks. Rather than shiver all night beneath the thin wool blanket, Danny would slip his fatigues over his Army-issue pajamas for a little extra warmth. Unfortunately he forgot all about his pajamas one frigid morning when they were awakened and marched over to the clinic for physicals. The flight surgeon roared with laughter when he discovered Danny's extra layer of clothing.

"Well, well, Private PJ. Nice and comfy cozy, are we?"

"Yes, sir. Thank you for asking, sir," Danny answered with a smirk.

"Then drop your drawers, Private. All of them!"

Danny could still hear the guy laughing when he left the room, rubbing his right cheek after the shot he'd just received.

For the most part, they learned the basics of soldiering while at Sheppard—the correct way to wear their uniforms, how to make up a bunk according to regulation, the basics of military language and the meaning of different orders, and lots and lots of marching in formation. But on their last Saturday on base, the troops were entertained by none other than Roy Rogers and the Sons of the Pioneers. Danny was thrilled, listening to all the great songs by one of his favorite movie stars. He didn't even mind that Dale Rogers hadn't joined them.

With basic training now under their belts, Danny's outfit was transferred to Lubbock, Texas, for "pre-pre-flight school." Danny had to chuckle when they were assigned dorm rooms in one of the Texas Tech residence halls. He vowed never to harass the male students on the Tech campus like the sailors had done at Northwestern, though it was certainly tempting. He was surprised to find himself back in college classrooms, required to take some basic collegiate courses, many of which he'd already taken at Northwestern. But he kept his mouth shut, did his school work, and tried to do the best he could.

Just like at Sheppard, they spent an incredible amount of time doing drills and calisthenics. But this time, they did so under the direction of Texas Tech's head football coach, Del Morgan. Some of his players—those who had not yet been called up by the draft—assisted Coach Morgan in these athletic endeavors. Danny found it all very strange, particularly as he remembered the PE requirements back at Northwestern and the massive "display" of athletic prowess that day at the Illinois vs. Northwestern half time at Dyche Field. Sometimes he wondered what he'd gotten himself into. He was growing weary of all the physical training. He wanted to fly!

At long last, his wish came true.

His first time up in the Piper Cub, Danny could barely contain himself. With an instructor in the seat behind him, the tiny plane gained speed heading down the runway until it finally lifted up, up, up into the air.

"WA HOOOO!" he shouted at the top of his lungs. He'd never experienced anything so exhilarating in his life! He couldn't stop grinning, couldn't stop laughing as he took in the amazing vistas beneath him and the blue, blue sky all around him. He drank in the moment, and realized this was what he was born to do! He let out another shout, then twisted around to see his instructor. The pilot smiled from ear to ear, obviously understanding the significance of the moment. Danny gave him a thumbs up which he promptly returned.

Over the next few days, Danny and his outfit fulfilled the required ten hours of flight time—which taught them the basics of flying while also weeding out those who couldn't fly without puking. The instructors handled take offs and landings, but up in the air, they turned the controls over to their students. First and foremost, the new pilots learned how to recover from a stall or a spin. The instructor would pull the nose up steeper and steeper until the plane finally stalled. The student quickly learned the right maneuvers to bring the aircraft back under control. Danny had never worn a seat belt before, but he was sure thankful for it the first time the plane rolled over.

In July, Danny and his outfit were transferred to Santa Ana Army Air Base near Los Angeles, California. He loved the warm dry air of California, but all that took a back seat as Danny and his buddies were put to the most severe testing yet. The Classification Center for the Western Training Command put them through a whole new level of endurance testing, both physical and mental. By far the most difficult experience he faced was the pressure chamber test. He blew out a long sigh of relief when he passed it with flying colors. The men were also subjected to a whole battery of psychological tests to further weed out anyone who might have problems functioning in flight. Again, Danny successfully passed those exams.

The day he was assigned to Pilot Training, he couldn't wait to tell his family.

"Congratulations, Danny! I'm so proud of you!"

He could hear the genuine pride in his mother's voice, though he knew she still had serious qualms about him flying. "Thanks, Mom. That means a lot coming from you."

"Your father's at the theater, but Joey's here. Hold on." It was muffled, but he could hear her shouting, "Joey! Danny's on the phone! He has wonderful news!"

After a lot of excited chatter in the background, his brother finally took the receiver. "Danny! What's the good news?"

"Joey, I did it. I've been assigned to Pilot Training. I'm gonna fly!"

"I can't believe it! No, I take that back—I CAN believe it. I always knew you could do whatever you set your mind to. Ah, Danny—I'm so happy for you. Couldn't be prouder!"

"Thanks, Joey. I should probably tell you . . . I may be the one learning to fly, but I'm doing all this for you too. I can't help feeling I'm finishing what you started, if that makes sense."

Silence filled the line for a moment. "I don't know what to say. That's . . . I'm honored. I really am."

"No, I'm the one who's honored. I just wanted you to know. But enough of that stuff. How's Millie? Have you all set a date yet?"

"We set it for the week you'll be home after graduation. Wouldn't think of getting married without you by my side."

"And I wouldn't miss it for the world."

They talked for a few more minutes as Danny promised to keep in touch, and Joey promised to pass along Danny's news to Dad.

A short time later, Danny was assigned to Flight School at Cal-Aero in nearby Ontario, California. With ideal weather conditions, Cal-Aero was considered the best of the best. He and five others were assigned to a flight instructor named Sam Holliman. A former barn-storming pilot, Holliman was a short man, very soft-spoken—at least on the ground. In the air was a different story.

Learning to fly in the Piper Cub had been a dream come true. But once he got to Cal-Aero and took his first flight in a Stearman, he realized how serious a job it was to get it right. The Stearman had an upper wing and a lower wing and an open cockpit. It also had a much more powerful engine than the tiny Piper Cub. Now, every time he sat in the cockpit, he remembered the old adage his instructors had drilled in his head: *There are old pilots, and there are bold pilots, but there aren't many old, bold pilots.*

After several flights, Danny was given a flight check by the Squadron Commander. After performing several maneuvers and shooting several landings at an auxiliary field, Danny got the shock of his life.

"You're ready to solo. Drop me off alongside the runway then show me what you can do."

Danny swallowed hard. None of the other guys in his group had soloed yet, and he hadn't expected to any time soon. He was scared spitless!

"Take it easy and just fly as if I was there in your back cockpit," his commander said as he stepped out of the plane onto the runway.

"Yes, sir!"

Following the hand signals of his instructor below, Danny did a series of take-offs, circling the field, then landing. After several landings, the commander motioned him over to pick him up again.

"Nice job, McClain. Congratulations."

They took off again to return to the main field. As they taxied to the parking area then deplaned, Danny proudly left his goggles on top of his head—signifying he had soloed. Until a pilot solos, the goggles were worn under the chin whenever he was on the ground. As the first in his group to solo, Danny couldn't help the proud smile on his face.

Holliman swore. "Well, I'll be."

As luck would have it, Cal-Aero was converted to a basic flight training center just as Danny completed his primary training. That meant he would stay put for the two months of basic flight training instead of transferring elsewhere. He couldn't help thinking his mother's prayers had paved the way for all these perfect situations. He'd have to remember to thank her when he got home.

34

January 1944

Moving into basic flight training took Danny's flying experience to a whole new level. With his Stearman days behind him, he and those in his class now flew the BT13 basic trainer. With a closed-in cockpit, radio contact, lights, and a much more powerful engine, Danny thought it must be like stepping out of a Model A Ford into a Rolls Royce—not that he'd ever been in a Rolls Royce. It was also his first experience flying at night. What a thrill!

A month later, when their training was completed on schedule, Danny was transferred to the Stockton Army Air Base for Advanced Flight Training. There he learned how to fly two-engine aircraft, as well as flying with a co-pilot. Each cadet took turns flying in the left seat or right seat, as pilot or co-pilot. Danny much preferred that left seat where he could be in control, but he knew how important the role of a co-pilot was.

As Danny's class neared the completion of their flight training, they were asked to fill out a form indicating their preference as to what type of aircraft they'd like to be assigned. The choice was an easy one for Danny. After reading reports about the exploits of Major Jimmy Doolittle and his group during the first bombing raid on Tokyo, Danny knew he wanted to fly the B-25. He was disappointed when he didn't make the cut, unaware that the B-25 was becoming obsolete. Of his entire 44E class, only two B-25 assignments were made.

Still, he was thrilled to see his name on the list of graduates. He was also surprised to find out that 20th Century Fox would be filming their graduation ceremony for the movie, *Winged Victory*. Sure enough, on May 23 the huge studio cameras recorded their entire ceremony, including a flyover of AT-7s flown by the class of 44F. They were disappointed to learn the film's star, Lon McAlister, was not in attendance. Apparently his part would be dubbed later in some Hollywood studio. But Danny didn't care. He was just excited to be graduating, and glad to hear his family would get to see the ceremony on film sometime in the near future. He could already imagine Dad and Joey holding a special matinee at the theater to "showcase" his cameo in the film.

But with graduation now behind him, there was only one thing on his mind—going home!

05 May 1944

Chicago, Illinois

"Oh sweetheart!" Mom cried as he swept her up in his arms at the airport, then twirled her around.

"Hi, Mom! I've missed you!"

"Put me down, Danny. I want to look at you!"

He gently set her back on the ground, still holding her as she held his face in her hands. "Oh, Danny, you look so handsome in your uniform. How are you?"

Before he could answer, she kissed him on both cheeks. "I'm great, Mom. Better than great now that I'm home." He looked over her shoulder at his father. "Hi, Dad."

His father, still walking with a cane, made his way closer, standing beside his mother. "Good to see you, son. How's the Army Air Force treating you?"

Danny shook his hand. "Fine, just fine. How's the theater?"

"Ah, it's plugging along. Joey's there now. He insisted I come along with your mother."

"I'm glad you came." When his father broke into a chuckle, Danny surprised him with a hearty hug. "I've missed you!"

His week-long leave flew by much too fast. Three days after he got home, Danny served as best man as Joey and Millie were married in a small ceremony at the church. Watching Millie walk down the aisle on the arm of her father, he'd felt a twinge of jealousy as he watched her eyes locked on Joey's. What would it be like to know without a single doubt that someone so beautiful, so wonderful, loved you unconditionally? He'd almost chuckled out loud when he sneaked a peek at his brother and caught a glimpse of his goofy, love-smitten grin. He'd never seen his brother so happy.

As Joey and Millie mingled with family and friends at the reception, Danny heard someone call out his name. He turned to find his former high school teacher beaming at him.

"Mrs. Zankowski! Nice to see you!"

She hugged him hard. "Oh, the pleasure's all mine. What a handsome best man you made! Why, I couldn't believe that dashing young man in uniform standing up there beside Joey was that skinny little guy who used to mow my yard. How in the world are you, Danny?"

"Great. I just graduated from flight school, and I have to say I'm feeling pretty good about that right now."

"Congratulations! That must have been so exciting! We're all real proud of you. I pray for you every single day. Your mother keeps me up to date on all your news."

"I appreciate that, Mrs. Z." He turned to look at Joey and Millie who were talking to some friends. "I guess you and I are family now, huh? Millie's a great gal. Joey's a lucky man."

"Isn't she a dear? And oh my, how she loves your brother. Watching those two fall in love—well, it reminded me there's still some good left in this old world after all."

He noticed a trace of sadness in her eyes.

"Any word from your family over in Poland? I think of them every time there's war news out of Warsaw."

Her face darkened as she looked away. "Oh, let's not spoil such a nice occasion. I thank you for asking, but a wedding isn't a place for such troubling talk." She gave him a trembling smile. "Never mind all that. How about you? I'll bet there are lots of pretty girls out there lining up for a smart, good looking fella like you."

"Well, I hate to disappoint you, but there's no pretty girls chasing after me and certainly no lines forming. I was just hoping you had another niece or two like Millie."

She laughed, looping her arm with his. "Well, I'll have to give that some thought. In the meantime, let's go have us a piece of wedding cake."

Four days later on his way back to California, Danny dug in his satchel for his journal. He'd been negligent lately, with so little time to jot down a note or two. But the long flight back to California gave him plenty of time to catch up.

I can't believe I'm already heading back. It was great to be home, but strange too. It's hard to even remember the kid I was when I used to live there. Same house, same family, same smells, same sounds . . . but I don't feel like the same person. Not at all. I wonder what it will be like when I come back from the war?

With Joey moved into the apartment, Sophie decided to spend her nights with me. I'd forgotten what it was like to share a bed with a beagle. But I have to say, I'll sure miss her. She's great company. And apparently the only kind of female company I can handle these days . . .

I couldn't help thinking about Beverly while I was home. I guess being so close to Evanston brought up all those old memories. I'm sure she's married by now to Mr. Football. I heard the Wildcats turned their season around and only lost two games this year. I guess I should be happy for them—the team, that is.

I came across the old cigar box with all my letters from Hans and Anya. I'm not sure why but something made me read all through them again. It seems like it's been a lifetime since I lived for the mailman's delivery, hoping to have a letter from Holland. It was hard reading the letters from Hans again. Even after all these years I still can't believe he died so young. It reminded me of how I felt after Craig died. We were never that close, but it still seemed like such a waste. I wonder how God chooses who will die young and who dies of old age?

I've thought about Anya a lot after reading through all her letters. I wonder what she looks like now. Does she still have those freckles? Has she grown into a beauty like her mother once was? Did she grow tall like Hans? Hard to imagine, after all these years thinking of her as "little Anya." I'm not sure why, but I stuck that picture of the Versteegs in my wallet. For old time's sake, I guess. In my gut, I want to believe she's still alive, but I don't know. The war seems like such a distant monstrosity, but whenever I think about Anya and her family, it seems very close and personal. I guess it should, since I could be smack dab in the middle of it soon. Sometimes the thought of it scares me more than I'm willing to admit. And sometimes . . . well, sometimes I can't wait to get there.

Las Vegas, Nevada

Upon returning from his leave, Danny and several of his fellow graduates were sent to Las Vegas Army Air Base in Nevada where they were first introduced to the mighty Flying Fortress—the B-17. Danny was in awe of the enormous aircraft, grasping at once the reasoning behind the legendary nickname. The four-engine bird was the biggest aircraft he'd ever seen.

It was here at the base in Las Vegas that Danny learned he would be training as a co-pilot. The training at the Las Vegas base served two purposes. Gunners were sent up for practice in the air while co-pilots used the same flights to learn the ropes of flying the Fort. Some flights were strictly for co-pilot training, a tremendous responsibility onboard the four-engine birds.

Shortly after their arrival, Danny and his buddies learned that D-Day was on and the invasion was underway. Time was of the essence.

Once they had mastered the B-17, Danny and his unit were transferred to Lincoln Army Air Base in Nebraska for crew assignment. Danny was glad to finally meet the men he would fly with, a diverse and interesting bunch. He looked forward to getting to know them better.

Pilot Dick Anderson hailed from Milwaukee, Wisconsin. Anderson, about six feet two with a shock of brown hair, seemed like a congenial guy, but Danny knew instantly he took his job seriously. Twenty-six year old Anderson would serve as the airplane commander, responsible for the safety of his crew. His leadership would set the tone for the morale and discipline necessary for them to function as a unit. Respect and confidence in the airplane commander was vital to the men who served under him. His word was final, regardless of the situation. Danny had a feeling Anderson could easily maintain those responsibilities.

Navigator Lane Pendergrass had the look and demeanor of an Ivy leaguer. With his black hair, blue eyes, and an air of self-confidence, he reminded Danny of the fraternity boys back at Northwestern. With a name like Pendergrass, the Boston native surely had blue blood flowing in his veins. But none of that would matter in the skies above enemy territory. A navigator needed the smarts to get his plane to the target and back in spite of weather, flak, or formation emergencies, while also calibrating all of the Fort's complicated instruments. Positioned in the Plexiglas bubble in the nose of the aircraft, the navigator would also man the nose gun when fighters attacked.

Sullivan "Sully" Thornton, a twenty-two year old from Atlanta, Georgia, would handle the toggelier controls for the crew. The primary function of a B-17 is to drop bombs on the target, which is no simple task. In the lead crew, bombardiers are responsible for calculating altitude, air speed versus ground speed, actual time of fall, drift, bomb trajectory and several other factors to make precision bomb drops. Toggeliers would control the bomb release switch in non-lead crews, following the signal of the lead crew.

As senior enlisted man on the crew, the flight engineer had to know more about the B-17—its mechanics, its armament, and the function of all equipment—than anyone else on board. He also served double duty as the top turret gunner. Paul "Shorty" Lowenstein, born and raised in Pottstown, Pennsylvania, didn't really look the part—at least to Danny. The five-foot five-inch engineer had a quick smile, and he constantly worked a wad of gum like it was the difference between life and death.

Radio operator Tony Franconi was a New York native from Staten Island with a thick accent to prove it. For the long hours of flight, the radio operator manned his desk in the middle of the fuselage with the constant crackling static streaming through his headset. He would give position reports every thirty minutes, while keeping headquarters informed of target attacks and results.

Ball turret gunner Don Michaels came from St. Louis, Missouri. As required for the cramped compartment beneath the belly of the B-17, Don was also a short guy, but he made up for it in strength. Danny had never seen a guy so chiseled. He didn't envy Michaels' vulnerable position in the ball turret. It gave Danny claustrophobia just thinking about it.

Tail gunner Dal Nicholson was a good looking kid from Sterling, Illinois. The eighteen-year-old's easy manner would hopefully be a calming influence on the crew. Danny had to admire anyone willing to crawl back around the tail wheel then man his position while kneeling on what looked like a bicycle seat. *No wonder they draft 'em young.*

Left waist gunner Francis McCabe called New York City home. Danny was quite sure the young kid must have lied about his age to enlist. But he took his job seriously and that's all that mattered. Nashville, Tennessee native Jimmy

Foster rounded out the crew as right waist gunner. Tow-headed and feisty, Foster always kept a deck of cards on hand "for a quick one." Waist gunners had the highest rate of casualties, exposed to the 150 mile per hour slipstream while manning the 65-pound machine guns in the mid-section of the Fort.

Danny liked the guys and felt confident they'd make a good team. It was a sobering thought to realize these complete strangers would play a significant role in whether or not they would return home after the war—be it safe and whole, wounded, or in a wooden box. It was a thought he chose to ignore.

After their crew was assembled, they were sent to Alexandria Army Air Base in Alexandria, Louisiana for Phase Training. Here, they would learn to operate as a unit, working in sync with one another to perform the necessary tasks for combat flying.

Over the next few weeks, they flew constantly, learning to work together and do the job as flawlessly as possible. But they learned early on how easily mistakes could be made. On a Saturday afternoon exercise involving a mock bombing mission, they witnessed the crash of a P39 Aircobra crashing into one of the B-17s—a maneuver that was definitely *not* in the planned mock-drill. In less than a minute, they'd accounted for all crew members on both planes—a miracle considering the extreme damage to both aircraft. The crash made an indelible impression on every one involved in the exercise that day. In the blink of an eye, everything could go wrong—a lesson Danny never forgot.

In another week, they boarded a troop train and headed back to Lincoln where combat gear was issued to each of them. By the type of gear they were given, Danny and his crew realized they would most likely be headed to the European Theater of Operations, or ETO. In the back of his mind, Danny had always assumed he'd be flying above the warm waters of the Pacific when the time came. But after a year and ten months of training, he didn't care where they were assigned. He just wanted to get there.

35

November 1944

He'd never seen a cruise ship before. The *Queen Elizabeth* was a beautiful vessel, massive in size, sailing beneath the Union Jack—and the main means of transportation for those like Danny, heading to his home away from home in England.

Halfway across the Atlantic, he took out his journal for an update.

> *After arriving at Camp Kilmer, New Jersey this morning, our crew boarded the "Queen Elizabeth" headed for England. The last place I expected to be on Thanksgiving Day was on a ship cruising the Atlantic. I have to admit, there's not a lot to be thankful for here. We're all crammed on the QE like sardines. She's a beautiful ship—the largest ship afloat these days—but there are 20,000 troops on board, plus another 2,000 of the ship's crew. As officers, we were assigned to bunk in staterooms. Sounds fancy and it is—except for*

the fact there are 48 of us squeezed into three-tiered bunks in these two-room staterooms which normally accommodate just two passengers!

To make things worse we've encountered unusually rough seas which has caused most of the troops on board to toss their cookies into their helmets. Thankfully, as aviators, we're used to motion sickness so it hasn't been a problem.

We were all hoping the meals served on the QE would be up to par for a ship this classy. The officers are served meals by British waiters in a special dining area, but much to our disappointment, the food is typical military grub and very bland. So much for tea and crumpets.

I've never seen so much gambling in all my life. The main ballroom has turned into an Officers Club, where every game of chance is played almost around the clock. I'm too cheap to take a chance on losing my hard earned cash, but some of these guys would mortgage their skivvies if they could. Pendergrass, our navigator, has already made $1000! Rumor has it a chaplain from the Bronx put the title of his new Buick convertible in the pot and LOST it! These guys are nuts!

But I'm so glad we're finally on our way to do our part in the war effort. We keep up with the war news as best we can. We hear the Allies are making huge progress in fighting the Axis powers since the invasion on D-Day last June. And all of us cheered when we learned that Paris had been liberated near the end of August. In September we heard about "Operation

Market Garden" – *the Allied assault on The Nether-lands. British General Montgomery's plan was for the Allies to drop paratroopers and supplies at Arnhem while at the same time marching a major force from Belgium in the south. When they met up, they would defeat the Germans, free The Netherlands, then have easy access to Germany through the Dutch border. But it all went horribly wrong. The Germans in Holland were much stronger than they'd expected, and the paratroopers dropped in Arnhem were quickly defeated. Not only was it a serious disappointment for the Allies, it had an extremely demoralizing effect on the people of The Netherlands.*

Of course, I never hear news of Holland that I don't think of Anya and her family. It's hard to believe it's already been four years since I last heard from her. I sure hope she's okay.

Something really bizarre happened today. I remember hearing about "Tokyo Rose"—the Japanese radio doll who attempted to demoralize the troops by propaganda. So today we were told that "Lord Haw Haw," the German's answer to Tokyo Rose, announced that our ship, the Queen Elizabeth, had been sunk by German subs and all hands were lost at sea! We had a good laugh over that one as we sailed along. We're told the QE is more than capable of outrunning any subs, so we're not sweating it.

I keep wondering what it'll be like to be in actual combat. Training can only take you so far. Sometimes I get a little queasy thinking about being up in the sky, dodging the Luftwaffe fighters. I'm not too anxious to fly through all that flak they've told us about. Then I remember why I'm here and all I can think about is swinging up into the cockpit of our own Fort.

On December 1, the *Queen Elizabeth* docked at Greenock, Scotland up the Firth of the Forth.

"Well, which is it? The fifth or the fourth?" Sully teased as they walked down the gangplank.

"No, it's a 'firth'," Pendergrass answered, pointing up at the majestic peaks surrounding them. "It's what the Scots call these inlets in the mountains."

"Yeah? So why don't they just call 'em inlets?"

"Because they're Scots. They can call them whatever they like."

"Yeah? So?"

"Listen up, men," Anderson interrupted. "We'll grab a ride on one of these troop trucks to the train station. From there, we'll board a train for a short trip to Warrington to the reassignment station."

Franconi moaned. "You've gotta love the Army. They can't just send us where we're going. We have to make twenty stops before we get there."

"At this rate, we won't get our birds up in the air until the day after the war ends," Jimmy whined. "All those months of training for nothing."

"Don't worry, Jimmy," Dal said. "We've called Roosevelt and asked him to keep the war going long enough so you'll get your chance."

"Called FDR, did you? Did you ask if Eleanor was there? I heard you've got a crush on her." He grabbed Dal's hat off his head.

"Nice one, Jimmy," the tail gunner quipped. "Now give me my hat back or I'll call your mother."

"Over here, men."

When they got to Warrington, they were assigned to the 390th Bomb Group housed at Framlingham near Ipswich, which was clear across the British Isles. The next morning, they boarded yet another train for a day long journey which put them in Ipswich in the early evening. When they arrived, the town was under total blackout conditions. Danny immediately felt a chill that had nothing to do with the cold, damp British weather or the mud squishing beneath their boots.

This is a war zone. We're finally in it.

He shrugged off the disconcerting realization as they checked in at the 390th. He couldn't tell much about the base under blackout. Since dinner had already been served on the base, they were told they could get something to eat at the Combat Mess. They made their way to the large Nissen hut walking on a series of planks to avoid the impossible mud puddles.

"They can't be serious," Franconi groaned as they picked up their grub. "Liver sandwiches?"

"What did you expect?" Shorty asked. "Spaghetti and meatballs?"

"Yeah, Franconi," Michaels taunted. "Stop your bellyaching and chow down. A little liver never hurt anybody. In fact, it's good for you. Full of iron."

"Who knows, Franconi," Shorty added, setting his tray next to the Italian, "maybe it'll make a man out of you yet. And not a minute too soon, sweetheart!"

The radio operator pealed back the day-old bread for a good look at the slimly calf liver. "A fine welcome to the 390th, that's all I've got to say."

Half an hour later, the enlisted men were taken to their Quonset huts, and the officers were taken to an empty officers' quarters by a corporal. "This will be your home, gentlemen."

The accommodations weren't fancy, but they'd have to do. He noticed some glowing coals in the small stove at the center of the room and another toward the opposite end of the hut. The room was only slightly less cold than the outdoors, which was miserable. He remembered layering up with all his clothes to sleep back in Wichita Falls, but he had a feeling the stoves wouldn't help much in these frigid English temperatures.

The corporal continued his instructions, pointing directions as he spoke. "Latrine is half a block to the east that way, and the cleansing center is just beyond that on your right."

"Cleansing center?" Danny asked.

"Yes, sir. That's where the showers are. The ablution center—that's where you can shave or wash out socks or whatever—that's behind the cleansing center. But you might want to wait until morning to find those. You'll be given a tour first thing after breakfast. Meanwhile, you can stow your belongings in those lockers there."

Danny noticed the long shelf that ran along the side of the wall of the Nissen, where he assumed he could put some of his belongings. Beneath it, a suspended rod provided a place to hang up his uniform. He would stash the rest of his gear in the footlocker provided below.

"Kind of big for just the four of us, isn't it?" Anderson asked as he dropped his duffel on a bed. "Where's everybody else?"

The corporal made his way back to the door. "The previous occupants were shot down in the Merseburg raid on 30 November. No survivors. Welcome to the 390th, gentlemen."

36

December 1944
Framlingham, England

It was so strange waking up and realizing once again I wasn't in America anymore—though I use the term "waking up" rather loosely. I'm going to have to find a way to make this so-called bed more comfortable. The cross-bar beneath my mattress hits me right at the hip. No way to get comfortable. I finally got up and stuffed some of my dirty clothes up over that bar. But that was nothing compared to the cold. Once the fire went out in the stove, there was no way to get warm. I think I finally just shivered myself to sleep around 3:00 this morning.

After we cleaned up, we made the long, muddy walk over to the Officers Mess for breakfast. I couldn't stomach powdered eggs this morning so I took some black bread and "toasted" it on the tent oven. I covered it with butter and jam and washed it down with several mugs of coffee. It would have to do.

When we finished eating, we were given a tour of the base. In daylight, we could finally see our surroundings. The base is set in a patchwork of fields and densely wooded areas located about seventeen miles northeast of Ipswich, England, and just ten miles from the coast of the North Sea. We were told the entire Eighth Air Force is based in a 40x80 mile strip that stretches north/northeast of London. Like most of the 42 bases of the Eighth Air Force, ours was built in the heart of English farmland. Rumor has it the neighboring farmers had kept their distance when the Americans first set up bases here, offering a cold shoulder to the Yanks for waiting so long to engage in this long-suffering war. They were often heard to say, "The trouble with Yanks is, they're overpaid, oversexed, and over here." But as time passed, I understand they've become more friendly, most likely because of the many overtures made to them—Christmas parties, concerts by visiting celebrities, and the generous gifts offered by our guys at a time of prolonged rationing here.

Like most bases over here, the living areas of each squadron are spaced far apart to lower the risk of a complete wipeout should the enemy send a bombing raid over here. I suppose I should feel comforted by that thought? The three runways form a triangle around which the rest of the base lies.

Each of the four squadrons here has its own site area which is actually nothing more than a quarter-

mile stretch of road lined with Nissen huts.
"Anderson's Crew," as we are now known, is situated
in Site 3, about a half mile from the Communal Site
which houses the mess halls, the Officers' Club, and
the Red Cross Aero Club for the enlisted men. On the
perimeter of the base, we saw the ammunition area,
the bomb drop, sick quarters, sub depots, and a huge
area that houses the technical site. They also took us
to the hut where the parachutes are maintained.
Watching guys pack those chutes gave me the willies.
When you fly, it's inevitable, I suppose—needing one of
those. But I wouldn't mind at all fulfilling my duty over
here without ever needing one.

Each squadron's site includes its own Squadron
Headquarters, an Orderly Room, and the living
quarters for officers and enlisted men, as well as the
latrine and the "cleansing" and "ablution" areas.
(You've got to love the Brits and the interesting words
they come up with.) All in all, it's pretty rustic but for
now, it's home.

Over the next few weeks, Danny did his best to get used to the
living conditions at the base in Framlingham. The cold,
miserable weather didn't help the flying conditions for their
numerous practice runs. Compared to previous training, they
were acutely aware of the fact that this was serious combat
training. Now they were learning how to operate as part of a
Squadron and Group. The elaborate, highly choreographed
formation flying had required hours of grueling practice back
in the states. Now, as they rehearsed in the frigid skies above

England, they flew in sync with other Fortresses of the 390th. Returning to base, they would fly low over the fields of Framlingham, veering left in sequence as each group landed one by one.

When they weren't flying, Danny and the other officers participated in constant briefings about the war effort and the 390th's role in it. The Allies continued to make progress in the Continent (Europe), but the job was far from completion. With its incredible success of daylight bombing raids, the Eighth Air Force had given the Allies a much-needed boost to defeat the German Luftwaffe. But plenty of targets deep in Germany—Nazi refineries, munitions and armament plants, marshaling yards, rail lines and shipyards—continued to dominate the daily mission lists of the Eighth Air Force, including the 390th.

One afternoon, following a particularly bothersome briefing, Danny stepped outside of the Squadron Headquarters into the drizzle. As he stopped under the awning to put on his cap, a fellow officer joined him.

"Makes you wish for those warm summers back home, doesn't it?

"You can say that again. I used to moan and grown about all those stiff winds off Lake Michigan, but I'll never complain again after this."

"From Chicago?"

"Yes, and you?"

"Born and raised in St. Louis. I suppose you could say we were once neighbors." He held out a gloved hand. "Name's Charles Janssen, but my friends call me Charlie."

"Danny McClain," he said, shaking his hand. "Nice to meet you, Charlie."

As they stepped out into the light rain, Janssen asked, "How many missions, McClain?"

"None, yet. Just got here a little over two weeks ago, but we're hoping to get the call any day now."

"Well, you're not far behind us. My crew arrived here on Thanksgiving Day. Flew our first mission on 11 December. Flew our second mission the next day."

"What was it like?"

"Good to get under our belts, that's for sure. I couldn't stop shaking for hours after we got back to base after that first one. I've flown in all kinds of weather, in all kinds of planes, even flew through a monster electrical storm one night back at Las Vegas. But I'm here to tell you, that's all kid stuff compared to this."

"I keep hearing that. Hey, I'm heading over to the Officers' Club. Can I buy you a cup of coffee?"

"Sure thing," Janssen said as he turned toward the Club. "But we all got home in one piece, so I'm thankful for that."

They ordered coffee and found a couple of leather chairs by the fireplace. "What was the worst part of it?" Danny asked. "What do I need to know that they haven't told us yet?"

Janssen took a sip of the hot brew. "Everything they tell you about the flak is true—times ten." He shook his head, looking into the glow of the fire. "What a nightmare. I'll take a fighter any day compared to that stuff."

"Did you encounter fighters as well?"

"Did we ever. Our target was Koblenz, Germany. In fact, Koblenz was our target both days. Picked up our first fighters just after we'd crossed the North Sea. Came out of nowhere. Thankfully we had some Little Friends along for the ride. Don't know what we'd do without those Thunderbolts running cover for us. Watching them swarm all over those Jerries—what a relief."

Danny leaned forward, elbows resting on his knees as he cradled the coffee mug in his hands. "Charlie, how'd you handle the shakes while you were up there? I'm in the right seat and our pilot, Dick Anderson, is the best there is. Still, in the middle of the night, I keep having these dreams about losing it . . . I forget everything I've been taught and I just sit there, unable to function. Drives me nuts, those dreams."

"Well, the good news is, you're not alone. We all fight the fear, one way or another. And the thing is, I never really panicked or had the shakes up there. Wasn't til I got back to base. Funny how that happens, y'know?"

"I guess," Danny answered, not really convinced.

"The hardest part is all this waiting. It gives you too much time to think about all that stuff. Once you get that first mission behind you, it'll make a world of difference. Like I said, we flew our second mission the very next day, and I wasn't near as rattled on that one."

"Good to know."

Janssen set his mug on the side table. "So tell me, which is it, McClain—Cubs or White Sox?"

"What kind of choice is that?" Danny laughed. "The only team in Chicago, of course—the Cubs!"

"Yeah? We're a two-team baseball town as well." He paused, scratching the back of his head. "Remind me again—who won the World Series this year? Was it St. Louis? Or was it St. Louis?"

"Is this where I'm supposed to chuckle?" Danny teased.

Charlie threw his head back, laughing. "Yes, I believe it is. McClain, I have a feeling you and I are gonna be good friends."

37

Framlingham, England

Charlie Janssen was right. The waiting was about to get the best of Danny McClain. The abysmal weather conditions had caused numerous missions to be aborted which set most everyone on base on edge. At this rate, he wondered if they'd ever get off the ground again.

On his way back to his quarters after lunch, Danny dug his gloved hands deep into the pockets of his leather flight jacket. He chewed his gum aggressively, wishing he could shake the worrisome shadow hanging over him. He hadn't been this edgy since his last few days at Northwestern. He'd tried to shake it off, this nagging feeling just beneath the surface, but it wouldn't let him go.

Plus, something was going on with his pilot. Dick Anderson had grown increasingly quiet, which concerned Danny more than he cared to admit. They bunked in the same quarters, they attended the same briefings, they often ate at the same table in the mess hall. But no matter how hard he tried to make conversation, all he got was the bare minimum when he responded. Sure, they were all cranky from being grounded so long. But why weren't they communicating? Danny told himself it was just Dick's way. *Funny, I used to hear Mom say the same thing about Dad's moods. Thankfully, Dick's nothing like Dad. Then again, there's nothing in the manual about a pilot and co-pilot having to be friends . . .*

"Hey, Danny!" Charlie hollered, waking Danny from his thoughts. "We're going into town for a while. Come with us."

He looked up just as his friend and some of his fellow officers poured out of their quarters. "Where you headed?"

"Who knows? C'mon. You got something better to do?"

Danny picked up his pace. "Well, there's that letter I owe Rita Hayworth, but I suppose it can wait."

A barrage of teasing and laughter filled the air as he joined them and continued as they loaded a troop truck headed for Framlingham. They huddled as the wind whipped through the back of the truck, its tarp cover doing little to buffet the chilly air. They almost lost Charlie's navigator when the truck hit a deep hole in the mud-filled road, but no one seemed to mind the bumpy ride. A few miles down the road they passed an enormous castle sitting high on a hill overlooking the town. Danny remembered seeing it from the air on their many practice runs—a massive circle of walls and chimneys, ringed around an empty, vacant area.

"Framlingham Castle, right?" someone asked.

"Right so, right so," answered a co-pilot named Banks in a pitiful attempt at an English accent. "You see, the castle dates all the way back to the seventh century when it was founded by some Saxon king. But early in the twelfth century, Lord Hugh leBigod built a great and strong castle—"

"By god, I think he built it!" someone quipped.

"As I was saying," Banks continued, "the strong castle which was later rebuilt by Roger leBigod—"

"By god—*another* by god?"

"Yes, mate, Roger leBigod, Earl of Norfolk. But the history of the castle doesn't get really interesting until the reign of Henry the Eighth when—"

"By god, there's now a Henry?" someone else teased.

"Banks, pipe down, will you?" Charlie shouted. "You're reminding me of my history teacher back in St. Louis. Although I must say, you're much better looking than she was."

"I was only trying to give you chaps a lay of the land where we've made our temporary home," Banks pleaded, still feigning the accent. "We've basically butted our way in, leveled their farmhouses and fields, then rumbled their walls and shattered their fine china with the roar of our planes. The least we can do is respect their long and colorful history."

"Well said! Well said!" they all mocked, shouting and clapping.

"Now stuff a sock in it, Banks!"

As the walls of the castle disappeared in the truck's cloud of exhaust, the vehicle pulled into the quaint village town of Framlingham. A light snow had just begun to fall. In any other setting, it would be a beautiful place to visit, Danny thought. The steep cobblestone roofs of the shops and homes made for a picturesque setting, even in the wintry weather. People rushed about, their coats wrapped tightly around them, their heads covered against the blustery wind.

All of a sudden the truck lurched to a stop, tossing them all forward.

"I guess this is where we get out," someone joked.

"Cherry-oh!" Banks teased, hopping down to the soggy road.

"Right this way, gentlemen," Charlie added, pointing as he jumped down. "Quincy's Pub is just across the road there."

Danny shook his head. He'd had a feeling they'd end up in one of the many pubs he'd heard about here. Drinking seemed to be the favorite past time both on and off base, so he wasn't surprised a trip into town would include a pint or two. Or three.

It struck him as funny that things weren't really so different back home at Northwestern. Weekends on campus meant fraternity parties, dorm parties, and dance parties. Come to think of it, just about any excuse was good enough for a party. Between work and studies, he'd never been a part of those occasions. Well, except for a couple of dances he and Beverly crashed.

That would be Mrs. Ronnie Wentworth now.

"McClain! Over here!" Charlie called.

He followed the guys through the crowded, smoke-filled room to a rustic table in the corner. A young woman with a white apron tied around her waist approached their table.

"What'll it be, Yanks?"

"Aye, and aren't you a lovely sight for sore eyes," Banks said, this time in a messy Irish brogue. A round of groans cut him off.

"Not again, Banks," the navigator named Whitlow said, redirecting his attention to the waitress. "Hello, sweetheart. How about you bring us all a couple pints to start."

"I'd be more than happy to, Yank. But let's get one thing straight. I'm not your sweetheart. I'm the owner's daughter. See my Da over there? Yes, that's him. The one with the shotgun on the wall behind him? So stay as long as you like, drink as much as you can, be don't be calling me your sweetheart."

As she turned to go, they all stood and applauded, cheering madly as Whitlow shook his head in defeat.

"Whitlow, how is that you've already crashed and burned, and you haven't flown a mission yet?" a guy named Reid asked.

"You haven't flown a mission yet?" Danny asked.

"No, we've been aborted three times because of this stupid weather," the rascally kid said. "I'm not on Janssen's crew. I'm on Feeney's Crew. We've been waiting for weeks. Finally got our call Sunday, and three times they've scrubbed our missions before we got off the ground. I've gotta tell ya, it's making me a little crazy."

"Yeah?" Charlie said. "Well, don't be messin' with the owner's daughter, okay? We came to have fun, not to get our heads blown off."

The waitress returned with a tray full of dark brews in thick glass steins. She set them down on the table, sloshing foam here and there. "Anything else, gentlemen?"

"Would it be too much to ask your name?" Banks asked, without a trace of any accent.

"Not at all. My name is Sophie."

Danny opened his mouth, then clamped it shut.

"Was there something you wanted to say?" she asked.

He felt his face heating. "It's a lovely name. That's all."

"Well, thank you. Have a nice time, Yanks. I'll check back in a bit to check for refills."

"Thanks, Sophie," Charlie said with a wink. As she moved to another table, he turned to Danny. "What was that all about?"

He couldn't help his grin. "Nothing. Just the name of, uh—well, just reminded me of someone back home."

Charlie's eyebrows arched. "Is that so? Someone special?"

Danny laughed. "You could say that."

Charlie raised his glass. "To Sophie!"

They all raised their glasses. "To Sophie!"

The waitress looked over her shoulder, tossing them a smile as she shook her head.

As the snow began to fill the corners of the pub's windows, the guys spent the rest of the afternoon talking, drinking, singing, and drinking a little more. Danny sipped the dark ale slowly, careful not to overdo it. He'd never cared for the taste of beer, but something about the surroundings here prodded him to overcome all that. It seemed to defuse the stress of the last few weeks. After downing his second pint, he excused himself to the restroom. He was a bit woozy when he first stood up, but took his time, careful to walk as normally as possible. When he returned, the pub owner waved him over to the bar.

"Yes, sir?"

The weathered face of the old man suddenly warmed

with a smile. "I like that. A Yank with manners. You must be from a good family, son."

Danny sat on a stool at the bar. "Yes, sir, I am. And any manners I may have, you can thank my mother."

"I expect she's a fine woman. Raised a boy to respect his elders. Yes, a fine woman indeed."

"You had a question?" Danny asked, leaning his elbows on the worn oak bar.

"Question? Oh—yes. I wanted to ask where you're from. I like to know where our boys come from, you see."

"From Chicago, Illinois, sir. That's in the United States."

He laughed. "That much I got from the uniform. And how long have you been a guest in Framlingham?"

"Arrived three weeks ago. Haven't flown a mission yet, but happy to be here, sir."

The pub owner wiped off a section of the bar. "We don't thank you boys enough for what you're doing. A lot of folks around here—well, they have their reasons and I'll not fault them for it. But I want to thank you for your service. For leaving your home and coming to this cold, wet country so far from home."

"Thank you, sir. I appreciate that."

"My son is with the RAF. We . . . well, my son and I don't get along much these days. Which is why he doesn't often come to visit. But I'm proud of my boy. I'm proud of all of you. You're all so young." His eyes glistened. "So young. I see boys like you come in here and then some . . . well, some I never see again." He blinked several times then took a deep breath. "Well now, you didn't come in here to watch an old man cry. Go." He waved his hand. "Go back and join your friends."

"There you are. We wondered what happened to you."
Charlie slid onto the bar stool next to his.

"I was just having a nice chat here with—"

"Quincy. Patrick Quincy." He shook both their hands.

"With Patrick Quincy," Danny finished.

"Hit us with a couple more, Mr. Quincy," Charlie said.
"You have a very lovely daughter, sir."

Quincy's face tightened. "I do, but what is that to you?"

Charlie raised his hands. "No! I meant no disrespect! I
was merely paying you a compliment, I assure you. She
knows how to handle my buddies over there, and she's got a
smart head on her shoulders. I meant only to compliment
her—and you for raising her, sir."

Quincy set the two glasses on the bar. "Then I shall take
the compliment and thank you. She is her mother's daughter.
The spitting image of my Anna, God rest her soul."

"Anna?" Danny said after a rather large gulp of ale, the
foam still on his lip.

"Yes, Anna. Died three years ago Christmas day.
Sweetest woman on the face of God's green earth."

A group of enlisted men blew into the room, raising the
noise level considerably. Quincy made his way toward them,
leaving Danny and Charlie at the bar.

"So there's a Sophie *and* an Anna?" Charlie asked. "I
noticed your face light up when the old guy spoke of his late
wife."

Danny took another long drink, stalling for time. He
didn't realize he'd been so transparent.

"So?"

"No, there's no Anna."

"My mistake."

"There is, however, an *Anya*."

"Now we're getting somewhere. Tell me about your Anya."

"She's not *my* Anya. It's not like that at all."

And yet, Danny couldn't stop talking about the Dutch girl who used to write him. The feisty preacher's kid who couldn't stay out of trouble. The heartbroken young girl whose brother drowned while trying to save a child who'd fallen through the ice. An angry young woman who hated what Hitler and his Nazis were doing to the nearby countries in Europe. The troubled friend he'd grown to care deeply about. The one whose letters he couldn't wait to read—until the letters stopped coming when Holland also fell beneath the German jackboot.

"You're crazy about her, aren't you?"

Danny blinked at the question. "What?"

"Danny, you've got tears spilling into your ale. She's obviously more than just a friend, this Anya you've been gushing about for the last half hour."

He quickly dashed his wrist against his cheeks, embarrassed by the tears and puzzled by the fact he had not realized he'd been crying. He blew out a weary sigh. "I've had too much to drink. That's all."

Charlie draped his arm over Danny's shoulder. "It's not a sin to get choked up, Danny. And it's nothing to be ashamed of—caring for someone like your Anya. She sounds like the kind of girl that gets deep inside a guy's heart and won't let go." He patted Danny's chest for emphasis.

"Look, you don't understand. It's not like that. I've never even met the girl!"

"Sure you have! Hundreds of times on every page she ever wrote you. You don't have to see someone face to face to know them."

He waved Charlie off, anxious to change the subject.

"And tell me about Sophie. When our waitress said her name, your eyes got all big like a lovesick puppy."

Danny couldn't help it. He threw his head back and laughed hard.

"What's so funny?"

"Ah, nothing," he said, still chuckling. "An inside joke, I guess you could say."

"Yeah? C'mon, out with it. This Sophie—is she back home in the states?"

"She sure is."

"And by that forlorn and sappy look on your face, I'd say she's near and dear to your heart," Charlie said, warming up to the story.

"That she is. A loyal and faithful girl who can't *wait* for me to get back home."

"So is she pretty? What does she look like?"

"Oh, she's a real looker, I can tell you that much."

"Got a picture?"

Danny snorted then composed himself. "No, not on me. But take my word for it, she's a real sweetheart."

Charlie leaned closer. "And I bet she's a good kisser, eh?"

Danny fought it, forcing himself not to laugh. He leaned over to whisper near Charlie's ear. "Well, let's just say she keeps me warm at night." He waggled his brows for added effect.

Charlie patted him on the back. "Now that's what I'm talking about!"

Danny held up his hand. "But don't get me wrong—she's a good girl, my Sophie."

Charlie waited for more.

"Yes, sir, my sweet Sophie is one in a million."

"That's it, then!"

"That's what then?"

"Tell Anderson you want to name your Fort *Sweet Sophie*. You said he didn't care about naming the plane, and since you're next in line, that leaves it up to you, right? So name your plane *Sweet Sophie*—it's perfect! Named after your girl."

"Oh, well, I don't know, Charlie. She's not really—"

"Nonsense. It's perfect! And just think of how much that will mean to her once she hears?"

Danny dropped his head and laughed again. How crazy was this? Then again, he had to admit he liked the sound of it. And if the crew thought he had a girl back home named Sophie, well, no one had to know Sophie was a dog, right?

He slapped his palms on the counter. "You're right, Charlie. It's perfect!"

Somewhere a glass smashed on the brick floor followed by a raucous outburst by the American patrons.

"My friends! My friends!" shouted one of the enlisted men. Danny noted the sergeant stripes on the jacket of the stocky American as he jumped up on the hearth. "My friends! My friends! I beg for your attention for just one moment!"

The noise level diminished, but only slightly.

"I apologize for the broken glass. I'll gladly pay for it, Mr. Quincy. But today is a celebration. Today, I—Sergeant Cosmos Francis Benedetto from the great state of New

Jersey—along with all my friends from Ordnance Division of the 570th—am here to celebrate my twenty-first birthday!"

The room erupted again in cheers and the *thunk-thunk-thunk* of empty pints pounded on tables.

"Thank you! Thank you, my friends! And because it's my birthday—the next round's on me!"

Again the room burst into cheers.

"My friends! My friends! There's just one more thing!"

"'My-friends-my-friends,'" Charlie mocked. "If he says that one more time, I'm gonna deck him."

"The next round's on me BUT—"

"No buts! Please no buts!"

"—only after you give me a moment more to share something near and dear to my heart."

"Oh, please no."

"Shut up and buy the ale!"

"Let the guy speak! It's his birthday!"

"Yeah? Well, maybe it's MY birthday!"

"Yeah? Says who?"

"Says me, you lunkhead!"

The smack of fist hitting cheekbone sounded just before the room erupted in chaos.

"Uh oh, time to go," Charlie said as he stood and grabbed Danny by the arm. He stopped, dug out a wad of bills from his pocket and tucked them in the pub owner's shirt pocket. "I'll be back tomorrow if this doesn't cover our bill, Mr. Quincy."

As jabs and kicks and shouts and utter bedlam spread through the pub, Charlie, Danny, and their friends hurried out into the snow-covered night.

"Taxi!" Whitlow yelled, his hand raised as he dissolved into a fit of giggling.

"Whit, do you see a single vehicle anywhere?" Banks chided. "It's not like we're in Times Square."

"This way, gentlemen," Charlie called.

Two blocks down around the corner they found a couple of troop trucks. Charlie greased the palm of one of the drivers and off they went, accompanied by a bawdy version of "Jingle Bells."

When the song ended, they rode in silence—except for the hacking cough of the truck's engine.

Then, out of the quiet wintry night, a voice called out . . .

"My friends! My friends!"

"SHUT UP, BANKS!"

38

23 December 1944

Framlingham, England

The walls of the officers' quarters swirled along with the rhythmic pounding inside Danny's head. And he hadn't even lifted his head off the pillow yet.

"Looks like someone had a good time last night," Pendergrass teased as he buttoned his uniform shirt. "One too many 'Jingle Bells' last night, McClain?"

Something about that sounded vaguely familiar, but Danny ignored the comment. "What time is it?"

"Oh-seven-hundred. Better get that sled of yours out of bed if you want some of those tasty gray eggs."

His stomach roiled at the thought. "No thanks." He sat up but kept his eyes closed, hoping the room would stop spinning. *How do guys do this day after day?*

It took longer than usual to dress and bundle up, and by the time he stepped out of his quarters, he finally pitched his cookies.

I'm never gonna make it through this day.

But somehow he managed. He nursed several cups of strong coffee in the Officers' Mess where he'd found Charlie, Banks, and Whitlow scarfing up full trays of bacon, eggs, and toast. The smell alone was enough to send him running back outside.

"How can you eat? Am I the only one who's paying for last night's little adventure?"

Charlie looked around the table. "Apparently so. Course, most of us are seasoned veterans when it comes to the pints. Right?"

"Here here!" Banks said, spreading grape jelly on his toast. "Care for a shingle, mate?"

Danny held up a palm. "No thanks."

Charlie slapped him on his back. "You'll be okay, rookie. You just need more practice."

"I don't think so, but thanks for the advice."

As the others left, he yawned and made a mental note to stay far away from the pubs. Then he remembered the kindness of Patrick Quincy and his daughter's assertive spunk. He hoped the place wasn't a disaster after the brawl that ensued. Then he amended his mental note, allowing himself a return to Quincy's but only for tea and a sandwich.

The snow must have fallen most of the night, piling up a good four or five inches. He thought of the snows back home and all those sidewalks and driveways he'd shoveled over the years. Suddenly, a wave of homesickness blanketed him deeper than he'd ever experienced. *Must be this hangover. Who in their right mind misses Chicago in the winter?*

Danny headed over to the Officers' Club hoping to find

the latest issue of *Stars and Stripes.* With a fresh cup of coffee and a comfortable chair near the fireplace, he settled in to catch up on the latest war news. The headlines covered Hitler's grand attack known as the Ardennes Offensive—though nicknamed "The Battle of the Bulge" by the Allies. The story detailed Hitler's attempt to break up the alliance of Britain, France, and America with a massive, surprise attack on the Allied front lines. The Führer ignored the fact that his own military was in retreat, depleted of supplies and manpower following D-Day. But with bad weather grounding the superior Allied air power, he commanded his forces to bomb the Allies' front line followed by a ferocious armored attack.

With a panzer army of 970 tanks and armored assault guns, along with more than 300,000 troops, the four German armies rolled into Ardennes before sunrise on 16 December, catching the Allies there totally by surprise. Once again, Hitler ignored an important fact: an armored attack of this magnitude would require huge quantities of fuel to keep those tanks moving. And fuel was in short supply for the Germans, thanks to the constant Allied bombing runs over German fuel plants. Already, the tide had turned as the Allies fought back. The paper lauded the efforts of the Eighth Air Force saying, "Their dedication and perseverance under the worst imaginable conditions, helped cut Hitler's legs right out from under him."

Just then Charlie popped his head in the door of the Officers' Club. "I'm headed into town. Want to join me?"

"What?"

"I said, I'm heading into town. I want to stop by and

make sure old man Quincy survived the brawl last night."

"That's probably a good idea. But I'll take a pass. I'm afraid one whiff of ale would send me throwing my guts up again."

"You're probably right. Well, I'll be back in a while. Try to stay out of trouble, okay?"

"Will do."

Danny decided to walk over to the Post Exchange and see if he had mail. He'd only received one V-Mail from home so far, but kept hoping for more. He pulled his gloves on as he headed back outside. The snow had stopped and the skies looked as if they might actually clear. He wondered what the odds were that his crew would finally be put on alert to fly tomorrow. He zipped his jacket, chilled by the breeze but kept walking. He needed some fresh air to clear his head. As he approached the Post Exchange, he realized how much he was hoping for a card or letter from back home.

"Yes, sir. Here you go," the staff sergeant said, handing the familiar V-Mail envelope to him.

Danny recognized his brother's awful handwriting and couldn't help smiling. He tore open the envelope and began to read.

Dear Danny,

Sure was strange having Thanksgiving dinner without you yesterday. Mom put on quite a spread, as usual. I'm sure it was nothing compared to the grub they serve you over there. Ha ha. I had an extra slice of pumpkin pie in your honor. You're welcome.

Last we heard you were heading over to the EOT

on the Queen Elizabeth. Bet that was some ride. By now you've had a chance to get your feet wet (so to speak). It's probably real different than my experience, with you enlisting during a war and all. Probably scary at times. We're all praying for you. Millie and I pray together every night and always ask God to keep an eye on you. Yeah, I know—hard to picture me a praying sort of guy, right? That's what marriage will do to you.

Speaking of marriage, I wanted to let you know you'll be an uncle next summer! We just found out and surprised the folks with the good news yesterday. Made for a real nice Thanksgiving. Wish you could have been here.

Dad's doing okay. He has his days, but more good than bad lately. He's letting me take over more of the theater management, and I'm really enjoying that. Right now we keep filling seats with "Going My Way," Bing Crosby's latest film. It's not exactly my cup of tea, but it sells tickets. You'd have loved "Double Indemnity" with Barbara Stanwyck and Fred McMurray. A real steamer. Maybe they'll show it on your base sometime. But the one I can't wait to see is "Thirty Seconds Over Tokyo" about the Doolittle Raid. It just released, but we haven't gotten it yet.

Mom's good. Real happy about having a grandbaby. She talks about you all the time. She and Sophie have these ongoing conversations. It's pretty funny. You'd get a real hoot out of it. We're all doing our best to keep Sophie company, but she still prefers to nap on your bed.

Well, Danny, that's all for now. Take care of yourself. We're all praying this war ends real soon so you can come back home.

Love,

Joey

Danny reread the letter two more times before refolding it and tucking it in his jacket pocket. He headed back outside with his thoughts thousands of miles away. What he would give to be back home right now, away from all this tedious waiting. Away from the knot of fear that had camped out in his gut. Away from all these strangers.

He took a deep breath, continuing down the slushy road. A Red Cross Clubmobile rolled up to Hangar #2 where several Red Cross Girls got out and made their way into the hangar. Danny remembered the Christmas party planned for the local children that evening. For lack of anything better to do, he decided to check it out. As he walked in, he was surprised how nice the place looked with strings of Christmas lights hung here and there, tables set with pine branches and lots of big red bows. A bandstand was set up at the front as it usually was for the regular Saturday night dances. A few of the musicians ran through scales, occasionally playing a couple bars of a familiar carol.

The room bustled with activity. The Red Cross Girls had obviously dragged a lot of the guys into helping—not that it took much dragging. Hilda Edwards and her Red Cross Girls took the lead in these events, and they had never had trouble persuading the men to help.

"Lieutenant, could you give me a hand?"

Danny noticed the pretty redhead looking his way but assumed she was talking to someone else. He looked behind him and finding no one, turned back around. "Me?"

"Yes, you. We need to get all these boxes here moved over to that table in the back. Then once Santa's bag shows up, we'll stuff them inside."

Danny joined her beside the stack of boxes, each about the size of a shoebox, and following her lead, picked up as many as he could. "Are these for the kids, Miss . . .?"

"Miss Wells, and yes, these are the kids' gift boxes. We load them up with all the goodies you guys have contributed—mostly rationed candy and a few things sent from home. The kids have a ball opening them."

Danny followed her across the room. "Ah, that explains it. Our tail gunner has been bugging us for days, rounding up all kinds of goodies 'for the kids' or so he said. I have to admit, I wondered if he was stashing most of it for himself, but from the looks of all this, I'd say he came through for you."

She set her boxes on the decorated table. "What's his name?"

"That would be Dal Nicholson, ma'am. Nice kid, talks with a real southern accent even though he's from my home state of Illinois."

"I know Dal. He's wonderful! All our girls love him. He's been such a great help to us this last week." She looked around the busy room. "In fact, he was here just a few minutes ago helping us put up the tree. It was late arriving because of the weather, but I think we'll have it decorated in time. Quite a resourceful one, that Dal."

Danny followed her back for more boxes. "Yes, ma'am, that would sure enough be Dal."

"You said you're from Illinois, Lieutenant?"

"Chicago, born and raised. How about you?"

"Tallahassee, Florida."

"Whoa—from Tallahassee to Framlingham. You must have taken a wrong turn somewhere to end up all the way over here."

"Not at all. It's actually quite an honor to be selected as a Red Cross Girl. Lots of girls apply, but they're rather selective about who they send over here. They require us to be single, at least twenty-five years old, and we also have to be college graduates. Though I have to admit I often wonder how much my degree really helps when I'm up to my elbows in donut batter."

Danny chuckled. "Clearly it helps. We all love those donuts." *What a stupid thing to say. Smooth. Really smooth.* "So, what's it like, being over here and outnumbered like a thousand to one? Ever get tired of all the whistles?" He felt his face warm and wondered why he couldn't seem to keep his mouth shut.

"Oh, we go through some rather intensive training that covers all that. In fact, that's a big part of why we're dressed in these military-style uniforms. It sends a message. We're here to boost morale for our boys, but we know where to draw the line." She smiled at him as they both gathered more boxes in their arms.

Danny had seen many of the Red Cross Girls on base, but he'd never given them much thought. He'd noticed the way the guys made a big fuss over these American girls, always circling them as soon as one of the Clubmobiles drove up. He just wasn't the kind of guy who cared to elbow his way through a crowd of guys hoping to have a couple minutes of conversation with a pretty girl. Still, he'd heard plenty of the other guys talk about how nice it was to have someone from back home to talk to.

"But I'll be honest. I'd never really thought about joining the Red Cross while I was in college. But after my brother survived Pearl Harbor, I—"

"He did? My brother was on the *Oklahoma*."

She stopped, her face ashen. "Oh, Lieutenant—I'm so sorry."

"What? Oh—no! No, he's fine. I mean, Joey was injured pretty bad. Burned over fifty percent of his body, but he's okay now. In fact, I just found out he and his wife are going to have a baby. "

She set down the stack of boxes on the table and quickly put her hand to her chest. "Oh, thank goodness. For a minute I thought—well, it doesn't matter what I thought. I'm just glad he's okay."

"Your brother survived Pearl too?"

"Yes. He had a rough time of it, but he'll be fine. I mean, someday he'll probably be all right. It really messed up his head, if you know what I mean."

"I do. Some of the things Joey told me . . . well, it's a wonder any of them came out of that in one piece."

"After Richey came home, I just couldn't stop thinking about all those wonderful nurses and Red Cross people who were so good to him over there. And that's when I made up my mind to do my part, so I joined the Red Cross."

Danny followed her along with another stack of boxes. "He must be real proud."

"I guess he is. As much as he can be."

"Lieutenant McClain!"

Danny turned to see Dal Nicholson walking in with several of the girls, a huge tangle of Christmas lights in his hands and an even bigger smile on his face.

"Hi, Dal. Looks like you've got quite a mess there."

"Yes, sir, but I've got plenty of help, as you can see. Real nice of you to help out, sir."

"I could say the same for you."

"Yes, sir, you sure could."

"Come along, Dal," a tall blonde said, tugging at his sleeve. "Let's string these out and see if we can untangle them."

He gave Danny his trademark smile with a wink, then followed the girls to a spot in the corner of the room.

"Will you be joining us for the party tonight, Lieutenant?"

"Sure, Miss Wells. I wouldn't miss it. But please, call me Danny."

"Danny it is. Then you must call me Sally."

"Sally it is."

Later that evening, when Danny returned to the hangar, the room was filled to capacity with the local children and their parents. The band played Christmas carols, the lights twinkled in the soft light, and everywhere he looked, he saw smiling kids.

"Danny!"

He turned to find Charlie walking his way, surprised to find him holding hands with a rather striking female.

"You remember Sophie, don't you?"

"Sophie? Sophie! I'm sorry, I didn't recognize you—I mean without the apron and all." He couldn't believe it was the same girl. Her auburn hair curled just below her shoulders, a hint of make-up on her pretty face, and a deep blue dress. No wonder he hadn't recognized her.

"I suppose I could have worn my apron," she said, smiling demurely, "but I was afraid they might put me to work. And to be honest, I needed a night off."

Danny turned toward Charlie who beamed from ear to ear. "And I suppose your trip into town had nothing to do with this?"

"What? Oh, well, I fully intended to go see Sophie's father to make sure his place wasn't in complete ruins after last night."

"Which, of course, it wasn't," Sophie added. "Da never lets things get out of hand. Right after you all left, he fired off a warning shot, and they all scampered into the night like so many field mice."

Charlie slipped his arm casually around her slender waist. "When I stopped in to see him this afternoon and asked how it went, he didn't say a word. Just pointed up to the ceiling. That's when I noticed it was full of bullet holes."

"Da knows how to keep order."

Danny tried to picture the scenario. He turned his gaze back to Charlie. "Then Sophie just happened to be there and you just happened to ask her to the party tonight?"

Sophie put a hand on her hip. "I'll have you know a proper English lady doesn't accept a request for a date the day of. It's considered poor taste. Lieutenant Janssen invited me half-way through the evening last night. That would be about the time you and Da were having a bit of a chat."

He smiled at them. "Well, then. Happy to do my part."

The band started quietly playing "Here Comes Santa Claus" just as Colonel Moller stepped to the microphone. "Ladies and gentlemen, boys and girls—just moments ago, a whole herd of reindeer landed on the roof of the hangar, and rumor has it Santa is on his way. In fact, there he is now! Boys and girls, let's give a great big welcome to jolly old St. Nick!"

The kids squealed and rushed closer as Santa and his helpers made their way to the platform.

"Here, Danny, let me hold your punch glass so you can join the other children."

"Very funny, Charlie."

A few more announcements were made then the children lined up with their parents in tow, waiting for their turn to see Santa and receive a gift box from the man in red. Danny watched the excitement on the faces of the local children as Santa's helpers handed them wrapped boxes out of his big red bag—the same boxes he and Sally Wells had loaded into the bag earlier that afternoon. That's when he realized the bouncing red curls of one of Santa's helpers. In a red dress trimmed with white fur and a hat like Santa's sitting jauntily on her head, Sally seemed to be having as much fun as the kids around her.

As the music played on, Danny drifted around the room making his way closer to the front while watching clusters of little ones as they opened their presents. They all seemed delighted with the boxes filled with candy and toys, coloring books and crayons, socks and knitted gloves.

A young boy held up an orange. "Mummy, what is it?"

"Oh, it's a very special treat, William. It's a fruit called an orange. Would you like me to peel it for you so you can have a taste?"

"No, I want to save it for Christmas day."

Danny smiled, remembering the joy of saving special presents for the big day when he was a kid. *But an orange?* Then he realized the child, no more than four or five years of age, would never have known what it was like to live in a world not dominated by war and rationing. *No wonder the tyke had no idea what an orange was.* He looked up just as Santa's redhead helper approached him.

"Lieutenant McClain, you came!"

"I promised I would. You look quite festive, Miss Wells."

"Ah, this old thing? Just a little something I dug out of my closet."

"Somehow I doubt that. But you look—well, you look lovely tonight." Something flitted through her eyes just before she looked away. He quickly changed the subject. "It looks as though the kids are enjoying their presents."

"I never get tired of these parties, especially seeing their faces light up when Santa comes in. And every single one of them says a very polite 'thank you' to him. It always amazes me how grateful they are."

"I'd imagine they're extremely grateful under the circumstances. Would you like some punch?"

"Yes, that would be nice."

He extended his hand, gesturing for her to go first as they made their way to the refreshment table. He filled a glass for her then one for himself.

"Cheers," he said, raising his glass for a toast.

"Cheers," she mumbled, looking away again while taking a sip, her hand slightly trembling.

"I'm sorry," he began, "Have I said something to offend you? I can't help but notice there's something—"

"No, Lieutenant. I—"

"It's Danny, remember?"

She took another sip from her glass then set it back on the table. "Danny, I think I should tell you . . . that is, I probably should have told you earlier that I . . . you see, I'm engaged. And I wouldn't want to give you the wrong impression or lead you on." She looked down at her hands which she'd clasped together.

Danny studied her for a moment. She was definitely attractive. Actually, she was quite beautiful. And there was no question that he'd hoped to see her tonight. It had been a long time since he'd been around a woman or even entertained the thought of starting something again.

Then another thought crossed his mind. He reached out and took hold of both of her hands, giving them a squeeze. "Thank you."

"What? I don't understand."

"Thank you for being honest with me. But thank you even more for being faithful to that lucky guy who wants to marry you." He squeezed her hands again then let them go.

She smiled, releasing a long breath. "Oh, yes. Well, thank you. But, if you don't mind my asking, why would you say such a thing? Why thank me?"

He nodded for her to go ahead of him, pointing her toward the chairs around the outer perimeter of the room. As soon as they sat down, he took a minute, trying to figure out how to convey what he was thinking.

Finally he just looked up at her and blurted it out. "Because I was once in love with someone. I loved her, and I wanted to marry her, then we were apart for a few months one summer, and she got engaged to someone else."

"Oh, I see. Goodness, that must have been horrible."

"It was. Pretty much ruined my sophomore year at college, that's for sure. I'd never really dated much, so I guess I just wasn't 'up to par' on these things. I just assumed she was as crazy about me as I was about her." He stopped, nervously flicking his finger against the crease in his slacks. "I'm rambling and telling you a lot more than you need to know."

"Not at all, Danny. Remember this afternoon when I told you we go through a lot of extensive training? We learn all about being good listeners. I know I kind of joked about them teaching us where to draw the line when it comes to men making advances, but more than anything, the reason we're here is to be like that girl next door back home. Just someone to talk to. So please, go on. Your girlfriend got engaged to someone else. That must have been awful for you. "

He turned to face her. "It was. I'd never been so shocked in all my life. But the thing is, when you told me a minute ago that you were engaged, I wanted to hug you—and not for the reason you might think, but because you let me know you're spoken for. I really appreciate that. Instead of flirting or letting me think I could ask you out, you remained faithful to your fiancé." He ran his hand through his hair. "All I'm trying to say is, well, it's mighty refreshing to meet a girl who doesn't lead a guy on."

She pulled off her Santa hat and laughed. "Oh, thank goodness. I was afraid I'd hurt you or—"

"Not at all, Sally. In my own unbelievably *pathetic* way, I was just trying to say thanks."

"Well then, you're welcome. But I should probably be thanking you instead. You wouldn't believe how many guys aren't distracted at all when I tell them I'm engaged. In fact, if anything it seems to encourage them to try harder."

He shook his head. "Some guys have all the nerve."

"Okay, Lieutenant, you can cut the sarcasm." She stood up and placed the Santa hat back on her head. "I'm glad we had this talk."

"Me too. And I hope we can be friends. I'm running low on those right now."

"I'd love that. I really would. Well, I need to get back. See you around?"

"Absolutely."

39

29 December 1944

Framlingham, England

"Lieutenant McClain? Mission today, sir. Time is 0300. Rise and shine."

Danny felt the nudge on his shoulder and covered his eyes against the glare of a flashlight shining in his face. "Thank you, Corporal."

"Have a safe flight, sir."

He sat up, wiping the sleep from his eyes. He hadn't slept well. In fact, the orderly's wake up call had startled him. He heard the call repeated down the rows as the others who would be flying today were awakened, but assumed he was dreaming.

The sleep fog finally cleared as Danny realized the significance of this day. *First mission today. Oh, Lord, it's finally happening.* Butterflies danced through his gut.

He quickly dressed, gathered his shaving gear, threw on his coat, and trudged out the door with the others. The frigid air scattered away the last trace of sleepiness as he followed the others to the ablution center. How many times had they been reminded about the importance of a close shave on flight mornings? *In order for the oxygen mask to fit tightly and securely around your mouth, an extra close shave is imperative on flight days.*

After a quick stop back in his quarters, he hopped on the six-by-six truck with the others for a trip to Combat Mess. Flight crews were served real eggs instead of powdered on the day of their missions, along with ham, corned beef, pancakes, and lots of other options they didn't normally have. Danny wasn't the least bit hungry, but he knew it could be ten, maybe twelve hours before he'd have a chance to eat again. He tried to get down what he could, washing it down with strong coffee. He sat with Anderson and Pendergrass, and wondered if they were as nervous as he was. The room felt strangely surreal. The cigarette haze was nothing unusual, but the peculiar silence bugged him—silence occasionally interrupted by those acting out their nerves with horse play.

As Danny drained his second cup on his way out, Charlie caught up with him.

"Morning, McClain. How're you holding up?"

"So far, so good."

Charlie patted him on the back. "You'll do great today. Don't worry about a thing. Besides, I'll be keeping an eye on you, okay?"

"Yeah, you've got nothing better to do than watch out for the green horns at the back of the formation."

"That's what auto-pilot is for. Didn't they tell you?"

"Good to know."

A few minutes later they were back on the truck, whisked away to the Briefing Room located near the flight line. Once they filed in and took a seat on the long hard benches, Danny's jitters kicked into double-time. Even the smells in the room got to him—aftershave, sweat, and enough cigarette smoke to choke thirty chimneys. Regardless, he took a couple of deep breaths, trying to stay calm.

You've trained for this. You know the drill. You'll be fine.

He closed his eyes for a moment. As he did so, the image of his mother came out of nowhere—on her knees beside her bed, her hands folded in prayer. He'd seen her there so often when Joey was overseas.

Keep 'em coming, Mom.

He opened his eyes, staring through the hazy room to the front wall which was shrouded beneath a heavy black curtain. *Check out the yarn pulley on the left side of the map,* Charlie had told him earlier. *If the pulley is way down, you'll be home in time for dinner. If the yarn's all used up, say your prayers.*

"TEN-HUT!"

The thunder of boots hitting the concrete floor filled the room as everyone stood. A millisecond of quiet, then the quick, steady footsteps of the Group's leaders echoed as they made their way down the middle aisle and up onto the platform.

"Have a seat, gentlemen."

Colonel Joseph Moller, Commanding Officer of the 390th, began his introductory comments from the podium. "Gentlemen, your mission today is an opportunity to advance the cause of liberty in a substantial way. What you do today will have a tremendous impact on the outcome of this war. Do your best, and remember that those back home are proud of you, and so are we. Good luck, gentlemen. Colonel Waltz, Group Operations Officer, will now detail your mission."

Lieutenant Colonel Robert Waltz, second in command of the 390th, stepped up to the podium and nodded to the S-2 Security Officer assisting him. The lights dimmed as the black curtains parted revealing a map of Germany which filled the entire wall. "Gentlemen, your target for today is Frankfurt, Germany."

Groans and murmurs rippled across the room sending another wave of butterflies through Danny's stomach. He was starting to regret he'd eaten any breakfast at all. Then, like everyone else in the room, he simply busied himself taking notes as Colonel Waltz detailed the marshaling yards they would bomb in a matter of hours. Danny studied the elaborate map, their course plotted by yarn stretching across the outlines of Britain's coastline, the North Sea, and across the Continent into the Führer's backyard.

Following Colonel Waltz's comments, the S-3 Officer from Operations and Planning described the pertinent operation details. The S-2 Officer representing Intelligence described what they could expect as far as flak and enemy fighters. The Weather Officer then listed current conditions for the flight over, but more important, the prediction for conditions above the target. Danny knew his would be the final word in determining whether their mission would get the green light.

Colonel Waltz returned to the podium, checking his wristwatch. Everyone in the room did the same. "Time-tick. Gentlemen, it is now four-thirty-four minus thirteen seconds . . . ten, nine, eight . . . three, two, one—Hack!" With the official synchronization, the meeting adjourned.

As they filed out of the room, Dick Anderson and the other first pilots stayed in the briefing room for any last-minute instructions, while Danny and the other co-pilots headed to the changing room. He knew that Pendergrass would join the other navigators in a separate room to draw up their flight plans. Sully would go to another room set up for bombardiers and toggeliers to finalize the check points and receive the *flimsy sheets* that would help identify the target. Chaplains, both Protestant and Catholic, roamed the entire area, available for prayer or encouragement to anyone who wanted or needed it.

In the changing room, Danny handed over all his personal effects which were catalogued and held until he returned. He knew this procedure assured that no personal information would be available to captors in case the plane was forced down. Next, Danny received his flight bag which included his folded silk parachute. He swallowed hard when a corporal handed him the bag containing prisoner-of-war aids and rations.

At this point, he stripped down to his long johns to put on the blue heated flight suit beneath his uniform. Next, he put the heated slippers inside his combat boots. By the time he was dressed again, a thin layer of sweat made him clammy beneath all the layers. How much of that was from the extra layers and how much was from nerves, he couldn't tell. Danny slipped on his parachute pack, strapping it securely, then pulled on his life jacket—known affectionately in the Army Air Force as *Mae West*—over his head.

Once they were all suited up, they loaded their gear back on a six-by-six for the trip out to the hardstand where *Sweet Sophie* stood in readiness. He admired the fancy big letters painted for her nose art. When the base artist asked what kind of picture he wanted to accompany her name, Danny told him that wasn't necessary since "no picture could do her justice." Now, seeing her name written in script, Danny smiled, loving the fact that his entire crew thought Sophie was his girl back home.

Now, in the darkness, *Sophie's* interior lights glowed as if welcoming her boys. The gunners were already on board, mounting their fifty-caliber guns and stocking their clips. While the ground crew attended to last minute details, the Ordnance Crew finished loading bombs into *Sweet Sophie's* bomb bay. A gas truck lingered to top off the tanks.

Danny and the other officers joined them after hopping out of the truck. Nervous chatter assured Danny he wasn't the only one feeling the first-mission jitters. While Anderson made a final check of *Sweet Sophie's* exterior, Danny grabbed his gear and headed toward the front of the plane. He tossed his bag inside, then turned to attend to one more matter before climbing aboard. In the bushes ringing the hardstand, he joined several of his crew for one last "comfort" stop. *Twelve hours is a long time to hold it,* Charlie had said.

Finally, Danny hoisted himself up into the front end of the plane. After stowing his bag, Shorty handed him his flak jacket. He climbed into the cockpit after Anderson, slipping into his seat on the right. After strapping on his flak jacket, Danny went through the pre-flight checklist with Dick and tuned in to the Control Tower for any last minute changes. As co-pilot, Danny then requested the crew's roll-call.

"Toggelier, checking in."

"Navigator, checking in."

"Top turret, checking in."

"Radio operator, checking in."

"Ball turret, checking in."

"Right waist gunner, checking in."

"Left waist gunner, checking in."

"Tail gunner, checking in."

Danny took a deep breath as he kept his eyes glued to the tower, watching for the green flare which would signal time to start their engines. As he waited, another annoying round of butterflies flitted through his abdomen, so he tried to pray.

He had never doubted there was a God. But right there, at that particular moment in time, he wished he'd spent more time with the Lord. Mom had always been the praying one in the family, but he was smart enough to know he couldn't very well ride her spiritual apron strings into battle. With his eyes still open and watching for the flare, he prayed silently.

God, I feel kind of stupid calling on You now when I'm facing such a dangerous situation. Seems like I should've prayed a lot more before all this. But the fact is I've trained two years for this. And in a few minutes, we'll be flying out of here through some treacherous skies with a belly full of bombs beneath us before we dump them in the heart of Germany. I'm as ready as I'm ever going to be, but I'm sure You can tell I'm scared to death. Lord, I'd be awfully glad if You could take these nerves away from me so I can do the job I need to do. I promise I'll do better and spend more time with You when this is over. Amen.

Ten minutes later, a green flare arced through the air above the Control Tower. Danny and Anderson went through a final checklist then flipped all four ignition switches. The noisy engines coughed and sputtered then roared as *Sweet Sophie* came to life. Soon after, at a snail's pace she turned to the right out of her hardstand onto the perimeter track, and took her predetermined place in the taxi lane. As they reached the end of the runway, as soon as the plane ahead of them was on the roll, Anderson taxied out and lined up for take off. Both he and Danny stood on the brakes as the engines revved to their highest pitch. With a full bomb load and full fuel tanks, building up airspeed was critical to lift off before they ran out of runway. The B-17 shook violently as if every rivet on the plane would surely pop out. Then, with engines screaming, Anderson gave the sign to release the brakes, and they were on their way.

40

Since this was their first mission, *Sweet Sophie* flew the "tail-end Charlie" position at the back of the formation. As predicted, the fog and low ceiling complicated the well-rehearsed assembling of aircraft into their formation. It took just under one hour for the entire division to unite into combat box formation and turn east toward the Continent. As they flew, Danny took in the heavily peppered sky filled with B-17s and B-24s. Then, as they gained altitude, chalk-like contrails formed by crystallized vapor began to stream behind each plane. A beautiful sight to the untrained eye, but it felt like they were flying blind-folded through those eerie contrails of the planes ahead. Both pilot and co-pilot held their breath, anxious to clear the stuff.

"This is a whole lot worse than I expected," Shorty said, chomping his chewing gum. As flight engineer, he stood directly behind the cockpit between the pilot and co-pilot's seats. There he kept a keen eye on all the instruments, making sure everything worked as it should. "Sure wasn't this bad in all those practice runs."

"Let's just hope it's not a sign of things to come," Anderson said.

"Captain, we're over the Channel," Sully said from his position in the nose. "Permission to arm the bombs?"

"Roger that," Anderson responded.

As Sully left the nose to make his way down to the bomb bay, Dal Nicholson inched his way back to his position as tail gunner. Don Michaels crawled into the ball turret and strapped himself in.

A short time later, Anderson said, "Time to test your weapons, gentlemen."

Shorty slipped up to the top turret position soon joining in the *tat-tat-tat-tat-tat* of machine gun fire that rattled the fuselage. From front to back, top to bottom, the gunners shot off their weapons sending the pungent odor of gun smoke whipping through the aircraft.

"Little Friends at three o'clock high," Dal announced from his position in the rear of the plane. "Nice to know we've got escorts, huh?"

"Yeah, but they don't come along just for the heck of it," Franconi chimed in. "Must be bandits up here too."

"We're at ten-thousand feet, men," Anderson announced. "Time for those oxygen masks. Check in."

"Ball turret, checking in."

"Top turret, checking."

"Radio, checking in."

The rest followed, one after another.

Diane Moody

"Keep checking those masks for oxygen flow. At these altitudes, they'll freeze and you'll pass out if you're not careful."

"Yeah, Franconi, you heard the captain," Jimmy teased from his post as left waist gunner. "No drooling today. We wouldn't wanna have to carry your sorry corpse outta *Sophie* tonight."

"Shut up, Foster."

"All right, that's enough," Danny said. "We're all a little tense, so let's cut the cheap shots."

"Stay sharp, men," Anderson ordered. "We're crossing the European coastline. Watch for those fighters and call them out the second you see them."

"Captain, I see flashes down below!" Michaels yelled from the ball turret. "You seeing flak up ahead yet?"

"I see it," Anderson answered. "Coming in heavy at one o'clock low. Men, make sure you've got those flak jackets on."

Danny spotted the black puffs of smoke popping up all over the sky. Soon the plane rocked hard as they encountered the dreaded explosive shells for the first time. Each jolt seemed to slam the B-17 harder.

"Geez, it feels like we're dancing through a mine field!" Danny yelled.

"Better get used to it," Anderson growled. "The closer we get to target, the worse it'll be."

"I hate this stuff!" Michaels shouted, adding a string of expletives.

"Three bandits! Coming in level at three o'clock!"

"Thunderbolts fanning out! Knock 'em outta the sky, Little Friends!"

342

The B-17 slammed hard again, thanks to the dense flak.

"OUCH!" McCabe screamed. "That one got me!"

"Waist gunner! Where are you hit?" Danny shouted.

"I'm okay! I'm okay! Just some shrapnel on my cheek."

Another explosion rocked the plane as hot shrapnel bounced through *Sophie's* mid-ship.

"Fire! Fire!" Jimmy shouted. "Balls of fire all over us!"

"Put it out! Put it out!"

"Tony!" Anderson yelled. "Can you put it out?"

"I've got it!" Franconi answered. "Fire extinguisher blowing as we speak, sir. I think we've got it—"

"Over here, Franconi!" McCabe shouted. "There—in that corner."

For three more hours, they battled German Messerschmidts and Focke-Wulfs while dodging the unrelenting flak. The constant *ping* of shrapnel and the hollow *clanging* of cartridge casings flying around the middle section of the plane all grated on Danny's last nerve, an audio background to the visual madness.

A few minutes later, they watched helplessly as *Dream Boat* took a direct hit on its left wing. The engine caught fire and the ship quickly started losing altitude, then spiraled out of control. Then, before a single chute was spotted, she exploded in a huge fireball, wreaking havoc on every ship in her immediate area. Anderson struggled to keep control of *Sweet Sophie.* As the initial shock swept through the plane, the intercom went silent, but only for a moment.

"Dear God . . ." Danny's breath caught as his heart pounded.

"Those guys didn't have a chance."

"Did anybody see a chute? Surely somebody—"

"No time for chutes."

"My buddy Mickey," Dal croaked. "Mickey was on *Dream Boat*."

"Get us to that target so we can take out those Nazi—"

"Gentlemen, take a breath," Anderson said.

Danny did, and with it gave himself a mental slap in the face to focus on his job. Nothing could help those guys now. Not even a prayer.

Anderson called for another oxygen check. The crew sounded off in order.

"Captain, we're five minutes, thirty seconds from the IP," Pendergrass stated.

The sky was nearly black with heavy clouds of flak as they drew ever closer to their first target. Anderson fought hard to maintain as level a path as possible.

"Bomb bay doors in the lead plane opening!" Danny shouted as he watched the streamers of pure white smoke cascade from the lead plane.

"Opening bomb bay doors," Sully answered from the toggelier. Then, following the lead plane, Sully flipped the switch, releasing the payload from *Sophie's* belly.

"Bombs away!"

All around them, the ships flying in their formation dropped the five-hundred pound bombs right on target. Danny had never seen anything like it. As their craft still bounced along the flak-filled sky, he looked down, marveling at the explosions rippling across the landscape below. For a moment, the intercom remained silent. Danny wondered if the rest of the crew was experiencing the same emotions he was—pride at a mission accomplished, as well as a peculiar check in his spirit at the loss of life below. It wasn't regret. Not in the least. The Germans certainly had it coming. The atrocities and bloodshed at their hands were the sole source of blame for the war here in the European Theater. Still, an odd and quite unexpected sense of sadness drifted through him, knowing there were also *innocent* lives lost below. Yes, war was necessary and he was honored to do his part. But that didn't make it palatable.

Danny called for another check-in, and once completed, the crew's nervous chatter once again filled the intercom as they banked to the left to begin the long ride home. The trip back to England was much like the trip over, dodging the incessant flak and constant enemy fighters. Yet, knowing they'd fulfilled their first mission supplied *Sweet Sophie's* crew with an adrenaline they'd never experienced.

Several hours later they crossed the North Sea, thrilled to spot the famous white cliffs of Dover. Just as they'd taken off, they approached the base at Framlingham in formation flying in low circles until they peeled off and at last, touched down. And only at that moment, did Danny take a breath; one he felt sure he'd been holding since they'd left here before dawn.

As they taxied on the way to their hardstand, the ground crew lined the flight line as was their custom, welcoming them home. These unsung heroes always waited patiently on mission days, keeping careful count as each plane appeared on the horizon. Danny wondered if they ever realized how much the flight crews appreciated all these guys did. He blew out a long sigh of relief and thanked God for *Sweet Sophie's* safe return.

When *Sophie* made her final stop back at the hardstand, Anderson cut the engines. He sat silent for a moment before reaching his hand out toward Danny. "Good job, McClain."

Danny shook his hand heartily. "Great job, Captain."

As the boisterous crew went about collecting their belongings, they all slapped each other on the back for a successful first mission. Danny was relieved too, but far too fresh from the experience to be cutting up with the rest of the guys. Once they all exited the plane, a truck showed up to ferry them to the Briefing Room. Once there, they looked around, wondering what they were supposed to do.

"Danny!"

He turned as Charlie waved his hand above the crowded room. Danny waved back as his friend closed the gap between them then gave him a hug.

"How'd it go, Rookie?! Feel good to have that first one under your belt?"

"You can say that again." Danny laughed, raking his hand through his hair.

"Flak was pretty heavy up there today. Any trouble?"

"Nothing too serious, but it sure felt good to get back on the ground. How about you?"

"Not exactly a milk run, but we managed. C'mon. I'll buy you a drink."

"Ah, that's okay, I'd—"

"Danny, it's part of the routine. Compliments of the United States Army Air Force. Calms your nerves before debriefing." Charlie chuckled as they neared the table of drinks. "Don't worry. I won't let you get drunk again."

All over the room he watched officers knock back shots of whiskey. "All right, then. If it's protocol."

Charlie handed him the tiny glass filled to the rim, which promptly spilled from his trembling hand. "Whoa, you were right about the shakes."

"Just be glad you're all in one piece and able to hold it at all." Charlie winked then held up his own glass. "To your first mission."

"To my first mission." They clinked glasses and Danny downed his whiskey. "Whoa," he rasped, feeling the liquid burn all the way down.

Charlie patted him hard on the back. "See? Just what the doctor ordered. I'll see you after debriefing."

Danny shook his head to still the alcohol buzz then found his way over to the table with his crew. The Red Cross Girls supplied them with plenty of hot coffee and donuts as the S-2 Officer started the intense questioning. Danny wondered if Sally might also be helping out, but with the interrogation underway, he had no chance to look around the room. The Security Officer asked each crew member questions pertinent to the mission. Clearly, they were all ready to unleash the tension they'd held in for the past twelve hours, filling in all the details until at last the session was over.

Danny felt like he was still in a haze the rest of the evening as everyone chatted over dinner. They talked about the day's mission, the close calls, the planes and crew members who didn't make it back, and the usual horse play that follows such a nerve-wracking day. Mostly, Danny just wanted to get some sleep, but on the way back from dinner, he stopped by Operations to check the roster for tomorrow's mission. Sure enough, Anderson's Crew was listed.

That night, when his head finally hit the pillow, Danny uttered a silent prayer of thanks. As he rolled over on his side, he had one last thought before he drifted off to sleep.

And tomorrow we do it all again.

41

31 December 1944

Framlingham, England

"Hamburg. Why'd it have to be Hamburg? It's New Year's Eve, for crying out loud!"

"Franconi, knock it off," Pendergrass growled from *Sweet Sophie's* nose. "Uncle Sam didn't ask for your opinion and neither did we, so shut up."

"Yeah, but three missions in a row? You'd think they'd at least give us a day off so we could—"

"So we could what? Go celebrate at Times Square?" Lowenstein asked. "In case you haven't noticed, we're in a war here."

"Maybe so, but I'm with Tony," Michaels chimed in from the ball turret. "It's not fair, sending us up three days in a row."

"That's enough, men," Anderson snapped from the cockpit. "Unless you're calling out a fighter, I don't want to hear another word. Just do your job so we can get back to base in one piece tonight."

"Yes, sir," Franconi and Michaels answered in unison.

Once again, *Sweet Sophie* flew in one of the last groups. Danny had assumed by their third mission, he'd be used to the anxiety—at least partially. But the knot in his gut pinched every bit as hard as it had the last couple of days. Today the flak was brutal and getting worse the closer they got to Hamburg. They'd been warned during briefing about the possibility of intense flak, but Danny had never seen the sky so black. The plane bounced and slammed as shrapnel peppered the exterior, harder than any hail storm back home. Once they passed the Initial Point, Anderson fought to maintain as straight a line as possible to the Drop Point. The moment came, the bomb bays all around them opened, and once again Sully Thornton flipped the switch.

"Bombs away!"

Anderson leaned to his left to watch the impact below from his side window. Thinking he'd do the same out his window, Danny turned to his right just as a B-17 at one-o'clock high took a direct hit. Before the words could form in his mouth, the plane exploded. The fireball was coming directly at them! He slammed Anderson's right arm to get his attention. As the pilot casually glanced back, he immediately spotted the fireball and quickly but steadily pulled up on the steering column, allowing what was left of the crippled Fortress to slide right beneath them. *Sophie* bucked and slammed and rocked, but she kept course.

"DID YOU SEE THAT?!" Lowenstein shouted from the top turret.

"It's the *Lazy Susan!*"

"Look for chutes! Look for chutes!"

"I see two!"

"I see three!"

"Geez, look at it! There's nothing left!"

"McClain! We've lost power on engine number three!" Anderson shouted.

Danny looked out his window at the engine closest to him. "Number three all torn to shreds. Globs of oil coming out!"

"Feather three!"

"She's not responding. She's dead, Captain!"

Unable to stop the lame propeller from spinning, its blades created drag on the already beleaguered B-17. Quickly losing altitude and dropping out of formation would make them easy pickings for the Luftwaffe.

"Navigator! Anderson shouted. "Give me a heading to get us out over the North Sea as soon as possible!"

"Roger that, Captain," Pendergrass answered. A few seconds later he called out the heading which would place them over the mouth of the Elbe River. Banking hard to make the turn, the river came in sight.

"Captain! Flak barges on the river and they're all firing!" Jimmy Foster shouted from midship.

The nasty black puffs of smoke soon engulfed them, shaking the plane from nose to tail.

"Captain! We're losing altitude! Twelve thousand feet and falling!"

Anderson drove *Sweet Sophie* like a race car on a severely pot-holed track, but moments later they outran the black madness as they sputtered over the open sea.

"Thank God!" Dal shouted from the tail.

"Great job, Captain!" Sully cried.

Danny shook his head. "Unbelievable."

"Captain! Bandit at six o'clock!" Dal screamed just before blasting off his guns.

"Bandit closing in fast, Captain!"

"Here come our Little Friends!"

"Knock 'em outta the sky, Little Friends!"

As if obliging their cries for help, the P-47 Thunderbolts swooped in and shot the German ME 109 out of the sky.

The cheers of the crew filled the intercom, thankful the fighter pilots had once again provided protection.

"Men, we've got to lighten our load or we're not going to make it to the coast," Anderson barked. "Toss everything you can overboard, and I mean everything."

They'd all heard too many stories from other crews who credited these North Sea dumps with saving their lives. They quickly threw out guns, ammunition, and anything not nailed down in an attempt to lighten the load and get *Sophie* across the water.

"Mayday! Mayday!" Danny shouted on the Emergency Channel to alert Air Sea Rescue to their position. They still had a long way to go before they could hope to see the white cliffs of Dover. He looked out his window and wondered how cold the sea water below might be then prayed he'd never have to find out.

Finally, the English coastline appeared ahead. Danny let out a heavy sigh—just before a plane blew right across their path!

Anderson tried hard to fight the bird's slipstream. "What was THAT?"

"British Air Sea Rescue, sir!" Lowenstein shouted.

"Don't those idiots listen to the tower?"

"Hey, thanks for the rescue, jerks!"

With their plane approaching stalling speed while flying at an extremely low altitude with her nose up, Danny gulped hard when he noticed white caps just below them.

"This is gonna be close!" Anderson cried.

"There's the Brit's Norwich Airfield!"

With no time to call for clearance, Anderson aimed for the closest runway.

"Hold on, everybody!" Danny shouted.

Seconds later, they landed. *Sophie* skidded all over the runway. By the feel of it, Danny wondered if the tires had taken some flak. But thankfully, they were back on the ground and still in one piece. A few minutes later while exiting the damaged aircraft, the crew started counting flak holes—astounded that the plane had survived. They stopped counting at two hundred.

As they waited for a truck from the 390th to come for them, the British offered hot coffee and refreshments in a hangar that was chilly at best, but at least out of the elements. They all talked at the same time, reliving the close calls and applauding their captain's incredible landing which prevented them from ending the year—and possibly their lives—with a freezing swim. A few moments later, the pilot from the Air Sea Rescue plane arrived. Anderson lit into him for cutting so close across their path, forcing them to fly through his slipstream.

Danny stepped between them. "Dick, take it easy. We're fine. I'm sure it was an accident."

"Sorry, mate, but to be honest, you gave *me* quite a fright as well," the Brit said, still holding his helmet. "I was looking for you in the water below! I couldn't believe you were still airborne, what with your nose just above the drink and flying at stall speed? I couldn't believe you and your crew weren't all wet!"

"Yeah? I'll *show* you who's all wet!" Anderson snarled, trying to push Danny aside.

Danny held on, blocking him. "Captain Anderson! Let it go!"

Anderson's chest heaved repeatedly until he finally grumbled a few choice words then walked away.

Their truck showed up several hours later, long after the stroke of midnight. The tired crew spoke little on the trip back to base, most of them sound asleep despite the bumpy ride. Danny tried to sleep, but couldn't. His mind still whirling, he wondered how many close calls a guy gets before he uses them all up. He wondered if his mother's prayers had been responsible for keeping him alive one more day. He couldn't help wondering what the new year would bring.

Then he wondered if he would live long enough to find out.

42

Following our harrowing mission to Hamburg, we were given our first 48-hour leave along with several other crews, including Charlie's. We all headed to London to see the sights. What an impressive place it is. The history alone would make it a great place to visit, but it was mostly nice just to be away from the war for a couple of days. Well, I guess I shouldn't really say that. London has had more than its share of bombing—it was bombed more than 71 times during the 8-month Blitz back in the early days of the war. So many historic landmarks were decimated, others took serious damage, and some were flattened altogether. Even while we were there, a couple of air raid sirens went off, but we never bothered to go into a bomb shelter.

When we returned to base, we had a few more days off while the ground crews worked on our plane. Sophie took a lot of damage, but nothing major, thank goodness. I still smile when the guys ask questions about my "mystery girl" back home named Sophie. The more evasive I am, the greater the fantasies they create about her.

I've seen Sally a couple of times and we've had a chance to catch up. It's really nice having a friend like her to chat with, especially since we're just friends. Though I have to admit, I'm usually a little jealous whenever I see the other guys hogging all her time.

The crew and I put in for a Distinguished Flying Cross for Dick Anderson. He sure deserves it. If it hadn't been for his superb handling of Sophie during the Hamburg mission, we might all be pushing up daisies right now. I sure hope he gets it.

I had a letter from Mom earlier this week. I think the Almighty knows when I need a good dose of encouragement because her letters always seem to arrive when I need them most. I don't think I'll ever be able to tell Mom how much her prayers mean to me, but I'll sure try.

On the third day of February, Danny and his crew took part in the biggest mission the Eighth Air Force had ever flown. Across England, almost a thousand heavy bombers lined up in formation then headed east to Berlin where they would attack the Berlin Tempelhof marshaling yard, one of Germany's biggest. With the 390th positioned toward the rear of the bomber stream, Danny and his crew marveled at the sight of the sky before them literally filled with bombers as far as the eye could see.

But flying in that rear position also put them in an unusual situation. By the time they reached their target, Berlin was completely covered with smoke from all the exploding bombs, compliments of the Eighth Air Force. Instead of wasting their bombs on a target already demolished, the 390th was instructed to take "a target of opportunity." They picked a canal bridge and barracks area in a part of Berlin which had seen little bombing. After dropping their bombs, they banked a hard left and headed back to England. Clearly, the Eighth Air Force had done its job well as they encountered no flak whatsoever on their return flight.

Over the next few weeks *Sweet Sophie's* crew flew several more missions, eventually earning themselves another leave. While they were taking some time off in London, another crew was instructed to fly *Sweet Sophie* for a couple of missions. It wasn't unusual for planes to be "borrowed" if another crew's plane was damaged, requiring major repairs. They'd simply use the plane of a crew on leave.

But once Danny and his crew returned to *Sophie,* they knew immediately that something wasn't right. If he hadn't known better, Danny would've sworn *Sophie* was out of sorts after flying several missions with strangers. Then again, he reminded himself, the plane was just a flying machine—not a temperamental woman.

In late February on their first mission following their leave, they had no problem making it to their target in Leipzig. But on the long trip back to Framlingham, Dick and Danny knew they had a serious problem. Their gauges indicated they were running seriously low on fuel. Flying in formation used fuel at a much faster rate than going it on your own. So even though they were still over France, Anderson called the Group leader asking for permission to leave formation for a straight-in flight back to the base.

"Request denied."

"We'll never make it," Danny muttered to Dick with a sick feeling.

"We have no choice," Anderson growled along with a few expletives.

For the next fifteen minutes, they sweated it out watching the fuel gauges drop lower and lower. Yes, they might make it back across the English Channel, but the long, intricate process of waiting their turn to land in the formation line up would surely drain the last drop of fuel from their tanks.

Once again Dick requested permission to leave formation. Once again, his request was denied.

"We've crossed the coastline of France, and we're out of harm's way," Danny fumed. "What possible reason could he have to—"

"*Sweet Sophie* to Group leader!" Dick shouted as he dropped out of formation. "We'll see you back at the base—*if* we make it!"

Precious minutes ticked by as they flew straight toward the base. As the shoreline of England appeared in the distance, Dick called "Tightboot"—code for the 390th tower—and requested clearance for approach.

"Permission granted. Bring it in."

Danny and Dick looked at each other in surprise. "Was that Colonel Moller?" Danny asked in disbelief, surprised to hear the Commander of the 390th at the radio.

Dick nodded, his eyes wide. "Guess we can't get any higher clearance than that."

Lo and behold, after they landed and taxied to their hardstand, they found a gasoline truck waiting for them. Danny swallowed hard, knowing the presence of that gas truck meant their remaining fuel would be calculated as they filled the tank. As the crew disembarked, both pilot and co-pilot knew their butts would be in a sling if *Sophie's* tanks weren't all but dry.

In debriefing, they were told the ground crew had proved them correct, adding that there wasn't enough fuel to make a second try if they hadn't set her down when they did. But why had their full tanks not lasted the entire mission? They'd even flown element lead which meant their gas consumption shouldn't have been as much as those that flew on their wings. They should have had more than enough to spare.

Danny had no answers. He was just thankful they'd made it back. He went out of his way to thank Dick Anderson for getting all of them back safe and sound. He might not be the friendliest pilot in the 390th, but he did his job and did it well.

"Cup of coffee, Lieutenant?"

Danny turned at the sound of Sally's voice to find her holding a mug of steaming coffee toward him. "Don't mind if I do, Miss Wells." He took the mug and wrapped his hands around it, welcoming its warmth.

"Tough day?" she asked, gathering up some empty mugs from a nearby table.

"You don't even want to know. But thanks for asking."

"Actually, that's what I'm here for, remember? Sometimes it helps to talk it out after a rough day in enemy skies." She stopped for a moment, as if waiting for his response.

"I know, but I'd rather hear about your day. I'm sure it's far more interesting."

She gave him a playful look, but seemed to understand. "Well, let's see. This morning I visited the boys over in sick quarters for a couple of hours. I helped three of them write letters home. I played cards with some fellows over at the Officer's Club. This afternoon I made around two hundred donuts, making sure we'd have plenty for you guys this evening, and then I started brewing coffee. Lots and lots of coffee. Same old, same old."

"Not such a bad day, if you ask me," Danny said. "Any news from Geoffrey?"

Her face brightened. "Yes! He's back in the states now and anxious for me to come home so we can get married."

"That's great, Sally. I'm happy for you. I really am."

She beamed as she lifted the tray of empty mugs. "Thanks, Danny. That means a lot to me."

"Here, let me carry that for you." He took the tray and followed her back toward the coffee cart. "So how does it work—you serving in the Red Cross? Do you have to finish a tour of duty or can you leave any time?"

"No, we make a commitment to serve a tour of duty just like you do. I'll be here until the end of May, unless the war ends sooner."

He set the tray down with the others. "That must be hard for you, knowing he's home and you can't leave yet."

She pushed a curl out of her eyes. "Yes, it's hard. But I love what I do here, and he knows that. Besides, it won't be that much longer. Oh, by the way, your friend Charlie was here earlier. He said to tell you a bunch of the guys are heading to Quincy's tonight if you'd like to join them."

Danny closed his eyes, shaking his head. "I don't know how they do it after flying for twelve hours. All I can think about is calling it a night."

"That's because you're the smart one."

"I'll take that as a compliment, Miss Wells."

"As you should, because it was, Lieutenant."

"Goodnight, Sally."

"Goodnight, Danny."

43

28 March 1945

"Bombs away!"

After successfully dropping their payload on the marshaling yards in Hannover, Germany, Captain Dick Anderson followed the lead element, banking sharply to the left to begin the trip back to England. On this, their eighteenth mission, the flak had been unusually thick—always the case near important target areas. The closer to target they'd flown, the heavier the anti-aircraft fire. They always felt like sitting ducks up there, but never more so than near the target. How many times had they limped back to base after one of these box barrages? The enemy would aim for a section of sky where they knew the planes were heading on their bombing run then bombard that area, filling it with exploding shells. Some crews called it an "iron cumulus" because the air looked much like a solid cloud of black. On approach to target, they were unable to veer one way or the other to avoid the nasty stuff. They had to fly right through it.

Sweet Sophie bumped, rattled, and rolled through the tremendous onslaught of anti-aircraft fire. As they completed the wide turn before settling in for the ride home, Danny called for the routine check-in following the drop.

"Tail gunner, checking in."

"Ball turret, check—"

Suddenly, *Sophie* slammed hard once, twice, and a third time before pitching a sharp left then back right. Even from the cockpit, Danny could hear the explosions ricocheting through the cabin and the frantic voices of his crew.

"We're hit! We're hit!" Jimmy yelled from waist gunner. "We've got—"

"Somebody help me! I'm hit!"

"I can't breathe! I can't breathe!"

"We've got shrapnel—help me! Help!"

"Jimmy's down! Oh God, no! Half of Shorty's head got blown—"

"CHECK IN! That's an order!" Danny shouted, unable to tell who was saying what. As he turned to ask Anderson a question, he stopped cold. His pilot sat hunched over his steering column.

"Dick!" Danny yelled, reaching over to pull him back. But Anderson's wild eyes stared back at him, pleading, begging—his bloodied hands seemingly frozen in front of him even as blood poured like a fountain from a hole in his neck. A split second later, his eyes rolled back and he fell limp.

"PILOT DOWN! PILOT DOWN!" Danny shouted as he quickly grabbed his own steering column, fighting to keep control of the plane.

"Waist gunner down! Both waist gunners down!" Franconi yelled. "Top turret down!" "Lieutenant, we—"

"IT'S GONE! IT'S GONE! Get me outta here!" Michaels screamed from the ball turret.

"Somebody get Don out of the ball turret!" Danny shouted. "Tony! Lane! Get down there!"

"Lane, help me! Pull me up! Oh God, I don't wanna die!" Michaels cried.

"I've got you, Don!" Lane shouted. "Look, you're out, buddy! I've got you. You're safe! You're safe!"

As he fought *Sophie's* stubborn pull downward, Danny could hear Don wailing in relief. "Everybody else, check in! That's an order!" he repeated.

"Lieutenant, Jimmy's out cold. I can barely detect a pulse!" Franconi shouted. "And Sully's . . . oh God help us, Sully didn't make it!"

Danny eyed the controls knowing he was fighting a losing battle. "Navigator, give me our location!"

"We're approaching the German border into Holland," Lane shouted. "About ten miles out."

"Lane, get up here. Now!" Danny tried to visualize their position. The southern portion of Holland had been liberated back in September, but there was no way to know where they were in relation to that demarcation.

Something to his right caught his attention. Flames on engine number three danced wild around the edges. He flipped the lever to feather it but nothing happened. He flipped it up and down, up and down. Nothing.

"I'm here, Danny, what—" Pendergrass said, then stopped, gripping the pilot. "Captain!" He raised Anderson's head and found his glassy eyes. "Danny, he's dead!"

"I know, I know. Talk to me. What's the status of the crew?"

"It's just you, me, Donnie, Tony, and Dal. Everybody else is—"

"Get Dal to—oh, no NO NO!" Danny shouted, looking past the slumped body of his pilot. "Fire on number one! Three's still burning! Lane, sound the bell. We've got to abandon ship!"

Seconds counted as the reality of those burning engines prompted Danny to get out of the cockpit as fast as he could. He put the plane on autopilot, then quickly pulled out of his seat and headed for the bomb bay.

"Don and Dal are already out!" Pendergrass shouted.

"Tony! Abandon ship!"

The radio operator made his way down to the door. He froze, his hands gripping the frame. "I can't! I can't do it!"

Lane stepped beside him. "Yes, you can, Tony! Your chute will carry you down. Just don't forget to pull the—"

"GO GO GO!" Danny yelled even though he knew they couldn't hear him over the engines.

With that Lane gave Tony a thumbs-up. "You 'n me, Tony. Let's do this!" And with that, they disappeared out the door.

As Danny stared down through the open bomb bay doors, the image of his mother kneeling in prayer beside her bed once again flashed into his mind. The thought gave him comfort, and with one final prayer of his own, Danny came to attention and jumped.

The *whooshing* of the wind roared in his ears as he tumbled downward. *Be sure to wait a proper amount of time before pulling the cord in order to avoid getting tangled up with the plane.* The warning from his training manual came out of nowhere, but boy, was he glad it did. *Not yet, not yet, not yet!* He tried to look for the other chutes but couldn't see them through the clouds whipping past him. *How could Lane and Tony be out of sight so soon?* Then, it occurred to him that his flight downward wasn't as quiet as it was supposed to be.

Pull the ripcord, you knucklehead!

And he did.

OUCH! So that's why the leg straps are supposed to be so tight that you walk bent over . . . Clearly, his weren't tight enough as he felt the mind-numbing pain shoot through his groin. For a moment he saw stars, then despite the pain he couldn't help enjoying the peaceful quiet as he gently descended slowly downward. A litany of random things rolled through his mind. The night he found Sophie in the alley behind the store; the feel of her protruding ribs beneath her filthy coat. The letter from Anya telling him that Hans had died. The homecoming dance at Northwestern where he and Beverly twirled to the music of Kay Kyser. The sticky blood pooling beneath his father that night the thugs beat him with a baseball bat. Sally's smile earlier that morning when the Red Cross Girls brought them coffee at their hardstand.

They say your life passes before your eyes right before you die. A chill passed over him. *Is this it? Am I going to die?*

The huge blast from an explosion not so far away would be his last memory of *Sweet Sophie* and the crew members who went down with her. He turned to see the fireball and felt the loss deep in his gut. So many things rushed through his mind. Then, he gave himself a mental slap and tried to focus on his landing.

He looked below him as the earth came into focus. The afternoon sun glistened, sending rays into the forest as if he were looking at a painting by Michelangelo. The easy, peaceful descent surprised him, especially after the trauma of the last half hour.

Wait. A forest? I'm about to fall into a bunch of trees?

He looked all around, unable to see a clearing he could shoot for. Then he realized the breeze around him had kicked up considerably, wreaking havoc with his billowing chute. He hiked his knees up, hoping to shield himself from as much harm as possible.

And just that fast, he fell through the upper branches of several trees, tossed about like a rag doll; the snapping of tree limbs piercing the silence like a wild, unrestrained drum solo pounding in his ears. He raised his arms to protect his face as the slapping and scraping continued. Suddenly he found himself a human canon falling much too fast.

"This is gonna HURT!"

Part V

44

As Danny struggled to wake up, he had a feeling he wasn't back on base. He tried to lift his head but a bolt of pain shot through it, taking his breath away. He rested a moment before lifting one eyelid only to find everything blurred.

He remained still, needing to get his bearings even if he couldn't see anything at the moment. *Where am I? How did I get here?* He was in someone's house or a building of some kind, by the sounds of it. He could hear voices speaking quietly somewhere, but couldn't tell what language they were speaking. Panic quickly swept through him as he realized those could be German voices.

Wait. Think. What's the last thing I remember? Oh . . . we had to bail! Sophie's engines were on fire . . . The crew! Are they here too? No, that can't be right. I was the last one out. We would have landed several miles apart. Or at least I think so?

But no matter how hard he tried, he couldn't remember a thing after standing in the bomb bay preparing to jump. He searched his mind but came up blank.

The voices grew louder. Danny tried again to open his eyes, noting immediately that the room was mostly dark except for a soft glow off to his right. He blinked repeatedly then started to wipe his eyes but found his arm too sore to lift. He closed his eyes again, frustrated by his inability to do something as simple as rubbing his eyes.

A door creaked. Footsteps approached. Danny held his breath.

"Awake?" someone said with a thick accent. *A woman. German? Dutch?*

"Where am I?" he asked, surprised by the graveled sound of his voice.

He felt the warmth of someone's hand on his forehead. "Ja, fever still."

"Please, can you tell me where I am?" He tried again to lift his head and immediately felt a wave of nausea. "Uh, I think I'm gonna—"

The women muttered something he couldn't understand, but soon he felt the coolness of a bowl placed beside him. Suddenly the blurry room spun and he leaned over, emptying the contents of his stomach into the bowl. The sudden movement made his head feel like it would explode. When he finally stopped throwing up, he felt a cold cloth pressed on his forehead.

"There, there," the woman said.

He fell back against a pillow, biting his lip so he wouldn't scream out from the excruciating pain gripping his head. He felt something roll down the side of his face and into his ear. And just as he wondered if it might be his own tear, everything went black.

He had no idea how long he'd been asleep, only vague memories of drifting in and out of consciousness. As Danny tried to wake himself, he noticed something near him smelled pleasant. Something fresh. Maybe it was nothing more than the absence of the usual smells—the strong scent of *Sophie's* motor oil, the smoky stove in his quarters at the base, the constant stench of sweat, his own and that of his crew. Yes, this was something clean. He carefully lifted the back of his hand to his nose, thankful the pain in his arm had diminished somewhat. He breathed in.

Ah, soap. Yes, that's what it is. Soap. But how . . . did I take a shower? Impossible. I couldn't have slept through a shower. Oh. Then that means . . . somebody gave me a bath?

He carefully blinked his eyes open, relieved to find his sight no longer quite as blurred. He blew out a sigh, thankful he could finally look around. The room, still dark, was lit only by an oil lamp resting on the table beside his bed. Yes, a bed. He was lying in a bed, covered with a quilt or blanket of some kind. He moved his hand gently across the soft fabric. He touched his face, feeling the stubble along his jaw line, then looked down, surprised to find himself in pajamas instead of his uniform. He blinked, hoping to clear his eyes. *Pajamas?*

He peeked under the covers. *Make that a night shirt.*

His eyes darted around the room looking for his clothes and not finding them. The nerves kicked in sending his imagination in too many directions at once. He moved his legs under the covers and quickly discovered another injury when a sharp pain jolted his left foot.

This is worse than I thought.

"Hello?" He coughed and tried to clear his throat. "Hello? Is anyone there?"

He rested his head back on his pillow and tried to listen. Somewhere a radio cackled though he couldn't make out what was being said—or what language. Just then, the door opened wide.

"Ah, you are awake, Lieutenant?"

Danny watched the man approaching his bed. He looked about six feet tall, his wiry salt and pepper hair sticking out from beneath a faded, worn cap. His deep set eyes seemed kind enough, feathered by lots of wrinkles on his weathered, gaunt face.

"Can you tell me where I am?"

"Ja, you are in The Netherlands in a village just outside of Enschede."

"I don't know—"

"We found you in the woods. You fell from the sky, no?"

Danny tried to read his expression, unsure how much he should say. "I don't remember." It seemed the safest answer.

"No, I doubt you do. You are American?"

Danny looked away, wondering who this man was. "Yes, American."

"Then we are friends."

He looked back at the man, finding a wide smile on his face. "How so?"

The smile faded a bit. He turned, then took a seat in a chair beside the bed. "Your uniform. You are American pilot, ja?"

"But how—"

"Your tags there."

Danny felt the dog tags against his chest.

"And this." The man slowly held up Danny's wallet. But Danny knew it contained no personal identification. He'd turned those over to the corporal before his mission. Just pictures of his mom and dad, one of him and Joey when they were kids, a few others. He waited, knowing there would be more questions.

"We are friends, Lieutenant, because your country fights with our Allies to stop the Germans. That makes us friends. The Nazis have tried to destroy our country. They have occupied our homeland for many years now, but never have we given up. When America joined the Allies, we knew it was just a matter of time before we are free again."

Danny felt his heart rate soar. "The war is over?"

"No, not yet. But soon, I think. Very soon."

Danny wondered how much he could trust this Dutchman. If he was, in fact, Dutch? "You speak English. Do all Dutch speak English as well as you?"

"Ja, I speak English. Before the war, I was a school teacher. Years ago, when I was studying at university, I took English because I was curious about the culture of our neighbors across the Channel. It has served me well." He paused for a second. "But never so much as now."

Danny waited then asked, "Why now?"

"These are things we shall talk about later," he said, standing again. "For now, I shall leave you and have one of our women prepare you something to eat." He turned as if to leave, then stopped. He opened Danny's wallet and pulled something from inside it as he returned to Danny's side. "Before I go, I wonder if you could tell me why you carry this picture?"

Danny reached for the faded photograph. His hand trembled as he stared into the faces of Reverend and Mrs. Versteeg, their son Hans, and little Anya. He looked up and found the man's eyes trained on him, all traces of friendliness vanished.

45

"These are childhood friends of mine. Nothing more," Danny answered, stalling as he tried to gather his thoughts.

"And that windmill? I did not know America has windmills such as this."

He didn't respond and avoided eye contact as he attempted to sit up straighter, grimacing with the effort. "I would like to get dressed. Where are my clothes?"

The man stared at him a moment longer, then turned, slipping Danny's wallet back into his coat pocket. He reached into a closet and brought out some clothing. "You can wear these for now." He dropped a shirt, sweater, and pair of pants on the bed. "It's best you not put on your uniform while you are our guest."

Danny tried to stand up but the room started spinning again. "Whoa . . ." He promptly sat back down.

"Perhaps you should rest a while longer," the man said, again heading for the door. "The doctor thinks you had a concussion, among other things."

"Doctor?"

"Yes, and your foot is badly sprained but not broken."

"My foot?"

The door creaked shut. Left alone with his thoughts again, Danny eased himself back on the pillow. With his eyes more accustomed to the darkness of the room, he looked around as he tried to make himself think. *Why was he so interested in that photograph?* He tried to remember the map of Holland he'd once studied. He recognized the name of the town, Enschede, but couldn't place it. *Did he recognize that particular windmill? Didn't Hans once tell me that each windmill had a name and families often chose a favorite?*

Or is it the people in the photograph that intrigue him? Is it possible he knows the Versteegs? The thought both excited and frightened him. If Enschede was close to Utrecht where the Versteegs lived, was it possible he might find them? If he asked the man about them and found out where they lived, would he finally meet this family he'd known for so many years?

Then again, what were the chances he'd parachuted into Anya's backyard? Slim to none. And if he asked about the Versteegs, would he be putting them in some kind of danger? The man called him "friend" simply because he was an American, but that didn't mean he could be trusted.

Danny huffed, frustrated to be in this mystery place and unable to ask the questions he needed answered. He turned his head to the left and only then noticed what appeared to be a hand-carved cross hanging on the wall between two windows. *Christians?*

A siren wailed in the distance and quickly grew louder. Just as Danny realized what it was, his door flew open and two men rushed into the room. They spoke in urgent tones though Danny had no idea what they were saying. They moved him into a sitting position then helped him to his feet, taking most of his weight as they lifted him between them. He was thankful the nightshirt was long as they rushed him out of the room. Anxious voices filled the many rooms of what looked to be an old house.

The two men jostled him through a series of halls and rooms. As they entered a large storage room, a man and woman pushed aside a wooden rack of floor-to-ceiling shelving, then shoved a heavy rug out of the way. One of them pulled a rope, lifting an opening in the floor.

"*Schiet op!* Hurry, hurry!" she said, waving them down.

Danny's escorts clumsily helped him down the steep stairs. The awkward movements pushed and pulled at him, painful reminders of injured parts of his body he hadn't yet realized.

Others trampled down the steps behind them, all barking orders in what he assumed was Dutch. They led him to the lower bunk on one of a half dozen bunk beds lining the far wall. As they helped him onto the mattress, he knew at once this was no ordinary house.

The ground shook above them, shaking dust from the rafters. The others seemed indifferent to the explosions, busying themselves with different tasks. In the center of the crowded room, long tables covered with maps and instruments were anchored by numerous oil lamps. In the far corner to his right, two men wearing headsets sat huddled around what looked like an ancient oversized radio, another one tapping out Morse code. The other side of the room looked like a well-stocked arsenal of weapons, boots, heavy coats, and enough tools to fill a hardware store.

Danny could feel his heart racing, wondering how well those rafters above him would hold under such intense bombing.

"You eat," a woman said, appearing with a tray. She motioned for him to sit up in the bunk, which he did in spite of his pain.

She seemed unfazed by it all, as if serving him a meal was the most natural thing to do in the middle of a bombing. But he was too hungry to refuse her offer. She set the tray on his lap, then pulled off the cloth napkin covering it. Except for a small loaf of dark bread, nothing looked remotely familiar. It didn't smell too good either, but he didn't care. He thanked her then dug in. The dark purple soup had thick chunks of something chewy in it and tasted horrible, but he hid his displeasure, plastering a fake smile on his face.

"Goed, no?"

"Very good," he lied. "What's in it, if you don't mind my asking?"

"Beet soup with tulip." Her smile faltered as she nodded, as if assuring him it was all right for him to eat the stuff.

Danny forced himself to take another bite. As he crunched the peculiar morsels, a thought came to him. He looked into the strange concoction, stirring it slowly with his spoon. *These are chopped tulip bulbs? Holland is famous for their tulips, yet they're forced to eat these precious bulbs . . .*

His eyes stung, feeling humbled by the sacrifices these people were making.

Tearing off a bite of the bread, he watched the others around him as they worked. Each had a task, all of them focused in their endeavors. Even the woman who'd just served him was busily making more coffee in the small makeshift kitchen. As he sipped the hot nasty liquid, it dawned on him that everyone in the room was bone thin. Every single one of them. Belts cinched tight around the men's waists hiked up pants that no longer fit. The women's tattered dresses hung from their emaciated frames, their faces gaunt, their wispy hair peeking out beneath scarves tied under their chins.

Danny slowly lowered his mug as he continued studying them. Their wrinkles and furrowed brows served as further evidence of lives rudely interrupted by a madman's insatiable quest for power. *These are the faces of war. What has it been like for them, so many years under Nazi occupation? How have they survived, living in constant fear?*

The man who'd talked to him earlier approached him, his eyes lifted toward the ceiling. "This is a bad one."

"Must be the RAF boys," Danny said. "We only fly daylight missions."

The man pulled up a rickety chair and took a seat. "That may be, but it is ten o'clock in the morning. Those are indeed Allied bombs. We are so near the border, we seem to taste a little of everyone's arsenal."

"But it was dark outside when the sirens began," Danny argued.

The man nodded his head in understanding. "It was dark inside your room because all our windows have blackout shades. It's a bright and sunny day up there."

Danny took another sip of the wretched coffee, then set his mug back on the tray. "Do you have a name?"

"Yes, of course. Forgive me for not introducing myself. I am Eduard van der Laan." He held his hand out to Danny.

Danny shook his hand. "Danny McClain. But of course you already know that."

Eduard smiled. "Yes, Lieutenant McClain, we know your name."

"Mr. van der Laan, this is no ordinary house. Would I be correct in assuming I'm in a safe house?"

"You must call me Eduard, but yes. This is a safe house."

"Then can I also assume you and these other good people are part of the Dutch Resistance?"

He smiled even bigger. "Ja, that would be a wise deduction on your part."

Danny let out a long sigh, resting his head back. "Thank God."

The ground shook again but Eduard seemed to ignore it. "Thanks be to God, we are still alive. Thanks be to God, He led us to you before the German pigs found you and dragged you away to their god-forsaken prisoner of war camps."

"Do you know if anyone else from my crew made it? Five of us parachuted from our plane before it exploded."

"You were the only one in this area. We can check with some of the other safe houses for you."

"I'd appreciate that."

"After you eat, write down their names for me. But first, I must ask again about the photograph we found in your wallet. We cannot be too careful, Lieutenant McClain. To find such a picture on an American pilot is most unusual. Do you know those people?"

"Please, call me Danny." He took a final sip of the awful coffee, still hesitant to identify the Versteegs. *He seems honest enough, and he and these others have risked their lives to save mine. Still . . .*

"Then, Danny, I wonder why it is you evade my questions regarding this photograph? Could it be you are hiding something, Lieutenant?"

"No," he said, choosing his words carefully. "It's just that . . . you see, when I was younger, one of my school teachers—one not unlike yourself—gave us an assignment to find a pen pal in another country."

"Yes, I am familiar with pen pals. Many students here have them."

"Well, I drew the name of a boy here in The Netherlands. I wrote to him and we became good friends. He sent me that picture years ago."

"I see." Eduard rubbed his face. "But why would you carry this picture with you all these years later?"

"I can't really say. Before I left home, I happened to notice it and tucked it in my wallet. I didn't give it much thought at the time."

Eduard watched him carefully, but Danny still couldn't decipher the man's continued interest in the photograph.

"When was the last time you heard from Hans Versteeg?"

Danny tried to remember, then paused. "Mr. van der Laan, I never mentioned my friend's name."

They stared at each other for several seconds, neither saying a word. Finally, Danny asked, "How is it that *you* know his name?"

Eduard slowly leaned forward, his elbows resting on his knees. "Because I know this family."

46

As the last siren faded, the cluster of Resistance workers bustled about, preparing to go up and check for damage. Someone called for Eduard's assistance, and before Danny could ask the question, he was gone.

"Eduard!" Danny shouted, shoving the food tray aside. "Mr. van der Laan!"

He watched helplessly as the man disappeared up the stairs along with some of the other men.

"You not eat?"

Danny turned as the older woman lifted his tray. "Oh, no, I'm sorry. My, uh . . . my stomach doesn't seem able to handle any food just yet." He rubbed his stomach hoping to validate the lie. "But it was really good. Thank you for sharing."

Her face clouded then she looked away. "You eat more later. You rest now."

She took the tray and walked across the room to the small kitchen area. He watched as more of the dozen or so people milling about took the stairs, leaving only the radio guys and a couple of women behind.

"Hey, can somebody help me?" he called out, anxious to get upstairs to find Eduard.

No one even looked his way. "Please? Can somebody . . ." He fell back against his pillow, unable to hold himself up any longer. He closed his eyes and uttered a silent prayer asking God to take away the intense pain in his head so he could think more clearly. He'd never been one to have headaches and had no clue how to find relief from the throbbing. He touched the bandage on the back of his head and wondered just how much damage he'd done when he fell from the sky.

Danny could feel himself slipping beneath the shadow of depression. He recognized the signs well after his long lapse after his breakup with Beverly and the dark days following his roommate's death in college. Both seemed like distant memories, but the downward tug of deep sadness felt all too familiar. He couldn't give in to it. Not here. Not now.

He opened his eyes and looked across the room. The kind old woman who'd brought him food was stuffing the remains of his meal into her mouth. She turned to see if anyone was looking. Danny quickly averted his eyes, unwilling to let her find him staring. *Poor old girl. How hungry would you have to be to eat someone's leftovers? Especially such tasteless morsels as those?*

Of course, he knew the answer to his own question. Hunger drives behavior, throwing out all codes of conduct. Who was he to judge? He chastised himself for such a thought and tried to relax. In a few minutes, he fell fast asleep.

Danny slipped his hand under the cloth napkin covering his mother's homemade biscuits. His dad was praying. He thought that odd, especially considering the expression of gratitude that seemed to flow so naturally from his father's mouth. Danny lifted the biscuit, its warmth and aroma tantalizing his taste buds. He peeked across the table at Joey . . . surprised to find a baby seated in a high chair between Joey and Millie. The baby, toothlessly gnawing on a big fat biscuit, giggled when she noticed Danny watching her. The basket of biscuits were still beside his plate. *How'd you do that, kid?*

Someone elbowed him, but his eyes stayed glued on the baby. She waved her tiny fingers at him, as if they were sharing some wonderful secret. Then someone tapped on his shoulder. Couldn't they see he was preoccupied with his cute little niece?

"Lieutenant?"

He opened his eyes and looked at the man standing beside his bunk. "Yes? What do you want?"

He stepped back, staring at Danny with narrowed eyes. He tilted his head to one side as if to study him.

It took Danny a moment to realize he wasn't actually home, there weren't any warm biscuits, and there certainly wasn't a baby sitting across the table from him. He rubbed his face, trying to wake up. When he looked at the young man again, he noticed the tattered appearance. The jacket, sagging and rough, as if made from burlap, was at least two or three sizes too big for the guy's small frame. Same for the pants and filthy boots. A worn leather cap pulled low on his forehead shadowed his face.

"Who are you and what are you doing here?"

The tone surprised him—a husky, mellow sound—making it hard to discern if it was indeed a man or a woman trying to pass as a man. He tried to sit up and couldn't, his head screaming in protest. He fell back and closed his eyes. "Where's Eduard?"

"He's upstairs."

"Could you ask him to come down here? And could you ask someone to take me back upstairs?"

Silence.

He raised a lid, surprised to find the young man standing closer. "Look, I'm not sure what you—"

"I asked you a question. Who are you?"

He studied the face, not at all sure he wanted to play this little game. Danny smirked in response. "Who wants to know?"

The man stepped back then walked over to grab a small wooden table. Dragging it across the planked floor, he placed it right beside Danny's bed. He stomped to the left and grabbed the same wobbly chair Eduard had occupied earlier, then dragged it beside the table. He plopped himself into the chair, crossed his arms across his chest, and glared at him from beneath the cap's bill.

"I asked you a question. I shall sit here all day and all night until you give me an answer." He pushed the cap up an inch or two on his forehead. Danny couldn't help noticing the dirty fingernails.

He rolled his eyes. "Fine. Although I'm sure they've already told you, I'll tell you myself. I'm Lieutenant McClain,

United States Army Air Force."

The man said nothing but something fluttered through his eyes. "I told you, so now it's your turn. Who are *you*?"

"How did you get here?"

"I had to bail from my airplane."

"You're a pilot?"

"A co-pilot."

"Where's your crew? Who's your pilot?"

"You sure ask a lot of questions."

"Where is your crew, Lieutenant?"

"I don't know. Four others jumped. I haven't seen them since."

"Where were you going? Were you on a mission?"

"No, I was out for a Sunday drive. Germany is so lovely this time of year, don't you think?"

He didn't crack a smile or even blink. "Were you on a mission?"

"Yes."

"Where?"

"Where what?"

His lips drew tight. "Answer the question. Where was your mission target?"

He wondered if Eduard had sent this brash young man to dig for more details. He blew out a breath of impatience. "Hannover. That's in Germany, in case you don't know."

"Hannover? So you were part of the mission that bombed their marshaling yards on Wednesday?"

How could he possibly know that?

"Lieutenant?"

"Yes, but—"

Diane Moody

"Well done. Our sources tell us you boys of the 390th completely demolished those train yards."

Danny watched him, uneasy at the comprehensive amount of information he seemed to possess. Granted, if he was here in this safe house bomb shelter, he was obviously a member of the Resistance. But why all the interrogation? And why now? *And where the heck is Eduard?*

"Look, it's been really swell chatting with you like this, but would you please go up and ask Eduard to come down here? I answered all your questions, so if you could please just do me a favor and—"

"They told me your plane was called *Sweet Sophie.*"

Now it was his turn to glare at this stranger. "Who's been feeding you all this information? How could you possibly know the name of my—"

"And you—" he paused, as if unable to continue. He pulled off his cap, releasing a tangled brunette mess which came cascading down—and only then did realize this stranger was—a young *woman?*

She twirled the old leather cap in her hand, watching it. She tried again to speak, then swallowed hard instead. She dipped her head down for a moment, then raised it, leveling her gaze at him as she spoke, her voice husky with emotion. "And you named it after your dog—a smelly beagle mutt you found behind—"

"Anya . . .?" he gasped.

Her nod was all but imperceptible. As a lone tear tracked down her dirty cheek, her face softened just barely as she breathed his name.

"Danny?"

47

Anya hadn't cried in years. She had learned long ago to steel her nerves and stop the ridiculous show of emotion. At twenty-one, she wasn't a child any more, and she had no time for such weakness. But in this moment, as she stared at the friend she'd never met, she couldn't help the tears pooling in her eyes.

Earlier, when Eduard searched her out across town after the bombing, he'd insisted she come with him to the safe house. It annoyed her, these fellow Resistance fighters always bossing her around. She'd arrived in Enschede late the night before after a long and difficult journey delivering two orphaned twins to their aunt and uncle in Zwolle. While in Zwolle, her contacts told her to go to Enschede where she'd often helped with the pilot lines—the secret routes set up by the Resistance to help downed Allied pilots return to England. Since she'd arrived in town long after curfew, she stayed in the home of a fellow Resistance member, not willing to walk the final three miles east of town to the other safe house and risk being arrested.

When the bombing began that morning, she'd rushed to the nearest shelter with everyone else. Not long after she emerged, Eduard had come racing toward her, insisting she come with him. He'd rambled on and on about some American pilot they'd rescued. She hadn't bathed in days and couldn't have cared less about this or any other pilot at the moment. But the ever-dramatic Eduard wouldn't hear of it, all but dragging her across town. There, he'd shown her an old photograph he'd found in the pilot's wallet. She knew immediately why they'd sent her here.

Now, as Danny reached out his hand toward her, she could hardly breathe. Her chin seemed to take on a life of its own, trembling against her will. Suddenly, she stood up, the chair scraping in protest before clanging onto the floor. Anya dashed away the stupid tears then crossed her arms across her chest.

He let his hand fall back on the bed. "I . . . Anya, I can't believe . . . it's really *you*."

She didn't respond, even as she watched the disappointment flutter across his face. She couldn't trust herself to speak. In her mind, Danny McClain was still the American kid she wrote letters to long ago. How silly to think he was still that boy in the picture with his brother. This was no kid. This was a young man—a handsome young man with thick brown hair framing his kind face, his firm square jaw line visible beneath his dark stubble. She searched his deep blue eyes which, at the moment, seemed to pierce her soul.

He scratched his eyebrow. "I've wondered about you a thousand times since your last letter. When I heard The

Netherlands had fallen, I prayed that you and your parents would be—"

"You should've saved yourself the trouble," she scoffed. "God left us the day the Germans marched into our homeland."

He didn't say anything, but she couldn't miss the sympathy in his eyes. She turned her back to him, picking up the chair. "But if praying made you feel better, then good for you."

"Anya, why are you—"

"But don't worry." She set the chair back beside the table. "We'll make sure you get back to your base across the Channel. We're quite good at helping you boys get back to your nice warm barracks. We wouldn't want you to miss another hot meal."

"Can you cut the sarcasm for a minute and just talk to me?" He tried to sit up and couldn't, his face pinched in a grimace.

Instinct sent her toward him but she stopped herself. How badly was he injured? Eduard hadn't mentioned he was hurt. "Are you all right?" she asked, trying to sound indifferent.

"It's nothing," he said, touching the bandage on the back of his head. Apparently I bonked my head pretty good when I landed." He motioned for her to sit. "Can you please just have a seat and talk to me?"

She tried to think of a smart come-back but came up blank. She lowered herself back into the chair.

"I don't even know where to begin," he said. "How long has it been since we wrote—four years? Five?"

"Five. When the Germans came in May of 1940, they shut down our mail system."

He nodded. "I wrote several more letters, but I guess you never got them."

"No, of course I didn't."

"How are your parents?"

Her bouncing foot stopped. "They're dead."

"What? No!"

Seeing the shock on his face, she glanced away. "They were picked up and sent to a concentration camp in Germany. I was told Mother died before they got there. Father was shot later for helping another prisoner who had fainted." She looked up at him with defiance, hoping he'd see how much the war had toughened her. He'd seen her tears, now he'd see how thick her skin was.

"I'm so sorry."

"Why? You never met them."

"Anya, please . . . must you be so belligerent? Of course, I never met them. I never met Hans either, but that didn't stop me from caring about you and your mother and father after he died."

She shrugged, toying with her cap again.

"How have you managed? What has it been like for you?"

She crossed her legs, noticing a streak of dried mud on the hem of her pants. She scraped at it for a moment, her foot still bouncing. "Where would you like me to start? The day the Nazi swine started rounding up all our Jewish friends to ship them off to the death camps? Or would you prefer to hear how they raided and pillaged all of our possessions and let us starve? Or maybe you'd like to hear about the mind games they play with us, pitting one against another to see who would rat out their friends first? Huh? Or the time a German soldier—"

He grabbed her wrist. "Stop it, Anya!"

She tried to jerk her hand free but he held it tight. She glared at him.

He shook his head. "Hans always told me you were a stubborn little thing, but I had no idea."

"Don't!" She twisted her wrist and freed it, then pointed at him. "Don't you *dare* speak of my brother."

"Anya?" The voice came from behind her. "What's going on here?"

She turned, finding Eduard at the bottom of the stairs. She put her cap on her head and blew past him, stomping up the stairs without a word. Once up in the house, she shoved past several workers then out the back door, letting it slam behind her. She ran to a stand of trees near the barn and climbed to her favorite hiding place, a perch high up in its strong branches.

Anya looked out across the village, watching columns of smoke from the countless new bomb craters. How many times had she found comfort in the arms of this tree and so many others like it across her country? She was much too old to be climbing trees, but she didn't care. She couldn't stand the moments after the sirens stopped, when everyone climbed out of the shelters. She couldn't stand hearing their same sorrowful comments, over and over. And she couldn't stand seeing all the damage inflicted all around her. How much more could her beloved country bear?

Up in these branches, she always found the solace and

privacy she craved. She needed to be alone with her thoughts and somehow bolster her wretched emotions back in place. The carefully constructed dam around her heart had held for years. She'd witnessed despicable atrocities and never shed a tear. She'd stolen anything she could get her hands on to help the cause, feeling no shame. And she'd killed her share of Nazis without a single trace of regret.

Oh, she'd heard the gossip. They said she had ice in her veins. She had smiled the first time she heard it, confident at last that her walls were securely intact.

Until today.

From the moment she saw him, she'd come completely undone. In that split second, her entire childhood flashed through her mind, dashing all restraint in the blink of an eye. The sudden precious memory of Danny's letters pulled the single thread that had held her together for so long, unraveling her from the inside out. He was a living, breathing remembrance of her life before the war. Through their letters, she'd found hope again after losing Hans. Until the Occupation—even thousands of miles away—Danny McClain had always been there for her.

And now he's here.

"Do you feel better?" Eduard asked as he assisted Danny from the upstairs bathroom.

"Yes, thank you. I can't remember a bath ever feeling so

good."

"You are lucky. Not always is the water warm. The ladies, they heated water for you."

"Please tell them how much I appreciate that."

"I will, but it is their honor to do so. We all wish to help, even in the small ways, those who have come so far and risked so much to help us."

With Eduard's help, Danny sat on the side of the bed, slowly easing himself back against the pillows propped against the headboard. He let out a long sigh. "And I have to admit, it helps just having some clothes on again. I really appreciate your help, Eduard."

The man stepped back. "It is my privilege. We will never be able to thank you enough for helping fight for our freedom."

"And I can never thank you enough for rescuing me before the Germans shot me."

"Yes, well, it seems we are both thankful." He chuckled, a broad smile warming his face.

"May I ask you a question?"

"Of course." Eduard took a seat on the bedside chair.

"Why is Anya . . . I mean, what did she . . . well, why did she—"

"You would like to know why she is so angry?"

"Yes. I was so shocked to see her, to finally meet her after all these years."

Eduard's brow creased. "You mean, you've never met?"

"Not face to face. We were pen pals, like I told you earlier. I mean, at first I was pen pals with her brother Hans before he died—"

"Such a tragedy that was. For his parents, but especially for Anya."

"Yes, I know. She was the one who wrote to tell me about the accident. Then, over the course of time, we just continued writing each other. I was . . ." Danny felt his face warm. "I was very fond of her—in a brotherly way, of course."

"Of course," Eduard added with knowing eyes.

"But once the war started, that was the end of our correspondence. I was worried sick about Anya and her parents. But that was long before the United States got into the war. I never forgot about her, but life went on for me. I went to college for a couple of years, then enlisted, and . . . the rest is history, I guess you'd say. Literally, in this case. But I never imagined finding Anya in the middle of a war like this. Yet, here I am and there she was."

"Sometimes our life stories are written in spite of us," Eduard said. "No one here in our country ever imagined we'd be under German rule. Ours is a neutral country. Always has been. And yet, we have been occupied now for almost five years. That is, those of us who still live. So many are gone." He shook his head. "So many . . .

"But as for Anya, you must understand how difficult it has been for her. She has lost everything. But instead of breaking down or being debilitated by this nightmare, she has worked hard for our Resistance. Tirelessly. Never complaining. She just does what she has to do. As we all do."

Danny tried to imagine how hard it must have been for a girl growing up in a country torn apart by war. The young woman he'd met earlier was hardened and gruff. He never would have known her had their paths crossed otherwise, so little did she resemble Hans' rebellious young sister standing with her family in the old photograph.

"Eduard, how can I help her? What can I do to get through to her?"

"Be patient, my friend. Let her learn to trust you again."

Danny wondered how long he would remain in this shelter before he was sent back to Framlingham. Would he have enough time? Would he even see her again?

"I shall leave you," Eduard said, standing. "Get some rest. If you feel up to it later, you'd be welcome to join us for dinner."

"Thanks. I'd like that."

As Eduard closed the door behind him, Danny's thoughts swirled around the strange and awkward moments he'd spent with Anya earlier. He'd often wondered what it would be like if he ever had the chance to meet her face to face. How interesting that he'd never wondered or speculated on the sound of her voice. Hearing it now with the unusual mix of Dutch and English accents blended with such a unique, natural raspiness to it, he realized how perfectly it fit her personality. Even the way she pronounced his name— sounding more like "Donnie" than Danny—surprised and intrigued him.

But what puzzled him most . . . had he just imagined the level of friendship written in those letters so many years ago? Did he read between the lines, thinking she cared for him on some deeper level? Or was he nothing more to her than a distant substitute brother?

No. He knew better.

Be patient. Let her learn to trust you again.

48

Later, Eduard returned to help Danny into the large kitchen where several people were gathering for the evening meal. He took a seat at the round table as Eduard introduced him to the others in the room. They all seemed cordial, though only a few of them spoke English. Greta, the woman who had given him food in the shelter downstairs, brought a large soup tureen to the table.

She gave him a gracious smile. "You hungry now?"

He smiled, nodding at her, wondering what was in that covered soup dish. *I'm so hungry I could eat a . . . then again, maybe not.*

As everyone took a seat at the table, he looked up just as Anya walked into the room. At least he thought it was Anya. She'd obviously cleaned up, her long brown hair hanging just below her shoulders, the natural curls still damp on the ends. Danny couldn't take his eyes off her. A wisp of long bangs feathered along her forehead. She didn't need make-up with skin that perfect, though a natural blush seemed to warm her cheeks. But it was her eyes that caught him completely off-guard. When they'd met earlier, they were mostly hidden beneath matted hair hanging over her brow. He'd not seen how incredibly beautiful her eyes were—the perfect blend of blue and gray, framed by dark lashes.

But she was much too thin. They all were. The long peasant-style blouse, cinched at the waist with what looked like a braided rope, did little to hide her slender frame. The khaki military-style pants seemed to swallow her whole, but at least they were clean.

Then, all of a sudden he noticed her freckles. The freckles on the young girl in the photograph were still there. A bit faded perhaps, but still sprinkled across her nose and cheeks. Something about seeing those humored him.

"What are you smiling at?"

Hearing her voice, he blinked and quickly realized everyone at the table was looking at him. "I was just thinking . . . well, I remembered your, uh . . . you look lovely, Anya."

She looked down, tearing off a piece of bread then passing the loaf.

"He's right," Eduard added. "You look very nice tonight, Anya."

"Only because you all have hoarded the only soap in all of The Netherlands. Frederic, have you been stealing from the black market again?"

The man beside Danny laughed. "Right under the nose of the Gestapo. Not that any of those vermin would know what to do with soap."

Eduard repeated the words in Dutch then everyone else

chuckled. Greta ladled something brown and lumpy into a bowl and handed it to Danny. He prayed it was stew.

"Thank you, Greta." He tried very hard to still his face at the strange aroma. She continued giving each person one full ladle of soup. Or whatever it was. He was fairly certain the chunks were more of the chopped tulip bulbs, but the rest of it remained a mystery. He stirred his portion as the conversation continued around the table, mostly in Dutch. He looked across the table at Anya and caught her watching him. He smiled before tasting the soup.

Good Lord, that's awful! He held it in his mouth, afraid to swallow while careful not to physically react to the assault on his taste buds. He heard a snicker and looked across to find Anya quietly laughing at him. It was the first time he'd ever seen her smile. He smiled back, completely forgetting not to swallow. He blinked, his eyes watered, and it took the greatest effort not to cough or groan. Across the table she hid behind the curtain of her napkin, but he could still see her shoulders shaking.

Oblivious to the two of them, the others continued chatting.

Anya put down her napkin, sat up a bit straighter, and filled her spoon with soup. With her eyes locked on Danny's, she swallowed the soup while making a great show of savoring it. Not to be outdone, Danny dipped his spoon in the soup again, and with his eyes still locked on hers, swallowed it in one gulp. Though desperate to gag, he stifled the urge. Anya took another spoonful, her eyes daring him to do the same. He did. She took another and again, he followed her lead. But for the life of him, this time he could not make himself swallow another drop of the vile stuff. The gag reflexes kicked in and he knew it was just a matter of time before he spewed it all over the table. With his face contorted, he forced it down then grabbed his glass of water to wash it down. When he finally looked over his glass at her, she had her lips pressed together though her eyes danced. Then, just that fast, she lost control and burst out laughing.

Everyone around the table froze at the sound of Anya's unrestrained, wheezing laughter. Watching Danny continue to guzzle the rest of his water, she laughed even harder. The dinner guests looked back and forth between them, mystified. But so contagious were her giggles, the rest of them joined in until the room was filled with raucous laughter. Several made comments in Dutch, but Danny didn't need a translator to know what they were saying. He rolled his eyes at her then grabbed a piece of bread and stuck it in his mouth.

Eduard stopped and held up his hand, ending the laughter abruptly. The haunting wail of the air raid siren grew loud, dispersing them immediately toward the makeshift cellar. The guy named Frederic helped Danny to his feet, but before they could move, an explosion rocked near by, crashing them all to the floor. Everyone seemed to shout at once, frantic to get down to the shelter. Danny tried to get up, but failed. Frederic draped Danny's arm over his shoulder, practically lifting him as he dashed to the stairs.

Their awkward movements down the steps landed Danny below in a pile, his injured foot bent beneath him. Before he could open his mouth to cry out, another explosion rattled the rafters. Fredric grabbed him again and quickly deposited him in one of the lower bunks.

"Are you all right?" Anya shouted, coming to his side.

He nodded, his jaw clenched hard as he leaned back trying to absorb the searing pain in his ankle. She responded but he couldn't hear her. He cupped his ear. "What?" he yelled.

"You're a liar!" she shouted, leaning close to his ear. "You're obviously *not* all right!"

He waved her off as another rumble shook dust from the beams above them. At least this one was farther away. She shrugged as if utterly uninterested in what he had to say and turned to leave. He reached out for her hand. She looked down at his hand on hers, then slowly tracked her eyes to his.

"Don't go," he said.

He watched her, wondering if she'd pull free of his grasp as she had last time, but she didn't. Instead, she lowered herself to sit on the edge of his bed, turning slightly toward him. She looked around as if concerned what the others might think, then tipped her head to look up at the ceiling.

"I think the worst is over now," she said quietly. Her eyes met his again. "Your foot. It's very painful, isn't it?"

"*Killing* me. If it's possible to re-sprain a sprained ankle, I believe that's what just happened."

The slightest smile lifted a corner of her mouth. "Frederic is many things, but a gentle man, he is not."

"I would have to agree."

She looked back down at her hand, still in his. "So you liked very much Greta's stew?"

"Please, don't remind me," he groaned. "Stew, was it? I'm almost afraid to ask what was in it."

"You don't want to know," she said coyly.

"Then don't tell me. I'll just savor the memory."

She raised her eyes to his. "Good. Because there's more where that came from. I can bring you some, if you like?"

"It was good to see you laugh, Anya."

She shrugged, looking away again. "Fatigue. Nothing more."

"Regardless, it was nice to see you smile. For a moment, I could almost imagine the war had ended and we were still friends . . . after all."

She didn't say anything, but he hoped she understood his meaning. He brushed his thumb along the back of her hand, surprised how soft her skin was. Her short nails were free of dirt and snags now, and he wondered how long it had taken her to scrub them clean. He slowly raised his other hand to finger a curl of her hair. She stiffened, but didn't pull away.

"Danny, I apologize about . . . earlier."

Her voice was so quiet, he wasn't sure he'd heard what she said—except for his name.

"It was unfair," she continued. "I had no right to treat you that way." Her gaze remained on their joined hands.

"No apology necessary. I really can't imagine what it's been like for you or what you've been through. To see me here in this place, in the middle of this nightmare, well I'm sure it must have been a bit of a shock."

She looked up at him; the hint of a smile had returned. "Yes, I suppose you could say that."

"And how is our pilot?" Eduard said, interrupting them as he approached the two of them.

Anya stood up, dropping Danny's hand. "If you'll excuse me." And then she was gone.

"I'm all right, I guess. Though I think I may have re-injured my ankle."

"I was afraid of that," he said, putting his hands on his hips. "I'll have our doctor stop by tomorrow if he can get here. In the meantime, I think perhaps we should keep you down here for a while. With so many air raids, the trip up and down those stairs won't help your recovery."

"That's fine with me."

"Good. I'll go up and take a look at the damage, then come back later. Perhaps I could ask Anya to redress the wrapping on your foot?"

Danny felt his face warm. "Oh? Yes. Well, perhaps."

Eduard lowered his voice as a gentleness filled his face. "Do you know, I have never once heard the sound of her laughter? At least, not since the war started. Not once."

"Really?"

"It's true. I think you are good medicine for her, Lieutenant." Eduard winked, then turned to leave. "I'll see if the women were able to salvage any of our dinner. If so, I'll have them bring you something."

He disappeared up the stairs before Danny could tell him not to bother.

He leaned his head back against the pillows and let his eyes close. He remembered the sound of her laughter as if a recording of it played over and over in his mind. How her eyes and nose crinkled as though she could do nothing to stop the giggles spilling out of her; as though a great reservoir of long forgotten laughter had just been rediscovered.

She's still there, he thought. *The little girl in the picture by the windmill is still there inside.*

As his mind gazed at the memory of her blue gray eyes, he prayed for the beautiful young woman she'd become, despite the war. He prayed for the horrors still haunting her and the unspeakable loss of her short life. *Lord, if You're listening, please help her find her way back from the nightmare she's lived. And if it's all right with You, Lord, let me . . . let me be the friend she needs now.*

49

The cellar remained a swarm of activity through the next several hours. Sirens came and went as the rumble of distant bombings continued. Danny felt trapped and restless. He dozed from time to time, but his mind wouldn't stop fussing. What was going on up there? Were those Allies bombing them? It made no sense as most of the 390th missions were German targets. But over the course of the last few months, they'd decimated the Luftwaffe for the most part. Eduard had said they were near the border here, but he wondered just how close they actually were. It all troubled and irritated Danny, to be sitting there useless in a time of great need.

He hadn't seen Anya for several hours. He wondered if she was offended by his simple gestures. He hadn't meant to frighten her. When they'd laughed across the dinner table, he felt a long forgotten stirring of all those feelings he once held for her when they'd been writing each other. How was that possible after all he'd been through? After all those years since the letters stopped? After all those months at

Northwestern when his thoughts were of no one but Beverly? Through all those long months of training after he enlisted? How could the confused feelings of the teenager he was back then survive through all that and show up here?

But deep inside he knew. He'd never forgotten her. He'd always wondered what might have happened to her. And as best he knew how, he'd pray for her and her parents. Yet here he was in a safe house in Occupied Holland, and all he wanted or cared about was seeing her again.

One of the radio guys took off his headset and crossed the room. "Lieutenant, Eduard wanted me to let you know," he began with a thick Dutch accent, "We have contacted all of the other safe houses within one hundred kilometers, and no one has word of your crew mates."

Danny refused to accept the implication. "Do you have ways to get in touch with my base back in England? I'm stationed at Framlingham with the 390th. Maybe they know something."

"Ja, we reported to our people who speak directly to bases in England. We passed along your name so they will know you are here and safe."

"Thank you, but is it possible for your people to find out if they've—"

"*Dank je wel,* Maarten," Anya interrupted, tapping the young man on his shoulder. She spoke softly to him in Dutch, but Danny couldn't understand. As the radio operator returned to his station, Anya explained. "We have contacted all our sources both here and in England, and we have no word of your crew."

"I'm sure they're either hiding out somewhere or . . . or

maybe they just haven't made contact with anyone yet."

"Of course."

He wasn't fooled. He knew what she was thinking.

"Would you like some tea?" she asked, pointing toward the kitchen.

His mind was elsewhere, trying to pinpoint where Don, Dal, Tony, and Lane could have landed and why they hadn't reported in yet. Surely they'd been able to—

"Danny?"

He blinked. "Yes?"

She studied him for a moment. "I'm going to have some tea. I'll make some for you as well."

He watched her cross the room but felt uneasy about the news he'd just heard. Surely they'd survived as he had. Surely it was just a matter of lousy communication. This was war, after all.

A few moments later she returned, carrying two mugs of hot tea. As she handed him one, he asked, "How far are we from the German border?"

"Only a few kilometers. A stone's throw, as they say. Not far at all." She took a seat on the same rickety chair. "That is why we have so much activity here—all the bombings and anti-aircraft fire. Just across the border, not far is the Ruhr and Rhine industrial region. Always we hear the planes of our Allies, day and night, as we lie below their bombing runs into those areas. Which is why the Germans constantly fire off their anti-aircraft, with their explosions raining down shells all around us. Ja, we are too close here. Much too close."

He took a sip of tea, surprised it actually tasted like tea. "Where did you get this? It's very good."

"Frederic is not the only one. I know a thing or two about the black market."

"Is that right?"

"When the Germans invaded us, they took everything. They raided our homes, our stores, our farms. It was difficult to find food, though we managed. We were required to use ration coupons for this or that, and even if you had enough rations, the store shelves were mostly empty. Still, we survived.

"Until last September, that is. Back in 1940, just before the invasion, our Queen Wilhelmina escaped along with much of our government to England. There, they could send coded messages to us on the BBC and stay in constant contact with us. Last September we received word from our queen that our railroad workers were to stop working and go into hiding in order to paralyze rail movement for German troop reinforcements. And that's what they did. At first, the Germans merely retaliated by cutting our food rations, hoping to starve us all to death. But we didn't care. We thought for sure our liberation was at hand.

"At the same time British General Montgomery put into place a plan called 'Market Garden'."

"I remember reading about that and how horribly it all went wrong," Danny said.

"At first, when we saw all the Allies storming in, we felt sure our liberation had begun. People were celebrating in the streets, girls were kissing the Allied paratroopers—it was one big party. Then Montgomery's plan failed miserably. The Germans were furious with us for thinking we could overthrow them, so they cut us off in every possible way. They destroyed our ports and bombed most of our railroad facilities. They blasted our dikes and flooded much of our lowland areas which ruined almost all of our crops. Some areas had their electricity completely cut off. Seyss-Inquart, the German Reichskommissar over our country, halted all food supplies."

"In effect, trying to starve all of you," Danny added.

"Yes. I'm sure Hitler knows all too well that hungry people are much easier to rule. But of course, that wasn't enough. Later, in November, they rounded up as many of our men as they could to work as 'volunteers' in their labor camps." A touch of humor lit her eyes. "Of course, we Dutch are a smart people. Our men who were forced to work in the German ammunition factories conspired to build 'duds' as I believe you call them. We always wanted to thank those brave Dutchmen whenever the Germans fired near us and their shells did not explode. A sort of sweet vengeance, I suppose you could say."

She tucked her foot beneath her and continued. "The winter was brutal. We had no heat, no food . . . no hope. At times when I was out on a delivery, I would see people walking along the road and they would just drop dead in their tracks. Sometimes many along the way. You have no idea what it's like to see that. So many died through the winter, and there was no wood for caskets. Bodies were wrapped in cloth, if they could find some, then piled with all the others."

"I can't even imagine such hunger," he said softly. "What it does to you—not just your body, but your state of mind. How do you function, how can you think about anything *but* how hungry you are?"

"It consumes you. Yet, even that was not as bad as the bombings. You think nothing can be worse than starving and the numbing cold, but the bombs . . ." She shook her head, as if searching for the right words.

"I remember, it was February of last year. February 22nd—my first time back to the safe house in Nijmegan in many months. I'd gone there to rest. I was so tired, so exhausted. I'd crawled into a bunk bed in a far corner of the cellar—not unlike these here—and I'd only been asleep for a couple of hours when the air raids went off again. Everyone started coming down the stairs, stomping and making so much noise. I pulled the pillow over my head, wishing to ignore it all.

"But that was not to be. The Germans hit us hard. In the middle of the day, the bombs fell. For hours, they fell, flattening everything. Thousands died. The churches were destroyed, so many beautiful churches—just gone. One of the Montessori schools was flattened. All the children—gone. It went on and on and on. Everything was on fire, huge pillars of black smoke filled the air, and no water to put out the fires. And the wind. I remember the wind kept blowing so hard . . .

"When the bombs finally stopped falling, everyone came out of the shelters, searching for loved ones in the destruction. Everyone crying, everyone frantic—such screams you can't imagine in your worst nightmare. Others walking in a daze, lost and confused. But most were never found. Thousands and thousands of them. Only the body parts. So many body parts . . ." She paused, her voice hushed. "I saw . . . I saw a baby crying in her mother's arms . . . but there was only her mother's torso."

He watched as she fell silent. *She's there again, hearing the screams, smelling the smoke, and seeing that poor baby* . . . As the image rolled through his mind he watched a tremor pass over her.

"Anya?"

His voice seemed to break the spell as she turned to him.

"Anya, could I ask you a favor?"

She shuddered again. "Yes?"

"Could you help me sit up better?" Of course he could do it himself, but he hoped to distract her from the memories.

She set her mug down and stood, looping her arm beneath his to help him sit up. She pulled the pillows out, plumping them before stuffing them back behind him. "Better?"

"Almost."

"Almost?"

He patted the bed beside him. "Sit with me."

She turned to look around the room.

"Who cares what they think? Sit."

She turned back to face him, and he watched a visible change come over her. Gone were the haunting memories, quickly replaced with a flash of challenge in her eyes, her chin thrust forward. Then, without a word, she scooted in next to him, mostly sitting up, her back straight as a board. He moved over an inch or two—no more—to give her room, turning just enough to better face her.

"There. Isn't that more comfortable?"

"I don't know yet." She paused, looking at the foot of the bunk bed. "I'll let you know."

50

Anya didn't want to sit so close to Danny, but she wasn't about to let him win the dare she'd heard in his voice and seen in his eyes. Did she care what the others thought? Well, no. At least she didn't think so. Still, she had a reputation to maintain, one she'd worked hard to establish. And she knew the others would have plenty to say about this close proximity.

After all, we are in bed together, she thought. A second thought whipped through her mind. *No, we are on a bed together. There's a difference.*

Sensing the chill of those dark memories slipping away, she tried to focus on Danny. She still couldn't believe he was really here. It felt as if a past life and her present life had accidentally collided, leaving her off-kilter somehow. She was also bewildered that the young American kid in the picture with his brother at some ball game was in fact this handsome Allied flyboy. He'd matured in a way she hadn't expected. Not that she'd spent hours speculating on the subject. Well, only a few, perhaps. And that was long, long ago.

Yet now, here he was beside her—this young man with a profile not unlike that of a Roman god. But even as the thought traipsed through her mind, she scolded herself for such a silly notion.

"Now, where were we?" Danny said, breaking her thoughts. "Oh, yes. It was a very difficult, cold winter here. I have to say, it's chilly in here now, but I would think the winter must have been so much worse. How did you stay warm?"

Relief wound through her, thankful to be distracted from thoughts she must avoid. "We did *not* stay warm. We stole anything we could to burn in our hearths. We bundled up as much as possible. But mostly we were hungry. *So* hungry. And we still are, as you may have noticed. They tell us there's not a rat or cat or dog in all of Holland."

"Oh no," he groaned, putting his hand over his stomach. "Please don't tell me that was rat stew at dinner?"

"No, of course not," she scoffed, acting insulted.

"Thank goodness, I'm not sure I could—"

"It was *dakhaas*."

"Which is?"

"Some people call it 'roof rabbit' but it's actually cat meat."

"What?!"

She felt a chuckle rise to the surface as she watched the expression on his face. "We haven't seen rabbits in at least a year or more. So people kill whatever kind of animal they can find, then cut off the tail and head, skin them, and sell them as rabbit meat."

"Wait, how can you know for sure that was cat meat in tonight's stew?"

"Because of its pungent odor and taste. Dog meat is much more flavorful."

He leaned his head back. "I think I'm gonna be sick. Again."

She rather enjoyed making him squirm. "It's an acquired taste, Danny."

He turned to give her a sick smile. "Evidently."

"Now rat meat, on the other hand—"

"No!" he said, holding up his palm to her face. "No more food talk."

"Are all Americans so weak-stomached?"

"Of course not. But can we please change the subject?"

She blew a sigh, louder than necessary. "If we must."

"You spoke earlier of making deliveries. What did you mean? Is that part of your work with the black market?"

"Trust me, our black market does not make home deliveries."

"Then what did you mean?"

She folded her arms and tried to focus on anything apart from the compassion in his face. "From the beginning, most of my work with the Resistance has been transporting people here or there. Most of them Jews, mostly children."

"Anya, that's incredible. You save lives! In all this madness, you're saving people's lives. That must be very rewarding."

"This is war, Danny. Hardly anything feels 'rewarding'."

"Maybe when it's all over, you'll look back and see it that way. But it also sounds extremely risky. Is it?"

"Always. But then everything is a risk now."

It was so easy talking to him. Before she knew it, she

was telling him all about her work and the many children she'd taken here or there. She always called them by name, her "little ones" who often clung to her, frightened and wanting nothing more than to go home to their parents. She told him about her many close calls and the various acting roles she'd had to play whenever the Gestapo began to nose around.

She never forgot he was there beside her, letting her talk. He seemed to hang on every word, all the while watching her. At first it made her uncomfortable, such scrutiny by someone sitting much too close. Then, the more he asked questions, she began to relax.

When telling of a fellow Resistance worker who'd been arrested, she lost her voice for a moment. When it returned, she couldn't hide her emotion, hearing the graveled attempts in her own voice.

"We know what goes on in the prisons. We have infiltrators who report back to us what happens in those places. Things no human should ever have to experience. The beatings, the rotting, bug-infested food, the filthy conditions, and so much sickness. Many die from illness soon after they arrive. With so little nourishment, most of us have no way to fight off infection or disease. But those are the lucky ones. For those who survive, they face unspeakable abuse. Every time I hear of this one who was assaulted by a guard, or that one who was shot for no reason at all—every time, I wonder what it must have been like for Father in one of those places." She straightened her back, speaking through clenched teeth. "And I admit to myself how glad I am Mother died before she got there. Better to die than endure such horror."

She stared at nothing, seeing everything, tired of talking about it.

Danny gently took her hand in his, slowly entwining their fingers. She knew she should pull back, but she didn't. As much as she wanted to, she couldn't.

"I used to think people were inherently good," she said, barely over a whisper. "That deep down, most people try to live good lives and be kind to one another. But I know that's not true. I believe it's quite the opposite. The good ones are few and far between."

She grew silent, gazing down at their hands and finding it hard to swallow. She felt him still watching her and wondered what he was thinking. Did he think she was crazy? Did he think she was bitter, merely finding fault with others? No doubt he still believed the world was full of good and kind people. After all, he was one of the Allies—one of thousands from all over the world who had joined together to stop Hitler's madness. Who would do such a thing, risking their lives for people they didn't even know in countries on the other side of the globe?

"Anya, tell me. What was the last good memory you had? I mean, before the war. When was the last time you remember being happy?"

She tilted her head, facing him. "What? That's a silly question to ask."

"Maybe so, but I still want to know. Think back to the last time you had a good laugh."

"You mean, other than at dinner tonight?"

He rolled his eyes. "Please, let's not bring that up again."

"Why do you want—"

"Humor me. So much heartache here. So many awful memories. I just thought you'd like to think back on happier times. Like that snotty girl you sucker-punched in Girl Scouts."

She smiled. "Ah, Tilly."

"Yes, that's her name. I remember now."

Anya shrugged. "She had it coming. I'm still not sorry, even though Father made me apologize to everyone. I'd do it again, if I had the chance."

"Do you ever see any of your old friends?"

"No, not many. Everyone stays to themselves as much as possible. It is best not to draw attention to yourself. Ever. From time to time I see people I've known, but we rarely speak. You become very suspicious. You have to be. No one can be trusted. So many traitors all around us and most of them, people you'd never suspect. But of course, turning friends and family over to the Gestapo is quite lucrative."

She took a deep breath and stretched, weary of it all, dropping his hand in the process. "I talk too much. Talk, talk, talk."

"Not at all. We're just catching up. It's been such a long time since our letters."

Anya wondered what time it was, then realized she didn't care. She turned to rest on her side facing him, propped up on her elbow, her head resting against her fist. She felt drowsy and relaxed and strangely comforted here beside him. How long had it been since she'd felt so . . . secure? She brushed away the thought.

"Then it's your turn," she said. "Tell me how you got here. Last I heard you were working for your father at the theater."

"Whoa—that seems like a lifetime ago."

"It *was* a lifetime ago." She pulled at a thread on his sleeve and toyed with it. "So tell me, did you go to university? What was the name of it?"

"Northwestern?"

"Ja, that's it. Did you go?"

"I did. Dad eventually recovered from the beating those thugs gave him—I wrote you about that, didn't I?"

"Ja, I remember. It was horrible, how badly they hurt him."

"It was bad. I wasn't sure he'd ever really get over it. But he was finally able to go back to work. In the meantime, I'd saved up enough to get me through the first year—barely— but I made it. Even lived on campus."

He stopped for a moment. She could tell he was remembering something. She watched him, studying every detail on his face. *It's a good face. A kind face.*

"What was I saying?"

"You said you lived on campus. Did you like this university, Northwestern?"

"I did. At least at first."

"What happened?"

He scratched his chin whiskers. "Well, that's a long story and not a particularly happy one."

"Surely it is more happy than mine?"

He nodded. "You have a point."

"Then tell me. What was it like, living on this Northwestern campus?"

"Great. Well, sort of. I had this roommate named Craig. He was such a carefree spirit, at least on the surface. And boy, did he love the girls on campus. And they seemed to love him just as much. I never saw much of him, unless he'd run out of clean clothes or needed a textbook for class. Not that he went to class much. I think his college experience had more to do with carnal knowledge than anything he learned in the classroom."

She felt her face warm, shocked by such a statement. "You're making that up."

"No, if anything I'm sanitizing the situation."

"Sanitizing?"

"Cleaning it up. He seemed to hop from one bed to another, and never seemed to run out of willing partners."

She felt her brows arch high on her forehead. "Surely you are exaggerating? Is this normal in Chicago, America? This bed-hopping?"

"No! Well, I mean, I guess it goes on, but nothing like— well, no. Certainly not."

"You don't sound very convincing," she teased, enjoying his reaction.

"It's just that . . . well, the thing is—"

"Danny, did you also have many girlfriends at Northwestern?" She continued to play with the renegade thread on his sleeve, twisting it around and around on her finger. She raised her eyes slowly, waiting for his response.

"Nothing like that, I assure you."

"Not even one girl you fancied? Even a little?"

"Well . . . okay, yes, there was someone." He nodded, looking down at his ankle. "Do you think maybe I should rewrap my ankle? Or just check the—"

"What was her name?"

"Who?"

"Danny . . ."

"Oh. Her name was Beverly."

"Was she pretty, this Beverly?"

"Oh, well, yes. She was very pretty, actually."

"Does she write you letters?"

He twisted his mouth to one side. "No, we broke up before I enlisted."

"What happened? Why did you break up with her?"

He huffed, his eyes widening. "Well, if you must know, *she* broke up with *me*."

"What?" She lifted her head off her hand. "Why would she do a stupid thing like that? *Een dom meisje.*"

"And that means . . .?"

"A stupid girl."

He smiled. "Should I have sucker-punched her, you think?"

Anya pursed her lips, recognizing the tease. "I should hope not, as you are a gentleman. But this Beverly obviously didn't deserve you."

He took a deep breath. "As it turns out, we were apart that first summer. I stayed for summer school and she went to her family's lake house. And while she was there, she fell in love with her brother's best friend who came to visit. He and her brother both played football for Northwestern."

She shook her head. "What is it with you Americans and your sports? Always the baseball or the football—"

"And I seem to remember how much you truly loved hearing about my Cubs."

She pressed her lips hoping to camouflage her grin.

"Back to the girls. Were there others? Surely she wasn't the only one."

"Well, sad though it may seem, she was. But what about you? I know there's been a war going on, but have you met anyone along the way? Another Resistance worker perhaps? Frederic's kind of handsome, don't you think?"

"If you like a man who's fascinated with his own belching and other bodily noises."

He laughed. "Ah. How very romantic. But no one else?"

What a thing to ask, she thought. "I don't know what it's like for the Allies, but here in The Netherlands, we've hardly had time for romance." She didn't mean to snap at him but knew that's how it sounded. "What with the war going on, as you said."

"What about that guy . . . what was his name? The one at the farm where you used to help out."

She never saw it coming, the knife he'd just shoved in her heart. His question took her breath away. She could only stare at him, unable to form a single word.

"Come on, you know who I mean—Willard? William?" His eyes danced. He seemed to enjoy his line of questioning.

"Wim," she whispered.

"Yeah, that's it! Wim. He broke his leg, right? As I recall, he had a crush on you, right?"

She dropped her eyes.

"C'mon, you can tell me. Were you in love with him?"

His playful grin only twisted the knife in her heart. She couldn't bear it. Without a word, she rolled back on the bed, then stood up.

"Anya, I'm sorry—I shouldn't have pried. I didn't mean

anything by it. Hey, I was mostly just teasing."

She turned around to face him, her fist knotted over her mouth. She shook her head.

"Anya, please—" He reached out for her, but she pulled back her hand.

She turned, rushed across the room, and fled up the stairs.

51

"Anya! Please don't go. Come back!"

Danny couldn't believe he had been so insensitive. He had no idea what had caused her to up and leave like that. Still, with everything else she'd been through, he should have been more cautious. He should have known to tread carefully with such personal questions. *Why didn't I just keep my mouth shut?*

He leaned back against the pillows, mentally kicking himself for being such an inconsiderate fool. He looked around and found only a few of the guys looking his way. Had they heard everything? Did they know something he didn't?

"You Americans, you are . . . how you say—fumble?" Frederic came around the corner, puffing on some kind of cigarette. It smelled like dried manure.

"I don't know what you mean," Danny said, wishing the conversation was already over.

"You have Anya here," he said, pointing his cigarette toward Danny's bed, "but now she's gone. You fumble." He shrugged as if Danny should clearly understand his meaning.

"I didn't know football was so popular in The Netherlands."

Frederic's bushy brows drew together. "Eh?"

"Never mind," Danny said, waving him off.

Frederic rattled off something in Dutch then punctuated it with a perfectly timed flatulent. He offered a proud smile then wandered off.

Wonderful.

Before he could brow-beat himself further, a sudden burst of commotion came barreling down the stairs. Everyone was talking at once, shouting in both English and Dutch. Then, out from the middle of the knot of people, a scruffy man in uniform broke free.

"Danny!"

"Lane!"

The navigator rushed to Danny's side as he tried to stand up. When he did, Pendergrass hugged the stuffing out of him. "Where on earth have you been?" he croaked.

"I can't believe it's really you!" Lane said, finally stepping back. "They told me a co-pilot had been brought in a couple of days ago, and I hoped it was you. Are you okay?" he asked, just then noticing Danny's faltering stance.

"I'm fine, I'm fine! Come here and have a seat."

"Lieutenant, we need to debrief Lieutenant Pendergrass," Eduard insisted, finally reaching them.

"And you will," Danny said, "but just give us a couple of minutes, okay?"

Eduard held up two fingers. "Two minutes and not a second more."

Lane helped Danny sit back down on the side of the bed.

"You're obviously hurt," he said, falling into the wooden chair.

"Just a sprained ankle, nothing serious. I can't believe you're here! I've had them asking all over about you and the other guys. Are they with you?"

Lane's face fell. "No, I was hoping to find them here. No word? Nothing?"

"Nothing. These Resistance folks even contacted the 390th for me, but they were told I was the only member of *Sophie's* crew they'd heard from. What happened? How did you get here?"

"I landed somewhere in Germany, not far from the border." Lane pulled his hand roughly over his face. "Never did see Tony after we jumped. We got separated on the way down. Somebody up there must've been looking out for me, because I landed in the middle of nowhere and was never approached by any Germans. Not once. I gathered up my chute and made a run for it. I heard their tanks coming, but I hid in a ravine surrounded by a bunch of bushes."

"Is that where you've been all this time?"

"At first, I thought better safe than sorry. If no one knew I was there, better to stay put and keep it that way. Then early this morning just after midnight, I decided to take my chances. Took me a long time, trying to stay out of sight— darting here and there, always watching my back. Once the sun came up, I hunkered down in a bombed out church. Crawled up in the chimney. Stayed there all day.

"Then long after the sun went down this evening, I made tracks and finally crossed what I thought must be the border. Came across those other guys," he nodded toward three RAF men huddled around a table with some of the Resistance workers. "They'd just jumped from their Lancaster," he said, pointing at the Resistance men, "and those guys were there picking them up. I'm here to tell you, it *had* to be a miracle. A minute before or after, and they would've been gone and I'd still be out there. Those guys work fast."

Danny reached for Lane's hand with both of his. "A miracle. Had to be. I'm so glad you made it, Lane."

"Glad you made it too, Danny. Real glad."

Eduard patted Lane on the shoulder. "Now, I must insist we spend some time with Lieutenant Pendergrass." Eduard handed the navigator a cup of tea. "Are you hungry?"

"Starving," he answered, both hands on his stomach.

"While we chat, I shall have the ladies prepare you a bowl of stew."

"Thank you. That sounds great. I'm absolutely famished." Lane patted Danny on the knee then followed Eduard across the room.

"Enjoy," Danny said with a smile, picturing his navigator chowing down on kitty cat stew.

Anya never came back downstairs. Danny couldn't get her off his mind, but had no idea what to do. Once the guys finished their questioning with Lane, they took him upstairs for a midnight meal. Danny hated to miss out on watching that, but decided not to try the stairs. He'd no doubt hear all about it later.

One of the RAF pilots came back down and chatted briefly with Danny, updating him on the progress of the Allied efforts. Most everyone seemed to believe the war would soon be over. "We're liberating towns and cities left and right. Besides, apparently there are so few targets left to bomb, there's precious little left to do. We've all done our part and Jerry's all but finished. Any day now. Any day."

Lane showed up a while later, clean from a shower. "That'll wake you up," he said, still towel-drying his hair.

"What's that?" Danny asked.

"That shower. Whew!" He shook off a shiver. "I think my goose bumps have goose bumps!" He threw his towel on the bunk above Danny's.

"That's why I took a bath."

"Wait—you took a bath? Was it warm?"

"Warm enough. The ladies heated some water over the fire and filled the tub for me. Nice and toasty."

"You're lying."

"So how was your dinner?"

Lane pulled his chair close to Danny's bedside and lowered his voice. "Do I even *want* to know what that was?"

"Nah. But keep it to yourself. These poor folks have had it rough. And just so you know, someone most likely skipped a meal so you could have it."

Lane propped his feet up on the end of Danny's bed, crossing his ankles. "I kinda wondered about that. They're all paper thin." He shook his head while raking his fingers through his damp hair. "I can't even imagine, can you?"

"No. But I'll tell you one thing. It sure makes what we do worthwhile."

"That's for sure. All of it."

Danny leaned his head back against the pillows. "I've been thinking a lot about our crew. The guys who went down with *Sophie.* I still can't believe they're gone."

Lane took a deep breath then slowly let it out. "I kept thinking about them the whole time I was out there hiding. And I realized, when you get right down to it, we're all just a bunch of kids. Barely out of high school, some of these guys. And yet here we are, on the other side of the world, flying these great big Fortresses—"

"Like sitting ducks—"

"Like sitting ducks. But I look around here and see these people . . . and I think, they're why we do it. I never really thought about that before. Up in our birds, we don't see them face to face."

"You have no idea. Spend some time talking to them and you'll understand even more. The stories they tell are—well, there aren't even words to describe them."

"I would but they're sending me back to base in the morning."

"What?" Danny sat up.

"I guess you'd be going too, but with your injuries they didn't want to risk it. Speaking of which, why didn't you tell me you had a concussion?"

"It's not important," Danny said, waving him off. "How are you getting back? They can't exactly put you on a flight out of here."

"I'm not sure. They didn't tell us." Lane stood up and stretched, then climbed to the upper bunk. "Apparently it's a bit of cloak and dagger, so they'll tell us only when we need to know. They have a team that does this regularly. Sure hope they know what they're doing."

"A team?"

"A guy and some girl I haven't met yet."

Of course. Eduard had told him Anya often helped run the pilot lines.

"Danny?"

"Yes?"

"You got awfully quiet. You okay?"

"Yeah."

"Well, buddy, I haven't slept in two days. I'm beat, so I think I'll—"

"Goodnight, Lane. Glad you made it here safe, buddy."

A freight train roared from the top bunk in response. Danny smiled, then climbed under the covers. He socked both pillows, trying to get comfortable. His foot was bothering him and the dull headache wasn't so dull anymore. When he finally settled in, he felt a troubled wave wash over him. It had nothing to do with his physical ailments.

Anya was leaving in the morning—with Lane and those RAF guys, who all happened to be shaking the rafters with their snores at the moment. Danny turned on his side to face the wall, jamming one of the pillows over his head to muffle the roar.

But no matter what he did, Danny couldn't push the image of Anya's face from his mind. The sadness in her eyes made his heart literally ache in his chest. But it was more than that. What worried him most was the wall he sensed going up between them again.

And you have no one to blame but yourself.

52

Pre-dawn, 01 April 1945

Danny awoke early from a restless sleep. He couldn't stand the thought of roosting in his bed for another minute. Besides, he needed to find a bathroom. An oil lamp cast a soft light in the corner near the radio. He spotted the kid with the red hair, his head resting on folded arms on the table, the headset askew on his head. Otherwise the room remained dark. He mustered the strength to sit up and pivot, putting his feet on the floor. As he sat there, trying to figure out how to get across the room, he spotted a broom. He hopped over to it and practiced balancing as much of his weight as he could. Satisfied, he made his way to the stairs and began the long ascent.

Finally reaching the first floor, he got his bearings then quickly maneuvered his way to the tiny bathroom. Afterward, he limped into the kitchen. Maybe I can make myself a cup of—

"Goedemorgen."

"Ah!" Danny jumped, almost losing balance. "You scared me half to death!"

Eduard hopped up to help Danny to the table. "I assure you that wasn't my intent."

"What are you doing, sitting here in the dark?" Danny said, taking a seat.

"I do my best thinking when it's quiet, before the day begins. Could I fix you a cup of coffee?"

"Yes, thank you," he said, hoping it tasted better than Greta's brew.

"What brings you upstairs this time of the morning—other than nature's call?"

"Couldn't sleep. I thought the guys in my quarters back on base snored a lot, but I had no idea. Those guys down there could do some serious damage to your foundation with those snores."

Eduard chuckled. "Yes, I suppose that's true. But they all need their rest. Particularly those we picked up last night."

Danny propped his foot on one of the other chairs. "Lane told me you have a team taking them back to base today."

"Yes, that's true. They won't take them across the Pond, but they'll deliver them safely to the shore. Fishing boat will take them the rest of the way. When pilots come in with no injuries, it's best to move them out as soon as possible. We never know when we'll have more coming in. It's much more difficult to move twelve or fifteen than just a handful."

"I can see that."

Eduard returned with a mug of coffee. "There you go. I'm sorry I can offer you no sugar."

"Not a problem. So how does this work, your team taking them back to base? They can't exactly just walk out of here."

"That's true," Eduard said, taking a seat. "We have a complicated system of contacts in place. We alert them ahead of time how many we are transporting and when. Of course, we'll outfit them in civilian clothing so they blend in."

"Makes sense," Danny said after sipping the tolerable coffee. "I'd think such a system would be quite risky."

"You'd be correct."

Danny leaned forward, cupping his hands around the mug. "I've been meaning to ask. How is it that you do all this under the nose of the Germans? So many people coming and going is bound to arouse their suspicions? Does the Gestapo never knock on your door?"

"Since we're located so near the border, we must stay constantly alert. You see, we're only a few kilometers from Gronau, the closest town just over the border in Germany. So it was quite easy for the Germans to set up a command center here when the Occupation began. In fact, it was one of the first established in The Netherlands and one of the first Dutch cities to fall when the invasion began. But we've played the game well."

"Meaning?"

"We have people placed in strategic locations to alert us in *all* aspects of those who rule over us."

"Do you mean you have Resistance workers posing as members of the Gestapo?"

Eduard leaned back, his finger tracing the rim of his chipped mug. "Lieutenant, I do not wish to be rude, but it is best you do not know the details of our operation here. For your protection and for ours." Eduard pulled out his pocket watch and stood up. "Frederic should be waking the boys any time now."

Anya appeared at the door, her eyes fixed on a button she was fastening on her sleeve. "Eduard, have you heard from The Hague this—"

"Good morning, Anya," Eduard interrupted.

She looked up then turned her eyes in Danny's direction. "Oh, I'm sorry." Her smile didn't reach her eyes. "I didn't know you were here."

"Hello, Anya," he said quietly.

"Hello."

Eduard looked back and forth between them. "Yes, well, I shall check downstairs to see if the boys are up and see about our arrangements." He shuffled down the hall toward the stairs.

Anya made her way to the coffee pot. "I didn't realize you'd be up so early."

"I couldn't sleep. I was restless, so I dragged myself up the stairs. I suppose I needed a change of scenery."

She didn't respond, her back still toward him. He noted her clothing—a worn black shirt at least a couple of sizes too big, a black, baggy pair of men's pants, black boots, and her hair tucked inside her leather cap. From the back, he wouldn't have known it was a woman.

"Lane tells me you'll be accompanying them on their journey today."

She turned, sipping from the cup. She winced. "I shall never get used to this."

"The coffee?"

"You're most kind to call it that. Actually it's—"

"Don't tell me," he said, waving a palm toward her. "I'd rather not know."

A faint smile showed, nothing more, as she leaned against the kitchen counter. "No cats or rats or dogs. Just brown beans which are burnt to look like coffee beans. Unfortunately they do not taste much like coffee. But it has to do."

"It's fine." He cleared his throat then spoke quietly. "Anya, could we please talk?"

She looked down into her cup. "I think now is not the time."

"Only for a moment? I can't bear to see you go until I can apologize."

She shook her head. "It is not necessary."

He tried to stand, and she came closer. "Your ankle. You should not be standing on it."

"Then will you come sit here? Please?"

She inhaled, then slowly let her breath out as she took the seat beside him. "Danny, you are very stubborn, I think."

"Funny, that's what Hans used to say about you," he said, settling back.

She looked up at him so quickly, he felt sure he'd blown it again. Then a trace of her smile was back. "Yes, I would imagine. How I loved to annoy him."

He said nothing for a moment, trying to gather his thoughts. He fought the urge to reach for her hand. "I can't forgive myself for causing you such pain last night. I have no excuse. I didn't think, I just . . . but if you could possibly find it in your heart to forgive me, I promise I'll never hurt you again."

She kept her eyes on the cup in her hand. "Do not make such a promise, Danny."

"Why not?"

She paused. "Because war is not the time for such things."

When she said nothing more, he asked, "Will you come back? After you take the men, will you come back here to this safe house?"

"I don't know. It depends where I am needed."

"You're needed here—*I* need you. Can you please just try to come back? We need to . . . I believe there's a reason we—"

She abruptly stood. "You ask too much." She took her cup to the sink.

He stood up, grabbed the broom, and hobbled over to her. "Anya, listen to me."

She turned, surprised to see him beside her. "What are you doing? You should not be standing." She took his arm as if to help him back to the table.

He wrapped his arm around her waist and drew her to him even though she stiffened at his touch. "What do I have to do to get through to you? I'm not the enemy, Anya! It's me—Danny. And all I'm asking is your forgiveness for opening my stupid mouth!"

She searched his eyes, mere inches from him now, and the nearness of her drove him nearly mad. Still, he fought the desire to pull her closer, knowing one more wrong move would be the end for them. "Please don't push me away," he whispered.

He sensed the slightest change in her, if only a little—not quite so rigid. Still, she studied him, as if searching his face for answers. Then, ever so slowly she closed her eyes and melted against him, her head on his shoulder. "Oh, Danny."

He held her silently, so afraid to spoil the moment, afraid she'd bolt from his embrace. He leaned his head on top of hers, holding her close, breathing in the fragrance of her. "Please, Anya, just give me a chance. Don't push me away. I need you."

"But I'm so scared to let you—"

"Don't be scared. I'm here for you. Let me be here for you. We can—"

"Well, well, well!" Lane said, stepping into the kitchen.

She pulled away from him, putting distance between them as Danny turned around, almost losing his balance.

"There, now, McClain, let me help you," his navigator said, leading him back to his chair.

"I'm fine. Really." Danny plopped into the chair as Lane went to Anya's side.

"I don't believe I've had the pleasure." He held out his hand. "I'm Lieutenant Lane Pendergrass, United States Army Air Force, happy to make your acquaintance. And you are?"

She busied her hands, tucking her hair more firmly under her cap. "I am Eva. Along with Gastön, I will be accompanying you and the others today."

Danny wondered at the false name she'd given, but assumed it was part of the routine. He avoided eye contact with Lane as the other RAF men crowded into the kitchen. They all wore rugged clothing, looking nothing like airmen.

Eduard followed Frederic into the kitchen. "Gastön, if you will brief the men, Eva and I will load up the supplies in the truck. We have packed some food for this first part of your journey. You will be fed at the next safe house once you arrive.

"If you will follow me," Gastön/Frederic instructed, leading the men into the living room known as the *zitkamer*. As they shuffled into the next room, Lane paused beside Danny, shaking his hand. "Sure hate to leave you behind, McClain." He leaned over, lowering his voice substantially. "Here's hoping for a slow recovery, eh? She's a real looker." He patted Danny on the back and left before Danny could say anything.

Danny stretched the kinks out of his neck before looking back at Anya. She and Eduard put a large bag into a box along with some tins of what looked like crackers. Eduard hoisted the box and made his way to the back door.

"Anya—"

"I must go," she said, sticking some tulip bulbs into her pockets. At least he assumed that's what they were.

"Will you come back?"

She stopped beside him, her hand on his shoulder. "Yes, Danny. I will come back. A day or two."

He placed his hand over hers, squeezing it gently. "Good. I'll see you then."

She met his eyes briefly, then she was gone.

53

They'd just passed through their third roadblock, once again rumbling down the horribly pitted dirt road. Frederic's impeccable German kept the gated stops well greased, along with his many generous donations of Lucky Strikes to the German soldiers, most of whom knew him well. To them, he was Gastön van Dam, a Dutch truck driver and German sympathizer who never stopped complaining about his "insatiable wife Mathilde." The German soldiers loved to hear of Gastön's many bedroom escapades with his young, eager, and adoring wife. They'd long ago stopped checking Gastön's cargo, which he'd assured them time and again were important supplies for Seyss-Inquart, the German Reichskommissar over Holland—never giving more than a cursory look at the bed of the truck. Had they investigated more carefully, they might have noticed the many cartons loaded in the back of the truck were the same ones he carried week in and week out. Had they investigated even further, they might have discovered the false front of the truck's bed where the more precious cargo was hidden—Allied airmen on their way back to England.

Instead, Gastön's German buddies at the roadblocks preferred to crowd around the cab where the driver gave them colorful, graphic descriptions of his husbandly duties. They never paid much attention to Anya, disguised as Gastön's fictitious mute brother who always slept through these visits. "Not even God himself could wake my lazy brother!" he often lamented. With loud laughter and a good many animated gestures, the guards enjoyed their visits and sent them on their way. Anya understood enough German to know the wild web of lies about the non-existent Mathilde. As long as the ruse got them through the roadblocks, she didn't care what "Gastön" said.

As they neared Utrecht, Anya's heart grew heavy. Her hometown looked vastly different from the beloved place where she grew up. Like much of Holland, the war had taken its toll on Utrecht, leaving wide areas with nothing more than pile after pile of rubble. Whole city blocks were left in ruin with mangled beams of steel, twisted and ugly in the smoldering ashes. It was the same everywhere, but it bothered her here most of all. She hadn't been back to her city block or the house she'd called home in years. She didn't have to see it to know it too was probably gone. She'd rather not know.

With sunrise only moments away, they pulled up to the large stone safe house just outside of town to the east. Once Frederic pulled around to the back of the house, he backed up the vehicle to the sheltered side building and shut off the engine. Anya quickly made her way around the truck, hopping inside to the camouflaged secret door. Unlatching it, the men inside spilled out.

"Where are we?" one of the RAF pilots asked, yawning.

"Just outside of Utrecht. Please, come this way," she said, showing them into the building. Inside, the aroma of cooked meat made Anya's stomach growl. A long table was already set for breakfast. She ushered the men inside.

"Eva! Good morning! Come, give me hug. "

Anya stepped around the men as they took their seats at the table. "Hello, Helga," she said quietly as she fell into the dear woman's embrace.

"Hello, my dear Anya," Helga whispered so no one could hear. "How are you?" She grasped both of Anya's hands in hers. "You look more like a twig every day, child. Come. You must eat today."

"We'll see," Anya said, gazing at the plates of food being carried to the table. "I see your friends have been shopping again at the black market."

Helga, looped her arm with Anya's. "Yes, our shoppers did quite well this week."

Anya nearly gasped. "Is that smoked sausage?"

"Yes, and you must have some. Farm fresh eggs as well."

"But how—"

Helga placed a finger on her lips. "Best not to know, though I suspect a certain Reichskommissar in town will miss his usual hearty breakfast. I say, let *him* eat beets for a change. But enough of that. You sit. I'll bring the bread."

Anya took off her cap and stretched her arms behind her back. It was always good to see her mother's friend whenever her pilot runs brought her through Utrecht. Still, the mere sight of Helga always filled her heart with a deep melancholy longing for her parents. It couldn't be helped, such feelings, though Anya always hid it from the older woman.

The only seat left at the table was on the end next to Danny's friend. She wasn't in the mood for conversation, but her hunger pangs won out. She slipped onto the bench just as one of Helga's co-workers brought her a steaming plate of food. She looked down at it, trying to remember when she'd last had a real meal other than beets or the onion-tasting tulip bulbs they'd nibbled on earlier.

"Is there something wrong?" Danny's friend asked.

"No."

"You should have a bite. It's really good. Much better than the powdered eggs we get back at the base."

She bit the side of her lip in an effort to silence a sarcastic response. He didn't know any better, she reasoned, whining about those powdered eggs.

"You probably forgot, but I'm Lane."

"Yes, I know." She picked up a fork and moved the eggs around on her plate.

He ate a sausage patty in one bite. "And you're Eva."

She took a sip of coffee, savoring the hot brew in her mouth, trying to ignore him. *Coffee. Real coffee. With cream and sugar, no less.*

He wiped his mouth with his napkin. "I should apologize for interrupting you and Danny this morning."

She forked a small bite of eggs. "There's nothing to apologize for."

He chuckled. "Hey, it's nothing to be embarrassed about. This is war, after all. Be happy you found each other, even if only for a day or two."

She turned to face him directly. "You have no idea what you're talking about, Lieutenant, so I'd appreciate it if you would drop the subject."

He held up both hands. "Hey, I'm just trying to apologize. Don't get so defensive."

Helga leaned between them, placing a basket next to Anya's plate. "Some fresh bread for you. Still warm." She gently patted Anya's shoulder and moved on down the table with another basket.

"Here, allow me," he said, holding open the cloth covering the thick slices of dark bread.

She took a slice and put it on her plate without acknowledging him. They ate in silence for several moments as she noticed most of the men gobbling down their food. She knew better. Like every other Dutch citizen, she knew that eating too much after months of too little could cause serious stomach cramps or worse. Almost everyone had hunger-related illnesses in one form or another. She'd learned the hard way to eat only enough to get by while on these travels, or face dire consequences while on the road.

Anya also knew that the staff here always fed the hungry airmen first. She looked toward the kitchen, knowing they'd be lined up there as they always were. They would not eat until their guests were fed. It was their way of thanking these men for their efforts to liberate The Netherlands. Even if the bounty stolen from a German officer was enough for all of them, she knew those fellow Resistance workers would not eat until their English and American guests were finished. By leaving something on her plate, she knew it would not go to waste.

"I think there's something you should know, Eva," Lane

said quietly, leaning toward her. "And I only tell this to you for your own good."

She reached for her coffee. "What's that, Lieutenant?"

"Your friend Danny . . . well, I think you should know he's got a girl back home."

She held her mug between her hands, wondering where this was going. "Is that so?"

He leaned his shoulder against hers. "Yes, and he's crazy about her. And I do mean *crazy*."

"And how do you know this? Does he talk of her often?"

He shrugged. "Not much, really. Just this one time. He was at a pub with a bunch of guys from another crew. Rumor has it he got pretty drunk, and at one point they said he was sitting at the bar crying in his ale over this girl back home."

She watched him, knowing perfectly well his intention. He was handsome enough, but she had no doubt he had an ongoing love affair with every mirror he ever laid eyes on. She couldn't resist, so she played along doing her best to sound heartbroken. "Oh no. Does this girl have a name?" she asked, lifting the coffee mug to her lips.

"Oh sure." He leaned even closer, whispering against her ear as she took a sip. "Her name is Sophie. Even named our plane for her."

Anya spewed coffee clear across the table, showering Frederic in the process. He jumped up, ranting at her in Dutch as he wiped off his face and jacket. She hadn't seem him so riled in all the years she'd worked with him.

"Het spijt me zo, Gastön!" she said, apologizing as she covered her mouth to stifle her giggles. "It was an accident! I promise!"

He carried on—mostly for effect, she thought—then finally sat back down, shaking his head. She noticed the coffee shower didn't seem to harm his appetite as he continued shoveling in the rest of his drenched breakfast.

"What was that all about?" Lane asked, leaning back from her.

"Oh, I . . . it's just . . ." Then it came to her. "It's the name Sophie. You see, that was my grandmother's name, my Oma. And she . . . she was very dear to me. I always get very emotional whenever I hear her name." She poured it on, quite the grieving granddaughter. When she felt the laughter starting to bubble up inside, she quickly stood and excused herself. Once outside she laughed so hard, she thought she might lose what little she'd eaten.

It took a while for her to calm back down. When she did, she leaned against the building and wiped her eyes. *I can't wait to get back and tell Danny.* She imagined his laughter, even rowdier than hers just now. She smiled, longing for the sound of it. She closed her eyes, lost in an unexpected fantasy of being in his arms, the sound of his laughter soothing her soul. It occurred to her that the only other time she had laughed in years was just last night, watching him try to eat the roof rabbit stew. Then just now, with the "great Sophie secret" told to her so seriously by Lieutenant Pender-whatever his name was.

Oh Danny, only you could make me laugh in the middle of this despicable war. Only you.

Immediately, she scolded herself. What had happened to the resolve she made sitting in that tree by the house in Enschede? Where was her thick skin she'd worked so hard to maintain? How was it possible, in the middle of all this, she'd suddenly given in to feelings so long forgotten? She felt the icy fingers of a chill skitter down her spine. *It's dangerous, so very dangerous, letting him get to me like this.*

She had only to remember the teasing way Danny had mentioned Wim's name. As if Wim was just a farm boy who'd merely toyed with her affections when she was just a girl. The thought of it sealed off any childish illusions she may have allowed, cautiously locking out any silly fantasies that may have drifted through her unguarded thoughts.

Anya took a deep breath, letting it stretch her lungs as full as she could. And as the reality of her loneliness was carefully mortared back in place, she stuffed her hands in her pockets, and went back inside.

54

With the Allied airmen safely on their way to England, Anya
and Frederic started on their trip back to Enschede. With a
full tank of stolen fuel supplied at their last stop, they should
be able to make it back before midnight. As Frederic rattled
on, as he always did, sharing his dream of going to America
once the war was over, Anya tried to bolster herself before
seeing Danny again. As much as she might secretly wish to
open her heart to him, she knew she couldn't. Eventually,
growing weary of the argument between her head and her
heart, she tuned back in to Frederic's latest idea.

"A movie star. I'm a natural, don't you think?"

"You? Starring in American cinemas?"

"Yes! Like the Clark Gable or the Lawrence Olive."

"Olivier."

"What?"

"His name is Olivier. Lawrence Olivier."

"Ja. As I said. What do you think? I have a certain

flare—a mystique, no?" He tilted his head, waving his hand as if giving the performance of a lifetime.

"Not mystique. More like a *mistake*, Frederic. Why do you allow yourself to think such things? You could die tomorrow. Why, you could die tonight, here on this road. Look all around you. Everywhere, the reminders of war. It's a waste of time to dream such silly dreams."

"But if we do not dream, we shall not survive, Anya. What good is life if we see only gloom and doom, eh?" He reached over to nudge her on the arm. "We are much too young to give up. Look at us! We have survived many years of war! And they say liberation is close—so very close! It could happen any moment, Anya. Even tonight!"

He burst into song, proudly singing the Dutch national anthem. Anya shook her head at his continuous antics, suddenly feeling exhausted. As the serenade continued, she leaned her head against the door and closed her eyes, trying to ignore the bumpy ride.

She wasn't sure how long she'd slept when the truck came to a halt. But instead of the safe house in Enschede, they were parked in front of her home in Utrecht. The overcast sky didn't dampen the glorious sight in front of her—her home? Still standing, as if welcoming her home from a long journey?

"Frederic, what are we doing here?"

"I was told to bring you here before I continue on. Do you need me to walk you inside, or will you be all right?"

She stepped out of the truck, anxiously looking around to see if Nazis still patrolled the neighborhood. But all she saw was her beautiful home. Even her mother's beloved tulips lining the front walkway were in bloom. How could they have survived the war? Yet there they stood, as if proudly saluting her homecoming. As she knelt beside them, cupping her hands around the brilliant red, yellow, and white petals, she heard the loud grinding of the truck's gears.

"I'll see you in a few days!" Frederic called as he backed the truck down the driveway.

"Goodbye!" She waved without watching him drive out of view.

"Anya!"

The shock of hearing her mother's voice vacuumed the breath right out of her lungs. "Mother!" she cried, running up the cobbled walkway and into her mother's outstretched arms. "Oh Mother! I knew it was all a lie! You're alive!"

"Yes, dear Anya! I am here, I am here."

They hugged and laughed and cried until Anya thought she'd pass out from sheer joy.

"Come," Mother said, turning her toward the house. "Someone very special has come to see you."

"Father? Is Father here?"

"No, child."

Her heart ached. "He is dead, then? Did he die in the concentration camp?"

"What?" Mother looked perplexed. "No, no, he's at the church practicing his sermon. Come inside and see for yourself."

They walked up the steps, arm in arm. But as the door opened, the interior of the home she loved was . . . missing? In its place, the ice-covered canal. She turned to ask Mother about it, but her mother was gone. *No doubt making those special tea cakes I love so much*, she thought happily.

"Anya!"

It can't be! It can't . . . But there, out on the ice, stood her brother waving at her. "Anya! Come skate with me!"

"Hans!" She flew across the snow-covered field, hardly believing her eyes. "Hans, how can it be? We thought you died!"

And suddenly, he scooped her up in his arms, whooping and hollering. "My little Anya! I have missed you so! Where have you been?"

"There was a war . . . and the Germans, they did such horrible things . . . and Hans, there were so many bombs!"

"What? Don't be silly," he chided, putting her down on the ice. "There's no war. The only bombs are over the border. We are safe. Always, the Dutch are safe. Oh, Anya, it's so good to see you again!" He hugged her tight once more, then took her hand. "Come! Everyone's here! You're just in time for our skating party!"

She pulled back hard, shaking her head. "No, Hans. We mustn't. It's not safe."

He turned to look back at her. "Don't be such a silly girl. Look there—all our friends! They'll be so surprised to see you!"

She followed him, despite a haunting sense of dread and foreboding. Looking down, she noticed her favorite skates on her feet, laced and glistening as she glided along behind him. "But how . . .?"

"Look, everyone—Anya is here!"

They all crowded around her, all their friends, everyone wanting a hug.

"Rieky!" she cried, "Oh my goodness, dear sweet Rieky— you're *alive*? I thought you and Hans drowned beneath the ice!"

The little girl giggled behind her mittens then skated off to join the other little girls.

"Anya? Is it really you?"

Anya turned at the sound of her best friend's voice. There, beyond Rieky and her friends was her best friend Lieke doing figure-eights on the ice with little Inge in her arms.

"No! No, it cannot be. Lieke? But I thought you . . . I was there when the awful German soldier put a bullet in Inge's head. How can she be here?"

Suddenly, something way down deep inside released a horrible shiver that stretched from Anya's head to her skate-covered toes. While everyone laughed and skated and carried on, she heard a piercing cry in the distance. Someone somewhere was in trouble. But where? She pushed through the crowd, so terribly frightened of what she might find, yet unable to stop herself.

"Please, someone! Help me!" the voice cried.

I recognize that voice . . .

Her heart pounded as she kept skating toward the cries. She turned her head back to where her friends were—but they weren't there? They were gone, every one of them except Hans. "Please, Hans! Come help me! Someone is drowning!"

"Oh, my little Anya, you were always such a melodramatic child. No one is there." He pointed beyond her. "Look—no one."

He was right. No one was there. Then she heard it again, a desperate cry.

"Please! I can't hold on much longer!"

That's when she saw the enormous jagged crack in the ice. And there, between the thick walls of ice, a mittened hand reached up from the icy water, waving frantically before disappearing again.

"Hans, we must save her!" But when she looked back, Hans was gone. She was all alone. She would have to make sense of it later. Now, it was entirely up to her to save whoever had fallen through the crack.

She got down on all fours, crawling her way closer to the edge of the fissure. She lay down on the ice reaching her arms down toward the person. "Give me your hand!"

"I can't! I can't! Please help me!"

Anya froze. The person she watched batting at the frigid water . . . was her?

And just that fast, she became the one in the water fighting for her life. The freezing water took her breath and her voice. *It's so cold! I can't bear it! Please! Save me! Save me!*

The realization came to her—with no one there to help, this would be her last dying breath. She must force herself up one more time.

Oh God, please! Send someone to save me!

As her face then arms broke through the water, she saw him! He grasped beneath her arms and easily lifted her out of the freezing grave and into his arms.

"Oh Anya! Thank God!"

Her teeth chattered so hard she couldn't speak and her body trembled violently, but she couldn't take her eyes off him. He wrapped his coat around her then pulled her close against him as if willing his body heat to warm her. Tears fell from her eyes blurring her view of him.

"Thank God . . . oh, thank God," he said over and over.

Unable to speak, she breathed his name . . . *"Danny?"*

55

"Anya! Anya, what's wrong?"

It felt so good to be there in his arms. A feeling unlike anything she'd ever experienced—an overpowering sense of warmth and security and protection all rolled into one. As though nothing would ever harm her again. As though this was her destiny, where she'd always belonged. Even with her clothes still soaked by the freezing canal water, she felt such tremendous relief in Danny's arms. "Nothing's wrong," she murmured, content to stay right where she was for the rest of her life. "Nothing."

"Anya!"

She looked up, startled by the sound of someone else calling her name. Only then did she realize she was still in the truck, though it was no longer moving.

I don't understand. Where is Danny?

"It's about time," Frederic growled as he stepped out of the truck. "Come along." He belched. "It's late, and I'm exhausted."

She waved him on then sat there a moment longer

watching him go inside the house—not her home in Utrecht, but the safe house in Enschede. "Oh no." She dropped her head in her hands. *It was only a dream?* Her hands wore no wet mittens. Her clothes were dry. And she wasn't nestled in Danny's warm embrace. She was sitting in the smelly cab of the old truck.

Anya clamped her teeth together. What could possibly have caused such a cruel scene to play out in her mind? She yanked the cap off her head and raked her hand through her hair, thinking she must surely be losing her mind. She held the cap pressed against her face and rocked back and forth, wondering why she couldn't just die and get it over with. What was the point? Life held no meaning any more. Not like this. Better to rot in a grave than have her heart broken and stomped on by something as foolish as a dream.

Someone tapped on the truck's window, scaring a scream out of her.

"I'm so sorry!" Danny said as he opened the door.

"You scared me to death!"

"I know, but I didn't know how else to get your attention. Why did you have your hat over your face?"

As her heart started beating again, she huffed. "Don't ever sneak up on me like that! I could have shot you!" She jumped down from the truck's cab onto the ground beside him.

"Are you carrying a gun?"

"Of course. I always carry a gun." She slapped the hat back on her head. "What are you doing out here anyway? It's almost one o'clock in the morning. It isn't safe to be out."

"I was worried when you didn't come in with Frederic."

She started walking toward the house, then paused,

looking back at him. "Where did you get that?" she asked, pointing at the single crutch beneath his arm.

"Eduard got it for me from one of the other safe houses."

She looked him over, carefully avoiding his eyes. "Well, come inside before you get us both arrested." She opened the back door, holding it as he hobbled through, then closed it behind them.

"When Eduard told me you all were on your way back, I waited up."

"I can see that, but you shouldn't have." She pulled off her gloves and stuffed them in her coat pocket. Still standing in the back entry hall, she looked around him at the uncovered stairway leading down to the cellar. "You should get some rest. Is everyone else asleep?"

"Yes, I believe so. And Frederic went downstairs as soon as he came in." He limped to her side. "Anya?"

She pulled off her jacket and cap, hanging them on the peg beside the door. "What is it, Danny?" She didn't mean to snap at him. He was only being kind to her. Why was she always finding excuses to be rude to him?

She stopped abruptly, frozen where she stood—her back to him, her hands still on the jacket she'd just hung up. The fresh, vivid memory of the dream roared through her, filling her with the same compelling warmth and security she'd felt in his arms.

Anya heard him closing in behind her. "Anya, I was just hoping we could—"

Without a single trace of hesitation, she turned and grabbed his face, pulling it down to hers, kissing him with a passion she hadn't known she possessed. Her heart pounded in her chest as his arms wrapped around her, his crutch banging against the floor where it fell. He kissed her with such hunger, holding her so tight, so secure in his arms, she could hardly breathe. As she lost herself in his embrace, she realized—it was just like in her dream.

And just as in her dream, Anya could no longer deny it.

This truly is my destiny, the place where I belong. I know that now. But how? How can it be? After all these years, how is it possible?

Danny was afraid to open his eyes. Could this really be happening? He kissed her tenderly, then pulled back. "It's really you. I can't believe—" He leaned his forehead against hers. "Anya, it's really—"

"I had a dream," she whispered, her voice warbled. "I was back at home and Mother was there, and Hans, and all our friends. And then we were on the canal skating, and I could hear someone crying for help, and I skated to the crack in the ice. And then I looked down and stretched my hand out . . . and it was me! I was the one drowning!"

She was talking so fast he could hardly understand her. So he simply held her as she wept, her face buried against his chest, her body trembling in his arms. "Shhh. You're not drowning, Anya. You're here, safe in my arms."

She looked up, searching his eyes as tears streamed down her face. "I know—that's what I'm trying to tell you. I was so scared and frightened and—and *so cold*. I knew I only had one last chance. I pushed up once more from the water . . . and you lifted me up, Danny! It was *you*."

He pushed a strand of dampened hair out of her eyes, then cupped his hand around the side of her face. "Well, there you have it."

She hiccupped. "Have what?"

"It must have been a dream because I'm not much of a skater."

She laughed and cried and burrowed deeper into his embrace, all the while murmuring, "You saved me, Danny. You saved me."

He rested his chin on her head. "I would lay down my life to save you, Anya, if you'd let me."

She wept quietly in his arms for a long time. When she finally took a long rugged breath, he released her. "Could I be a bother and ask you to help me into the other room?"

Anya seemed perplexed, but willingly wrapped her arm beneath his, letting him lean on her as they made their way to the bedroom. At the doorway, she hesitated. "Danny, I don't think—"

"Anya, we'll leave the door open," he said smiling. "And we will sit *on* the bed, not *in* the bed. We have so much to talk about, but I can't stand any longer because of this blasted foot. I assure you, my intentions are that of a gentleman."

She smiled through her tears and helped him into the bedroom where he'd first stayed. "Then we shall sit *on* the bed, not *in* the bed, and I shall assure you *my* intentions are that of a lady."

She stacked pillows behind him as he settled onto the bed, then slowly made her way to the door. "But we shall *not* leave the door open, Lieutenant McClain, because it is none of their business what we do."

"Well, I, uh . . . then if, uh . . ." He swallowed hard.

She climbed on the other side of the bed and snuggled up against him, pulling his arm around her. "Wait," she said, reaching down for the quilt folded at the foot of the bed. She wrapped it over them and returned to his arms.

"Now *I* am the one dreaming," he said, taking hold of her hand. "And if I am, then I never want to wake up."

She looked into his eyes. "When you found me in the truck, I was furious, Danny."

"Why?"

"Because Frederic had just awakened me from that dream, telling me we were back here. I felt so angry, so cheated. I'd been in your arms, but then I wasn't."

"That's why you were mad at me?"

"Yes! Well, no. I wasn't mad at *you*, I was just so disappointed. If you must know, I was mad at myself for having such delusional dreams." She laid her head on his shoulder. "For so long I have . . ."

He waited, not wanting to rush her but praying she would share her heart with him. "Go on."

"For so long I have wanted no one to come close to me. I couldn't . . . I *wouldn't* let anyone get near to me. These people here, they are co-workers only. Nothing more. I respect most of them, but never do I let them become my friend. Except perhaps Eduard. He is more of a father figure, I guess you would say."

She paused, and he waited again. He stroked her hair, giving her as much time as she needed. He would wait as long as it took for her to tell her story.

"It is because—I knew if I lost again, I would not survive. I have lost *everyone*."

He listened for more, stroking her hand with his thumb. When she finally spoke again, her words were slow. Deliberate. As if each was harder to speak than the last.

"Hans. Mother. Father . . . and Wim."

For hours, he had wondered. The entire time she was gone, he had tried to think what possibly could have happened to Wim that the mere mention of his name could cause her such sorrow. He knew Wim must have died, but how he died, Danny had no idea.

"Tell me about him. I know he meant a great deal to you."

She nodded, her head still resting on his shoulder. A moment passed then another until she finally began to tell her story. She told of traveling with Wim to transport children from one safe house to the next. She told of close calls and frightening situations, their lives always in danger. She told him of their clandestine return to Utrecht and making their way to Wim's farm. She lost her voice as she told of finding little Inge, her friend's baby sister, alone in the field beyond the farmhouse. She grew animated as she described Wim dashing to bring the baby out of that field and their unbridled fear, both of them knowing that something was terribly, terribly wrong.

Anya grew quiet again. He said nothing but silently prayed for God to give her courage. When she continued, she fought to get the words out. "Wim insisted on sneaking up to the house to find out what had happened. Almost as soon as he left my side, I felt a gun pressed against the back of my head. I was so afraid . . . I held little Inge close, so frightened we would be killed. The soldier came around to stand before me, moving the gun to press it against my forehead."

Danny swallowed hard. He wished he knew how to spare her this pain.

"I begged him not to hurt us. But all of a sudden, he turned the gun to Inge's head and . . . he shot her. He *shot* her!"

She sat up, pushing her hair out of her face with trembling hands, then cradling her arms as if holding a baby. "She fell limp in my arms. And I wanted to kill him. I was so . . . but then I threw up, and he kicked little Inge's body aside. He pulled me up by my hair, then . . . then suddenly, he just fell to the ground. Wim had smashed a rock over the German's head! And he was there with me. Wim was there with me, and he held me . . ."

Danny held his breath as he listened. He grieved for the wild look in her eyes, knowing she was reliving the horrible scene. He knew she had to do this, and so he remained silent.

"Wim told me the Germans had . . . it looked as if they had lined up his family along with the Jews they'd been hiding beneath their barn, and . . . and they executed them. His parents, Lieke—all of them." She paused to wipe away the endless tears. "And then as he held me—"

She stopped. He said nothing.

"A shot rang out. And I looked over Wim's shoulder and saw the German soldier—we'd thought he was dead but he wasn't. And just as I saw the smoke coming from the gun in his hand, I felt Wim's body slump against me. And I knew he'd been shot. The soldier—he moved the barrel of his gun, pointing it straight at me—" Anya fought to find another breath. "I knew he was going to kill me. And I *wanted* him to kill me!" She shook her head back and forth. "But the gun fell from his hand and his head fell into the dirt."

Danny watched as she cried silently, her body quaking now and then with the remnants of her grief. He watched and waited. Then he gently gathered her into his arms, tucking her safely beside him. "Oh, Anya, I'm so sorry. I'm so sorry."

She wrapped her arms around his waist and leaned her head against his chest. They remained that way for more than half an hour. At first Danny murmured assurances that she was safe now, that he would protect her. Eventually, he felt her breathing grow more relaxed and hoped she would fall asleep. The images of what she'd described were now seared into his mind and his heart broke for her. How could anyone so young have endured so much? How had she survived carrying so much pain, so much despair?

When he was sure she'd fallen asleep, he laid his head back against the pillow, closed his eyes, and prayed.

Lord, none of this is news to You. I don't begin to understand why . . . why she's lost everyone in her life, why so much evil is all around us, and why so many have lost so much. It wears me out, wondering about all of it. But somehow, through all this pain and sorrow, You brought me to Anya. And just now, I know it was You who gave her the courage to open her heart. I don't know what You have in store for any of us, Lord, but I'm begging You from the bottom of my heart . . . let me guard and protect her. Don't let this war come between us.

God, please just give us a chance.

56

Danny woke as someone tapped on his shoulder. He looked up to find Eduard standing beside him, a gentle smile on his face. He nodded toward Anya.

"At last she has found rest."

Danny looked over to find her sound asleep beneath the quilt, her back curled up next to him. In any other situation, he might feel embarrassed, but there was no need. As he turned back to respond, Eduard continued.

"I'm sorry I must disturb you, but it is necessary for us to move you."

"What? But I thought they told me to—"

"Come. We must talk."

Eduard had brought his crutch and helped him to his feet. Danny tried to move off the bed without disturbing her.

"Danny?"

He turned. "I'm sorry, Anya. I had hoped not to wake you."

She sat up and yawned. "Eduard, what is it?"

"We have received word that we must move out all of our Allies. It seems our liberation may soon be happening, but the Germans will not go easily. Already they have begun going house to house with a greater sense of urgency, intending to eliminate any remaining Jews and those who have taken them in. But far more valuable to them at such a time as this are the Allies who have slipped by them. Downed pilots, paratroopers who came in to work behind enemy lines, everyone. It is imperative we get all of you out of here as soon as possible."

"But won't it be more dangerous to travel with Allies in our vehicle?" Anya asked, climbing off the bed to join them. "We'll be stopped at every roadblock. And if we are, I doubt Frederic's tales will deter them if they are as desperate as you say."

"That may be, but no one is safe here now. Already our friends in the other safe house across town have been killed—"

"What?"

"It seems an infiltrator had joined ranks with them. Always we are told to be careful, to be suspicious. This is why. Now, we have all been compromised."

"Who? Who was the traitor?" she demanded.

"It does not matter now. The infiltrator tipped off the Germans about a meeting scheduled in their safe house cellar. When they all gathered, the Germans threw live grenades below and killed them all, including the traitor."

"Will it never end?" she cried, knotting her fists. Danny pulled her to his side, wrapping his arm around her shoulder.

"Yes, it will end. And soon," Eduard said. "All around us,

they fight to free us. But we are not free yet. If anything, we are in more danger now than ever before. Which is why we must hurry."

Only then did Danny notice the uniform shirt and trousers Eduard was wearing. It wasn't one he'd seen on any of them. But before he could ask, Eduard interrupted his thoughts.

"I have already sent the rest of our staff to their homes. Frederic and I will drive. We must stop in Apeldoorn to pick up three more airmen who came in over night. Anya, you will ride in back with Lieutenant McClain and the others we pick up."

"But he's in no condition to travel," Anya argued. "If something should happen, how could he—"

"I'll be fine," Danny said. "But Eduard, I want Anya to come all the way to England with me. How can we make that happen?"

"No!" She backed away from him. "I cannot leave now! There is too much to be done here. Tell him, Eduard."

Instead, Eduard headed for the door. "There is no time for such an arrangement now. Get your things. We move out in five minutes."

Danny hobbled to her side again. "Anya, you have to come with me."

"No, Danny. I can't leave. Not like this."

"Like what? You board the fishing vessel with me and the other Allied airmen. You help others do it all the time, now it's your turn. I want you with me where I can protect you." He reached for her hand but she raised her palms, taking another step back.

"You cannot protect me. None of us can protect each

other. You should know that by now."

He grabbed her wrist, holding firm, and made her face him. "Please. At least think about it. You said yourself, you've lost everyone here. Come with me. At least we will have each other. At least—"

"No, Danny." She pulled her hand free and started toward the door. "I can't."

"Then I won't leave without you."

An exasperated huff escaped her lips as she turned back toward him. "Now who's being stubborn? You cannot stay."

He made his way toward her. "Me? Stubborn? I thought you had the corner on that market." He reached for her hand then dropped his voice. "It took all these years to find you, Anya. I can't risk losing you now. I *won't* risk losing you."

She dropped his hand. "So 'all these years' you have been searching for me?" she asked, moving into the hallway. "No, you did not. You went to college, you enlisted to fight the war—"

"Which brought me to you," he said, following her. "I don't believe in coincidences."

She shook her head as she grabbed her jacket and cap. "And I don't believe in happy-ever-after fairy tales."

"Anya!" Frederic summoned from the back porch. "Let's go!"

She held up a weathered coat. "Put this on, Danny. We must hurry."

As he climbed into the coat, he pleaded with her. "Just tell me you'll think about it. Promise me you'll at least think about it."

When he turned around, she rolled her eyes while

placing a worn Fedora on his head. "I make no such promise. Now come along. I'll help you into the truck."

As she helped him down the back steps, he stopped dead in his tracks at the sight of a member of the Gestapo in full uniform. "Wha—"

"Don't worry," Anya said tugging him down the final step. "Say hello to the Lieutenant, Frederic."

The soldier belched, sending a waft of the same disgusting odor Danny remembered from the manure-like cigarettes Frederic often smoked. "Guten tag, Herr McClain," he said, clicking his heels together and throwing out his right arm in the familiar salute. "Heil Hitler!" Then he promptly turned and spat on the ground.

"Lock them up. Let's go," Eduard barked, emerging from the back door. He too wore the uniform of the Gestapo, still fastening the collar of his jacket. "Anya, you and Lieutenant McClain must keep utterly silent, especially when we are stopped. Not a sound."

"I know," Anya answered as she and Frederic helped Danny up into the back of the truck. They made their way through boxes and trunks all labeled in German. Liquor, cigarettes, firearms, and numerous other black market goods, all containers stenciled with the menacing swastika. Anya opened the camouflaged secret door and helped Danny into the compartment. She guided him toward the bench on the right side.

"How is this—?"

A metal door rolled down closing them in, effectively answering his question. In the pitch black, Danny held his breath, hearing a succession of thuds from the other side.

"They stack the trunks two-deep all the way to the top in front of the door," she explained, her voice placing her directly across from him. "From out there, it looks like a packed cargo of goods—all bound for German officers of the highest rank, according to our false paperwork. At the roadblocks, Frederic and Eduard will donate a crate filled with booze and cigarettes. The guards are used to these gifts and always let us through. At least they always have before."

Danny tugged at his collar. "Is there sufficient ventilation in here?"

"Yes, of course. When your eyes grow accustomed to the darkness, you'll see a random cluster of small holes above us in the roof. Undetectable from outside, but we must always be silent whenever the truck is stopped. Always."

The engine came to life followed by a grinding gear change. Then the truck backed up, changed gears again, and began rumbling over the rough ground, bouncing them around. He reached across the darkness, searching for her hand and found it. At first she entwined her fingers with his but said nothing. Then, a few moments later when the truck hit a particularly deep rut in the road, she moved to sit beside him.

"Not exactly the romantic setting I had in mind, but I guess it will have to do."

"Always, you find the humor."

"I can't see your face yet so I have no idea if you're smiling."

"Only a little."

"I can do with a little."

"We shall soon pick up the others, so any romantic

intentions will have to wait."

"Let's see if Eduard and Frederic will let these other pilots ride up front with them. Then we'll have more time. Alone."

She didn't say anything, and even though his eyes were starting to see the pinpoints of light from the holes above them, he still couldn't see her face. "You're quiet. What are you thinking?"

"I'm thinking that I wish I could have met you when you were that boy writing me letters in the back of your father's movie theater."

"Yeah?"

"You didn't know, of course, but I always loved getting those long letters. Always I waited for the postman to bring our mail."

"And I used to race upstairs after school to my bedroom. Mom used to place your letters on my pillow. Finding one there was always the favorite part of my day."

"Mine too. Except if you wrote about those silly cowboy movies."

"Hey! Those are my favorites. Have some respect."

"Those and your Cubs baseball. Such a boring sport."

"Ah, but you've never been to a real live baseball game. I'll take you when all this is over. We'll ride the trolley car to Wrigley Field, we'll eat hot dogs, and we'll try to catch home run balls."

The truck hit another rut and bounced them again, but she said nothing.

"What? You won't even try one single Cubs game with me?"

Silence.

He pulled her closer, resting his chin on her head. "Look, I know we can't be sure how all this will end. I know it's mostly wishful thinking to talk about baseball games and all that. But I need to believe there's a future for us. Together. That's why I want you to come with me."

"Danny, please don't ask that of me."

"What is so wrong with asking you to come with me? Your country is still at war and still extremely dangerous. I mean, look at us! We're hidden in a truck driving across German occupied territory. Why is it so wrong for me to care about your safety?"

The truck slowed down. Anya stiffened. "Shh! Say nothing," she whispered.

The complaining gears once more groaned as the vehicle came to a stop. Danny held his breath. He could hear German voices, obviously barking orders. Eduard responded in fluent German in a tone that suggested nothing unusual, merely routine. Next, he heard Frederic's additional comments in a much more animated version of German. Laughter rang out as the guards clearly enjoyed whatever Frederic had said. Danny allowed himself a breath, relieved to hear laughter instead of gunfire.

The conversation continued, back and forth. He could hear the squeal of the outer rear door opening. Anya squeezed his hand. Then, the door slammed shut again. Danny visualized Frederic handing over a crate of stolen goods. The resulting comments from the guards sounded favorable. In a moment, the truck roared back to life and they were on their way.

"Thank goodness," he said just above a whisper.

"We should be near Apeldoorn shortly," Anya said. "It is not far now."

"Then I haven't got much time to convince you to come with me, do I?"

"No, you don't, and I will not change my mind, so save yourself the effort."

"What is it that holds you back? What could you possibly have here that's worth risking your life every single day?"

She stiffened again and pushed away from him. "And what right do you have to tell me what to do? To tell me I must go with you? What if it were *your* country under occupation? Would you run away? Would you have someone tell you to leave? To simply—"

"To simply do whatever it takes to save my life? Of course, I would! Who in their right mind prefers living in a war zone when they have a chance to live in freedom?"

"Oh, so now you would say I'm crazy? That I am a fool because I won't drop everything and run away with you?"

He could hear the passion in her voice, the rising anger he'd stumbled back into. "Anya, no. I would never say that. I just—"

"You just want to protect me. I know. I've heard it all before."

"So that's it?"

No response.

"There's nothing I can say or do to convince you to come with me?"

They rode together in silence for several minutes until the truck made a quick turn and lurched to a stop. Someone inside the cab knocked twice then once then three times.

"That is Eduard's signal that we're at the safe house. No, Danny. There is nothing you can say. Please do not bring this up in front of the other men when they join us."

He could hear a flurry of commotion on the other side of the compartment, then the door was rolled up. Frederic stood there with his hands on his hips, silhouetted against the darkness. "Well, then. We must make this quick. If you need to go to the—"

"Yes, I do." Anya slipped out the door, leaving Danny behind.

Even in the darkness, he could see Frederic's eyebrows disappear beneath his helmet as he looked back at Danny. He lit an actual cigarette, no doubt one of the stolen Lucky Strikes. He blew the match out with a teasing smirk. "Again the fumble?"

Danny ignored the comment. "How much farther once the other men join us?"

"It is not the distance. Distance means nothing. It is the many stops along the way. Tonight we try a different route to avoid the many blockades. We will try to stop in Utrecht."

"Gentlemen," Eduard interrupted from the rear of the truck. "Make your introductions after we get going. All the way to the back. Hurry now."

Three individuals dressed in civilian clothing like Danny's hopped up into the truck and crouched their way forward around the trunks and crates before entering the compartment. Even with both doors open, the light remained almost completely dark as the men crowded into the close quarters. He moved as far against the wall abutting the cab as he could, hoping to keep his foot from getting stepped on.

"Come on in," he said, trying to ease the tension. "It's crowded, but I think we'll all fit."

"Danny?"

He recognized the voice at once. "Charlie?"

"Oh, thank God!" his friend cried, climbing over the others to reach him. They stood in a clumsy embrace, patting each other on the back.

"I can't believe it! How did you end up here?" Danny asked.

"Move it!" Anya shouted sounding like a kindergarten teacher losing patience with her young students. The metal door was rolled back down after she entered. "You'll get used to the darkness in a moment. Until then, sit still and don't move around."

"Danny! It's so good to see you—well, to almost see you. Can't we light a lantern or something? It's pitch dark in here."

"No, we cannot light a lantern," Anya answered. "Unless you would like to send up a flare to let the Germans know you are here?"

"It's okay," Danny added. "You'll see pinpoints of light from the roof soon. Charlie, what happened? Were you shot down?"

"More like shot to hell and back. Yesterday we caught anti-aircraft fire on our way back from a run to Kiel. It was unbelievable. Only Banks and Kearney bailed out ahead of me. Haven't seen them since."

"The rest of your crew?"

"Lost them all. All of them," he said, his voice cracking.

Danny patted his friend on the back. "It's tough. I'm so sorry. I know what that's like. Only five of us made it out of *Sophie.* And as far as I know, Pendergrass is the only other one who made it."

It took Charlie a moment to compose himself. "I'll be glad when all this is over and we can all go home."

The other two men echoed in agreement. They introduced themselves—both crew members from *Crazy Lady* out of the 95th Bomb Group—tail gunner Gerald Morrison and waist gunner Larry Fogelman. Finally getting used to the tiny shafts of light, they shook hands and exchanged more small talk. When the conversation stilled, Danny remembered Anya.

"I forgot to introduce our 'guide' on tonight's excursion. This is—"

"Eva. My name is Eva."

He wasn't sure why the cover names were necessary at this point, but he wasn't about to go against her wishes. "Eva. She has been most helpful."

"Nice to meet you, Eva," Charlie and the others said. "Thank you for your help getting us back to our bases."

He hated that she was across the cramped aisle at the other end, even if it was only four or five feet away. Every moment that passed was one moment closer to watching her go. He knew he could never convince her to change her mind. She made that abundantly clear.

With the tight quarters and sparse ventilation, Danny fought the slight tinge of claustrophobia that crept through him. The men obviously hadn't had a chance to clean up, filling the stuffy air with a combination of sweat and stale tobacco. Uncomfortable with the awkward silence, Danny asked them to update him on the war news, which they did.

"It's just a matter of days now," Charlie said. "At most, maybe a few weeks."

Danny noted Anya's silence. He could see her silhouette and wondered if perhaps she had fallen asleep. To be so near yet so far from her as their time together evaporated, so crowded in this stifling box drove him mad. He leaned his head back against the panel and closed his eyes. Instantly the image came to his mind as it so often did—that of his mother on her knees praying for him.

For now, that would have to do.

57

Late morning, 03 April 1945

The truck slammed to a stop sending all of them toppling into each other.

"What the—"

"Shhh! Say nothing!" Anya whispered. Thankfully, the men stopped their bewildered comments and heeded her warning.

She could hear the angry voices shouting German demands outside as well as the distinct report of numerous guns locking into place. Bright lights outside illuminated their hidden cabin from above so they could see each other better—most likely from headlights of several vehicles pointed in their direction.

Something was very wrong. Eduard would have signaled had this been a routine stop. *Wait* . . . She thought she heard a gentle tapping against the front wall. "Let me through," she whispered, climbing over the airmen's tangled legs. She pressed her ear against the wall, listening for further instructions. The coded message made her heart stop.

Mercenaries. Better they had encountered Hitler himself than these ruthless thugs.

Danny leaned over to whisper in her ear. His warm breath did nothing to stop the icy fingers of fear in her stomach. "What should we—"

She clamped her hand over his mouth as Eduard began speaking on the other side of the wall.

"Ah, a victory celebration! Mind if we join?"

"What is your business here? Where are you going?" the soldier barked.

"On our way to Utrecht to deliver supplies to Reichskommissar Seyss-Inquart. Here, you can see our orders."

"Ah, yes, yes. Always the orders. Your papers are of no value to us."

"No? And why is that?" Eduard asked.

A sudden blast of gunfire erupted. "Down down down!" Anya whispered frantically as several bullets pierced the cab wall. In a split second between shots, she heard a loud grunt across from her. The man in the middle fell limp, a stream of blood pouring from his head. The other two men attended to him but it was too late. The man nearest the front—the one named Charlie—must have ducked just in time, leaving a straight path to the young man named Fogelman. The tail gunner held a hand over his own mouth to stifle a groan as he pulled his dead crew mate against him, rocking in silent grief.

Anya held a finger to her lips and stretched out her other hand, shaking it in the men's faces. "Shhh! Not a sound!"

Anya mouthed silently. "They must not know we're here!"

She didn't have to see the gory evidence of what just happened to know Eduard and Frederic were dead. Her heart pounded as her mind sought a means of escape.

Danny pressed his mouth against her ear. "Can they find us in here?"

"Yes," she answered against his ear, "but only if they loot all of the cargo first."

The soldiers' voices moved toward the back of the truck. Anya held her hands up again, cautioning them to remain silent. Even the shaded sight of Morrison's tears didn't deter her sense of urgency. She slowly dug her firearm from the back waistband of her pants and slowly, silently cocked the hammer into place.

A single shot at the back of the truck drew laughter. "What shall we find?" one of them teased. The others joined in, obviously anxious to see what treasures could be pillaged.

She could feel the slight movement of the truck bed; probably several men hopping up inside.

They could hear the cracking of crates being pried open, and with each one a swell of laughter at its contents. Through their shouts of joy, she knew they'd found the many crates of liquor and cigarettes, readily pronouncing themselves the luckiest men on earth. The weapons were discovered, delighting the mercenaries with their good fortune and the promise of huge profits from their sale.

Inside their compartment, Anya and the men held their breath. From time to time they'd look at each other, wondering what was going on just feet from where they hid. When confused eyes would turn on her, she shook her head and held her finger to her lips again.

Eventually the Germans took their party back outside, removing crates and boxes from the back of the truck. Anya knew the truck was packed from back to front—the most valuable goods nearest the back door; the more mundane things such as socks and kitchen utensils and soap farther in. The strategy worked. As the men opened the boxes closer to their secret hideout, they soon grew bored, weary of the quest when their comrades were already imbibing in the spoils.

Convinced no one remained inside the truck, Anya leaned forward, motioning the three men toward her. "We will wait them out," she mouthed more than whispered. "We have no choice."

The others nodded in agreement. Charlie quietly pulled the scarf from his neck and placed it over Fogelman's head. They couldn't risk making noise by attempting to move his body, so it remained slumped between Charlie and Morrison. The young tail gunner dropped his head in his hands. She watched as Danny reached over to gently pat the young man's knee.

Through the long hours before daybreak, the Germans drank and sang and danced. Anya could smell wood burning and assumed they had built a bonfire to keep them warm. As the headlights of their vehicles grew dim, she caught the flicker of firelight dancing through the air holes above.

Her mind worked all the angles of their predicament as she tried to determine their options. Even if every last one of the German swine fell sound asleep in their drunken revelry, it would be much too risky to crawl their way out and attempt to escape. Or would it? She pictured herself crawling out of the compartment, foraging through the heavy boxes stacked just on the other side of the rolling door—then imagined herself jumping from the truck bed only to find an armed soldier watching her every move.

But to stay? Eventually the soldiers would wake up and drive their stolen truck to wherever they happened to go. At some point, they would empty the remaining cargo and find the hidden door. They would be shot—or worse, tortured before execution.

They had no choice. They had to escape and do it now. Anya knew their only chance was to slip away before the sun came up.

In whispered tones, she told the men what they must do. They understood the urgency of her plan and agreed to it. Quietly, Charlie and Anya moved to the door. She reminded him to help her lift the rolling metal door as slowly as possible to alleviate any potential noise. Inch by grueling inch they raised it, until it was all the way up. They could see slices of light between the trunks but nothing beyond. They knew they must work swiftly, moving the trunks without making a sound.

This will take a miracle. Anya shook off the thought.

Carefully, slowly, urgently they worked. It seemed like hours but Anya knew it was probably no more than half an hour at most. Finally they could see the rest of the truck bed, its contents strewn haphazardly. She spotted an open box of weapons and silently by way of hand signals told Charlie to grab a few along with some ammunition. He worked silently as Anya walked back into the compartment, every step made slow and deliberate.

"Morrison, you will need to help Lieutenant McClain, but you must both be absolutely silent. Take it slow and watch your step."

"But what about Sergeant Fogelman? We can't just leave him here," his friend pleaded.

She placed her hand on his shoulder. "I'm sorry, but we have no choice."

The young man blinked a couple of times, took a deep breath, then nodded.

She and Morrison quietly helped Danny to his feet.

"Anya, are you sure?" he whispered in her ear. "I'll slow you down. You know I will."

"Not another word. Just hang on."

They continued their slow journey around the trunks and crates of the long truck bed. Charlie handed them each a loaded gun, filling his own pockets with ammunition. Anya went first, peeking just enough to get a lay of the situation. The German mercenaries appeared to be sound asleep around the dying campfire which was several meters from the truck's side. If they carefully exited the truck and immediately moved to the other side of it, they should be able to remain out of view of the sleeping pigs. She turned to face her three charges, giving them directions again with silent hand motions. Morrison gestured the sign of the cross. She hoped his silent prayer helped.

Charlie and Morrison helped Danny down from the truck, each movement measured and silent while Anya kept them covered. Hidden from view once they moved to the other side of the truck, Anya considered their options. Daybreak was moments away. They needed to get out of there and fast. Charlie pointed toward a cluster of trees and they slowly made their way in that direction.

Suddenly a soldier emerged from behind the trees, his attention focused on his zipper. Anya was on him in a flash, shoving a scarf in his mouth at the same instant she kneed him hard in the groin. His eyes bugged briefly before rolling back as he passed out. She helped him fall to the ground to avoid a loud thud, then grabbed his head and swiftly snapped his neck. She relieved him of his pistol and rushed back to join the others.

They stared at her with stunned expressions as if paralyzed until she waved them forward, motioning with her gun. "Move it!" she whispered angrily.

As the men disappeared into the trees, she looked back over her shoulder for one last glance. There, Eduard's lifeless body hung half way out of the truck's cab, his unseeing eyes staring wide. Just beyond him, Frederic's body sat slumped over, his head resting against the blood-smeared window.

She fought the despair, swallowing hard against the bile in her throat, then forced herself to follow the Americans.

58

Danny hated this. Twice he'd tried to convince the others to just leave him and go, but they wouldn't listen. He'd never known such pain as that in his injured foot each time it made contact with the ground, and now his headache seemed intent on competing with the pain in his foot. Charlie was doing his best to help lug him through the forest, but the frustration was wearing thin.

"Charlie, please. This is ridiculous."

"So help me, Danny, if you say that one more time, I'll punch your lights out and hoist you over my shoulder. Knock it off. We're not leaving you, so shut up, will you?"

"We're not far now," Anya said, falling back to join them. "We should be near Utrecht soon."

"What is your plan, Eva?" Charlie asked.

"I will find some place for you all to hide, then I shall make my way into town and survey the situation."

"We can't let you go by yourself!" Danny argued.

"It's far less risky for me to go alone. You three would

draw too much attention. You'd be walking targets."

"Anya, please!" Danny pleaded, then caught himself. "I mean, Eva. Please let Charlie or Sergeant Morrison go with you."

"I know you may find this difficult to believe, Lieutenant, but long before you Americans finally decided to come to our rescue, we learned how to play this game called war. So don't insult me by treating me like some helpless damsel in distress."

"I didn't mean to insult you. I'm simply—"

"Over here." Anya cut a path to their left. "This will be a good place for you to hide until I get back."

They followed her into a dense covering. Charlie helped Danny onto the ground. The relief of being off his feet overwhelmed him. He laid his head back against a tree and tried to compose himself.

"Ma'am, I mean no disrespect," Morrison began, "but I have to agree with the lieutenant. I'm sure you're more than capable of taking care of yourself and all, but I'd sure feel better if you'd let me come along. Just in case something happened."

Danny could have hugged the guy. Surely Anya would listen to reason—even if it had to come from someone else.

"I appreciate your offer, Sergeant, but it's much safer for a woman to travel alone under the circumstances. Most every man in our country has been carted off by the Germans to work in 'volunteer' labor camps. So if the Germans should see you, they'd know something was wrong."

"So how did Eduard and Frederic elude their detection?" Danny countered. "Weren't they also making frequent 'deliveries' just like you?"

She looked at him a long time before answering. He couldn't believe he'd said something so insensitive. Her fellow Resistance workers had just been gunned down. "Anya, I'm so sorry. I shouldn't have said that."

"Who's Anya?" Morrison asked.

"I am Anya. Apparently Lieutenant McClain is unable to keep a confidence. We do not use our real names in our work because it is far too dangerous." She cocked her head at an angle, folded her arms over her chest, and turned her gaze on Danny. "But at this point, we'll have to forego all of that, and try to get through this without getting us all killed. *If* that is all right with you, Lieutenant?"

He looked away, unwilling to see the fire in her glare.

"Fine," she snapped. "Now stay out of sight until I return. Under no circumstances are you to leave. Is that understood?"

They all nodded, though Danny did so under protest.

"Good. I'll be back as soon as I can." She turned to go then stopped. "Oh, I almost forgot. Here are some bulbs if you get hungry," she said, digging them out of her deep pocket. "Hopefully I can find something more substantial once I get you settled." She handed Charlie the bulbs and started to make her way out of the thicket.

"Anya?" Danny called out to her.

She stopped and looked back at him.

"Please . . . please be careful."

For a split second, he thought he saw a trace of tenderness in her eyes as she nodded. Then she was gone.

How many times had she walked these roads? How many miles had she put on her feet? Long ago, they'd bled and cracked and ached when she had walked long distances. Now they were calloused and rough to the touch, but that didn't stop the aching. If she thought about it long enough, she would drop down where she was and never get up again. At this point, she could easily convince herself to give up and be done with it all. But that was not an option. Not with three Allies needing her help. And so she must focus on them and keep going.

Anya was torn. The closest place to go was the Boormans' farm, but she couldn't. She didn't have the stomach to face the demons of that place and what happened the last time she was there. No telling who was occupying the house now. Where could she go? Eduard had said all the safe houses were compromised after Enschede was infiltrated. She couldn't bear to think of them all murdered, but neither could she risk going there.

Home? Can I go home?

How desperately she wanted to run the rest of way, fling open the door, and find her family waiting for her with open arms. But that would never happen. They were all gone. Did she have the courage to go there? And if she did, would she find refuge for herself and the three Allies? For Danny?

No. I can't bear it. I refuse to go there now. But where else can we find shelter?

She wouldn't pray. Even though they escaped from the German mercenaries in an impossible situation, she wasn't ready to give God credit for saving them. And she certainly couldn't thank Him. Wasn't she the one who came up with the plan to leave before the soldiers woke up? Wasn't she the one who found the courage to lead them out of that situation? Of course she was. So why should she resurrect the God who had long forgotten the Dutch just to thank Him for something *she* did?

Think. Where can I go? Where can I take these men and be safe?

It came to her immediately. She picked up her pace, determined to find the help she needed and the one she knew would give it. Another kilometer north then two blocks over.

Fifteen minutes later, she spotted the familiar house and ran up the front walkway and the six steps up to the porch. She knocked quietly, afraid to call out. She knocked again, trying to see through the lace curtains on the door's window.

The door flew open. "Anya!"

"Oh, Helga!" Anya rushed into her friend's arms. "I'm so glad you're home! I didn't know where else to go."

"I can't believe you're here! Are you all right?" the kind woman asked, steering Anya toward the kitchen.

"Yes, I am fine. But I need help."

"Sit. I shall make us tea."

"I don't have time, Helga. I have three Allied airmen hidden outside of town. I must get them to safety, but I—"

"Don't go to the safe house! Haven't you heard the news?"

"Yes, Eduard told us we've all been compromised after Enschede was infiltrated."

"Yes, we've abandoned ours as well. They have names and descriptions and they know our routines. None of us are safe. None. Please, sit. Just for a moment. We must figure out what to do with your airmen."

Anya took a seat at the table then Helga joined her, placing her hand over Anya's. "Where are Eduard and the others?"

Anya looked her straight in the eye and shook her head.

"Oh no, Anya, no!" she cried. "What happened?"

As quickly as she could, she relayed the events of the past day. Even hearing the words coming from her own mouth, she couldn't believe they'd escaped. It couldn't have happened but it did.

"Helga, I must hurry. Will you let me bring the men here? Do you have some place to hide them?"

"Of course. I have a place much like the one your parents had. We can hide them here until we can find a way to get them to the coast. I will get word to someone."

Anya stood and hugged her. "Thank you. I will go and bring them back as soon as I can."

"Good. Be careful, dear," she said, following her to the door. "Try to be back before curfew."

"I will."

Anya pulled her cap over her head and hurried back the way she had come. She dismissed any thought of danger, focused solely on returning where she left the men. She had seen hardly anyone on her way into town, weaving her way in and out of trees and shrubbery to stay out of view as much as possible. She hoped the same would be true on the way out.

The rumble of a truck sounded in the distance behind her. She scoped her surroundings and found nothing but a small tree in the distance. But to run to it now would draw attention to herself. *I have nothing to hide. I'm merely a Dutch woman walking to a farm somewhere to bargain for food. Women do this every day. I can do this.*

She didn't look back but knew the truck was approaching. She heard the gears change as it slowed alongside her.

"Fräulein, would you like a ride?"

She paused and looked at the man on the passenger side who'd spoken to her. *German soldiers. Play the game.*

She scratched her head through her cap. "No, I appreciate very much the offer," she answered in German, "but I would like to walk." She scratched her elbow vigorously and continued walking.

"But it looks as if it could rain," the soldier asked as the truck kept pace with her. "Would you not prefer a dry ride to a wet walk?"

She played the idiot, raising her face to the cloudy sky while scratching under her arm. "Oh, I see what you mean." She stretched out her neck like a giraffe and gave it a good scratch, then leveled her gaze back their direction. "Well, I suppose—"

The gears changed and the truck started rolling. "Sorry, Fräulein, but we just realized we have no room." And off it went in a cloud of dust.

She pressed her lips together to stifle her smile. How many times had she used this ploy, always with the same results? Her imaginary infestation of lice had always served her well, scaring off many a German. She blew out the breath she'd been holding, thankful for the ruse and thankful for the German aversion to all things crawling.

Once again she picked up her pace, anxious to get back to Danny and the others.

Oh Danny . . . why must it be so complicated? He was absolutely right. She had nothing to stay for. No family. Only a handful of Resistance workers, all scattered and under the radar now. And of course, Helga. But how could she leave her beloved country? How could she desert the other workers when so few were left to fight?

Behind her, she heard the rumble of another truck. *I can't believe it. With no fuel left, still the trucks roll.* She fought her frustration and gave her head a good scratch. Just in case.

As the truck drew closer, it too slowed down. She fought the urge to look, preferring ignorance.

"Anya?"

She slowed, but didn't respond.

"Anya, Helga has sent me for you."

She turned to find a familiar face, but one she couldn't immediately place. Better to act dumb until she could remember. "Helga?"

"Yes. She got in touch with us. I was not far so they sent me to help you."

"Yes?"

"You don't remember me, do you?" He smiled and she vaguely recalled seeing his kind face . . . and the same truck, but—

"I gave you a ride into Utrecht. You and your friend. You

had stayed with Mr. and Mrs. Hildebrand after—"

"After getting off the train with the children. Yes, I remember you now," she said, approaching his truck. "Though I can't seem to recall your name. I apologize."

He leaned over and threw open the passenger door for her. "Nathan. But no need to apologize. These are difficult times."

She climbed up into the truck and closed the door. "Yes, they are most difficult." She looked down at her hand, still gripping the door handle, remembering the last time she was in this vehicle. Wim had been seated where she now sat. The memory of what happened not long after they'd watched Nathan drive away curled in her stomach. She closed her eyes, finding it hard to breathe.

"Are you all right?" he asked, touching her arm.

Her eyes flew open, and she turned toward him. "Yes, I . . ." She shook her head hard. "I'm sorry, yes. I'm all right. And I'm very glad to see you. I'm afraid I'm a little exhausted. That's all."

He put the truck in gear and they were on their way. "You'll have to tell me where we're going. Helga told us you were transporting three Allied airmen and needed to pick them up."

Ten minutes later, the men were loaded in the back and they were on their way.

"Nathan, if we're stopped, we're all dead. The Germans won't be fooled by a few blankets thrown over the men back there."

"I know. That's why we're not going back to Helga's."

"What? But she's expecting me. I told her we'd return as

soon as we could."

"Anya, you have to trust me. I sent word to Helga. She knows we've had a change of plans."

She pulled her cap off, irritated. "What change of plans?"

"We have passage for the men but we must get them to the coast today. With the Allies making so much progress now, the Germans are desperate. We have reason to believe the vessels leaving today may be among the last to get out until it's all over. There's no time to lose."

"How can we possibly make it to the coast without being stopped? I've made these deliveries. I know how this works."

"As have I. But today, we will go a route that bypasses the roadblocks all together."

"Oh, that's original. That's how we got in this mess in the first place. We took the back roads and ran right into the heart of German mercenaries. No, turn this truck around. We are not going through this again!"

He spoke with confidence as he looked over at her. "Anya, you have to trust me."

And here I thought Nathan was a decent fellow. He's just like the rest of them. Bullheaded, stubborn, and—

"Last week we sabotaged three roadblocks along this bypass route. The German guards are in fact our own people. We've been able to monitor all their activities as well as let our own people have safe passage through this area. We've got one coming up. I'll show you exactly what I'm talking about."

And he did. Much to Anya's disbelief, they went through a routine roadblock much as any other, except that these "German" soldiers were merely play acting the part. This,

Nathan told her, was done in case any Germans were coming through dressed as civilians. With the Allies closing in, some of the German soldiers had laid down their machine guns, changed out of their uniforms, and made an effort to blend in rather than face arrest or worse. But even a deserter couldn't be trusted. So these Resistance workers acting as German soldiers went through the motions, even checking the cargo portion of the truck without flinching.

"Everything checks out. On your way, now," the guard told Nathan in perfect German. Almost in disbelief, Anya had watched the send-off exchange including a barely imperceptible wink from the guard as they drove off.

She leaned back in her seat. "If I had not seen it for myself, I would not believe it."

"You have to admit it gives you pride to know your fellow countrymen—and women—have far exceeded all our expectations when it comes to fighting our enemies."

"I suppose," she said, letting her eyes close as fatigue and momentary relief washed over her. "But many have paid the ultimate price as well."

"Yes, that is true. But we never give up. I love what that English chap, Prime Minister Churchill said—'Never give in! Never give in! Never, never, never, never!'"

With her eyes still closed, Anya mused at her driver's rather perfect English accent and optimism. And with that thought, she fell sound asleep.

59

04 April 1945

After the third roadblock, Nathan pulled off the road to check on Danny, Charlie, and Morrison. They'd been cramped in the back of the truck beneath some smelly tarps and blankets for hours. As Charlie helped him down off the truck bed, Danny winced at the annoying pain in his ankle, aggravated even more by their long journey on foot to Utrecht.

"How's the ankle?" Anya asked.

Danny hadn't seen her standing on the other side of the truck. "Not worth discussing, I'm afraid. How are you holding up?" he asked, taking a seat on the tailgate.

"Not worth discussing."

Her eyes held the hint of a smile even if her mouth didn't.

"How much further to the coast?"

"Another ten kilometers," Nathan answered, joining them. "About half an hour at the rate we're going, but no more roadblocks."

"How do you bypass the Atlantic Wall?" Charlie asked.

"What's that?" Morrison asked.

"Hitler knew the entire western coastline was vulnerable to attack," Anya began, "so he created the Atlantic Wall which is basically a system of fortifications that stretches the entire length of that coastline. From France, Belgium, our Netherlands— all the way up to the northern tip of Norway."

Morrison seemed perplexed. "You mean there's an actual wall all along those coastlines?"

"Not a literal wall," Nathan answered, "but a series of fortifications. A good many of them are concrete pill boxes housing machine guns and anti-aircraft artillery. Some are right on the beach, others are more inland. Then there are the mines." Nathan shook his head. "Those scare me more than anything."

"We've lost three vessels to mines," Anya added. "There must be thousands of them, and not just on the beach. The most dangerous are the ones off shore."

"No disrespect, but isn't there a safer way out of here without taking such a risk?" Charlie asked.

Nathan took off his hat and ran his hand through his hair before putting it back in place. "I'm afraid we don't have that luxury, Lieutenant. In fact, we need to load up and get moving so we don't miss our connection. Anya, make sure they're covered then come along."

Morrison climbed up in the truck bed. "So how can you be sure we don't find one of those mines?"

"You just need to trust us," Anya said as she started to help Charlie move Danny.

"Charlie, give me a second, will you?" Danny asked.

"No problem," his friend answered.

Danny grabbed Anya's hand. "Please tell me we'll have time to talk before we get on that fishing boat?"

"I cannot make such a promise, Danny. It is very dangerous there."

"I can't just leave you like this, Anya. There's still so much to be said."

The truck rumbled to life. Anya looked up at him. "We need to get you covered." She raised her voice and called out, "Charlie? We need to get you guys back under the tarps."

Danny pulled her hand to his mouth and kissed the top of it. "This isn't goodbye."

He could see the confusion in her eyes and wanted nothing more than to pull her into his arms. But no sooner had the thought crossed his mind, than she pulled her hand free.

"C'mon, buddy, let's get you hidden from the Krauts," Charlie said.

Danny wanted to scream. He was sick to death of all the hide and seek. Sick to death of this despicable dance he and Anya were playing. And sick to death knowing that once he boarded that boat, he might never see her again.

The faintest whiff of salt air permeated their cover, causing the tension in Danny's gut to tighten even more. It wouldn't be long now. When the truck slowed then turned, he amended his thoughts, thinking they'd arrived sooner than he expected. But the vehicle continued, the road—if it was a road—rutted and bombed out, by the feel of it. With a squeal of brakes, it stopped.

They heard muffled voices, then the slow dropping of the tailgate.

"We arrived ahead of schedule, so we stop here to wait," Nathan said, throwing the tarps off them. "Here we have cover.

On the beach, we are most vulnerable."

"Okay if we climb down and get some fresh air?" Morrison asked. "Those tarps really stink."

"Yes, I know," Nathan said with a broad smile. "Very nasty. But wait until you board *De Roos.*"

"De what?"

"*De Roos.* Your transportation across the North Sea. A fishing trawler called *The Rose.*"

"How much time do we have?" Danny asked as Charlie helped him to the tailgate again.

"Ten minutes. Not a second more," Nathan answered after checking his watch.

"Then I'm going to ask a favor," Danny said as he scooted to the edge of the tailgate. "I need to speak to Anya. Privately."

She had just stepped into his line of vision as his request caught her by surprise. "What?"

"You heard me. Guys, if you'll get lost for a few moments, I would really appreciate it."

Their sheepish, knowing grins might have embarrassed him, but he had no time for formalities. That was the problem— he had no time! They shuffled away in the direction of the truck's cab, leaving him alone with Anya.

"Would you mind?" He held his hand to the spot beside him, hoping she'd join him.

"Danny, what's this all about?"

"Please, just have a seat."

She hesitated. He could almost hear a ticking clock inside his mind, desperately aware of the moments he had left with her. Finally, she hopped up beside him. "What is it?"

He stared at her, mentally memorizing every feature of her face, the exact color of her hair, the shape of her eyes, and the mystery they held. He fought the pounding of his heart to say what must be said. "Anya, I can't believe it's come to this. I would give anything for it to be different, you know."

"I know," she said softly. "But we have no choice."

"Well, it's no secret how much I disagree with you on that particular subject, but I won't spend the valuable moments we have left arguing about it."

She turned to look at him and he saw the relief in her gaze. "Good. I couldn't bear it if you kept after me. Not now."

He reached for her hands, slipping the gloves off them, finger by finger. "I understand. But that doesn't mean I'm giving up on you." He held her hands in both of his. "And it doesn't mean I'm giving up on *us*."

He could see the rise and fall of her chest beneath her coat as conflict troubled her face. He reached for her chin and slowly turned her face toward him.

"Danny—"

"Anya, I love you. And I have loved you for such a long time. All those letters—sure, at first I just needed to keep a connection with you because I—well, I just couldn't believe Hans was gone. But even if I never admitted it to myself, I knew it was more than that. I didn't continue writing you letters just because of Hans. I grew to love every one you sent, every word you wrote to me.

"All those years went by, and I never forgot you. I kept wondering if you'd survived, if you were all right. Then all these years later—in the middle of a war no less—I jumped out of my Fortress and landed in Holland. What are the chances of such a thing? And for some inexplicable reason, before I left home I grabbed that picture of you and your family and tucked it inside my wallet. Why did I do that when we hadn't exchanged letters in years?

"Then, because I was rescued by members of the Dutch Resistance, your colleague found that picture and notified you.

These are not coincidences, Anya. That night you came to the safe house cellar questioning me . . . when I realized it was you, all I wanted to do was take you in my arms and keep you there forever. I knew it then as I know it now—I love you, Anya. And I've never been so sure about anything in my entire life than the simple fact that I love you."

She lowered her eyes and shook her head as if trying to dismiss such a thought. She tried to speak and couldn't.

He wrapped her in his arms. "I've been such an idiot. I've wanted to tell you for so long and here I've waited until the last possible moment." He pulled back to look into her eyes. "And the thing is . . . well, I may be blind about some things, but I'm pretty sure you love me too." He couldn't have stopped the wide smile on his face if he'd tried. Then, without a moment's hesitation he leaned down and touched her lips with his. He hadn't thought beyond this moment, but he knew there was no turning back now. He kissed her once, then kissed her again.

At first she held back. He knew she was warring with her emotions again. Why did she always do that? Was it merely instinct? Or was it the same barrier she'd tried so hard to hold up between them? Then he felt her begin to relax in his arms and return his kisses. Her tears dampened his face and she clung to him, her arms wrapped around his waist. Oh, to be anywhere but here—in the back of a dirty truck in the middle of a country still occupied by Germans, within easy earshot of three others.

She slowed her kiss then looked up at him. "I've been so afraid, so scared of my feelings for you." She wiped at her cheeks. "I knew I couldn't bear it if I lost you, but I knew I would. Of course this day would come when I'd have to watch you go. I knew it from the beginning. And it just all feels like some cruel joke."

He pushed a strand of hair from her eyes. "But it *isn't* a cruel joke. It's real. This isn't goodbye, Anya. Even if you won't come with me, it isn't goodbye. I will come back for you—"

"Don't be ridiculous. Don't you understand? We have no assurances, no certainties. We live from one moment to the next and nothing more."

He put his finger to her lips. "That's the talk of someone exhausted from a long war. That's all it is. And we both know the war is about to end. All around us the Allies are liberating one town after the next. It will all be over soon, and I will come back for you."

"How? Will you just hop in one of your planes and fly over to get me?"

"Maybe? Who's to say? It doesn't matter. Whatever it takes, I will come back for you. Just tell me where I can find you. Where would you go if the war ended this very day?"

She leaned her head against his shoulder. "You're such an optimist. As if everything always goes the way you want it."

"We have to believe, Anya. We have to find hope, even when it seems hopeless. How else would we have survived this long? Any of us?"

She grew quiet and he prayed she was considering all he'd said. He had no idea how he'd get back here or how he'd find her. But there wasn't a trace of doubt that he would.

"I'm just so tired. I can't think straight anymore. I wouldn't begin to know how to believe or hope about tomorrow when we have no guarantees for today."

"Then I'll believe for you. I'll hold on even if you can't. We were meant to be together, Anya. It's so obvious. After all these years, we were meant to be."

He kissed her again, first on her forehead, then on the tip of her nose, then on her trembling lips. She murmured something, pulling her arms free and cupping his face in her hands. "I love you, too, Danny," she whispered through her tears. "I've just been too much of a coward to admit it."

He held her hands between his. "I had a feeling that was the problem, but I'm sure glad to hear you say it. And all I've got to say is—it's about time."

"Lieutenant, it's time," Nathan said after clearing his throat.

"All right. Thanks," Danny answered. He looked back at her as she swiped another tear from her face. "Tell me where I'll find you when I come back. Where will you be?"

"How can I possibly know that?"

He placed his fingers against her lips again. "Shh. Think for me, Anya. If this all ended tomorrow, where would you go?"

Pressing her lips together, she looked away for a moment. With a ragged breath, she looked back into his eyes. "I would go home. I just want to go home." Her face crumbled and she wept openly. "I just want to go home," she whispered through her tears.

He leaned his head against hers. "Then one day soon, I shall knock on your door in Utrecht and hope I'll find you there."

He kissed her once more, sealing his promise.

Part VI

60

"Come on, Danny. You need a change of scenery. It'll do you good to get off base for a while."

He knew Charlie was right. After three weeks back at the 390th, Danny was about to lose his mind. He'd spent the first week and a half in sick quarters staying off his foot as much as possible. But all that lying around only amplified the frustration knotting up inside him. He couldn't get Anya off his mind.

He'd busied himself, first making sure his parents were notified he was no longer MIA, then wrote them a long letter. He wondered what they'd been told and when they'd heard the news. After all they went through worrying about Joey when Pearl Harbor was attacked, he hated to think they'd experienced those fears all over again. Did they fear receiving another telegram? Were they afraid the blue star in the front window would have to be exchanged for a gold one?

The day after he got back, Sally had stopped by to see him in sick quarters. He was surprised how happy he was to see her even though she'd actually come to say goodbye. Her papers had finally come through and she was going home. They visited for almost an hour as Danny told her about his detour through Holland and finding Anya. She promised to pray he'd find a way to go back for Anya once the war was over. They exchanged their home addresses, promising to keep in touch after the war. She hugged him and wished him well, then she was gone.

"Hello in there?" Charlie teased. "Anybody home?"

"Huh? Oh, yeah. Sorry."

Charlie dragged him outside and over to the Jeep. "Come on, hop in. I'm headed to Quincy's. Sophie said she'd make us some shepherd pie. If I can't convince you to get out of here for a while, maybe Sophie's cooking will."

"All right, all right. Enough of the begging. I'll go."

With only a slight limp now, he made his way to the battered vehicle and climbed into the passenger seat. It was another gray and foggy English day, but he didn't care. The weather matched his mood. The fresh air and breezy short drive into Framlingham awakened his senses if not his spirits. Charlie was right. If nothing else, the change of scenery woke him out of his aggravating doldrums.

When they'd first arrived back on base, everything felt off-kilter. It was bad enough being confined to sick quarters, but even there he picked up on the restlessness among the men of the 390th. The war would soon be over, and they were all anxious to get back home. Every conversation seemed focused on who would do what or where they'd go once they got home—

topics that didn't resonate with Danny. His mind and heart were still back in Holland.

Then on April 12 came word of President Roosevelt's passing at "The Little White House" in Warm Springs, Georgia. News reports indicated that Roosevelt had complained of a terrific pain in the back of his head then immediately slumped over in a coma. He was carried into his bedroom where he died a short time later at 3:35 p.m. His attending cardiologist diagnosed his death as a result of a massive cerebral hemorrhage. Roosevelt had been president for twelve years, and his sudden death was a shock around the world—especially to those still fighting the war. Now they had a new Commander-in-Chief. Vice-President Harry Truman was immediately sworn into office as the 33rd President of the United States.

On that same day, the largest Nazi concentration camp was liberated by the 6th Armored Division of the Third Army. Reports about the atrocities of those imprisoned at Buchenwald spread like wildfire, increasing the urgency of the Allies to free other prisons like it. Millions had died.

Still, the job the Allies had come to do wasn't finished. The bombing raids had continued through the previous week until April 20, when the 390th—on its 300th mission—led the entire Eighth Air Force in finishing off targets in southern Germany. With the Luftwaffe annihilated, the Allies stood down in their strategic missions, now attempting the final blow to the Nazi regime.

For months, the Allied commanders had wrestled over the rumored "National Redoubt"—a final stand by Hitler and his Wehrmacht, supposedly based in the rugged mountainous terrain in Bavaria and Austria. With the Allies and Soviets both racing to capture Berlin, it was believed that the dictator and what was left of his army would hide out in the Alps then reclaim a new Germany headquartered there. With railways busily transporting goods to be stockpiled in those areas, the obvious solution was to bomb those rails and cut them off.

Now, as Danny and Charlie made their way into Quincy's, he pushed all of those thoughts aside and hoped the quaint pub would buffet his spirits, if only for a while. The pub wasn't officially open since it was Sunday, so they were the only guests.

Sophie was the first to greet them, welcoming him with open arms. "It's about time you came to see us!" She hugged him hard and planted a kiss on his check. "Do you know how many prayers have gone up from this place for you?"

Danny hugged her back. "I'm guessing whatever was left over from those for Charlie here."

"Nonsense. You were gone longer. I barely even knew Lieutenant Janssen was missing."

Charlie engulfed her in his arms. "That's Lieutenant Janssen *Darling*, and don't you forget it."

Danny smiled as he moved toward a nearby table while the two carried on.

"Oh, now, what's all this?" Patrick Quincy fussed, appearing from the kitchen door. "A father can't stand by and watch his daughter get smothered with kisses by her suitor."

"With all due respect, Mr. Quincy, I think *I'm* the one being smothered here." He dug out his handkerchief to wipe the lipstick off his face.

"Oh Da, you gave your blessing, so button up." Sophie snuggled beneath Charlie's arm.

"Now see what you've done! For pity's sakes, I didn't even see our dear Lieutenant McClain here!" The proprietor hurried over to give Danny a hug. "Welcome home, son! Welcome, home! You had us all worried, that's for sure. But thanks be to Almighty God for returning you to us!"

"Good to see you too, Patrick. And thanks for the prayers. I have a feeling those are the reason I'm finally back here."

"Sit! Sit! Let me serve you up a nice plate of shepherd's pie," he said, making his way back to the kitchen. "Sophie made it. Fresh from the oven. I can't offer you a pint as it's the Lord's Day, but I expect a nice cup of tea would taste just fine on a dreary Sunday."

"Yes, it would, Patrick. That sounds perfect."

"Sophie? Serve the men a pot of tea, will you, daughter?"

"Sure, Da." She placed a quick peck on Charlie's cheek. "I'll be right back."

Charlie took a seat across from Danny and looked around the pub. "Kind of nice, having the place all to ourselves, eh?"

Danny fiddled with a salt shaker, twisting it around and around. Charlie reached over and took it out of his hand.

"Take it easy there, buddy."

Danny sat back and folded his arms. "Sorry."

"Too bad Patrick can't sneak us a couple of pints. Might help settle those nerves you're fighting."

"Not really. I'm clearly not cut out to be much of a drinker."

Sophie returned with their tea and meals. "There you go, gentlemen."

"Can you join us?" Charlie asked.

"I'd love to." She took a seat beside Charlie. "Danny, Charlie told me about your time over in Holland. That must've been very frightening for you."

He took a sip of his tea, pleased by the heat of it going down. "It was. But I'm thankful to be back. I keep hoping the rest of my crew shows up. Well, the ones who are still alive, that is."

"I know." She placed her hand on Charlie's shoulder. "We pray every night for the other two members of Charlie's crew who parachuted before him. As much as I tired of Lieutenant Banks' silly accents, he's a good and decent man. I hope they both show up soon."

Danny noticed the slight tremble in Charlie's hand as he lifted his teacup. He knew his friend still grieved for his lost crew. Charlie had flown a few missions since they returned to base, but each time it was with a different crew. With the war wrapping up soon, there was no need to make permanent crew assignments. Danny hadn't flown again yet. He wondered about his own crew members who were still MIA and kept hoping they'd show up any day. He and Pendergrass still bunked in the same quarters, and the empty cots reminded them daily of their lost friends.

Danny shook off the thought and tried to change the subject. "What's this I hear about wedding bells?"

"Quite a surprise, isn't it?" Sophie said with a laugh. "I couldn't believe it when Charlie here took my hand and dropped to his knee."

Danny smiled. He loved the way Sophie pronounced her fiancé's name—*Chah-lie*. He had a feeling Charlie liked it too.

"Only wish I'd had a pretty ring to place on your finger." He placed his hand over hers on the table. "But next time I get some leave, we'll head over to London and find one."

"I'm not too concerned. As long as I've got you, I'm a happy girl."

He looked across at Danny. "I hope it's all right that I told Sophie about Anya."

Danny blinked, caught by surprise. "Oh? Sure, I mean, there's not much to tell, really."

"Not much to tell?" Sophie said. "I think it's terribly romantic how it all came about. What with all those love letters—"

"No, they weren't really love letters. At least I didn't intend them—"

"And then all those years passed, and there's a war, and suddenly, there she is . . ." She paused with a dreamy look in her eyes. "And right there in the midst of chaos and war, you found each other. I find it all *very* romantic."

Danny eyed his friend. "Sounds like someone's embellished the story a bit?"

"Who me? I just tell it like it is, McClain."

"And Charlie says you can think of nothing else but going back to find that dear girl." Sophie planted her chin on her hand and gazed at him with love-filled eyes. "I think it's the loveliest thing I've heard in years."

"I thought *I* was the loveliest thing in your life these days?" Charlie teased, leaning close for a kiss.

Danny sighed. "Yeah, well, it's all very 'romantic' right up to the part of getting over there and actually tracking her down."

"Y'know, I've been giving that some thought," Charlie said after swallowing a bite of food. "I think you should call in a favor or two."

"Meaning?" Danny asked.

"Remember the night your crew came gasping back across the Channel sputtering on fumes?"

"Yeah. So?"

"Didn't you tell me Colonel Moller was on the radio, personally giving you all permission to return to base?"

"Yeah. Like I said—so?"

Charlie scratched his chin. "Well, I was just thinking you could ask the Old Man for a favor."

Danny pinned him with a glare. "Are you out of your mind?"

Charlie raised a palm. "Now, hear me out. I'm just thinking you go in there, request to see the Colonel, then remind him about that night."

Danny stared at his friend, wondering where on earth such a lame brain idea came from. "First of all, he would never remember that night. Who knows why he answered the call anyway? It's insignificant."

"But you never know—"

"Second, I would never 'ask' our Commanding Officer for *any* favor, much less for permission to hop across the Pond when this is all over to find her. He's our Commanding Officer, Charlie—not some resident flunky playing Cupid."

Charlie laughed. "Well, I guess I see your point."

Sophie used Charlie's fork to steal a bite of the meaty pie on his plate. "I must say, it's a rather charming notion to think that the man I loved would do whatever it took to come and save me. A knight on a white horse and all that."

Danny pushed his empty plate back. "Look, I appreciate your interest, but I'm sure there's some way to work it out. I just haven't figured it out yet."

"You will, Danny." Sophie patted his hand. "You will."

The pub door flew open as a couple of MPs entered. "There they are," one of them said pointing to Danny and Charlie.

"Sirs," the MPs saluted.

Danny and Charlie stood and returned their salute. "What is it, Sergeant?" Charlie asked.

"Special called briefing on base at 1300 hours. All 3rd Air Division officers are required to attend by order of Colonel Moller. We're rounding up everyone who's off-base. Just now spotted your Jeep outside."

Charlie checked his watch. "At 1300? That's thirty minutes from now. We better move out."

The MPs saluted then quickly departed.

"What was that all about?" Patrick asked, wiping his hands on his bib apron.

"Meeting on base. Gotta run," Danny said, putting his flight jacket back on.

"Sorry, sweetheart," Charlie said, pulling Sophie close to his side. "I'll be back as soon as I can."

"TEN-HUT!"

"At ease."

The usual shuffling filled the room as the 390th officers took their seats. Up on the platform, Colonel Moller stood at the podium as Colonel Waltz took a seat.

"Gentlemen, as you know, our combat missions have concluded with the imminent fall of Germany. We expect that to occur any day now. And while we have not yet declared victory in the European Theater, we are standing down from any further missions—"

A rowdy cheer broke out as the men cheered and whistled.

When the celebration ebbed, he added, "—except for one last mission."

A communal groan waved through the room.

"However, this mission is like no other. This is a mission of mercy. At the directive of General Eisenhower in cooperation with our English Allies, food drops will commence today in the occupied western portion of The Netherlands to aid more than three million Dutch who are starving, thanks to their German occupiers."

Charlie elbowed him as Danny sat up straighter. *A food drop in Holland?*

"As you know, in retaliation for Holland's part in last September's Operation Market-Garden, the Germans cut off all shipments into Holland. The resulting 'Hunger Winter' that followed led to extreme hardships on the Dutch, including widespread starvation. Even aid coming in from Sweden's Red Cross was primarily hoarded by the German occupiers. Meaning, many of the Dutch have no food, no electricity, no fuel, and no hope unless we intervene."

Danny didn't need to hear Colonel Moller's assessment of the situation. He'd been there. He remembered the old lady at the Enschede safe house who had eaten his leftovers. He'd tasted the onion-like tulip bulbs and remembered well the symbolism of such a desperate thing. And he remembered the feel of Anya in his arms—her thin, fragile body without an ounce of fat, the feel of her cheekbone against his palm as he caressed her face. His hands fisted at the thought of all she and everyone in her country had endured.

Moller continued. "The situation is now so critical, General Eisenhower has ordered us to proceed immediately instead of waiting for the official end of the war, however close that may be. Apparently the remaining German divisions in western Holland have no intention of surrendering and as a final desperate effort, they have cut off all remaining supply lines by blowing up dikes, mining the canals, and flooding the lowlands. Our only recourse is by air.

"Several heavy bomber groups of the RAF will take part in these missions, primarily the Lancasters. They have dubbed this *Operation Manna*. As for the Eighth Air Force, the entire 3rd Air Division comprised of ten bomber units will participate. For our part, we have named this mission *Operation Chowhound*.

"The British began flying their mercy missions today. Due to our dense ground fog here, we are not able to join them. God willing, we'll be wheels up first thing tomorrow morning. And now Colonel Waltz will detail the missions you will be flying."

As Moller traded places with Waltz, the latter stepped up to the podium. "Gentlemen, in compliance of the agreement, the drops will be made in specified locations during daylight hours. You will fly at one-thousand feet or lower, dropping your cargo on white crosses which will be laid out at specified locations.

"After negotiations with Reichskommissar Seyss-Inquart, it has been agreed upon that Allied planes taking part in the drops will not be fired upon."

"Might as well put a target on our bellies," Charlie mumbled. "Jerry's not about to miss an easy shot like that." Others made similar comments under their breath.

As if reading their thoughts, Colonel Waltz continued. "Of course, no one takes Seyss-Inquart at his word. That is why extreme measures are in place through the agreement prohibiting all participating aircraft from being fired upon while flying to and from these drop zones—most of which are in abandoned airfields or open field areas."

Danny tried to imagine such a thing. The huge Flying Fortresses, flying so low to the ground, unleashing all manner of food to be rained down on the ground. Even at low altitude, how would such cargo not be destroyed on impact? He thought of all those starving Dutch people and imagined them running out as the food dropped from their planes. With German soldiers standing around?

"The Reichskommissar has been told in no uncertain terms that Germany will be wiped off the face of the earth if they do not comply."

Danny blinked, wondering how the colonel seemed to know his thoughts.

"Since these will be our last missions in the European Theater, General Doolittle has authorized our flights to include ground personnel as passengers to allow these hard working men to get a first-hand look at what they've been a part of. Assignments will be listed and posted at Operations.

"Finally, gentlemen, I would ask you to understand this operation for what it is. The aircraft you fly were built as vehicles of destruction, a means to fight a war against unspeakable atrocities committed on innocent lives. Now you will have the opportunity to use these same vehicles to deliver a message of hope, good-will, and in some cases, life itself. Do not dismiss the significance of what you do. Those are real people down there—men, women, and children—who will go on to live their lives because you made a final gesture of benevolence on their behalf.

"Godspeed. That is all."

61

Word of the successful Manna missions by the British had inspired the men of the 390th, but such reports also made them anxious to get across the Pond and do their part. Tales of the Lancasters, some flying as low as fifty feet from the ground at drop points, spoke of the powerful British planes barely skimming tree tops before dropping their precious loads. Such thoughts should have made him nervous, but Danny just wanted to get up in the air and take his turn. Unfortunately he had to wait a few days.

The ever-dependable soupy skies over Framlingham kept the B-17s of the 390th grounded for two full days. Located so close to the coast, their base was socked in where many of the others, including those of the Brits, had clear skies.

At Charlie's request, Danny was assigned to his crew for the Chowhound missions. With his foot healed enough to carry out his co-pilot duties, Danny couldn't wait to get back in the cockpit. Especially for a cause so near to his heart. He had only to think of Anya to put a face on the despair of the Dutch which Colonel Waltz had so poignantly described.

When the weather finally cooperated on May first, four hundred planes from the Eighth Air Force took part in *Operation Chowhound,* but Charlie and Danny's crew was still not included. Charlie tried to calm him down, reminding him they'd get their chance soon enough. There were only so many flights per day, and they'd just have to wait their turn.

With each passing hour, Danny grew more agitated, his imagination driving him crazy. It was bad enough, worrying about Anya before all this talk of the food drops. Now each hour filled him with an intense longing to fly over her country and help relieve the misery. When he recognized his feelings as outright jealousy toward those already making the food drops, he knew he was bordering some kind of ridiculous outrage. *Good thing I'm not a drinking man or I'd be three sheets in the wind by now.*

Not that he would or could. With missions pending on each early morning weather call, the red light blared brightly at the Officer's Club on base making alcohol unavailable.

Instead, Danny used the time to write his family again. He'd received one letter from his mother since his return, pages filled with relief and joy and thanksgiving to know he was alive and back on base. He'd choked up reading her letter, remembering how often he'd thought of her praying for him. He knew those prayers were the reason he'd survived. He'd lost count of how many times he read her letter, feeling such a profound homesickness and at the same time, such a bittersweet conflict of emotions. Yes, he wanted to go home. He couldn't wait to see them all again, to bury himself in their hugs. To sit at the dining room table and eat real food again. To see Sophie dance in celebration at his return—and tell her of *Sweet Sophie* and the secret joke he'd played on his crew.

How he longed to spend time with Joey talking about his experiences and how much Joey had inspired him.

And Dad. He wondered how his father would react at his homecoming. Would he be proud? Would he be emotional? He'd often thought of his father's awkward but meaningful embrace after driving him to the train station when he first reported for duty. His dad would forever remain a mystery to him, but deep in his heart, more than anything he wanted to make his father proud.

He grabbed his paper and pen and headed over to the Officer's Club. Writing a letter while sitting alone in his quarters would tempt the depression which seemed to nip at his heels. At least at the Club, he could enjoy a cup of coffee and a warm fire.

He'd written three pages when someone sat down across from him.

"Mind if I join you?"

Danny looked up and immediately flew out of his chair and threw a salute. "Colonel Moller, sir, yes, sir! It would be a privilege, sir!"

The Commanding Officer took a seat in the wingback chair across from him. Danny tried to imagine how on earth he could have missed the commotion when the colonel had arrived. He felt his face heat, wondering if everyone else but him had failed to salute the Old Man when he entered.

"At ease, Lieutenant. Please, have a seat."

"Yes, sir. Thank you, sir." Danny sat down and tried to gather the pages he'd dropped in all the excitement.

"Where do you call home, Lieutenant?"

"Chicago, sir."

"Cubs or White Sox?"

"Oh, Cubs, sir. Tried and true."

"Good man. You know I was working for Pure Oil there in Chicago before I was called up for duty when this all began."

"Yes, sir, I knew that."

Moller smiled then pointed to the letter in Danny's lap. "Writing the folks?"

"Yes, sir, I am. After our Hannover mission on 28 March, I was MIA for about a week, and they were mighty worried."

The colonel crossed his legs and leaned back. "MIA? You must've been on Dick Anderson's crew. I'd like to hear your perspective on it, if you don't mind?"

Danny tried to bring his voice down a notch, fearing he'd squawk like an adolescent as he told his story. He also tried to keep it brief, not wishing to impose on Moller's time, but the colonel seemed to have all the time in the world.

"How is it you knew this girl—Anna, was it?"

"Anya. Anya Versteeg." As Danny explained the long history, he found himself growing more relaxed. At forty-five years of age, Moller came across quite fatherly, no doubt the reason his men nicknamed him the Old Man and "Uncle Joe." With occasional questions and comments, Moller seemed genuinely interested in the details of his journey in Holland—and Anya.

"I have tremendous respect for the Dutch Resistance," Moller added. "I'm not sure any of us can ever fully grasp the hardships those folks have suffered. It's why I'm so pleased the 390th was tapped to take part in Chowhound. Seems to me, it's the least we can do for them."

"I agree, sir. I'm anxious to get over there myself."

"I flew one yesterday, and I can tell you one thing—that's one mission I'll never forget."

Danny smiled knowing Moller's record, flying more than forty missions while assigned to the 390th. "Uncle Joe" was hands-on all the way—a fact that only endeared him even more to his men.

Moller smiled then stared into the fire. "So Anya insisted on staying there in Holland, despite the immense danger and starvation?"

"Yes, sir, she did."

"Well, I have to say I admire that kind of loyalty. I'd like to think I'd do the same, but who's to say? Speaks well of her character. But I don't suppose I need to tell you that. What are your plans, Lieutenant?"

"Excuse me, sir?"

"Surely you're not planning to just go home and never see her again?"

Danny swallowed hard. "No, sir! I could never do that, but I don't, uh . . ." He honestly didn't know what to say.

Moller leaned forward, elbows resting on his knees, his hands wrapped around the coffee mug. "Now, I may be just an old man, but I know how important it is to find a good woman. So I'll ask again. What are your plans, Lieutenant?"

"I'm not quite sure. I suppose it all depends on what happens these next few days." He dipped his head, embarrassed to say what was on his heart.

Then, Colonel Joseph Moller, Commander of the 390th Bomb Group of the Eighth Air Force, leaned across the space between them, patted Danny on the knee, and said, "Go back for her, son. Sounds to me like she's worth going back for."

As the Colonel stood, so did Danny. "Yes, sir. I'm not sure how to do that, but—"

"Then you come see me. Understood?"

"Understood. Thank you, sir!"

Moller shook Danny's hand, winked, and walked away.

Then, Lieutenant Daniel Howard McClain of Chicago, Illinois, took a long cleansing breath and smiled.

"From what I hear, you can almost walk across the sky, there are so many Lancasters up there carrying food over to Holland," Charlie said, moving the toothpick to the other side of his mouth. "And with our guys up there now, I'm guessing the Dutch will see more aluminum than blue sky. They're probably just saving the best for last. That would be you and me."

"Yeah, right."

"What, were you expecting Uncle Joe himself to ask you to ride shotgun with him today?"

Danny rolled his eyes. "Very funny."

"Well, I may not have as much brass, but I promise we'll get the job done. Hey, at least we get to fly together before all this ends. That's good for something, right?"

Danny spent the rest of the day reading back through his journal. He wasn't altogether sure why he picked up the worn leather book, other than just a way to pass the time and get his mind off Anya. In a strange way, the scattered entries comforted him. Sure, the abrupt end to his relationship with Beverly still irked him. No guy likes getting dumped for someone else. But as he read his own recorded thoughts and emotions, he felt detached from that Danny McClain—as if someone he hardly knew anymore had written those words. After his father had been beaten, why had it taken him so long to accept the fact he'd have to wait another year to go to college? Why had he bruised so easily after Beverly rejected him? Why did he wander all over Evanston in the middle of the night after Craig's father told him his roommate had died? Who *was* that guy who let the roadblocks in his life almost destroy him? And for what?

Then, reading some of his later excerpts, he began to see a slow but sure maturing of that young guy who seemed to always wear his heart on his sleeve. Somewhere in those pages, he began to recognize a confident member of the United States Army Air Force fighting for his country. No matter what happened in the remaining days of this war, Danny knew he'd return home as someone quite different— stronger, prouder, wiser.

He closed the journal and decided to head over to the Officer's Club for a while. Just as he opened the door of his Nissen hut, Charlie raced up to him grinning from ear to ear.

"We're listed, Danny! Tomorrow we fly our first Chowhound!"

62

03 May 1945

What a sight, watching the ground crews loading boxes and bags of food instead of bombs into the plane. Danny couldn't believe the transformation of the Fortress they'd been assigned to. It and all the other Forts had been quickly adapted by outfitting the bomb bay with plywood "floors" hinged on one side to the bay, the other side attached to the bomb release mechanism. On these makeshift pallets, the food was piled high, filling every square inch of the bomb bay.

The flight crews marveled at the variety of food piled up on those plywood floors—coffee, tea, sugar, flour, powdered eggs and milk, meat, vegetables, cheese, and in some cases, even tins of chocolate. Many of these were "10-in-1 Ration" boxes filled with canned and tinned goods which would have a much better chance of surviving the free-fall drop to the ground.

The whole atmosphere around the hardstands felt entirely different as the crews gathered that morning. Where jitters and silent prayers often accompanied nervous laughter or terse responses before a bomb run, now a palpable sense of joy drifted through the air. And with the shocking announcement that morning of Hitler's suicide the day before, everyone had even more reason to celebrate. Charlie and Danny laughed along with the others at the comments bubbling out of everyone's excitement.

"Couldn't have happened to a nicer Kraut!"

"Guten riddance, Adolf!"

"Heil Hitler!" someone yelled, throwing the familiar Nazi salute. "Welcome to hell, Adolf!"

"Wish he'd done it five years ago and saved us all this trouble!"

"My friends! My friends! Such good news! It's a wonderful day!"

Danny and Charlie caught each other's eye at the same moment with identical puzzled expressions. *Why does that sound familiar?* They both turned around.

"Sergeant Cosmos Francis Benedetto, reporting for duty, sirs!"

There before them standing at attention with his hand in a sharp salute stood the chatty sergeant who had regaled Quincy's Pub back before Christmas. Slowly, Danny and Charlie returned the sergeant's salute wondering why he would be reporting to them for duty.

"I'm Lieutenant Charles Janssen," Charlie said as they all lowered their hands, "and this is Lieutenant Daniel McClain. But if you don't mind my asking, Sergeant, to what do we owe the pleasure?"

"I assure you, Lieutenant, the pleasure is all mine. It is

my honor, indeed my privilege, to be assigned to your esteemed crew today for the purpose of witnessing this most glorious occasion."

Charlie scratched his head. "Come again?"

"It is my good fortune to be selected to accompany you on your mission of mercy today at the request of Colonel Joseph Moller, our beloved commander."

"Colonel Moller selected you to ride with us?"

Danny patted Charlie on the back. "You remember, Charlie—the Old Man wanted all the ground crew men to have a chance to ride along and see from the sky what they've helped us do all these months."

"Oh yeah," Charlie said, pasting a plastic smile on his face. "Swell. Just swell."

Danny reached out to shake the sergeant's hand. "It's an honor to have you—Cosmos, was it?"

"Yes, sir. And thank you, sir."

Charlie followed Danny's lead and shook the crewman's hand. "A pleasure." Then, turning to Danny, "I'll see you in the cockpit after my final check."

Danny had to admit the kid was a pain. He was fairly short, stocky, with a head of curly black hair, and one hundred percent Italian. His Jersey accent bled so thick you could cut it. He seemed the perfect caricature of many of the ground crew men—hard working, tough as nails, and proud of it. He studied the sergeant's face trying to decide what made it so unique. Those eyes had almost a childlike wonder in them.

Bewildered. That's it. An interminable look of bewilderment on that face and in those eyes, as if every moment held unlimited potential.

Danny smiled. For all his annoying chatter, there was something refreshing about Benedetto's unmasked enthusiasm.

"Tell me, Cosmos, have you ever flown before?"

"No, sir," he answered, his face lighting up a notch more. "This will be my maiden voyage, as it were. I came over on the *Queen Elizabeth*—and a fine sailing vessel she was. But alas, my friend, this will be an unforgettable day for the son of Tony and Beatrice Benedetto."

"Your parents?"

"Oh yes, sir. Mama and Papa . . ." His chin trembled as he paused and briefly looked away. "I am the sole product of their loins and the pride of their union."

Danny bit his lip hard as he let the sergeant compose himself. "Yes, well, Cosmos. Climb aboard and we'll get you settled."

Unable to speak, Cosmos nodded and followed closely behind as Danny boarded the Fort through the hatch.

"This is Billy Henderson, top turret gunner and flight engineer today. Billy, this is Sergeant Cosmos Benedetto. He's our ground crew passenger on today's mission. How about you show him around then get him belted in the nose for take-off."

"Sure thing, Lieutenant."

Danny patted Cosmos on the shoulder and headed up to the cockpit.

"Danny, since you and Uncle Joe are such bosom buddies these days," Charlie started, "how about you call him up and see if we can't get the wonder child back there switched to another plane."

Danny slid into his seat on the right. "Ah, he's not so bad."

"Ten to one he pukes before we cross the Channel."

Danny laughed hard as he buckled himself in and got to work. Twenty minutes later, the Fort's engines roared in anxious harmony with the other B-17s as they barreled down the runway. From the cockpit, Danny couldn't see their guest below who was seated where the toggelier usually sits, but they could all hear him.

"MOTHERMARYOHMYGODHAVEMERCYONME!"

Over and over the sergeant yelled—except for the brief moment when he lost his breakfast.

Charlie shot his co-pilot a smirk. "Told ya."

"Oh God! Oh God! Help me, Jesus!"

"Sergeant Benedetto! Turn off your intercom!" Danny shouted.

"MOTHERMARYOHMYGODHAVEMERCYONME!"

"Billy! Get him off that intercom and I mean now!" Charlie ordered.

"Okay okay! I'm on it!" the flight engineer responded.

"MOTHERMARYOHMY—"

"Thank the Lord!" Danny quipped. He coughed, trying to suppress his laughter but failed miserably.

"McClain, don't make me order you down there to babysit your new best friend," Charlie balked.

Danny wiped his eyes and held up his hands in surrender. "I'm fine—really. I'm okay." He snorted a couple of times before taking a long cleansing breath. "Something tells me this is going to be an unforgettable flight in more ways than one."

Charlie just shook his head. "Y'know, I've looked forward to flying with you for quite a while now, but I'm wondering if I'll even survive it."

"No, buddy. I'm good to go. Honest." Danny pulled his hand over his face then shook it all off.

Charlie looked over at him.

"What?" Danny asked.

"All things considered I've got to say it's good to see you laughing again."

Danny looked out his side window, nodding his head. "Feels good too."

The flight engineer popped up behind them. "That guy . . . he was practically sitting on his intercom switch. White as a ghost. You'd think we were surrounded by bandits."

An hour later, with The Netherlands in the distance, Billy joined them again. "Speaking of bandits, did you all notice there's not a single Kraut in the sky? And no anti-aircraft fire or flak either. Ain't that somethin'?"

"Must be that milk run everyone always talks about. In this case, it really is."

In briefing that morning, they'd been told the remaining food drop missions would no longer be flown in formation. On the second day of *Operation Chowhound*, two bombers from the 388th Bomb Group had collided in midair as they attempted to keep in tight formation. There were no survivors. As a result, the bombers would fly in a single line, one after another, to avoid any more fatalities.

As they approached the coastline of Holland, they were

flying no more than 500 feet above the ground as they headed for Vogelenzang, a village in Bloemendaal, in the northwest corner of Holland. Danny could feel his stomach tensing at sights he'd never seen before. The first thing he noticed were the concrete pill boxes the Germans had built along the beaches, fortifying their so-called "Atlantic Wall." The Allies had done their job, bombing them repeatedly as evidenced by the craters on and around them. Beyond, he could see German soldiers standing at anti-aircraft gunneries, no doubt ready to fire if any of the planes flew outside the predetermined narrow corridor.

"Don't you know they're seething under those stupid bucket helmets?" Billy wondered aloud.

Thankfully, those in the 390th who had flown the previous relief missions had reported no instances of German aggression. At least for now, the truce seemed to be working.

Danny felt sure his knuckles hidden inside his gloves were white—and probably those of the entire crew as well. It felt so wrong to fly this heavy bird at such a low altitude and slow speed, as if any moment the Fort might drop down in a belly flop and kill everyone on board and those on the ground. He tried to steel the nerves chewing at his insides.

They were shocked by the vastness of the flooded terrain, evidence of Jerry's precise bombing of those dikes and canals. Everywhere they looked, fields were flooded. On many of the structures, only rooftops were visible. No wonder the Dutch had starved. With no agriculture and no means of transporting food in, it was a wonder they had a single beet or tulip left anywhere. Danny remembered how much Anya hated those beets. He also remembered the old lady who had eaten his leftover beet soup when he couldn't stomach it.

And once again he wondered—*is Anya still alive?*

But his troubled thoughts didn't last long. As they drew closer to Vogelenzang, everywhere they looked they could see people running and waving—some waving dish towels, some with white sheets, some jumping and dancing and throwing kisses.

He and Charlie couldn't help smiling as the rest of the crew chimed in, sharing the spectacular moment.

"Can you believe this?"

"Looks like they're mighty happy to see us!"

"Have you ever seen such an anxious crowd?"

"Hey, look at that guy on the roof over there! He's got a big sign that says, 'TOBACCO!' Too bad I can't throw him a pack!"

"Lieutenant Janssen, is it okay if I let Sergeant Benedetto speak on the intercom now?" the radio crewman asked.

Charlie glanced over at Danny. "Well?"

"Go ahead, Sergeant."

"Hello? Hello?"

"Yes, Cosmos, we hear you," Danny answered.

"HOLY COW! My friends, my friends! Have you ever seen such an amazing sight in all your life?!" he shouted. "Look at 'em—never in all my life have I seen anything so beautiful." His unrestrained weeping floated through the aircraft on the intercom, eclipsing his commentary.

"Check it out—over there at three o'clock!" Danny pointed at a field out his window. "Huge letters spelling out *God Bless America* on the ground." Suddenly, the sight of it lodged a lump in his throat and his eyes stung. He blinked several times realizing Cosmos wasn't the only one fighting his emotions. He cleared his throat a couple of times as he spotted the drop zone marker. "White cross straight ahead."

"Prepare to release the cargo!" Charlie ordered.

"Three, two one—now!" Danny shouted.

They felt the *whoosh* of air sweep through the craft as the bomb doors flew open releasing their 600-pound food gift to the Dutch people. Danny craned his neck to look back, catching a quick glimpse of the falling goods.

"Mission accomplished, Lieutenant!" the tail gunner yelled. "That is one payload that's a real pleasure to watch. I wish you all could see what I'm seeing right now."

"Well done, men," Charlie said. "Feels good, doesn't it?"

"If I may, Lieutenant," Cosmos began, his voice warbling. "In honor of this most glorious occasion and my own personal maiden voyage . . ."

Charlie dropped his head down momentarily, then glanced briefly at his friend in the co-pilot's seat. Danny laughed then said, "Go ahead, Cosmos."

"Thank you, sir. As I was saying, in honor of this most glorious occasion and my own personal maiden voyage as a guest on this magnificent bird, I wondered if you might allow me to share what's on my heart."

Charlie muttered under his breath while banking to the left to begin their trip home.

"Go ahead, Sergeant," Danny said, fighting a chuckle.

"I would just like to say that I shall never forget each and every one of you and the part you played in what surely must be the happiest day of my life. Not only did Colonel Moller assign me to you fine men, but with all my heart, I believe the very hand of God has reached down to pat me on the shoulder as He says, 'Cosmos? Do not ever forget what I have done for you this day.'"

Charlie leaned his head back and mouthed a silent scream while Danny flipped off the intercom switch on the pilot's steering wheel as a precaution. As they continued to watch the scene below them—the Dutch still waving at them in appreciation—Charlie flipped his own switch on. "Thank you, Sergeant. That was . . . well, words fail me at the moment. Now gentlemen, let's go home."

63

If the Chowhound mission they'd flown to Vogelenzang had been unforgettable, the return to the base had been nothing short of phenomenal. Everywhere, as crews disembarked from their planes, they whooped and hollered and celebrated as if ringing in the new year in Time's Square back home. Danny had never seen anything like it.

But stranger still came a penetrating wave of silence that drifted across the 390th's hardstands replacing the boisterous celebrations. One by one, the men fell silent, overcome by emotions too strong to fight. To a man, they wept. Every single one of them. Some turned their backs, brushing away tears. Others let their tears run freely, holding nothing back as though the long months of the job they'd come to do had somehow found release along with those bundles of food they'd just dropped on the fields of Holland. Then came the bear hugs as the tough airmen acknowledged the unity of their emotions and the incredible symbolism of what they'd done that day.

Food instead of bombs.

Life instead of destruction.

Hope instead of despair.

Not a bad day's work.

It would be three more days before Danny flew another Chowhound mission. But this time, instead of impatiently waiting his turn, he waited with excited anticipation, eager for another chance to fly another historic mercy mission.

In the meantime, he had another job assignment.

On the fifth of May, he served as best man in the wedding of Lieutenant Charles Janssen and Sophie Elizabeth Quincy. Deciding they couldn't wait another day—much less for the end of the war—the couple moved up their wedding date and tied the knot that Saturday morning at the quaint Reform Church just down the lane from Quincy's Pub. On such short notice, only a handful of witnesses joined them, seated on the worn pews of the church's chapel. But none of that mattered to the bride who smiled radiantly as she walked slowly down the aisle on the arm of her father.

And the groom? Danny had to admit Charlie looked downright handsome in his dress uniform, all shined up and sparkling clean. But it was the silly, love-happy grin on his friend's face that kept the best man in silent stitches through the brief ceremony.

Later, at the reception, Danny tapped Charlie on the shoulder to cut in on the dance floor.

"The least you can do is allow me to dance with your beautiful bride," Danny said as he took Sophie in his arms.

"Just mind your manners, McClain," the groom teased. "Remember *I'm* the one she goes home with tonight."

As the phonograph played *I'll Be Seeing You,* Danny

enjoyed a moment alone with the bride. "I still can't figure out why a nice girl like you settled for a nut job like Charlie. What's he got that I don't?"

Sophie smiled, her eyes sparkling with mischief. "Well, let me think. Oh, that's right—he's got *me*."

"True. It's even official now and everything."

"That it is, Lieutenant. But when all is said and done, it's actually a bit funny. You see, my father thought *you* would be the one to marry his only daughter."

"What?" Danny blanched with a smile.

"Oh, but sure. 'Now that Danny—he'd be a fine suitor, don't ya' know?' said my Da."

He twirled her around the small dance floor. "Well, I'd have to say he has good taste, that Da of yours."

"It's all that 'yes, sir' and 'no, sir' good manners you have, Danny McClain," Sophie said as if whispering a secret in his ear. "Impressed my father sure enough the first time he met you."

"Ah, well then. I'll have to thank my mother. She's to blame for any good manners I might possess."

"But Danny, what about Anya?" Sophie asked with smiling eyes.

"What about her?" he said, turning to avoid her gaze.

"You have to go back and find her. Surely you know that?"

He hummed along with the music.

She tilted her head to face him squarely. "You simply *have* to go back. How will you do it?"

"That, Mrs. Janssen, is the million dollar question. And for the record, one I've wrestled with every waking second since the moment I left her."

The song came to an end and Danny dipped Sophie ever so gracefully to conclude their dance.

Still arched back low in his arms, she said, "Then we must believe that love will find a way."

He lifted her back up and gave her a hug as the small party applauded. Charlie quickly took his place. A few minutes later, the bride and groom left the pub beneath a shower of rice and best wishes. Borrowing Patrick's ancient auto, they made their way to the inn on the other side of town. Charlie had hoped to honeymoon in London, but without a proper leave, he had to remain close to the base in case his crew was scheduled to fly another mission.

Danny chuckled later that evening as he read through the roster of flight crews for Sunday. It appeared the pilot-groom would have an abbreviated wedding night.

6 May 1945

Even the disgruntled remarks Charlie continued to make under his breath couldn't distract Danny's thoughts. Earlier, during briefing, he'd almost swallowed his gum when Colonel Waltz announced they'd be flying today's Chowhound mission to Utrecht. He'd coughed, sending the wad of Wrigley's against the back of a pilot sitting directly in front of him before dropping to the ground. Danny picked it up and stuffed it in a piece of paper.

Utrecht? What are the chances?!

Of course, he had no way of knowing if Anya was back in her hometown yet. She could be anywhere, for that matter. Even with all the previous food drops across The Netherlands, the fact remained—much of western Holland was still under German Occupation. Knowing Anya's stubborn streak, he had no doubt she was still in the middle of whatever covert activity might still be in place, despite the pending liberation.

Liberation. Any day now. Any day!

Later, as they made their way to their hardstand, the crew had chattered like a bunch of magpies, excited to finally get another chance to fly a mercy mission. Charlie remained silent, nervously chewing on his toothpick as he drove the Jeep with all of them loaded on it. He took a sharp turn, almost throwing Eddie, their tail gunner, off the vehicle.

"Hey!" the kid from Oklahoma cried. "Take it easy, Lieutenant . . . uh, sir!"

The others laughed heartily as the Jeep came to a halt beside their Fort. They all piled out and went about their business, preparing for the mission. Charlie threw his pack inside the hatch then turned to Danny as he tossed his toothpick on the tarmac.

"So help me, McClain, if that Cosmos character shows up today, I'm gonna—"

Danny held up his hand. "No way that's happening, so just calm down. We've got two cooks coming along this time. I've asked Billy to keep them quiet. Satisfied?"

Charlie blew out a huff and started his mandatory final check of the plane's exterior. Danny hoisted himself up into the plane and made his way to the cockpit. He tried to stay focused on the routine tasks at hand preparing for the flight, but his mind was way ahead of him. Of course, he had nothing to go by except the Vogelenzang mission they'd flown three days earlier. But in his mind he could see them, barely skirting treetops as they came into Utrecht. He visualized seeing Anya up on a rooftop—waving a scarf or something, anything to get his attention. He closed his eyes knowing if he saw her, he'd jump out of his seat, bolt for the bomb bay, and jump out with all the food parcels—if only he could.

Rationally he knew there was no way she'd know he was flying a mission today. After all the thousands of food drops from British Lancasters and American B-17s, did he really expect her to wait around in case he *might* be flying over today?

The ridiculous notions wrestled in his mind. He was relieved for the interruption when Charlie finally plopped into his seat.

Charlie busied himself stashing his gear and buckling in. "So, we're heading to Utrecht," he said without looking up. "Think you'll see her?"

Danny cocked his head and turned it sideways to pin him with a glare. "Could we just not talk about it?"

Charlie looked up. "Whoa! And I thought *I* was the one out of sorts? Sorry I brought it up."

Danny sighed and ignored the comment. "Let's just get this done."

They ran through their pre-flight checklist, then Danny checked in with the Control Tower for any last minute changes.

Billy showed up behind their seats. "Hey, did you all bring anything to drop?"

"What do you mean?" Danny asked.

"Y'know, these little parachutes." He held up a handkerchief wrapped around something, tied to look like a miniature parachute. "Everybody's been making these. We rounded up some extra stuff for the kids—candy, toys, whatever we could get the Red Cross Girls to help us find. Then we'll toss 'em out the same time we drop our cargo. From what I hear, the kids down there love 'em. The guys on *Crazy Eight* have flown four of these Chowhound missions already, and they even recognize some of the kids down there now. I heard some kid held up a sign thanking the *Crazy Eight* for the chocolate."

Danny smiled. "That's nice, Billy. Wish I'd known. I would've pulled something together."

"That's okay. Me and the rest of the guys have plenty. You can bring some next time." He disappeared calling the other crew members to gather their personal gifts for the kids.

"Too bad you, McClain," Charlie teased. "You could've dropped Anya some of that chewing gum you like so much."

"You're a real pill today, y'know that?" Danny scoffed. "But I understand. I really do. Had to be tough for you leaving the missus like that, especially being your wedding night and all."

A green glow distracted Danny then Charlie. They watched the green flare arc toward the ground from the Control Tower signaling time to start their engines.

Charlie laughed. "It's a real shame," he shouted over the first engine as it came to life. "I used to really like you."

"Yeah?" Danny smirked. "Well, the funny thing is—I

never liked you anyway!"

Charlie's laughter was lost over the roar of the engines. "Ready to roll, Lieutenant?"

"Ready to roll, Lieutenant. Let's do this!"

The silly banter in the cockpit seemed to cut the tension. Danny could never be mad at Charlie. In fact, he honestly felt bad for the guy. He knew the last place Charlie wanted to be was in this big, drafty bird, and who could blame him?

Out of nowhere, Danny found himself thinking about his friendship with Charlie. He couldn't imagine what this whole war experience would have been like if he'd never met the man sitting next to him. Charlie had been his friend from the moment they met. *Come to think of it, he's the best friend I ever had.*

The thought caught him off-guard, and made his eyes water. It didn't really surprise him, though he looked away to avoid ridicule. He'd been thinking about a lot of things lately. None of them knew how much longer they'd be over here. The war would end any day now, and that was all good. But it also triggered a lot of emotions he hadn't expected. His life was going to change drastically and soon. But *how* would it change? Any way he looked at it, it would be bittersweet. No one in their right mind would want to stay here at the muddy base where the sky was always gray and wet, where a trip to the latrine meant a long chilly walk, and where the greasy smells of the mess hall did nothing to improve the taste of the mysterious servings slopped on a tray.

Still, in a crazy way, Danny knew he'd miss it—for all those *other* reasons. The built-in, easy camaraderie of guys all experiencing the same life-and-death missions, day in and day out. The cozy ambience of the Officer's Club where a guy could sit by the fire and read or write letters home, or have a nice chat with a fellow officer—or even a colonel. The colorful characters he'd met along the way, especially his crew on *Sweet Sophie*. He still grieved the loss of those guys, but he wouldn't have traded knowing them for anything in the world.

And that was the thing he'd miss most of all—the friends he'd made, and no one more than Charlie Janssen. Danny never had a close buddy when he was growing up. He had plenty of friends, but no one who came close to being the kind of friend Charlie was. Maybe having a big brother like Joey had filled those shoes. It wasn't until he got to know Hans through all those letters that he understood what it meant to have a good friend. And then, Hans was gone.

Which once again brought him back to thoughts of Anya. How in the world could he ever even think of going home without her? He couldn't. Nor would he. But he still didn't have a clue how to do that—short of going AWOL, stealing a Fort, and flying back over here to find her. *Yeah, like that's gonna happen.*

"Coast of Holland straight ahead," Charlie announced, breaking Danny's thoughts. "This may seem like a milk run, men, but keep those eyes sharp for any Krauts still carrying a grudge. We'll do a fly by then circle back for the drop as instructed."

Once again they passed over flooded fields, identical to those they'd seen Tuesday. But Danny reminded himself this time it wasn't Vogelenzang—it was Utrecht. *Anya's* Utrecht. Butterflies flitted through his stomach. *In a couple of minutes,*

I could literally be within a few miles of her.

As they neared the city, he was surprised to see colorful tulip fields surrounding the magnificent windmills. For some reason he'd assumed the beautiful structures would have been leveled in all the bombing. Even from such a low altitude he couldn't tell which one had been the backdrop in the picture of Anya's family.

And the tulip fields—what a sight. They seemed to stretch for miles in every direction. In his naiveté, he'd assumed they too had all been dug up, their bulbs one of the few remaining sources of nourishment in this war-ravaged region. Yet there they were—vast carpets of vivid colors laid out like so many enormous blankets.

And then came the people. Everywhere they looked, folks rushed toward the field. "I don't know how it's possible, but it looks like there are at least three times as many folks down there as we saw the other day," he said.

Masses of men, women, and children crowded on either side of the field, many waving Dutch flags. As they made their initial flyover, he spotted a handful of people in a church steeple waving wildly. At exact eye level, he gulped hard and waved back wanting to believe Anya was with them.

As if on cue, Charlie dipped the wing in their direction. "You never know," he said with a smile.

"You never know," Danny echoed. Just then he spotted the large white cross. "There's the drop zone marker straight ahead."

"We'll circle and make the drop a bulls-eye on the way back, what do you say?"

The Fort banked to the left to circle back for the

approach. As it did, the crew men tossed out their makeshift parachute gifts to the crowds below.

"Enjoy the candy, kid!"

"Here's some chocolate from Uncle Sam!"

"Give these Lucky Strikes to your moms and dads!"

"Whoa, Krauts on the rooftop, up ahead at two o'clock!" Billy broke in.

Danny spotted the German soldiers, their anti-aircraft weapons pointed at them, tracking their slow circle. Not a single shot was fired. As the Fort leveled out, Charlie flew straight at them, as if to crash into them. The soldiers ran for cover—all except one. He stood indignant, shaking his fist at them and yelling as they passed barely over his head.

"Take that, you Nazi pig!" Charlie yelled, pulling up on his steering column.

The waist gunner named Rocko cheered. "Whoa, Lieutenant! That was close!"

"Yeah, and I'm guessing ol' Jerry there needs to change his skivvies about now."

The crew laughed hard and swapped some other colorful suggestions for the soldier.

"All right men, prepare to open the bomb bay," Charlie said.

"On my count, Danny said. "Five, four, three, two, one, let 'em fly!"

They all cheered again, enjoying the chance to play the ultimate Santa Claus to the ebullient Dutch folks below.

"I brought my camera this time so you can all see what I'm seeing!" the tail gunner said. "What a sight. Lord have mercy, what a sight!"

As the bomb bay doors closed, Rocko said, "Will you look at that?"

"Look at what, Rocko?" Danny asked.

"Two o'clock, way on top of that red brick building. An old man and a kid. See 'em?"

Danny searched and quickly found the building. They were so close he could clearly make out their faces. It was just the two of them—an old man standing at attention, saluting them as they passed by, the little boy also saluting with one hand while waving a small American flag in the other. Danny returned his salute and once more fought the boulder in his throat.

"I'll never forget that as long as I live," Billy croaked.

"None of us will," Charlie said. "Gentlemen, let's head back to the base.

Part VII

64

06 May 1945

Utrecht, The Netherlands

After five years of German Occupation, liberation unleashed a myriad of emotional responses in those who had survived. But to the Dutch who had witnessed the Allied food drops on their starving nation, they all wept—tears of joy, tears of relief, and tears of gratitude that the nightmare might actually be coming to an end.

Throughout the Occupation, Queen Wilhelmina and her government kept in constant contact with her people. By fleeing her homeland before the Germans invaded, she alleviated the risk of her country's "beheading" as so many other European leaders had experienced by remaining in their homelands. Tucked safely away in England, Wilhelmina had served her people valiantly by working with Allied leaders to fight the German oppressors.

At no time was that more evident than her plea to Prime Minister Winston Churchill, President Franklin D. Roosevelt, and King George VI on behalf of the almost four million starving Dutch who had suffered under German Occupation:

"Conditions have now become so desperate that it is very clear that if a major catastrophe, the like which has not been seen in Western Europe since the Middle Ages, is to be avoided in Holland, something drastic has to be done now, before and not after the liberation of the rest of the country!"

To Anya and everyone else in Holland, such pleading on their behalf by their beloved Queen was perhaps the last gasp of hope left in them. Words of hope, but would they translate into actual relief? How could they possibly put food into the mouths of so many before it was too late? Anya's main concern was the children walking about on toothpick legs, the haunting appearance of their sunken faces and vacant eyes, and the few surviving elderly whose shriveled bodies gave them precious little warmth on the still-chilly days of late spring.

She'd heard the rumors and reports of low-flying aircraft dropping huge quantities of food at various locations. But at this point, she didn't believe anything until she saw it with her own eyes. Besides, after walking for two days on her way home to Utrecht, she was bone weary and simply didn't have a single ounce of energy to waste on rumors—even rumors about food.

Anya might have been encouraged by the absence of German soldiers along her way home. She wanted to believe the announcements of liberation crackling over the radio day and night—first this section, then that, each followed by ecstatic descriptions of dancing in the streets. But deep down she could only dream of something good to eat and a nice warm bed to sleep in. She was just too tired to care about anything else.

As need for activity by the Resistance had slowly waned, Anya found herself thinking of home. She had no illusions— she knew it wasn't really home anymore. It didn't really matter to her if it had been ransacked by the Germans. As long as it was still standing, she just knew it's where she belonged. Throughout the long Occupation, after hearing her parents had been arrested, she had refused to think of going home. It would be too much, to walk in that house knowing both her mother and father were dead now. The house would surely feel betrayed and vacant, as though its family had deserted it somehow.

A house feeling betrayed, as if it were a living, breathing organism? What a silly notion. But such ridiculous ideas seemed to constantly imbed themselves in her mind— especially at times like this when she hadn't slept or eaten in days.

Then came the fantasies. They flitted through her weary imagination most often as she walked long distances. Giving in to them for a while helped numb her mind to the excruciating pain of walking such a long distance in shoes so badly worn, they offered no support whatsoever. No amount of rags wrapped around them could cushion the miles she'd accumulated over the past several years.

And so she dreamed. She imagined the younger, happier version of herself waking up in heaven. There, her steps brought no pain, and in wonderment she looked down to find the prettiest of wooden shoes upon her feet. Colorfully painted, comfortable, soothing reminders of her Dutch heritage. Then, looking up she gazed into the faces of her family—Mother, Father, and even Hans, all standing there at the pearly gates, their arms open wide to welcome her home.

Home.

The word rankled through her heart. Blinking, she looked around and remembered she wasn't in heaven, and she wasn't home. She was still on this crater-pocked road. She refused to cry, her tears long since dried up along with her hope. But as she looked around, she realized she wasn't far from Helga's house. She hadn't seen her since that day . . . well, it had been weeks. If she could just get there, she would find a bed, crawl into it, and sleep for a month or two.

Barely able to hold her eyes open, she finally spotted the little house. She had to tell her feet to keep moving—one step, then another—because she knew she only had a few more in her. As she turned to walk up the path to Helga's porch, the front door flew open.

"Anya! Oh, thank the Lord!" she cried, rushing out to meet her. "I have been so worried about you!" She smothered Anya in her arms.

"Hello, Helga," she mumbled. "If I could just come in for a few—"

"There's no time! You must come with me!" Helga turned toward the gate, pulling Anya along. "The planes are due any minute!"

"What planes?"

"Haven't you heard? The Allies are bringing us food! And today is our turn. Hurry! We don't want to miss it!"

Anya stopped. "No, I can't. I can't take another step. I'm

so tired, Helga."

Helga turned around. "Oh my dear child, I know you're tired, but you need to see this. You, of all people, need to see this miracle from the sky! You have worked so hard—we *all* have—and to miss this would be just . . . well, you mustn't!"

"Helga, please—"

"Come. You'll thank me when this is all over. Here, loop your arms with mine and lean on me. We don't have far to go. If I could pick you up, I would. Oh, Anya! It's all so exciting!"

They plodded along and soon neared the crowds of people rushing toward the field on the west side of Utrecht. Young and old, everyone was excited about the planes. Already people were pointing toward the sky.

"Here they come! Can you hear them?"

"It sounds like a buzzing bee—"

"Look! There they are!"

Helga hurried Anya to a spot alongside the wide, open field. People were lined up on both sides, like two long wiggling boundaries.

"Do you see the white cross there yonder?" Helga asked pointing toward the middle of the open area. There, white sheets were sewn together to make an enormous cross on the ground. "This is where they drop the food!"

"But the Germans!" Anya pointed to the soldiers standing on rooftops, their weapons drawn. "The planes don't have a chance!"

"No, Anya, no! They've agreed to a truce. They aren't allowed to fire upon these planes bringing—"

Whatever else Helga might have said was drowned out by the roar of engines as the B-17s drew closer. Anya was stunned how low they were flying—surely no more than three or four hundred feet. So low she could see the men inside the planes. She could even see the pilots and co-pilots as the planes neared them. She gasped—her heart pounding in her chest.

Danny? Could Danny be in one of those planes?

Until that moment, it hadn't occurred to her that he could be in one of them. Was it possible? There were so many of them coming one after another. How could she possibly hope to catch a glimpse of him—that is, *if* he was even flying today?

Out of nowhere—the unbidden, unspoken prayer tiptoed through her heart. She shook her head, physically dismissing such a thought.

Still . . .

Anxious, eager folks crowded all around them, blocking her view. People jumped up and down, screaming shouts of joy against the background roar of those mighty Flying Fortress engines.

"Helga! We must move away from everyone so I can see!"

"What?"

Anya saw her lips move but couldn't hear a thing. Obviously Helga couldn't either. She grabbed her friend's hand and pulled her away from the others. Her view finally clear, she watched as each plane dropped its load on the field. Huge bags and boxes slammed down on the ground, some exploding as they landed. She watched in horror as a child ran out to the field to grab something. Her mother ran after her, then struggled as the little girl tried to find something to put in her mouth.

As more planes flew over, people yelled, "KOM TERUG! KOM TERUG!" *Come back! Come back!*

The mother finally picked the child up and ran back to the side, the little girl bawling all the way even as another plane roared over and dropped its load right where the child had been standing. As it flew by, the crew members threw little white parcels out the side and back windows which drifted down to the ground like so many tiny parachutes.

Up and down both sides of the field, people jumped up and down, smiling and singing and dancing and waving Dutch flags.

"God bless America!"

"THANK YOU! THANK YOU!"

Anya felt warm tears track down her face as her heart overflowed with gratitude. *And to think I had no tears left,* she thought to herself. Helga was right. She never would have believed it if she hadn't seen it with her own eyes. So many planes! And still more coming, one after another!

Occasionally, there would be a break when no planes were in sight. People would run out and grab a bag or box and drag it to the side, then tear into it, sharing its contents with those around them.

"They're not supposed to do that," Helga said. "We were told the goods are to be gathered and taken to the Netherlands Food Distribution Service so that everyone gets a fair share."

"But can you blame them?" Anya said. "It could take days or weeks for them to sort out all the food." She pointed toward a man handing out potatoes from a large bag. They watched as people bit into the raw potatoes, too hungry to wait for them to be cooked. Beside them a man grabbed a packet of cigarettes. Real cigarettes made from tobacco had been scarce. She watched the man who started smoking almost as soon as he'd opened the pack and wondered where he'd found a match. He puffed and puffed, a look of serene pleasure on his weathered face—then he promptly coughed and sputtered.

People loaded carts and carried away what they could. Little ones laughed and carried on when the little handkerchief parachutes were handed around, their faces soon smeared with chocolate and other candies. Others unwrapped toys like tops and whirligigs and whistles. The air bustled with giggles and laughter—sounds she hadn't heard in years.

The distribution center would have more than enough to spread around by the looks of it. Cart after cart piled high with the goods made for an impromptu parade as they headed to the distribution center in town.

"Here come more!" someone shouted as another group of the Flying Fortresses filled the western sky.

Anya looked and hoped, wanting desperately to see Danny's smiling face, to see him waving at her. But after a couple of hours she finally gave up. "Helga, can we please go now?"

"Of course, dear."

They chatted about the miracle of the food drops and all they'd seen and experienced that day. As the made their way up the walkway to Helga's home, mischief lit her wrinkled face. "Now hold out your hands."

"What?"

"Hold out your hands!"

Anya lifted her palms and in them Helga placed a red

apple and a tin of chocolates. Anya gasped. "Helga!"

"Someone handed them to me back there. Look!" She pulled another apple and tin from her other pocket. "Tonight we shall dine like royalty, you and I!"

08 May 1945

For two glorious days, Anya slept. As exciting as it was to witness one of the incredible food drops, she was simply too tired to offer any more help or find out how she might be useful. It seemed as though she had not rested in years. Only now, in the comfort of Helga's home did she allow herself to truly forget everything else around her and just sleep. Helga's husband Lars had finally returned home from his own journeys, tying up loose ends of what was left of the Resistance. He delighted them with bags of food for which he'd patiently waited in line at the Netherlands Food Distribution Service warehouse. The simple taste of a good cup of coffee nearly brought them to tears, it tasted so good.

Then one morning Anya decided to get some fresh air by taking a walk with Helga. They'd only been out for a few minutes when word began to spread like wildfire.

"WIJ ZIJN VRIJ! WIJ ZIJN VRIJ!" *We are free! We are free!*

"The Germans capitulated! The Netherlands are free!"

"The Allies have liberated us!"

"The war is over! The war is over!"

Anya and Helga looked at each other then hugged and cried all at once. "Oh Helga, can it be true? Is it really over?"

The people of Utrecht poured into the streets, rushing from their homes to join the celebration. At first they felt hesitant to believe the wonderful news, but as reports of the armistice signed in Amsterdam filtered through the hordes of people, they dropped all caution and gave in to unrestrained joy. Suddenly, like a ripple of red, white, and blue water spreading through the streets, Dutch flags waved proudly once again.

Anya had never seen anything so beautiful in all her life. Somewhere a loud speaker blared the announcement, validating the wonderful rumor. The people shouted with joy then hushed once again, as the voice of Queen Wilhelmina came from the speakers, confirming the news of their liberation.

Then, even before they could applaud the comforting words from their queen, their beloved national anthem "Wilhelmus" played as their cheers turned to tears filled with longsuffering, patriotic emotion as they sang.

As she too sang along, Anya had a momentary thought. *If it is humanly possible for hundreds and hundreds of people to experience the same exact emotion at one given moment in time, surely this is that moment.*

When the song ended, the cheers rose again. Everyone hugged and kissed and danced, even with perfect strangers. Some fainted, too excited to take it all in. Some found refuge wherever they could find it and prayed out loud, giving thanks to God for giving them back their freedom. Church bells peeled, almost as if the Lord Almighty Himself had joined in the celebration.

Hours later, they chatted all the way home, wondering what would happen next and how they would begin to live again. As they approached the steps, a *boom-boom-boom-boom* pounded the air. They clutched each other in fear, jolted by the terrifying sound, until a rainbow of colors exploded in the sky above them.

"Will you look at that?" Helga marveled.

They stepped up onto the porch then turned to watch the fireworks. "It's all too good to be true, isn't it? I keep thinking I'm going to wake up and find it was all a dream."

"And if that's so, then let's hold onto the dream as long as we can."

"Dear sweet Helga," Anya began, leaning her head on the older woman's shoulder. "All these years you've been such a blessing—always to my family, and now to me. How can I ever thank you?"

"No need to thank me. Your father always preached about bestowing kindness on others. Jesus said, 'Whatever you do to these least of these, you do it unto Me.' And I am humbled to be His hands when others need a helping hand. Especially one as special as you."

65

In the days that followed, Anya felt her heart gradually begin to grasp what her mind already knew—Holland was truly free! Like so many others throughout her country, Helga and Lars opened their home to welcome the Allied heroes and feed them with *real* food as a gesture of thanks. Helping her friends prepare the meals, Anya thought she'd never tasted anything so delicious as those first bites of corned beef and cheese and eggs—even powdered eggs—with toasted bread and real butter. Where hunger had stolen their spirits, now each bite seemed to give them the strength and courage to live again. How better to celebrate this new beginning than by sharing their hospitality with those who had made it all possible.

Along the way, they began to notice their Jewish friends and neighbors gradually coming out of hiding. Too frightened at first, the Jews finally accepted the news, especially after hearing Hitler was dead and the Germans had been defeated. Anya witnessed many of these reunions of Jewish family members and friends, their tears and laughter all mixed and flowing freely. Many of them hadn't been outdoors in fresh air for years, and they couldn't seem to get enough of it. It was such a joy just to see them walking down the street inhaling deep breaths of the crisp, spring-like air.

In their new-found freedom, the Dutch could once again tune in their radios to hear the news they'd missed for years.

Of course, the news wasn't all good.

Through the BBC they learned that an American B-17 participating in *Operation Chowhound* back on May 7 was fired upon by German ground troops and crashed into the North Sea on its way home. Of its thirteen crew members—including two ground personnel on their first ever flight—only two survived.

Radio reports also told of the tragedy in Amsterdam which occurred just two days after the Germans surrendered. Excited crowds of Dutch citizens had gathered in Dam Square near the Royal Castle to celebrate their freedom. Then, in the midst of their dancing and cheering as their flag was once again raised above the castle, shots rang out across the wide open plaza. A band of drunken German soldiers standing on the balcony of the Grote Club began firing machine guns into the crowd. The heartbreaking irony—twenty-two people killed and one hundred nineteen men, women, and children injured as they celebrated their long-awaited freedom—was now mourned throughout The Netherlands.

Then came the news reports, photographs, and personal accounts about the atrocities that had taken place in concentration camps all across Europe. No one in their wildest imagination could fully comprehend the brutalities the Germans had committed on their captives—and not just millions of Jews, but millions of other victims as well. One report described American General George Patton's visit to the camp at Ohrdruf in southern Germany near Kassel. When the gruff and outspoken general who had led the U.S. Third Army to such great accomplishments, saw the piles of unburied corpses and the skeletal figures of those who had somehow survived, Patton vomited.

As the world began to learn what had been going on in the concentration camps, Allied commanders retaliated by requiring townspeople throughout Germany to tour the nearby camps and see for themselves what their silent indifference had allowed for so many years. Many wept and became ill. One mayor and his wife returned from such a tour and hung themselves. Allied commanders ordered the captured members of the SS who had run these camps to carry the corpses of thousands of their victims to mass graves.

In Holland, Nazi sympathizers were hunted down and arrested. When she heard that her former neighbors the van Oostras had been arrested, Anya couldn't help feeling a swell of satisfaction. How many lives had been lost because of their lucrative treason? And in a bold and symbolic act of revenge, all Dutch women who had fraternized with German soldiers during the Occupation were rounded up and their heads shaved in public as a mark of disgrace.

But along with so much sadness came the realization that those who had survived the war now had to go about putting the frayed and delicate pieces of their lives back together. For Anya and so many others there would be no reunions of laughter and tears. She had accepted the fate of her parents, and now it was time to bolster her courage and go home. To *her* home. Helga had offered to go with her. At first Anya declined the offer, but every time she pictured herself walking into her home, she felt her stomach knot and her knees go weak.

She hated the reaction. She'd always been strong and willing to do what she must and when she must do it. But the war had taken a toll on her, so much more than she wanted to admit. And if someone kind and considerate offered to help her make that first journey home, then so be it.

As they rounded the corner of her street, Anya could barely breathe. She hardly recognized the neighborhood for all the destruction. Thankfully, her block had suffered no direct bombing, still the damage overwhelmed her. As they neared the walkway up to her home, she stopped.

"Oh, Helga," she moaned, taking in the awful mess on the front lawn. A mattress was propped against a tree, obviously used for target practice—or worse. What was left of her mother's piano sat flat on the ground, its four legs and most of its keys missing. A heap of ashes revealed bits and pieces of furniture and clothing. Broken glass and china littered what grass was left on the lawn.

Helga's arm encircled Anya's waist. "Sweetheart, these are only things," she said quietly but with firm authority. "Just things. Yes, they hold memories, but they are nothing more than wood and glass and fabric."

She tightened her hold on Anya. "And you, my dear Anya, are alive." She paused, then whispered, "You made it. You *survived*. Through all of it, you survived."

Anya caught the sob in her throat when Helga's voice cracked. She didn't even try to speak.

"You can do this. Together, we can do this."

Anya swiped at her tears and took a deep breath, nodded, then started up the steps.

They were silent as they walked through the open doorway. Anya's eyes drifted over the remaining pieces of furniture and clutter. "Someone has lived here." The thought scared her. "What if—"

"I had Lars stop over earlier to make sure it was safe. There's no one here, dear."

Slow, wobbly steps took her through the entry hall into the kitchen area. There was little left, only a couple of chipped cups and a puddle of wax from candles in a saucer. She fingered the edge of the sink and turned the faucet on, but not a single drop fell from it. She stepped carefully over shards of glass and made her way down the hall. She wouldn't look in Hans' old room. Not now. Across the hall, her parents' room had only a filthy, stained mattress on the floor. Fingers of anger curled in her stomach at the disgrace of the bedroom that once housed her mother and father. Nothing was left. Only her father's old gray robe hanging from a nail on the wall. She started toward it, even reaching for it thinking she might still find a trace of her father's scent in its thick fabric. But she stopped, her hand in midair. *Father always hung his robe in the closet. Always. Someone else must have . . .*

A chill crawled up her spine and she turned abruptly, needing to flee from the images in her mind. She moved across the hall and stood in the doorway to her own bedroom. Surely she would find something of hers still here?

Nothing. Not the dresser where she kept her favorite things. Not a single piece of clothing. Not the worn stuffed bunny she'd slept with as a small girl. Nothing.

Of course it was all gone. She hadn't really thought she'd find anything left. But being here—finally returning home and standing in her own room—somehow the stark reality made it too much to bear. She fell to her knees and buried her face in her hands.

How can I go on? Why am I even here? Why did I survive when none of them did? Oh God, why didn't You just let me die?

Anya was thankful Helga had given her some privacy. She fell back on the floor in a heap, still holding her head in her hands, rocking back and forth. And when the last ounce of energy left her, she curled up and lay on her side. The wooden floor felt gritty beneath her as she tried hard to make sense of it all, tried to find some reason—*any* reason to go on. Oh, how she despised the incessant tears! No matter how hard she tried to rebuild her wall against them, she couldn't stem the flow.

But even the tears didn't disappoint her as much as God's complete and utter silence. No matter how much she cried out to Him, He never answered. Hadn't she tried one last time just the other day? That day at the field, as hundreds of B-17s flew over dropping their loads of compassion and hope, hadn't she prayed, extending her last olive branch to God?

Silently, she had prayed. *God, if You're there, let me see him. That's all I ask. Just let me see him.*

Now she felt so foolish. How stupid, expecting God to hear her silly prayer. Even worse, how ridiculous to still believe in God. After everything that had happened, why did she keep looking to Him for answers? Clearly, God was nothing more than a concept of wishful thinking.

And yet, in spite of it all, the unbidden words fell from her lips . . . *Oh God, I'm so alone.*

She lay there for some time before opening her eyes. Her view, at such an awkward angle skewed everything for a moment, and then . . . there, over in the corner . . . something. What was it? Silent hiccups quaked her body as she tried to sit up. She crawled across the floor, trying to see the tiny object barely visible in the late afternoon shadows. She reached out and grasped it, bringing it into the light. And as she opened her palm, what she saw took her breath away. There in her hand, with half a wing missing and a splintered snout, lay the flying piglet her brother Hans had carved for her so many years ago.

"When pigs fly," she whispered, cherishing the memory and missing him so much.

Footsteps sounded behind her, coming down the hall. She hid the pig in her pocket and dashed away her tears, not wanting Helga to find her blubbering like some helpless child. Clumsily she stood and turned to find Helga standing in the doorway, the woman's gnarled hands over her mouth and the strangest expression on her face.

"Helga, what is it?"

She pulled her hands from her mouth, revealing a quivering smile. "Anya, there's someone here to see you, dear." She stepped aside.

In full dress uniform with his cap in his hands, Danny McClain stepped into the room.

The space between them vanished and suddenly she was in his arms. "You're here, Anya. You're here!" he whispered into her hair. "I prayed so hard you'd be here."

She pulled back enough to see his face. "But how—?"

"I would have walked to the moon to find you." He pushed a strand of hair from her eyes and leaned down, gently kissing her lips. She felt so frail in his arms, so small—but so *right*. How he'd dreamed of this moment, as if a dozen tender kisses could make everything right in the world again. When he realized her response was tentative, he pulled back. "What is it? What's wrong?"

She started to say something then stopped, her eyes drifting downward. "I think perhaps I'm a little in shock." She looked back up at him, her gray-blue eyes filled with something he couldn't define. "Just now, before you came in, I . . . I cried out to God. I cried silently to Him, even though I wasn't sure He still existed. I just didn't think I could go on."

She reached down into her pocket. "And the next moment, I found this." She opened her palm, revealing a small hand-carved pig.

He smiled as he lifted it from her hand. "I know this pig. Hans made this for you, didn't he? It was his Sinterklaas gift to you."

She nodded. "Because whenever he asked me to do something, I always said—"

"—when pigs fly," he said along with her.

"And then I turned around and you were here."

He laughed. "Does this mean the pigs are flying?"

She tried to smile. "Perhaps they are."

He handed the tiny pig back to her and she returned it to

her pocket. Cupping her face with his hand, he brushed away her tear with his thumb. "I love you, Anya. I have loved you for so long. Since the moment I left you that night at the coast, I've thought of nothing but you." He wrapped his arms around her again, her head tucked against his chest. "You never have to be alone again. Ever."

"And what have I told you about making promises you can't keep?" she teased quietly.

He leaned back to face her. "Well, this is one I *know* I can keep."

"Ja? And how can you know this?"

"Marry me, Anya."

She stiffened, blinking up at him. "What?"

"You heard me. Marry me. And let me spend a lifetime keeping promises to you."

He couldn't tell if she was still in shock or possibly trying to make a decision. Another tear spilled down her cheek just as a trembling smile tried to take shape. He touched his lips to hers, and this time she responded eagerly. He could hardly think straight, his heart so full of love for her. How long had he dreamed of holding her again? He couldn't tell if she was laughing or crying, but it didn't matter. As long as she was here in his arms, he could handle anything.

When she finally eased back to look up at him, Danny stared into her eyes with an easy sense of belonging.

"I still don't know how you found me," she said. "How did you know to come here?"

"Don't you remember? The last time I saw you, you said you just wanted to go home." He took her hand and led her down the hall toward the front door.

"I know, but I didn't believe you'd ever come back," she said. "I wouldn't let myself believe it. I thought everything you said . . . I thought they were just meaningless words from a man who didn't know how to say goodbye."

They stepped out onto the front porch. "Shows how much *you* know." He quirked a smile at her.

They sat down side by side on the top step. "But how did you find my house?"

"I remembered your address. All those letters we wrote when we were kids—I guess I memorized your address without even realizing it. And when I got over here, I—"

"And how exactly *did* you get over here?"

"I guess you could say I hitch-hiked."

"What does that mean, hitch—"

"Hitch-hike? It means I caught a ride over."

Her brows crinkled as she searched his face.

"They've been transporting our POWs from the camps back to England. The planes are empty on their way over, so I climbed on board. And here I am."

"Just like that? You stowed away and no one saw you?"

"No, no, I had permission. Turns out the Old Man has a soft heart."

She shook her head, raking her fingers through her hair. "You always talk in such riddles, Danny McClain. Of the hitch-hike, of some old man—"

"Not some old man—*the* Old Man. It's a long story. Suffice it to say, my Commanding Officer sends his best wishes and told me to send him an invitation if the wedding is in Chicago."

"This officer, he is from Chicago, America too?"

Danny smiled. "Yes, he is from Chicago, America too." He leaned over to plant a kiss on her forehead. "So what do you think?"

"What do I think about what?"

"Should we invite him?"

Her smile began to fade, and she looked out across the scattered debris in her front yard. A trace of the former sadness drifted across her face. He knew what she was thinking.

Several moments later, she leaned her head on his shoulder. "Danny, I think I should like to meet your mother and father."

"Yeah?"

"And I think I should like to meet your brother Joey who steals biscuits during prayers."

He chuckled. "Yeah?"

"And I think I should like to eat a dog at Wrigley Field."

He threw back his head, laughing out loud. "I think you mean a 'hot dog'."

"Yes, then. I think I should like to eat a *hot dog* at Wrigley Field."

He smiled. "I think we can make that happen."

She reached into her pocket, then placed the tiny carved pig in his hand, and closed his fingers over the small wooden keepsake. Looking up into his eyes, she smiled. "Yes, Danny McClain, I will marry you. And yes, the pigs will fly."

He laughed, wrapping his arms around her and pulling her close. "Perhaps they will, Anya. Perhaps they will."

The Rest of the Story

Most Americans have never heard of *Operation Chowhound*. Most English have never heard of *Operation Manna*. But mention either of these life-saving missions to those of Dutch heritage, and chances are they will smile with knowing eyes. Mention these missions to the veterans who flew them, and chances are they'll tear up at the memory.

For the history books, *Operation Manna/Chowhound* was the first mission of its kind flown by military aircraft to drop help instead of destruction on those below. The war was winding down near the end of 1945, but those in western Holland faced certain starvation. While the southern part of The Netherlands was liberated, the highly populated areas of the northwest still endured brutal retaliation from the Germans. During the "Hunger Winter" the Dutch in those areas who had subsided on less than 600 calories a day, now had nothing. More than 16,000 men, women, and children died from hunger and the bitter cold.

Exiled Queen Wilhelmina begged the Allies to save her people before it was too late. What happened next was nothing short of a miracle.

In response to the Queen's plea for help, a plan was quickly orchestrated. On April 17, 1945, Air Commodore Andrew J.W. Geddes, Chief of Operations and Plans of the Second Tactical Air Force, was instructed by General Eisenhower's staff to formulate a plan to airlift food to the starving 3,500,000 people of western Holland. A few days later, Geddes presented a brilliant strategy which was immediately approved. An hour later he was on his way to Achterveld in The Netherlands where he would meet with German officials.

On April 28, the German officers arrived at the conference. It became quickly apparent that the four men had been sent on a fact-gathering mission with no authority to sign an agreement. They were sent away with terse instructions to return with whatever authority was necessary. They were also informed that General Eisenhower had ordered the food drops to begin the following day, April 29—with or without their approval. If a single plane was shot upon by the Germans, they were told "Germany will cease to exist."

Upon hearing that Reichskommissar Seyss-Inquart, the German commander over Occupied Holland, would be accompanying a large delegation, a prank of sorts was put into motion. Members of the Dutch Resistance had recently stolen the large black Mercedes staff car belonging to the proud Reichskommissar. Seyss-Inquart adored the vehicle. These Dutch Resistance workers had given the car to Prince Bernhard, the Commander in Chief of the Dutch Forces. That morning, Bernhard drove the vehicle to the meeting and parked it where Seyss-Inquart couldn't miss it—its license plate "RK-1" still attached. The German commander seethed upon seeing his beloved car now in the hands of his enemies.

But Seyss-Inquart, refusing to believe Germany would lose the war, stood his ground and refused to cooperate with regard to the food drops. It took several heated exchanges and outright threats by Geddes and other Allies to force the German to sign.

Between April 29 and May 8, English Lancasters and Mosquitos, and American B-17s flew almost 6,000 missions, dropping more than 12,000 tons of food and supplies to specific locations in western Holland. Some of these planes flew lower than 300 feet off the ground. The Dutch were thrilled with the food "raining down from heaven," but even more excited at the implication of these bizarre events. To see the Allied planes flying so low with no Germans firing at them could mean only one thing—the war was almost over! Liberation would soon be theirs!

When the long war finally ended, the Dutch slowly began putting their lives and their country back together. Queen Wilhelmina returned from exile and opened half of her palace to those of her people who had been in prisons and concentration camps. There, the heartbroken, beaten, and downtrodden found a place to rest and recuperate. Hundreds of others volunteered to help these wounded souls, and the queen insisted on visiting her "guests" each night and having tea with those helping them. No wonder they loved her so.

Many of the men who flew these life-saving missions remember them with gratitude, tremendously thankful for the opportunity they had to bring hope to a nation so desperately in need. Those messages of "MANY THANKS" and "THANKS, YANKS!" spelled out in tulips and other ways meant the world to them.

And to the Dutch men, women, and children who waved and cheered as they flew over them, the images and memories of those ten days have never been forgotten.

May *we* never forget.

Glenn Hale – Then and Now

1944 - 1945

Glenn with daughters Diane Moody
and Morlee Maynard in 2009 following
a flight on the Liberty Belle.

ABOUT THE AUTHOR

Born in Texas and raised in Oklahoma, Diane Hale Moody is a graduate of Oklahoma State University. She lives with her husband Ken in the rolling hills just outside of Nashville. They are the proud parents of two grown and extraordinary children, Hannah and Ben.

Just after moving to Tennessee in 1999, Diane felt the tug of a long-neglected passion to write again. Since then, she's written a column for her local newspaper, feature articles for various magazines and curriculum, and several novels with a dozen more stories eagerly vying for her attention.

When she's not reading or writing, Diane enjoys an eclectic taste in music and movies, great coffee, the company of good friends, and the adoration of a peculiar little pooch named Darby.

Visit Diane's website at dianemoody.net and her blog, "just sayin'" at dianemoody.blogspot.com.

Discussion Questions

1. Danny McClain grew up in a home with a mother who lived out her faith and a father who had little use for God. What kind of influence did each of them have on Danny's life?

2. Danny dreaded his class assignment to find a pen pal living in a foreign country, yet that simple task would eventually change his life forever. Have you ever faced a situation with dread then later realized it was a blessing in disguise? And just for fun, have you ever had a pen pal?

3. Anya was nothing like her brother Hans, yet her world changed forever when he died trying to save little Rieky from drowning. How did the loss of her brother change Anya? In what ways did that experience prepare her for the situations she faced during the German Occupation?

4. Compare and contrast Danny and Anya's backgrounds and their perspectives on the war. What specifically motivated each of them to "do something" in the war effort?

5. Even though Anya and Wim were just teenagers, they willingly risked their lives to help hide the Jews in Holland during the German Occupation. At such a young age, where does such courage come from? If you witnessed that kind of persecution to those around you, be honest—would you risk your life to save theirs?

6. Danny never forgot the image of his mother kneeling in prayer beside her bed. But at what point did Danny get serious about his faith, acknowledging his *own* relationship with God? Have you ever found yourself in a similar situation?

7. Even in the darkest of times, God promises us His presence. Was there ever a time you had to trust Him at His word, unable to see any trace of evidence of His presence? How did you respond in that situation?

8. How did God reveal Himself to Anya? What finally cracked her defense against the God she believed had forgotten Holland?

9. Most of us have never gone without a meal or faced such hardships as those in Occupied Holland. But try to imagine yourself as one of those who'd lived on nothing but sugar beets and tulip bulbs for months, maybe years. Then imagine yourself as one who witnessed the food drops. How would you react? What thoughts might you have?

10. What was your favorite scene in the book?

11. What was the funniest scene in the story?

12. Of the secondary characters, who did you find most interesting?

13. What is something you learned by reading *Of Windmills & War* that you'd not known before?

Acknowledgments

With overwhelming gratitude to my daughter Hannah Moody for the stunning book cover that brought tears to my eyes the first time I saw it. Thank you for using your God-given talents to bless this story with a cover so beautifully befitting its subject. But even more important, bless you for the heart you put into it on behalf of your grandfather. You're the best, and I'm so proud of you, sweetie.

As always, many thanks to my proofreaders—my good friend Sally Wilson, my husband Ken, and the ever-diligent Old Eagle Eyes himself, Glenn Hale. Dad, not only did you catch numerous typos, you made sure Danny's story was accurate—in Chicago, at Northwestern University, and all the way to the skies over Europe. He thanks you, as do I!

To Anita Van Melle for her expertise making sure I didn't embarrass my Dutch characters by putting the wrong words in their mouths. *Bedankt, Anita!*

To Melanie Beasley who likewise helped me with the German language, and to her friend Janne who also took a look at my Dutch. *Danke, ladies!*

To Bob Penovich, for your tireless dedication to teach the next generation about *Operation Chowhound* and the many accomplishments of the 390th. Thank you so much for loaning me your prized copy of *Memories of a Miracle: Operation Manna/Chowhound* by Hans Onderwater. Wow, what a gold mine of information! Thanks also for answering all those pesky email questions I kept sending you. You're a saint!

To Wendy MacVicar, for your friendship and inspiration on so many levels. Thank you for lighting the match back at the 2011 reunion that sparked this story and gave Anya a voice. How I thank God for you!

To Bill MacVicar, Wendy's father-in-law, who has so willingly served as president of our 390th Veterans Association for all these years. Thank you for all your hard work and that tender heart of yours that still beats for freedom.

To Iris Taggart, our dear friend of so many years. Iris's husband Robert "Tag" Taggart flew with the 390th, and though Tag died several years ago, Iris has faithfully attended every reunion. Her contagious passion for the B-17 and the other warbirds of WWII keeps her busy arranging air shows and inspiring young people to get interested in aviation through the Young Eagles program. We love you, Iris!

To Ray and Sally McFalone, thank you for the massive undertaking to videotape interviews with our 390th veterans. You have given their precious memories new life, enabling their stories to be heard for generations to come. Your insightful questions and meticulous editing have produced a beautiful history that we will never forget.

To my husband and best friend Ken who quite literally publishes and markets all our books. I couldn't do this without you. I love doing life with you more every single day—and then some. (P.S. My bags are still packed for Hawaii, in case you wondered.)

And finally, a special thanks to my dad, Glenn Hale. I have loved every minute working on this project with you. Thanks for answering my bazillion questions and always filling in the gaps with your colorful insight. If money grew on trees, I would have flown us over to Framlingham to soak up the local flavor and ambience of your memories there. How fun would that have been? Still, between your many resources and impeccable, precise memory, I think we did a pretty good job. Thank you for letting Danny share so many of your experiences. I hope you're pleased with him. Thank you for your service to our country and the uncompromised patriotic spirit that flows so strongly through your veins. I am so blessed, so thankful, and so very proud to be your daughter. Love you, Dad.

Resources

Eman, Diet with Schaap, James. *Things We Could Not Say.* Grand Rapids, MI: Eerdmans Publishing Co., 1994.

Freeman, Roger. *The Mighty Eighth in Color.* Specialty Press Publishers & Wholesalers, Inc., 1992.

Ippisch, Hanneke. *Sky: A True Story of Resistance During World War II.* New York: Simon & Schuster, 1996.

Kaplan, Phillip, and Smith, Rex Alan. *One Last Look: A Sentimental Journey to the Eighth Air Force Heavy Bomber Bases of World War II in England.* New York: Artabras Publishers, 1983.

Onderwater, Hans. *Memories of a Miracle: Operation Manna/ Chowhound, 29 April – 8 May 1945.*Rotterdam: Ad. Donker, 1995.

Sanders, Ronald. Translated and revised by Voyles, Hannie J. *Storming the Tulips.* St. Louis, MO: Stonebrook Publishing, 2011.

The Story of the 390th Bomb Group (H). Paducah, KY: Turner Publishing Company, 1947.

Van der Rol, Rund, and Verhoeven, Rian. *Anne Frank: Beyond the Diary.* New York: The Penguin Group, 1993.

Van Stockum, Hilda. *The Winged Watchman.* Bathgate, ND: Bethlehem Books, 1995.

WWII: Time-Life Books History of the Second World War. New York: Prentice Hall Press for Time-Life Books, Inc., 1989.

Wycoff, Johanna. *Dancing in Bomb Shelters: My Diary of Holland in World War II.* Bloomington, IN: iUniverse, 2010.

390th Bomb Group: 50th Anniversary Commemorative History. Paducah, KY: Turner Publishing Company, 1994.

The 1943 Syllabus: The Yearbook of the Junior Class of Northwestern University. Chicago: Students Publishing Company, 1944.

The 1944 Syllabus: The Yearbook of the Junior Class of Northwestern University. Chicago: Students Publishing Company, 1945.

Online Resources

The Dead of 7 May 1945. City Archives: Amsterdam Treasures, Second World War. Retrieved from: http://stadsarchief.amsterdam.nl/english/amsterdam_treas ures/second_world_war/doden_op_7_mei_1945/index.en.ht ml

Madison, James H. (Fall 2007). Wearing Lipstick to War: An American Woman in World War II England. *Prologue Magazine, Vol. 39, No. 3.* Retrieved from: http://www.archives.gov/publications/prologue/2007/fall/li pstick.html

Barris, Ted.(May 2005). Manna From Heaven. Legion Magazine. Retrieved from: http://www.legionmagazine.com/en/index.php/2005/05/m anna-from-heaven/

Myers-Verhage, Shelby. [1995]. Postmarked from Amsterdam: Anne Frank and Her Iowa Penpal. Reprinted from *Palimpsest* and used by permission from the State Historical Society of Iowa, as retrieved from: http://www.traces.org/anne.html

Operation Chowhound/Manna: 8th Air Force B-17 Food Drop over Holland, April-May 1945. [Video file]. Retrieved from: http://www.youtube.com/watch?v=4utm_gB_zs0

Operation Manna – 65 Years of Canadian-Dutch Friendship [Video file]. Retrieved from: http://www.youtube.com/watch?v=1HFWJ9GkNqE&feature= related

More Than Food: The Manna-Chowhound Food Drops. Retrieved from: http://operationmanna.secondworldwar.nl/

Other Books by Diane Moody

The Runaway Pastor's Wife
Available in paperback and Kindle

The Teacup Novella Series
Book One: *Tea with Emma*
Books Two: *Strike the Match*
Book Three: *Home to Walnut Ridge*
Book Four: *At Legend's End*
Book Five: *A Christmas Peril*
Available on Kindle

The Teacup Novellas – The Collection
(All five novellas in one volume)
Available in paperback and Kindle

Two Blue Novels
Blue Christmas
Blue Like Elvis
Available in paperback and Kindle

Non-Fiction Titles

Confessions of a Prayer Slacker
Available in paperback and Kindle

Also available from OBT Bookz

The Elmo Jenkins Series
Book One: *Ordained Irreverence*
Book Two: *Some Things Never Change*
Book Three: *The Old Man and the Tea*
Book Four: *A Tale of Two Elmos*
by McMillian Moody
Available in paperback and Kindle